WEDDING CHOCOLATE

WEDDING CHOCOLATE

Essence **Bestselling Author**

ADRIANNE BYRD

HARLEQUIN®KIMANI ARABESQUE®

WEDDING CHOCOLATE
ISBN-13: 978-0-373-09157-7

Copyright © 2014 by Harlequin Books S.A.

This edition published August 2014.

The publisher acknowledges the copyright holders of the individual works as follows:

TWO GROOMS AND A WEDDING
Copyright © 2008 by Adrianne Byrd

SINFUL CHOCOLATE
Copyright © 2009 by Adrianne Byrd

Recycling programs for this product may not exist in your area.

www.Harlequin.com

Printed in U.S.A.

CONTENTS

TWO GROOMS AND A WEDDING

Prologue

"Isabella Elizabeth Kane, what do you mean you're engaged to two men?"

With her head planted between her legs, Isabella waited for the nausea to pass. It wasn't going to happen anytime soon—especially not while her mother, Katherine, screeched at her.

"Answer me, young lady!" Her mother stomped her foot. "Do you realize the mess you've made?"

In response, Isabella released a long winding groan. Under the circumstances, it was the best she could do. Heck, she didn't understand how she'd gotten in this mess either. Well, she did, but it was all so unbelievable that she didn't know where to start.

Crash!

Isabella jumped from the bed, hiked up the hem of her white beaded Badgley Mischka wedding dress and raced to the bedroom window of her parents' two-story home.

Her mother and Isabella's team of bridesmaids/sorority sisters followed suit.

Outside, rolling around on the lush green lawn before hundreds of friends, family and Capitol Hill's most powerful elite, Isabella's two fiancés, Derrick Knight and Randall Jarrett, duked it out as if a world championship title was on the line.

Reverend Williams, bless his heart, jumped in to pull the men apart, but his efforts landed all three in the Lady Justice stone-garden water fountain.

Everyone gasped in horror.

"No. No. No. This can't be happening," Isabella fretted, turning away from the window to pace around the room like a mad woman. "Oh, God. What am I going to do?"

No one had an answer to that—especially since no one knew how she had managed to get herself engaged to two men at once.

"Izzy," Keri Evans, Izzy's best friend, spoke up. "You're going to have to do something."

Talk about an understatement.

Bam! Bam! Bam!

All the women jumped and gasped at the sudden hammering on the bedroom door.

"Isabella, open this door!" her father, Senator Tyler Kane, roared.

Shrinking from the rattling partition, Isabella returned to the bed and tucked her head between her knees again. Meanwhile, her mother rushed to the door.

"Everybody out!" her father barked.

The command was met with the loud rustle of silk as her bridesmaids bolted. Isabella wished she could join them, but she no longer trusted her legs' stability to carry out an escape attempt.

The Senator, as he was affectionately called, slammed

the door behind the women. Waves of heat pulsed from him and, if Isabella wasn't mistaken, the floor trembled as he stalked toward the bed.

"Well, little lady?"

"I'm sorry, Daddy," she croaked down at the pearl-colored carpet.

"Sorry? I have spent twenty years on Capitol Hill," he began, his voice laded with anger. "And I've never once been embroiled in a single scandal. Now my own daughter has managed to destroy my record in one afternoon. This is an election year for God's sake!"

"Tyler, calm down," her mother instructed softly.

"How can I be calm? The media is here."

Isabella's head snapped up and for her trouble the room spun. "Oh, Daddy."

"Don't 'oh, Daddy' me. You need to get out there and fix this."

Fix it? How on earth could she do that?

A quick knock and Keri rushed back into the room. "They're on their way up."

"Who?" her mother asked.

"The fiancés."

Isabella sprang to her feet, thankful they still worked after all. "Stop them! Don't let them come up here."

"Stop them?" Katherine questioned. "Honey, you can't stay up here and hide all day. You're going to have to talk to them."

"No. I—I can't," Isabella said, bordering on panic.

"By God! As much money as I have spent on this wedding, you're getting married today."

"To which one?" her mother asked.

"Derrick/Randall," her father and Keri answered in sync and then glanced at one another.

Only her mother thought to ask, "Well, which one do you love?"

"What the hell does love have to do with any of this?" the senator thundered. "She'll marry who I say to marry!"

"Tyler!" her mother screeched.

"What?"

Keri stepped forward. "Izzy? It's your decision."

Before anyone had the chance to refute the statement, the bedroom door banged open and Isabella's two bloodied and soaking wet grooms spilled inside.

"Randall, get out of my way!"

"Like hell, Derrick!"

Isabella leapt behind Keri, hoping to use her as a human shield while the men continued to scuffle.

Her brave father stepped forward and ended the tussle with the powerful boom of his voice. "Stop it, both of you! If you break one thing in this house, I'll have you both thrown in jail!"

The angry grooms sprung apart, but their heated glares continued the war.

"Isabella?" her father prompted and all eyes turned toward her.

Randall, her first fiancé, pulled his shoulders back and stood erect. His handsome face stared at her with confidence. "Will you tell this man—" he indicated Derrick, who stood to his right "—whom it is you wish to marry."

Isabella's eyes shifted to her second fiancé who towered over Randall by three inches and possessed shoulders as broad and strong as mountains. "Bella?" His dark eyes implored. "Tell them it's me you love."

Tears crested her eyes as she opened her mouth, but her throat clenched closed beneath everyone's expectant gazes. And then she did the one thing no one expected... she fainted.

Chapter 1

"Isabella Kane, will you marry me?"

A series of gasps traveled around the large dining table at Maestro restaurant. Handsome Randall Jarrett smiled his newly acquired veneers at his girlfriend.

Isabella dropped her fork and fluttered a shaky hand across her heart. Her eyes widened to the size of saucers. Surely she hadn't heard her boyfriend of eight weeks correctly.

"We're perfect for each other," he added, clutching her hand.

Perfect, she noted. Not "I love you with all of my heart" or "I'm crazy about you and I can't see myself living without you." Just a calculated "we're perfect for each other."

Isabella stared down at a breathtaking two-carat princess-cut diamond and had a hard time pushing the word "no" through her lips. How could she? Before Randall she had never had a serious boyfriend her entire life—let alone someone as gorgeous as Randall notice she was alive.

"Isabella?" Randall questioned with an awkward chuckle and then glanced at his parents and potential in-laws. "You're not going to leave me hanging here, are you?"

Isabella smiled; at least she tried anyway, and waited for the right words to come.

And waited.

And waited.

"Sweetheart?" Isabella's father spoke up and touched his daughter's elbow. "Are you okay?" he whispered.

"I think she's in shock," Randall injected with a nervous titter. "It's not every day a woman gets a marriage proposal."

Her parents joined Randall in his awkward laughter, giving Isabella sufficient time to break her silent trance.

"Yes," she agreed. "It's all so...unexpected. We've only been dating two months."

"Well," Randall's stepmother, Eunice, piped up. "I, for one, thought Randall would never settle down."

Embarrassment darkened Randall's face. "Mother."

"What? It's true," Eunice said and smiled. "And frankly, I don't think he could have made a better choice."

"Amen," the other parents chorused and then clinked their champagne glasses together in a quick toast.

So they had all known he was going to propose.

Isabella's face warmed beneath their open praises, but she couldn't help but feel Ms. Eunice stretched the truth a bit—well, actually, quite a lot. Fact was, Randall Jarrett with his athletic, six-foot-three body and creamy, peanut-butter skin could have snagged any woman he wanted off looks alone. His wealth and ambition were bonuses.

What surprised Isabella was that he wanted *her*—a

school-teased ugly duckling who'd survived her adolescence by burying her head in books. Before she knew it, she had sailed through high school without attending a single sporting event or prom. A late bloomer, she couldn't even fill her paltry "B" cups until she was a freshman in college. But luckily, she finally found a home with Delta Phi Theta sorority, where brains were exalted more than beauty.

Still considered a plain Jane, Isabella couldn't believe the direction her life shifted.

Randall, still on bended knee, held up his free hand. "We can't celebrate just yet. I'm still waiting for an answer."

"Well, of course she'll marry you," Katherine assured in her honeyed southern voice. "Isabella knows you two are a perfect match."

Everyone murmured in agreement and glasses clinked all around. Again, Isabella noticed no one said anything about love.

"If it's all the same," Randall said. "I'd like to hear her answer." His dark, almost black eyes bored into Isabella.

The table fell silent as Isabella swallowed the invisible lump in her throat while maintaining a synthetic smile. The war between love and common sense raged in both Isabella's heart and mind, and on this night, this very important night, there was no clear winner.

After one last nervous glance around the table, Isabella took a deep breath and rode to Randall's rescue. "Yes. Of course, I'll marry you."

Both sets of parents erupted in cheer, while Randall plucked a diamond ring from its velvet box and slid it down her slim finger. Honestly, it was the prettiest shackle she'd ever seen.

The senator leaned over and wrapped an arm around her waist and planted a kiss against her left cheek.

"Baby girl, you've made me *so* proud." He gave her a hearty shake and rewarded her with another kiss.

For the first time that night, Isabella's smile was genuine. She lived to make her parents proud, and tonight they looked just as proud as when she'd graduated class valedictorian from high school and summa cum laude in both college and law school.

All her life Isabella had done what was expected of her and being the only daughter of a prominent senior senator, great things were indeed expected. After obtaining her law degree from Yale, she interned at the White House. There she met Randall, a straight-laced, ambitious attorney who'd swooped into her life with the speed of a locomotive and then disappeared just as quickly. Three years later, he popped up again while she hammered into tax law with Smith, Bryant and Smith, LLC.

Sure, she was dazzled by his attention. The man was exceedingly handsome and came from a powerful and wealthy family, qualities her parents approved.

However, after a few dates, when the newness of Randall wore off, Isabella realized there wasn't much there. No sparks, no romance…no nothing. In fact, she suspected Randall was trying to construct an ideal power couple instead of searching for a true soul mate.

She suspected her father was doing the same.

Many times, she wondered what Randall saw in her. She wasn't ugly, but she certainly wasn't beautiful either. She'd seen pictures of Randall's ex-girlfriends. They all looked as though they should've had long careers in Hollywood or on the runways of Milan.

Isabella had often thought that the only pretty thing about her was her name.

Her mood flip-flopped for the rest of the night and passed by in a blur. There were smiles, laughter and champagne—lots of champagne. Not until her buzz kicked did Isabella relax. It also afforded her the opportunity to detach and watch the swirling excitement as if everyone was talking about someone else's life.

Not her own.

Randall caught her in the act and leaned over to ask, "Honey, are you feeling all right?"

The mindless chatter stopped and everyone refocused their attention on her.

"Of course, sweetheart," she assured. "I'm deliriously happy."

Smiling, Randall squeezed her hand while his dark eyes sparkled. "You can't be any happier than I am."

He was certainly right about that. But who knows? Maybe she would grow to love him.

And in Atlanta...

"Derrick, will you marry me?" Meghan Campbell stared up at her boyfriend with tear-glossed eyes. In her hands a black velvet box held a platinum band nestled in its center. "I know this comes as a surprise," she laughed. "But…I'm hoping you know in your heart of hearts, as well as I do that we belong together."

Derrick closed his eyes and expelled a long breath. After a nice evening out with his Kappa Psi Kappa Fraternity Alumni, he had not expected to come home to this. In hindsight, maybe he should have.

"You don't have to answer right now," Meghan rushed to say. "Just…think about it. I mean, we're happy, right? We have so many things in common. So why not get married?"

"Meghan—"

"Derrick, I know you're scared to settle down," she continued. "But you don't have to be. We don't have to get married right away. If you want we can have a long engagement. You know, so you'll have time to get used to the idea. We can even wait a few years to have children."

Setting his new Distinguished Service Award on top of the coffee table, Derrick fingered his tie loose and then stood from the leather sofa in order to put distance between them. "Meghan—"

"Derrick, please. I—"

"Meghan, stop. Please." He drew a deep breath and forced himself to stare into her sad brown eyes. "I can't marry you," he said as gently as he could. "I love you, but I'm not *in* love with you."

Snapping the velvet box closed, Meghan choked on a sob, while her entire body imploded before his eyes.

Derrick returned to her side, kneeling on the living room's plush carpet and pulling her trembling body into his arms. "I'm so sorry, Meg. I never meant to give you hope. I've always been upfront with you."

Meghan tilted her head, her eyes swimming in tears. "Maybe you could grow to love me?"

Sullen, he shook his head. "I'm sorry." He halfway expected more tears, prepared himself even. What he received instead was a burst of anger.

"You're sorry? Sorry?" With one strong shove, Meghan sent Derrick reeling backwards onto the floor. "Is that all you have to say after three years—you're sorry? Screw you!"

"Meg—"

"Don't! You lied," she screeched, jumping to her feet. "I never—"

"Not with your words but with your actions. You've always made me feel special."

"You are special to me."

"You showered me with gifts, offered me security. You've done everything to give me hope that I would be Mrs. Derrick Knight one day. My father is a Baptist minister. I'm supposed to get married."

Derrick wished with all his might that he could love her the way she wanted to be loved, but he couldn't make his heart do it. He couldn't lie to her or to himself.

Wailing, Meghan kicked over the coffee table, and even sideswiped a lamp on an end table as she stormed across the living room. "I wasted three years waiting for you!"

"I don't consider them a waste," he offered as he climbed to his feet, only to dodge a flying vase aimed at his head.

"I just bet you don't! I've done everything a good girlfriend should do. I've been faithful—"

"I never asked you to do that," he said. "We agreed that this was an open relationship."

Meghan's eyes widened. "You've been sleeping with other women?"

"We agreed—"

"Asshole!"

Another vase soared through the air. When it crashed inches from his head, a few shattered pieces ricocheted into his eyes. "Ow! Meghan you're being unreasonable."

"You're damn right I am." She snatched her purse and coat from the foyer's closet and then turned to give him a final glare. "I never want to see you again. I hate you!"

Derrick watched as she snatched open the front door and flinched when she slammed it behind her. It rattled in her wake. "Well that went well," he mumbled under his breath.

He looked around the high-rise apartment and realized he should be grateful she didn't cause more damage.

When he broke up with Mya, he had to hire a decorator to repair the place.

Sighing, he walked to the center of the room and picked up his award. A corner of the plaque had broken off, but it was nothing he couldn't fix. After another glance around, he promised himself he would clean the mess up in the morning before his flight to Washington. Right now, he just wanted to climb into bed and put this whole fiasco behind him.

In his bedroom, Derrick peeled out of his clothes, showered, and then slid between the bed's satin sheets. After two hours, he was far from dreamland. All he could see was Meghan's angry tears.

And Mya's.

And Genie's.

And Lana's.

Exasperated, he flopped onto his back and stared at the ceiling. They had all loved him. They had all expected a wedding ring. But he wasn't in love with any of them.

"Maybe it's time to face the truth," he said into the darkness. "Love just isn't in the cards for me."

Chapter 2

Isabella didn't float home on a cloud and she doubted she would dream of any happily-ever-after with her newly minted fiancé. Instead, Isabella wondered about the mess she got herself into.

"What do you mean, he proposed? You were supposed to break up with him," Keri thundered into the phone.

"I know. I know. But what was I supposed to do? He had invited our parents to dinner. Everyone was sitting there staring at me."

"You were supposed to say no."

Isabella sighed, and slumped onto the bed. She heard a loud rip, jumped up and ran to the mirror to see a long tear in the back of her dress. "Just great!"

"What happened?"

"Uhm. How soon do you need your green dress back?"

"Izzy, you said you'd be careful!"

"I know. I know." She sighed. Why was she always such a klutz? "It's just a small rip," she lied. "I can fix it." Balancing the phone between her shoulder and chin, Isabella struggled to reach the back zipper. When it jammed halfway down, she opted to pull the silk dress over her head, which caused her to lose her precious balance, drop the phone and crush her toes.

"Ow. Ow, ow." She hopped around the room blind on her good foot. Once the throbbing eased, she shouted down to the floor, "Just a sec, Keri." Isabella wiggled and pulled and after a few long seconds managed to work her way out of the dress. "I'm back."

"What happened?"

"Nothing. I dropped the phone." She sat on the edge of the bed and reached to take off her shoes when one heel came off in her hand. "Uhm, about your shoes…"

"Izzy!"

"I'm sorry. I just…I'm just sorry."

"Forget the shoes. What are you going to do about Randall?"

Isabella checked behind her before easing back onto the bed.

"Isabella, are you there? Hello."

"I'm still here," she mumbled.

"So what are you going to do? I mean, you're not going to go through with it, are you? You're not in love with Randall."

"I could learn to love him."

"What?" Keri shrieked. "Please say you're joking."

Isabella sighed. Was she joking? Really, what was wrong with falling in love *after* marriage? Does true love really exist? Hell, she didn't know anymore.

"Izzy?"

"I don't know, Keri. Randall *is* a good catch and it's not like there's a line of men banging down my front door. There never has been."

"Don't say it like that. What about that guy you met at the library?"

"You mean, Arthur? That was years ago. We went out one time and all he talked about was reaching some ridiculous level in some video game. Besides he had too many no's."

"He had too many what?"

"No's. No job, no car, no money and most importantly no personality. Consequently, he got married last year."

"You're joking."

"I wish I was. I was hard up enough a few months ago and called him again." Isabella grabbed a toss pillow, covered her head and proceeded to scream.

"Izzy? Izzy?" Keri shouted.

When her brief moment of anxiety and frustration passed, Isabella removed the pillow from her head and placed the phone back against her ear. "It's all right. I'm back."

"Okay. So Arthur is off the list. No big deal."

"No big deal? What does it say about the world when he can get hitched and I, an intelligent woman with a damn good job…and somewhat decent looking can only get asked out once every three years?"

"Izzy, stop putting yourself down. You're a pretty girl. Any man would be lucky to have you."

How come she only heard those words from her parents and friends? Acidic tears burned the backs of Isabella's eyes. The truth was the truth. She wasn't beautiful and she should count herself lucky Randall Jarrett ever gave her the time of day. "Randall would make a good husband."

"So you're just going to settle?"

"I didn't say I was settling."

"That is exactly what you're saying. You're letting Randall and your parents run your life."

"No, I'm not."

"Oh, please. Your parents chose your college, law

school, your condo, *half* of your friends and now they have thrown you into Randall's arms."

Isabella groaned at having the truth tossed back at her. The great thing about Keri was her wonderful way of telling it like it is. Sometimes she was a little too blunt, but love it or hate it, everyone always knew where they stood with Keri.

Sometimes Isabella wished she was more like her best friend. For one thing, Keri was gorgeous. Whenever she walked into a room, everyone noticed. Then there was Keri's no-nonsense attitude. She had no time for fools, or "dawgs" looking for a quick score.

"Take control of your life, Izzy," Keri said. "Do something. Stand up for yourself. This is your chance before they marry you off and pump you full of kids. Call Randall tonight and tell him you can't marry him."

"But—"

"No buts. Do it now. Tonight!"

Isabella fell silent while a knot looped and tightened in her chest. "Time to get a backbone," she mumbled.

"That's my girl," Keri encouraged. "Call him and then call me back," she instructed.

Isabella nodded and then rolled onto her back. "But what if he's not there?"

"Izzy!"

"Okay. Okay. I'm calling right now."

"Good. You're doing the right thing."

Then why did it feel like she'd swallowed a fifty-pound lead rock? Isabella disconnected the call, and stared at the phone. Just call him, she told herself. Her hands itched and her fingers tingled, but still she couldn't make the call.

Five minutes went by.

Ten minutes.

Twenty minutes later, Isabella reached for the phone, but after punching in one number, she hung up.

"I'll call him tomorrow."

Tomorrow she'd know what to say.

Derrick strolled through the doors of Herman's Barbershop flashing a wide smile and bobbing his head in greeting to the Saturday morning regulars. For nearly twenty-five years Derrick had been coming to the small shop.

A few men tossed a "Yo, Derrick," his way and he volleyed a "Whassup?" back at them.

Herman Keillor, a tall, robust man, who was in his early seventies, had owned the shop through some hellish times. Most customers came for his wonderful stories. Not only had Herman given Derrick his first haircut when he was just six, but the old man had often bragged about giving Derrick's father his first one as well.

"I was beginning to think you weren't coming this morning," Herman boomed from across the room.

"I always keep my appointments," Derrick said, shuffling across the room, dodging stretched out legs and chunks of shaved hair lying across the floor. "I do have a flight in a few hours, so we're going to have to make this quick."

"Bobby!" Herman shouted. "Get out here and sweep some of this hair up."

A second later, Bobby, Herman's seventeen-year-old great-grandson rushed from the back of the shop with a broom and quickly got to work.

Men in the neighborhood filtered in and out daily, but Saturday remained the shop's busiest day. Six barbers, ranging from old school to new school donned burgundy barber jackets with Herman's name scrawled on the back.

Despite residing in a red brick building that had clearly seen better days, Herman's Barbershop looked brand smacking new on the inside.

"Here. Have a seat," Herman instructed and reached for a black cape.

Derrick took his seat in the offered leather chair and made himself comfortable.

Herman's was the place to be to discuss women, politics and sports. It was a place where men were free to be themselves, get and give advice or just plain bond with one another.

On the suspended television set, some NASCAR race was well on its way, but none of the brothas were paying it any attention.

"Why do you have this stuff on?" Derrick asked.

"Cable is acting up. It's either this or Sponge-Bob," Herman cackled.

"Then never mind." Derrick laughed.

The bell above the shop's door jingled and Derrick looked up to see his buddy Stanley Patterson race inside.

The regulars greeted the lanky redhead with affectionate nicknames ranging from "Breadstick" to "Red" and even "Whitey." A couple of the new clients glanced at Stanley as if they were wondering if he was lost.

"Hey, you beat me here," Stanley said, panting. "I figured you and Meghan would still be celebrating your getting that award."

That comment caught a few ears and Derrick groaned. "Meghan and I decided to move on."

"What?" Stanley thundered. "Why? I thought you two had something going."

"It just didn't work out," he said and hoped that would be the end of it.

It wasn't.

"Did she find out about the others?" Stanley asked.

"My man Derrick be laying the pipe down for real," Bobby chuckled with a note of admiration.

"Humph," Herman grunted his disapproval.

"We had an open relationship," Derrick stressed. Why was everyone forgetting about that major detail?

"Hey, you can pass her my way." J.T., the neighborhood's merchandise peddler, said while showing off a tray of fake Rolexes to potential customers. "I saw you two at Phipps Plaza some time back. You sure know how to pick them. Lawd knows you do."

"You got that right," Stanley cut in before Derrick had a chance to answer. "Thick and curvy with a booty out of this world."

"Stan," Derrick hissed, trying to shut him up.

"What, man?" His buddy laughed. "Everyone in here knows how you roll. You hook up with the finest women in the A-T-L. You're the man."

Bobby stopped sweeping to ask, "How do you do it? Do you have a line or something?"

Just like that Derrick was the center of attention. Bobby looked like he was ready to bust out a pen and paper to take notes.

"Nah. It's nothing like that," Derrick answered modestly.

Disappointment crept slowly across Bobby's face and Derrick had the distinct impression the young man was suffering from a mild case of girl troubles. It wasn't hard to guess why. Acne blanketed the boy's face and his thick black-rimmed glasses looked as though they were a borrowed pair from his great-grandfather.

"It's not important the number of women you get," Herman said. Undoubtedly, he'd noticed Bobby's sullen expression, too. "It's finding that *one* special woman. This knucklehead—" he thumbed Derrick on the back of his head with a plastic comb "—is gonna realize that one of these days."

Derrick smiled and shook his head.

"Be still," Herman instructed.

Herman's declaration didn't seem to cheer Bobby any— in fact, it only won a few chuckles around the shop.

"I'm serious," Herman insisted gruffly. "You young folks." He tsked under his breath. "You just don't know what's important anymore."

"And what's that, old man?" someone questioned near the front door.

"Family," Herman said.

Derrick had mouthed the same answer and shook his head again. The guy by the door must have been new to the shop. The regulars knew Herman never missed an opportunity to climb on his soap box about how young men today where turning their backs on the traditional black family.

"It breaks my heart seeing all these beautiful sisters roaming around here raising these babies by themselves. It's a damn shame," Herman said.

"Hey, I don't have any baby mommas," Derrick said, feeling the need, once again, to defend himself. "And since I'm not ready to settle down, I make sure I practice safe sex."

"Yeah. Me too," Stanley added.

"Safe sex or no sex?" J.T. asked.

Another round of snickering ensued. Stanley's normally pale face bloomed a bright red. Still, it was amazing no one called his Irish friend out or ragged him about trying to date across the color lines. Derrick suspected it was because Stanley was not only a friend of his but was also a member of the Kappa Psi Kappa fraternity. The only white boy to do so.

Being a Kappa man gave Stanley mad respect in the neighborhood since the fraternity did a lot for the community.

"Shoot," J.T. chuckled. "It just don't feel the same with a condom."

"It's gonna feel worse when you catch something you can't get rid of," Herman huffed, and then added under his breath, "Lawd. Lawd. Please help these knuckleheads running around here." He clicked on his razor and started grooming Derrick's edges.

Minutes later, Bobby finished sweeping, Stanley was rapt into the NASCAR race and everyone else returned to their little pockets of conversations. However, Herman's thoughts were apparently still stuck on the previous discussion.

"Let me ask you something," the barber asked suddenly. "Are you happy?"

"Pardon?" Derrick asked, not sure whether he understood.

Herman turned off his razor. "Are you happy?" he repeated.

Again, Derrick didn't really know how to answer. "I, uh—"

"Uh-huh." Herman clicked his razor back on and went back to edging up Derrick's sides. "Let me tell you something while you're 'not ready to settle down.' Men and women were put on this earth to procreate. Marry and multiply. It breaks my heart to remember all the things we as a race had to overcome just for the next generations to become more lost than they ever were."

Derrick squirmed in his seat.

"All anyone talks about is money, fast cars and loose women." Herman tsked again. "We used to come in here and talk about how to advance the race. Now everyone's just hustlin' and only thinking about themselves," Herman said.

"I'm far from being a hustler," Derrick laughed, trying to lighten the old man's mood. "You know how long I've struggled to make a success as a political strategist, bouncing back and forth to Washington. It's a lot of hard work, long hours."

"Uh-huh," Herman said, unimpressed. "Nice slogan to put on your gravestone. Much better than something like: Derrick Knight—a wonderful husband and father."

Derrick swallowed.

"Let me tell you something, son." Herman clicked off his razor and turned the chair so that their eyes would meet. "There's nothing on earth better than the love of a good woman. You think you're a success now? Man, that's nothing compared to what you could do with a soul mate in your corner. Someone to hold you up when you don't think you can stand any longer. It's not about who has the deepest curves or the thickest backside, but someone who, when you look into her eyes, her soul speaks to you down in here." He thumped Derrick's chest, indicating his heart. "Love like that is better than some fancy job or fast car. Love like that is what it's truly all about. I know it and your father knows it, too."

Derrick's parents, now retired and living it up in Florida, shared a love that inspired everyone who knew them. But none of this changed the fact that Derrick had never experienced this ground-shaking love his parents shared.

Never.

Chapter 3

"You didn't tell him," Keri accused, marching into Isabella's apartment. "I should've known you would chicken out."

Isabella cringed and shut the door behind her steaming best friend. "I was going to call him…I just couldn't figure out what to say."

"You say: 'Sorry, Randall, but I can't marry you.' See? Simple," Keri said.

"Simple for you maybe." Isabella shuffled from the door and into the kitchen. She opened and slammed cabinets, while she prepared her morning coffee.

"I don't know why I even bother. You're never going to grow a backbone." Keri slumped into a chair at the kitchen's island. "From now on you're on your own. I'm keeping my two cents to myself."

"C'mon. Don't be like that." Isabella turned to her friend. "I need you in my corner more than ever."

"Need me to do what? Watch you throw your life away and marry the wrong man simply because you're too afraid to hurt anyone's feelings?"

"That's not what's going on."

Keri lifted a dubious brow and crossed her arms.

"Okay, it's sort of like that." Isabella turned toward the coffee maker and hit the brew button. In truth, up until now, she really hadn't minded her parents making all the decisions for her. Mainly because at twenty-seven Isabella still didn't know what she wanted to be when she grew up. How crazy was that?

In a sense, her parents gave her the much needed direction in life. As it turned out, Isabella was a damn good tax attorney. Maybe—just maybe, her parents really did know what was best for her—including who she should marry.

"I'm going to do it," she said softly, making a decision and ignoring Keri's narrowing gaze. "I thought all night about it and…well, I do have *some* feelings for Randall." She nodded more to convince herself than her best friend. "We're good friends and plenty of therapists and psychotherapists say that's the foundation for a strong marriage. Love will come."

"Nothing like putting the cart before the horse," Keri said.

Isabella's chin thrust forward while her intense gaze leveled with Keri's.

"Oh, God. You're serious."

"Love isn't like the movies," Isabella said, and then added in a sullen whisper. "At least not for me. If I turn this down, there's a strong possibility that I could end up an old maid."

"Oh, stop it," Keri snapped. "There's no such thing anymore. We're the same age. You don't see me rushing to the altar with the wrong man."

"That's because you have options. You've dated more men this year than I've dated my entire life. The rules for beautiful people are different from the plain Janes of the world. Beggars can't be choosey."

Keri stepped forward and placed a hand against her shoulder. "Izzy—"

"Don't." Isabella drew back, breaking contact. "I'm not trying to put myself down. I'm just facing facts. And the fact of the matter is: a proposal from Randall Jarrett is like winning the marital lottery. He's handsome, successful—"

"Okay. Okay." Keri said and threw up her hands. "Stop trying to sell him to me. You're marrying him not me. I'm just going to buy a big-o tub of popcorn and watch this fiasco from the sidelines."

"Keri—"

Her hands ascended higher in surrender. "Whatever you decide, I'll support you."

"Good." It was an obvious lie, but Isabella lacked the bravery to call her on it. But there was one thing she needed her best friend's help with. "Uhm," Isabella drawled and then swallowed the gigantic lump lodged in the center of her throat. "I, uh—"

Keri lowered her hands, but then crossed her arms while her eyebrows played a game of see-saw. "What? Surely this can't get any worse."

Isabella jabbed her hands onto her waist.

"I mean, better," her best friend corrected. "It can't get any better."

Isabella trudged past the arctic sarcasm. "Randall doesn't know I'm a virgin."

"Surely, it's not hard to guess."

"Will you please be serious?"

Keri's laugh erupted like a machine gun's rapid fire. "I was being serious."

Clenching her jaw in mutinous silence, Isabella poured

coffee into a ridiculous-size mug with the logo: *Geeks do it better!*

Keri read the mug and just shook her head.

"It's meant to inspire," Isabella said after following her gaze.

"Of course it is," Keri said with a roll of her eyes. "So, what's your point? Randall doesn't know you're a virgin. And?"

Her feelings still bruised, Isabella shook her head. "Never mind. Forget it."

"Izzy, spit it out before I strangle you."

Squirming while her face scorched with embarrassment, she plunged ahead. "I don't want to disappoint Randall. You know…on our honeymoon."

"As long as you have a pulse, it's fairly hard to disappoint a man in bed. And for some, a pulse is highly overrated."

Isabella's patience finally snapped. "Will you please be serious! I'm pouring my heart out to you and you think it's amateur night at the comedy club."

Keri's hands shot back up into the air. "My bad. What is it that you want me to do?"

"Teach me," Isabella said simply.

"Teach you what?"

"You know…how to, uhm, spice things up on our honeymoon." One look into her friend's amused face and Isabella regretted she'd ever brought it up, but Keri's next words surprised her.

"All right. You have yourself a teacher."

There were times when Derrick hated his job.

And flying to Washington in the middle of a thunderstorm was one of those times.

"You look green," Charlie Masters, one of his best

friends and frat brothers, shouted from the pilot seat. "If the storm is bothering you, why don't you just sit back and close your eyes?"

A jagged bolt of lightning appeared to strike dangerously close to the airplane's small wing. Derrick wondered how he let his buddy talk him into flying in this small death trap instead of him going commercial. These tiny things had a habit of dropping out of the sky.

"How the hell can you see where you're going?" Derrick snapped, trying to hide his fear. He didn't have much success given how the rain and the wind tossed the plane around like a paper kite.

"Relax," Charlie said with an irritating chuckle. "I'll have you on the ground in about twenty minutes."

Derrick's hard gaze speared his all-too-calm buddy. "You forgot to add alive and in one piece."

Charlie's hazel-green eyes twinkled with amusement. "Well, I'll do what I can." He laughed.

Derrick groaned because the alternative, punching the pilot, wasn't a smart idea. Out of the six tight-knit Kappa Psi Kappa fraternity brothers, Derrick and Charlie's friendship went all the way back to diapers—simply because their mothers had been best friends for over forty years.

The women had married around the same time and had even delivered baby boys ten days apart. The boys grew up thick as thieves. But where Derrick tended to be more aloof about his handsome looks, Charlie milked his *GQ* status for all it was worth with the ladies.

The plane's turbulence worsened and Derrick's hands tightened on the sides of his chair. "Charlie, land this damn thing."

"Roger that!" Charlie tipped the wheel shaft down and the plane tilted into a nose dive.

Derrick shouted a list of profanities.

Charlie, the jerk, laughed.

An hour later, a frazzled Derrick and a happy-go-lucky Charlie checked in to the Hamilton Crowne Plaza off 14th and K Streets. The front desk clerk questioned Derrick several times as to whether he was all right.

Derrick grunted while Charlie slapped him on the back. "He's just fine," Charlie laughed. "Just needs to learn how to relax."

Derrick shrugged off the heavy hand and cut a narrow gaze over his shoulder, however, the end result just further amused his traveling companion.

"I don't see why you're so upset," Charlie mused as they walked down the hallway of the fifth floor to their suites. "I got you here in one piece, didn't I?"

"Barely," Derrick muttered, stopping before room 519 and cramming his card key into the electronic lock. "I'm renting a rental car and driving back."

Charlie's bark of laughter rumbled through the whole floor as he stopped at room 521. "Now don't be like that."

Derrick entered his suite and back-kicked the door. He could still hear Charlie after the door slammed. "It's time to get a new set of friends," he mumbled under his breath as he plopped his suitcase and overnight bag onto the bed and then realized he'd been given a double instead of a king-size bed.

"Just great." At six foot six, a double meant he would either have to sleep diagonally or put up with his feet hanging off the bed—something he absolutely hated. "Don't sweat it," he coached. "You're only going to be here for two days."

He waltzed over to the window and opened the blinds. The view of the powerful political town was magnificent. The earlier thunderstorms had disappeared but left the day a blurry depressing gray. "Two days," he reminded himself. "It's probably going to be a living hell."

Isabella wandered through the aisle of the Capitol Hill Bookstore's Health and Wellness section, praying that she wouldn't bump into anyone she knew. Her lame disguise of being dressed head to toe in black—complete with a black duster raincoat, black oversize sunglasses and black fedora hat only seemed to draw more attention to her.

"Relax, relax," she mumbled and searched crammed bookshelves for the list of books Keri instructed her to buy.

A salesperson popped out of nowhere and asked, "Can I help you, ma'am?"

Isabella gasped and nearly jumped out of her skin before whirling around and physically blocking the bookshelf to prevent him from noticing the titles she was looking at. "Uh, no. I, huh, am just looking around." She beamed a nervous smile.

The employee stared at her with his eyebrows gathered at the center of his forehead. "All right. Well, just let me know if you need anything." He crept backward away from her like he was afraid to turn his back on a crazy person.

It wasn't until she was alone in the aisle again that she expelled the air burning in her lungs. "All right. Just grab the books and get out of here," she coached, snatching books like a wild hurricane.

Her arms full, Isabella performed a sort of walk/ run from the back of the bookstore up to the cashier counter. The only problem was there was a long line snaking around a gold post labyrinth. She lowered her head and mumbled a curse.

The giant in front of her turned around. "I'm sorry. Did you say something?"

Isabella's knees nearly folded at the incredibly sexy

baritone rumbling from above her, but no way was she going to glance up so he could get a better view of the books in her arms. Instead, she pretended like he hadn't spoken to her.

Sure enough, at her silence, he turned back around.

She chanced a peek over the rim of her dark sunglasses only to be startled by the sheer size of the man's broad shoulders and Texas-size back that narrowed into a trim waist. For a fleeting moment, she wished he wasn't wearing the long leather coat; she had a sneaking suspicion that the man probably had a nice butt.

Isabella's cheeks heated at the idea.

"Next in line," the bored, robotic cashier called out and everyone in line took a small step forward.

When Isabella stepped to where the potential hunk previously stood, she caught a whiff of the most seductive male cologne she had ever smelled in her life. It was so heavenly. She closed her eyes and imagined floating on a cloud. She drew in a deep breath and was unaware that her feet were moving on their own accord.

That is until she smacked into the Goliath's back. "Oh." Her eyes sprung open and her arms tightened on the books she nearly dropped. "Sorry," she mumbled, casting her eyes downward again.

A long silence, and then, "Not a problem."

Good God, she could listen to this man talk all night.

"Next, please."

The line crept forward.

Isabella's gaze returned to the man's backside and then slowly traveled down to the man's large feet. What had Keri said a man's shoe size represented? Surely not…oh, my. She struggled to gulp down the rising lump in her throat. Not to mention, it felt as if someone had shut off the air conditioner.

Guilt pricked her conscience. Why on earth was she salivating over a faceless stranger when she was newly engaged to one of D.C.'s most prominent bachelors? She laughed at herself and shook off the effects of Mr. Tall, Dark, and undoubtedly Handsome's hypnotic cologne and waited patiently for her turn at the cashier counter—which turned out to be another humiliating experience altogether.

"Did you find everything you were looking for?" the cashier asked, fluttering an amused smile at Isabella once she started reading and scanning the titles.

"Yes. Yes, I did," Isabella said and fumbled for her credit card from her purse.

One book the clerk picked up caused Isabella to turn a bright red. "Uhm," the clerk said. "You're going to love this one. My husband and I have the audio book."

"I'm sort of in a hurry," Isabella whispered.

"Oh. Of course." The woman turned off her friendly persona and quickly scanned the rest of the books. "Do you have a member discount card?"

Isabella's mystery man departed from the cashier next to her with a departing, "Have a good evening." And Isabella caught a quick glance at the man's handsome good looks.

The two cashiers and Isabella followed his departure with slack jaws and dreamy expressions. It wasn't until he disappeared out the glass door and into the gray afternoon that they were finally freed from the spell he'd cast.

"Oooh, girl. If I wasn't married," Isabella's cashier said to her colleague. "I'd jumped his bones right here at the counter."

"Shoot. Didn't you hear how he was flirting with me? I think he likes big girls."

Isabella cleared her throat.

Her cashier's face turned stony. "Your total is $98.54."

Isabella handed over her credit card and rushed through the remaining transaction. As she grabbed her bag, she caught the cashier's whispered words to her colleagues. "Now that's an uptight one. No wonder she needed those books."

The women giggled and then shouted, "Next in line!"

Humiliated, Isabella forced one foot in front of the other and slipped out of the bookstore.

"Stop, thief! He snatched my purse," a woman screamed.

Isabella barely had time to glance up before a lanky teenager plowed into her like a defensive linebacker. She was swept off her feet in an instant and when slammed backwards onto the concrete, every ounce of air rushed out of her lungs.

"Hey, let go of me," a boy squeaked somewhere near.

"I don't think so, buddy," came that familiar, sexy baritone.

Isabella opened her eyes, but quickly closed them again because of the light drizzle splattering against her face.

"Over there, officer," a hysterical woman cried.

Isabella groaned as she sat up. Everything ached—muscles and bones she had long forgotten about.

"All right. We got him. Thanks for your help, sir."

"Don't mention it," sexy baritone said.

"Ma'am, are you all right?"

The voice was now directly above her and it had the same effect on her as it did in the crowded bookstore.

"Ma'am?"

Isabella opened her eyes to see a giant hand extended toward her. Her gaze slowly climbed upward until she stared into a face that wiped all thoughts of her fiancé from her mind.

Chapter 4

Derrick grew increasingly concerned about the dazed woman on the wet concrete. She made no attempt to get up so he wondered whether she'd broken anything in that nasty fall. "Maybe I should get you to the hospital," he said. "You don't look too good."

"Huh? What? Oh." She blinked and shook her head. "I'm all right."

He didn't believe that for a second.

"Oh, God," she exclaimed, her eyes wide with horror as she glanced around at the books scattered around her. She frantically started snatching them up.

"Here. Let me help you," Derrick said.

"No! No. I got it."

Too late. Derrick picked up *The Complete Idiot's Guide to Amazing Sex* and *Sex for Dummies*. "Interesting reading," he joked.

The woman's sienna-hued complexion paled to a sickly brown. "Those are personal." She snatched the books out of his hands and then tried to lumber awkwardly to her feet.

Ever the gentleman, Derrick placed a guiding hand against her elbow. "I'm sorry. I didn't mean to offend you."

"Forget about it," she mumbled and turned with her arms loaded down with books. "Taxi!"

"Wait. Aren't these yours, too?" He bent down and retrieved her ruined hat and broken sunglasses. "Just keep them. Taxi!"

He laughed. "Don't be silly. Here you go."

A yellow cab drove up to the curb, which held about two feet of water, and caused a mini tidal wave to splash up and drench the hurried woman.

Derrick's laughter was out before he could stop it and when she slowly pivoted to meet his amused gaze, he couldn't remember ever seeing someone look so adorable.

"Sorry. It's not funny," he said in an attempt to smooth things over, but he didn't wipe the smile off his face.

Mute, the woman twirled back toward the cab. However, she now had a difficult time trying to open the back door with an armload of books.

"Here, let me help you with that."

"That's all right. I got it," she lied.

Derrick ignored her blustering and opened the cab's door and gestured for her to hop in. "After you," he said gallantly.

She rolled her eyes at his flair of dramatics and Derrick couldn't help but remain intrigued by the woman.

With a loud huff, she climbed into the cab.

He quickly followed suit.

"What are you doing?" she asked, scooting over to the other side behind the driver before he sat on her.

"Sharing a cab," he said amicably. "You don't mind, do you?"

She clinched her jaw and looked at him like she absolutely *did* mind.

"Great." Derrick shut the door without waiting for her answer.

"Where to?" The cab driver asked the question as he clicked on the meter.

"Okinawa Sushi & Grill," they answered in unison and then cut startled looks at each other.

"Well." Derrick settled back in his seat. "Looks like something else we enjoy."

"Something else?"

He didn't answer, but his gaze dropped to her bundle of ruined books while she tried to stuff them back into the bag.

She sucked in a breath and jerked her gaze away.

He chuckled, amused by how easy it was to fluster the young woman. While she wasn't looking, he took the time to assess his riding companion. Average height. Average weight. Add it all together, it somehow equaled adorable.

He couldn't pull his eyes away from her.

"Will you please stop doing that?"

"Hmm?"

She faced him again and he discovered that she had perhaps the longest eyelashes he'd ever seen. They framed her brown eyes beautifully.

"Stop staring at me," she ordered with a sharp thrust of her chin. "It's rude."

He smiled, unable to help himself, really. "Sorry," he said, but made no attempt to stop. "Oh, by the way, name's Derrick Knight."

Rolling her eyes, she returned her attention to the passing gray scenery while scooting farther away from him.

"Speaking of being rude," he began. "Are you ever going to thank me for helping you?"

That caught her attention. He was amazed she didn't get whiplash trying to meet his gaze again.

"Excuse you?"

Derrick's lips curled higher as he flashed his winning smile. "Forgive me for my stuttering problem, ma'am. It's apparently worse than I thought." Her eyes narrowed and drew attention to her cute pudgy nose. He had an insatiable urge to give it a little tweak.

"You want me to thank you for knocking me flat on my butt—"

"Ah, ah, ah." He waved his finger. "The purse snatcher knocked you down. I caught him and then helped you up and uh…helped you gather your books." He straightened in his seat and crossed his arms. "I'm a hero."

"A very modest one," she droned sarcastically.

He popped the collar of his raincoat. "Well. What can I say?"

They arrived at their destination and Derrick stopped her the moment she reached for her purse. "The fare is on me."

"I can pay my half," she protested.

"I'm sure you can, but I'm much too much of a gentleman to allow you."

"Allow?"

He nodded and handed the cabbie a couple of twenties. "Keep the change."

"Thank you, sir. Thank you," said the driver.

Derrick's mysterious companion bolted from the cab, and he found himself having to rush to catch up to her. "Hey! Where's the fire?"

The woman quickened her pace without sparing him a glance or answering his question.

"If you worry that I'm some sort of stalker, let me assure you I'm not."

"You could have fooled me." She sprinted through the

restaurant's door and scanned the place to see if she saw her mother.

He laughed, though he had to admit his behavior was a quagmire to himself. "Listen. I know we didn't exactly meet under the ideal circumstances, but uh—"

"There you are, Mr. Knight."

Derrick turned and smiled at Congressman Jamison Scott. "Hello, Congressman."

At that moment, Isabella caught sight of her mother waving from the other side the restaurant.

Derrick regretfully watched her slip away. Later, he realized, he never caught her name, but he could have sworn he saw an engagement ring.

"This is positively going to be the wedding of the season," Katherine droned from across the table. "Of course, I think we should have it in Martha's Vineyard, but your father insists on having it at our Arlington estate. What do you think?"

When Isabella didn't answer, her mother prodded her. "Isabella?" She waved a hand in front of her face.

"Huh? What?" Isabella hadn't heard half of what her mother was rambling about the wedding.

"The wedding?" her mother said. "I asked whether you wanted to have the wedding in Martha's Vineyard or in Arlington. Are you okay?"

"Yeah, yeah." She cleared her throat. "I don't understand why we can't just have a small ceremony," Isabella said, popping two pain pills into her mouth. "At this rate, I would prefer it if we just went to the courthouse and do this."

Katherine's face twisted in horror.

"It's just an idea," Isabella retracted.

"It's a terrible one," Katherine said, reaching across

the dining table for the travel-size tube of pain medication. "This is the social function of the year for the Kanes."

"I think you've said that already."

Katherine pursed her lips together and then tried another tactic. "Well, your father is on cloud nine about this political merger. A highly publicized wedding with the Jarretts in an election year is just what he needs to get the voters to forget about his backing that Davis Bill."

"I'm not cattle," Isabella mumbled and resumed playing with her smoked sea bass.

Her mother chased the pills with the rest of her champagne and then returned her attention to Isabella. "What was that, sweetheart?"

"Nothing."

"Of course, I think a lot of it has to do with Randall reminding your father how he used to be when he first arrived on the Hill." Katherine leveled a sweet smile at her daughter and then reached over and cupped one of her apple-plump cheeks. "My baby. I can't believe you're about to get married. Where has the time gone?"

Isabella smiled back at her mother and covered the hand on her cheek with their own. A measure of happiness bloomed in her heart. She loved being the cause of her parents' happiness. It was almost worth marrying someone she didn't love.

"I think it's time."

Confused, Isabella stared at her mother. "Time for what?"

Katherine cleared her throat. "You know. Time."

Isabella stared.

Her mother lowered her hand and shifted around in her chair. After making a few cursory glances over her shoulder, she leaned forward.

Still at a loss, Isabella followed suit and leaned closer as well.

"Time for...*The Talk,*" Katherine whispered. "You know."

"The Talk?"

Her mother nodded and resumed looking uncomfortable in her chair.

Finally, it hit Isabella. "Oh." A rush of heat surged through her. "Oh. *The Talk.*" Now it was her turn to shift uncomfortably. "That's okay, Mom. There's no need for that. It's okay." She reached for her untouched champagne and downed the contents in a single gulp.

Stricken, Katherine pressed a hand against her heart. "Isabella Elizabeth Kane, don't tell me that you've... that you're no longer...you know." She whipped her head around; making sure again no one was listening, and leaned forward to whisper, "A virgin."

The pain medication lost the war with Isabella's raging migraine. She couldn't believe she was having this conversation. "Of course I am," she whispered, equally appalled.

Her mother almost collapsed with relief. "Oh thank goodness. I knew I raised a good Baptist girl." She finally picked up her shoulders and straightened in her chair. "In fact, I'm sure it's one of the qualities Randall likes about you. You're so pure and innocent," her mother prattled on. "A man knows the difference between a woman you play with and a woman you marry—especially a political man."

Isabella went back to feeling like cattle. For the past week she'd tried to convince herself that Randall's proposal was based on love or at least a serious case of like, but her mother dismissed those notions with the same ease in which she'd told her that Santa Claus and the Easter Bunny weren't real.

Pressing her lips together, Isabella tuned out her mom

and went back to pushing her food around her plate. She lost her appetite over an hour ago. Not that her mother would notice.

"Isabella," Katherine snapped.

"What? Huh?"

Her mother's fork tumbled from her fingers. "You haven't been listening to a word I've said," she accused.

Isabella started to deny the charge but then decided to come clean. "Sorry. I just…have a lot on my mind," she offered with a smile. "You know: the wedding and all. What were you saying?"

Katherine still looked put out, but continued in a low voice. "I was talking to you about your honeymoon night."

Isabella fought all that was holy not to groan and roll her eyes.

"When your father and I—"

"Mom," Isabella cut her off. Despite being twenty-seven, and being the product of her parents' coupling, Isabella didn't want to imagine her parents ever having sex. "I know it's important for you to have this conversation with me, but I *really* don't think I can handle it."

Katherine looked hurt.

"It's just…awkward," Isabella covered. "Maybe I should learn about it like everyone else—from my friends."

Her mother rolled her eyes. "Please not from that Wakey girl."

"Waqueisha."

"Whatever. She'll probably tell you to charge for it."

"Mom."

Katherine waved her hand in the air. "Fine. Talk to your friends. But take my advice: it's best to lie still and recite the alphabet. It'll be over before you reach Z."

"Mother."

"Alright, alright." Her mother tossed her hands up in the air. "That's all I have to say."

Isabella sincerely hoped so.

Chapter 5

"You never caught her name?" Charlie repeated.

"I know. I haven't crashed and burned that badly since elementary school," Derrick told his friend at the hotel's bar while he tried to understand his disappointment every time he thought about the shy, skittish woman.

Charlie gave his buddy a good hearty pound on the back. "Well, don't beat yourself up about it. We all have one off day every once in a while. Never happened to me, but I've heard stories."

Derrick laughed. "Of course not."

"Drinks are on me, old man," Charlie chuckled. "It's probably all downhill from here. From now on you're going to have to start prowling for dates at the local bingo halls."

"Very funny."

"I'm just saying."

Derrick let the fact that Charlie was the eldest of the two by ten days slide because today Derrick's game was indeed off. He took another deep pull from his beer bottle and imagined for the umpteenth time what his little drowned rat would've looked like with dry hair and makeup. He hated he couldn't see what dangerous curves lay beneath her bulky, black trench coat.

But then there was that moment in the cab when their eyes had met. He felt…something. It wasn't sexual, though there was no question he had been attracted to her. It was…

"It's not about who has the deepest curves or the thickest backside, but someone who, when you look into her eyes, her soul speaks to you down in here."

Derrick gulped hard at the sound of Herman's gravelly voice floating in his head. He looked at the three empty bottles lined on the bar and decided he'd had too much to drink.

"Oh, it's just as well," he mumbled. "The last thing I need to do is screw up another woman's life."

Nestled in bed, Isabella pored through her clinical sex books with a growing sense of disappointment. Where was the hot, spicy or even juicy stuff that was going to make her a star in the bedroom? All her life, she'd heard how sex was such a big deal; from the whisperings in high school bathrooms to hormone-charged sorority sisters to every cable show in America.

Sex was a big deal.

True, she wasn't completely clueless. She knew the logistics, but not what unlocked passion. And passion was what she and Randall desperately needed.

Or at the very least a spark.

Derrick Knight's dreamy hypnotic eyes blazed to the forefront of her mind and her body tingled in response. Handsome failed to describe a man like that and undoubtedly women were reduced to silly putty beneath his twinkling gaze. She would have been too if it hadn't been for her complete mortification for toting sex how-to books around town.

The phone rang, snapping Isabella out of her make-believe conversation.

"Hello."

"*Mahogany* is on HBO," Rayne, another close sorority sister sing-songed over the line.

Isabella quickly searched among the books for the TV remote.

"You got it?" Rayne asked.

"Just a sec." Isabella found the remote and quickly tuned in to the spot where *"Do you know where you're going to?"* floated through the speakers.

"I love this movie," Rayne sighed.

"Yeah. Me, too." Isabella snuggled farther into the comforter and wished that she had a mug of hot chocolate.

"I heard you were engaged," Rayne said. "Congratulations."

Isabella winced. "I'm sorry. I meant to call everyone, but things are a little crazy around here."

There was a long silence and then, "I'm a little confused," her girlfriend said softly. "I thought things weren't that serious between you two. Last I heard you were, uhm—"

"Going to break things off," Isabella finished.

"Yeah."

Isabella would have to prepare an answer to this question, something better than the truth.

"What do you mean you can learn to love him? This is the twenty-first century," Rayne said once Isabella finished her story. "The only reason women should marry is for love."

Isabella glanced at the TV screen just as Diana Ross and Billy Dee Williams were embroiled in a heated argument. "Life isn't like the movies."

"Your family is pressuring you to do this, aren't they?"

"No."

Silence greeted the lie and Isabella had to backtrack a bit. "Not really."

Rayne clucked her tongue.

The friends returned their attention to the movie. Out of the many personalities of Isabella's close sorority sisters, she and Rayne were the ones with the most in common: highly intelligent, but shy introverts who were often pressured to the whims of their families.

On screen, came one of the famous lines from the movie.

"Success means nothing without someone you love to share it with."

Isabella and Rayne sighed dreamily.

"Life *should* be like the movies," Rayne commented. "Every woman should be rewarded with a nice happily-ever-after with a man as handsome as Billy Dee."

Or Derrick Knight, Isabella thought, but said aloud, "Amen."

When the credits finally rolled, the ladies said their goodnights and hung up. Isabella cleared the books off the bed, grabbed her teddy bear and curled into her pillow; but as she drifted off to sleep, she imagined that she wore Diana Ross's large white fur coat threading through the crowd at the end of *Mahogany* but the man guaranteeing that he could get her old man back was the exceedingly handsome Derrick Knight.

Randall Jarrett was a happy man. Not only was his career on track, he had closed the deal on obtaining the perfect political wife. He smiled while he lathered up in the shower. Senator Kane was a force of nature on Capitol Hill and Randall wanted to be just like him. Who knows? Maybe he would be the next Obama.

Already the Kanes and his parents were spreading the news to their family and friends. His phone had been ringing off the hook from stunned ex-girlfriends and old fraternity brothers. Charles and Taariq thought he needed to get his head examined for turning in his single's card so soon. Hylan and Stanley just couldn't stop laughing.

The only call that was missing was from his ex-best friend and frat brother Derrick. Randall and Derrick hadn't seen or talked to each other in years—ever since Randall caught Derrick in bed with Christina Faye, his girlfriend and first prospective wife. Derrick had fed him some cockamamy story about how nothing had happened, but Derrick's reputation made the declaration impossible to believe.

Boys will be boys, especially when the object in college was to score with as many women as possible, but Christina had been different. Randall had issued a "hands off" alert, but Derrick just had to stab him in the back.

But everything had worked out. He had Isabella now—and she would be the perfect politician's wife.

His mood only brightened as he whistled and enjoyed the bathroom's acoustics. After he scoured every inch of his six-foot-three frame, he stepped out of the shower and began dancing in front of the steam-covered mirror.

"I see you're in a good mood."

Randall jumped but then smiled at his long-legged visitor. "I have every right to be in a good mood, sweetheart. You're looking at the future president of the United States."

"Oh. Are we having that dream again?"

"A dream that's going to be reality. Mark my words. Give me 12-15 years, tops." He removed the towel from his waist and then snapped it against her ample bottom.

Randall's curvy guest just glared. "I can't believe you did it."

"C'mon." Randall squeezed toothpaste onto his toothbrush and began scrubbing his extremely straight pearly-white teeth.

"If you're going to marry her, then I can't see you anymore," she said.

Randall stopped scrubbing and turned his incredulous gaze toward her. "Why?" he asked, and then spat into the sink.

"You're kidding me, right?"

"But we talked about this," he said. "I *have* to marry Isabella. She is the perfect choice for my career. She has the breeding, a good reputation and hell, I think the girl is still a virgin. It doesn't get any better than that."

"Well, thanks a lot!" His girlfriend turned on her heel, and stomped away.

"Aw, hell." Randall turned on the water and quickly rinsed out his mouth before racing after her. When he had caught up with her, she had damn near reached the front door.

"Come on, baby." He twirled her around to face him. "What's gotten into you? We've been over all of this before."

"You just don't get it. Do you stop and think for one second about how all this makes me feel? What about me? I'm the one that should be your wife. I'm the one you've been screwing the last three years. I'm the one that puts up with your bull day after day."

"Bull?"

"Yeah, bull." She snatched her arm from his firm grip and then stabbed him in the chest with an acrylic nail. "Everything is about your career. The right school. The right job. The right wife. What am I, chopped liver?"

"No, baby." Randall lifted the hand planted in the center of his chest and brought it up to his lips to kiss her fingers. "You're my heart. You know, I can't live without you. You'll always be in my life."

"What—as your mistress?"

"As my true love." He pulled her stiff body into his arms. "You know how the game is played. I'm striving to be one of the most powerful men in Washington, and I can't do that without you in my corner."

"Then put a ring on my finger."

"I can't, baby. Not with your father's criminal record, and that bit of shoplifting you did back in high school."

"I was a teenager," she protested.

"What about that concealed weapons charge when you were in college?"

"It wasn't my gun. My ex-boyfriend—"

"It doesn't matter," he said. "You'd be crucified in the media and my career would be over before it ever got started."

"Jesus, Randall. What did you do, run a background check on me?" She tried to wiggle out of his arms, but he refused to let her go.

"Of course I did." He laughed. "I'm not taking any chances, and I don't like surprises."

"Let me go." She shoved at his chest while angry tears spilled over her thick lashes and raced down her cheeks. "Damn you. Let me go!"

Determined for her to see reason, Randall tightened his grip. "Baby, I'm doing this for the both of us," he cooed and rained a few kisses against her turned cheek. "Trust me. I'm going to always take care of you. I promise."

To his surprise, she began to sob.

"But I don't want you to marry her," she whined.

"I know, baby." Randall kissed her again. Slowly the fight drained from her body and he held her as she slumped to the floor. He gently pushed her thick mane of curls and tilted her chin toward him, so that their eyes could meet. "I want you to remember that even though I'm marrying Isabella, it's you that I love. Understand?"

A small whimper passed through her lips and Randall smiled and then proceeded to make love to her on the foyer's hardwood floor.

Chapter 6

After a month, Isabella slowly warmed to the idea of marrying Randall. At the very least, she was enjoying the attention her diamond ring brought. Family members, friends and even strangers would stop her and gawk at the sparkling jewel. Most of the women would cast coveted glances over at Isabella. They took in her plain attire, her uninspired hairdo and her clean but makeup-less face. She knew the question dancing in their minds: How did a plain Jane like her land a prize like Randall?

Isabella basked in their jealousy—mainly because beautiful women had never been jealous of her before. The whole experience was rather...nice.

This night, however, Randall and her parents were hosting one incredible engagement party. All of her father's big political movers and shakers on Capitol Hill put in an appearance and her fiancé looked as though he'd won the lottery.

She, however, endured an endless line of she-wolves. Randall's legion of female admirers smiled in her face and congratulated her; but the moment they walked away, their constant buzzing behind their pretty manicures launched Isabella's insecurities to an all-time high.

"She better keep a tight rein on Randy if she knows what's good for her," Felicia Ledford buzzed to her girlfriend as she sashayed past Isabella.

"Oh, just ignore them," Keri said, taking her by the arm and leading her to the bar where her other sorors, Rayne and Sylvia Graham, were already nursing their drinks. "They're just jealous."

"I guessed that much," Isabella mumbled.

Keri rolled her eyes and shook her head. "If you're going to be a politician's wife, you're going to have to develop tougher skin."

"You sound like my mother."

"Well, your mother is right—for once." Keri glanced around and drained the rest of her drink. "In this town when they sense weakness, they move in for the kill."

Realizing the truth of her best friend's words, Isabella stiffened her spine.

"That's my girl," Keri praised. "Now let's see if we can get ourselves another drink. Bartender," she called.

"There you are, Izzy," Waqueisha Tenney, another sorority sister, rushed over to the bar in a tight, gold metallic dress and surveyed the four women. "Looks like you guys have found the best place to hide."

The Italian bartender placed two cocktails in front of Keri and Isabella.

"I'll have what they're having," Waqueisha said, and then leaned over to whisper in Isabella's ear. "Girl, I hate to tell you this, but your parents sure know how to throw one boring-ass party. I figured you guys would have Jay-Z or Akon bumping in here."

Isabella laughed. "Yeah, right. You know Randall doesn't like rap music."

"Then what does he listen to—Tony Bennett?"

Isabella hid her answer beneath a loud cough.

"What? I didn't catch that."

"Alabama," she blurted.

Her two friends stared at her, and then Waqueisha asked, "You mean the country group?"

"They're not so bad…once you get used to them," Isabelle lied, shrugging.

After another long stare, her friends covered their crooked smiles by turning up their cocktail glasses.

"Next time," Waqueisha said when she came up for air, "you come to me and I'll hook you up with a *real* party."

"Speaking of which," Keri jumped in. "Where's my invitation to that Kidd Rhymes release party in Atlanta? Everyone's buzzing about it all over the blogs."

A smile exploded across Waqueisha's face. Her event planning business had taken off in the last two years with Kidd Rhymes being her biggest client to date.

"Hey, if you girls are willing to fly down, I'll be glad to hook you up."

Excited, Keri bounced on her toes and sloshed her drink. "Are you kidding me? Hell yeah, we'll come."

"Keri," Isabella hissed, too aware that her best friend's near squeals drew curious eyes in their direction.

"You'll come too, right, Izzy?" Keri asked, ignoring the subtle hint to calm down.

"Well, I—"

"You *have* to come," her sorors implored, their eyes begging.

"It'll be your last hoorah before you officially become a politician's wife."

"You mean my first, don't you?" Isabella joked. Both of them knew full well she was not the party type—especially when it came to attending some big rap party.

She could already see herself holding up the walls, afraid someone would and wouldn't ask her to dance.

Her girlfriends' faces fell in obvious disappointment, triggering Isabella's need to fix things.

"Well, I'm not saying 'no,'" Isabella covered, but was quickly interrupted before she could say anything else.

"Isabella," Randall said, rudely sliding in between her and her friends. "We're supposed to be networking. What are you doing hiding at the bar?" His arms wrapped possessively around her waist as he leaned in and whispered, "This is an important night, sweetheart. It's imperative we leave a good impression with these people. Any one of them could be my ticket into office."

Despite her irritation, Isabella clamped her mouth shut. Behind him, her sorority sisters rolled their eyes, expressing exactly how she felt.

However, her troubled emotions must have still shown on her face because Randall's next instruction was for her to "smile."

From across the room, she caught her father's eye and she forced the corners of her lips upward before quickly taking another gulp of her cocktail. She was definitely going to need plenty of drinks.

Keri gave Randall a pointed look and then maneuvered around him. "C'mon. Let's do like your fiancé says and mingle."

Isabella didn't have it in her to protest and allowed her friend to direct her away. However, she did catch Randall's irritation from the corner of her eyes. "Why did you do that?" she hissed at Keri.

"Why do you think?" Keri snapped back. "I can't stand that man."

"Keri—"

"Look, he wants you to mingle. We're going to mingle. Ah, Senator Winfield." Keri stopped and offered the Ken-doll look-alike a stunning smile. "So nice to see you."

Winfield perked up and returned the favor. After he imparted his congratulations to Isabella, his attention returned to Keri, despite the narrowed gaze from his wife.

Isabella, still enjoying the slight buzz from the champagne, glanced around the crowded room. It was her party and yet she felt like the loneliest woman in the room. Everyone appeared to be having a great time. She, on the other hand, wondered how much longer before everyone would go home.

"I don't know how she did it," a female's voice floated over to her. "She must be one of those closet freaks. You know how buck wild Randall is in the bedroom."

Isabella twisted around, trying to see who was talking.

"Girl, don't I know it," a short brunette near the fireplace confided. "Randy was the best lover I ever had. I want to scratch his fiancée's eyes out. I mean really—her?"

"I know," the voice said. "But if I know our Randy, he bores easy. Soon as he gets tired of her, he'll come running back and I'll keep the sheets turned down."

Isabella dropped her champagne glass, swiveled toward the two mysterious women, but ran smack into a waiter carrying a tray of hors d'oeuvres. A collective gasp rose from the guests as something with teriyaki sauce ruined her aqua blue cocktail dress.

"I'm so sorry, Ms. Kane," the waiter apologized profusely.

Slowly, Isabella lowered her gaze to the horrendous mess and felt tears brim in her eyes. However, before she had a chance to open her mouth, her mother along with her team of sorority sisters rushed into action. She was directed out of the room and shuffled upstairs to her old bedroom.

"Find something quick," Katherine commanded, throwing open the walk-in closet doors.

Problem was that Isabella hadn't lived in her parents' home since she graduated from high school and there wasn't anything presentable to wear in her old closet.

Rayne and Waqueisha unzipped the back of Isabella's dress while Katherine, Keri and Sylvia combed through a wardrobe that should've been donated to the Salvation Army at least a decade ago.

"What about this one?" Isabella's mother produced an oldie but goody Easter ensemble that rendered everyone else speechless.

"I'll take that as a no," Katherine surmised.

"Do you have anything in your closet she can wear?" Keri asked Katherine.

It was an innocent question, but the obvious answer stared Keri in the face. Isabella wore an average size eight while her mother would challenge anyone to a duel if they suggested her size eighteen frame was any higher than a twelve.

Waqueisha balled her hands on her hips. "Well, unless we're going to snatch the curtains down and pull a Scarlett O'Hara, we're going have to use one of your dresses, Ms. Kane."

A few minutes later, Isabella stepped into one of her mother's black sequin numbers and looked as though she was eight years old and playing dress up.

It was the perfect moment to have an emotional breakdown.

Boxes of Kleenex magically appeared and everyone patted Isabella on her back and head like she was a stray puppy.

"There, there. Baby, what's wrong?" Katherine asked.

Isabella just sobbed louder and mopped at her face. How

could she tell them the horrendous things those women had said downstairs? How could she tell them that she was beginning to have second thoughts about marrying Randall while she was at her own engagement party?

"Is it the dress?" Katherine asked. "I can go search for a different one."

Seizing on the convenient excuse, Isabella bobbed her head and then slumped with relief when her mother raced back out of the room.

"Okay. She's gone." Keri turned Isabella from the mirror to face her. "What's *really* wrong?"

Isabella wanted to hold it in, but before she knew it the words burst from her explaining about the two women downstairs. Four angry masks covered her sorors' faces before they all started removing their earrings.

Waqueisha pivoted on her heels. "Oh, we can handle this for you right now. Girls, let's roll."

"No. No." Isabella grabbed Waqueisha by the wrist. "Don't be ridiculous. You can't go beating up Randall's ex-girlfriends—even if we knew who they all were."

"What the heck are they even doing here?" Rayne asked.

"We should scratch their eyes out," Keri snapped.

"C'mon," Sylvia laughed. "One of the hottest bachelors in town? It's a woman's natural instinct to come and see who'd finally roped him into marriage."

"And then laugh when they see me," Isabella moped, snatching a new Kleenex from the offered pink box.

"Aww, now," the sorors chimed sympathetically.

Isabella shrugged away from them and turned to face the mirror. "Just look at me." She was a bigger mess now that her tears had ruined her makeup. "How did I land someone like Randall?"

"It's not the how that's important," Rayne said. "Only that you did."

"But I want to *look* like someone that belongs on Randall Jarrett's arm. And more importantly like someone who knows how to keep him."

"Just like you wanted to prep for your honeymoon?" Keri asked, crossing her arms.

"Say what?" Waqueisha asked.

Keri quickly brought the other girls up to speed.

"You told her to buy some books?" Rayne and Waqueisha asked, incredulous.

"Figured she needed to start with the basics," Keri defended.

Waqueisha rolled her eyes. "You need a new sex teacher and hot makeover. Lucky for you I'm available."

The girls nearly choked on their laughter.

Waqueisha ignored them both. "You're coming to Atlanta for my party, right?"

Isabella hesitated, but then decided why not and nodded.

"Great. While you're there I'm going to teach you how to rock Randall's world and give you a top of the line makeover." She took Isabella by the shoulder and turned her back toward the mirror. "Mark my words. When you return to Washington, you're going to be a brand-new woman."

Chapter 7

"Absolutely not," Randall shouted, appalled. "I *forbid* you to go gallivanting around Atlanta with those loose Delta Phi Theta sisters of yours. Need I remind you that we're supposed to be planning a wedding?"

Isabella stopped listening after the word "forbid." In the seconds that followed her back stiffened and her face grew hot. Before she knew it, she was up on her feet and stalking toward her fiancé with her hands on her hips. When Randall turned from his office desk to wag a finger, he jumped back, surprised to see her so close and doubly surprised to see the anger glaring up at him.

"What do you mean you *forbid* me to go?" she said in a near growl. "You don't own me."

Randall blinked.

Isabella drew a deep breath and took a step back. She didn't know whether it was the excessive amount of alcohol she had—three drinks—or residual anger from Randall's ex-girlfriends showing up at her party. All she knew was that she was tired of being pushed around. "You know what?" she said, wiggling her engagement ring off her finger. "I think I made a mistake."

"Whoa. Wait a minute." Randall tossed up his hands, refusing to take the ring back from her. "Let's slow down. I thought we were just having a discussion?"

"No. You were ordering me around like you thought this damn ring meant I was bought and paid for," she hissed and then threw the diamond at him. Never in her life had she stood up to anyone like this. She found the experience exhilarating. Pivoting on her heels, she marched toward the door of Randall's private study, but Randall made it there first and blocked her exit.

"Okay. Okay. Let's calm down," he said with clear panic written all over his face. "Obviously, I didn't handle this well. I'm sorry."

More like he was thinking about what a broken engagement would look like in the papers. "Move out of my way," Isabella said calmly.

"You're mad."

"No shit."

He jerked, stunned by the uncharacteristic language. "Fine. Fine. Go to Atlanta, if it means so much to you." He acquiesced as if she held a gun to his head.

She stared at him, enjoying the feel of her newfound power. "Why did you invite your ex-girlfriends to the party?"

"What?"

Surely, he wasn't going to play stupid. "They were all over the place, buzzing around hinting about…" She drew another breath; her courage waned at the thought of discussing his sex life.

"Hinting about what?"

"You know." She straightened her shoulder. "How good you are—you know—in bed."

He stared for a long moment and then finally burst out laughing. "Is *that* what all this is about? You're jealous?"

"I didn't say that."

"C'mon, Isabella. I know you've never...but you can't be that naïve. I'm thirty-two. Of course I've...dated around."

"You mean slept around."

He cocked his head at her; a bemused grin still on his face. "It's all in the past." He stepped forward and settled his hands on her shoulders. "I'm marrying you. Those women are only jealous and are trying to drive a wedge between us."

"But why were they *here* at our engagement party?"

"C'mon. This is Washington. You know you don't burn bridges in this town. Some of the women I've dated are some powerful women in their own right. What would it look like if I didn't invite them?"

He smiled, but he looked like a cheap car salesman when he did it.

"Tell you what," he said, dropping one arm and sliding the other across her to cradle her in a hug. "Go to Atlanta. Consider it a mini-vacation. If being with your friends is going to cheer you up then I'm all for it. But when you get back, I expect us to knuckle down on planning this wedding. I was thinking something like April 8th. What do you think?"

She didn't say anything. She wanted him to release her.

"Good. Good," Randall said, taking her silence as a yes. "Now why don't you go home and get you some rest, uhm?" He looked down at her; his cheap car salesman's smile still in place. Again, he took her silence as an agreement and he leaned down and planted a kiss in the center of her forehead.

When his arm finally fell from her shoulder, she headed toward the door.

"Wait. Wait." Randall glanced around the floor and then rushed over to the other side of the room and retrieved her ring. "Don't forget this." He held up the diamond.

Isabella stared at it and then at Randall. "You keep it." She opened the door and strolled out.

Whatever freedom Isabella felt was short lived. By morning, she woke with cotton mouth, a migraine and a massive hangover. After she managed to crawl out of bed and shuffle toward her morning shower, she wondered how long it would be before her father would send her mother over to fix her broken engagement. An hour or two at most.

While she stood motionless beneath the steaming hot water, she replayed the events of last night and smiled at the image of her throwing her diamond ring at Randall. The man truly looked as though he was about to have a heart attack.

She snickered and then wished that she would be able to conjure one tenth of last night's courage when her mother came calling. Looking for her when her cab dropped her off, she had the foresight to take the phone off the hook. If she hadn't, she would have been besieged by phone calls.

Finally clean and somewhat alert, Isabella shut off the shower, dried off and slipped into her favorite robe and made her way to the kitchen.

Only someone was already waiting for her.

"You look well rested."

"Daddy."

"Coffee?" he asked, holding up her favorite mug.

"Sure," she said. This was really serious if her father came to handle her himself. "Black. No sugar."

"I remember." He poured two cups. "I heard you and Randall had quite a fight last night."

There wasn't going to be any beating around the bush.

"Those things are normal," her father said. "The stress of planning a wedding can do those things."

"I don't..." *C'mon. You can do this.* "There's not going to be a wedding."

"Of course there is," her father countered without missing a beat. "You just have wedding jitters."

Isabella stared up at her father, swallowed whatever retort she had since his tone made it clear that this wasn't up for discussion.

The senator walked out of the kitchen to hand her coffee. "It's hot."

She accepted the mug. "Thank you."

Her father smiled. "You know how much this—arrangement means to me, don't you?"

Isabella didn't answer.

"This wedding is bigger than you. I mean, Randall has so much potential." He placed his fingers beneath her chin and forced it up so that their eyes remained level. "And so do you. If everything goes as planned, we can put you in the White House. Think of all the good you could do. The power and influence."

"But he's not in love with me," she whispered.

"Hmph. Love is...overrated—especially in a marriage. Love is fleeting and painful. And it always disappoints. But a marriage built on sturdier things: friendship, respect and a commonality have the potential to last. A different kind of love can be cultivated from that. You and Randall have more in common than you think. You could do great work together."

With every word her father spoke, Isabella felt her heart break more and more.

"Go to Atlanta," her father said as if granting her permission on an elementary school field trip. "Have some fun with your friends and when you come back, I'm sure you'll see things my way."

Chapter 8

"I think I'm ready to settle down," Derrick blurted to his frat brothers in the middle of halftime of an Atlanta Falcons game.

Stanley hit the TV remote's mute button and all eyes zoomed to Derrick.

"Not you, too," Charlie moaned.

Derrick frowned. "What do you mean?"

"You haven't heard? Your old boy, Randall, got engaged," Charlie informed him. "Damn shame." He shook his head and turned to Taariq. "Pass me those chips over there."

Derrick bobbed his head—not totally surprised at the news. "So he's finally found the nation's next First Lady?"

"Apparently," Taariq said, handing Derrick the bowl of chips. "When I talked to him the girl sounded about as exciting as a game of cricket. I kept trying to pump him for information, and all he said was how well-connected her family was and how perfect her personality was for the whole political game. We all know that's code for—"

"She's a dog," the frat brothers chimed together.

Derrick fell silent as he listened to his brothers discuss his ex-best friend and pretend he wasn't bothered by being cut out of Randall's life. To this day, he couldn't believe his old friend actually believed he'd had sex with Christina Faye. Sure Randall had found them in bed together—naked, but Derrick had been clueless of how she'd gotten there. After Christina sobered up, she admitted that she was too drunk and had climbed into the wrong bed.

A simple mistake.

Randall didn't buy it and ended his relationship with both of them. Hell, because of Derrick's reputation, *no one* bought the story. But it was the truth.

Nothing happened.

"I'm happy for him," Derrick finally said and meant it. He glanced around. "Frankly, I think old Randy may be onto something."

His boys stared at him with their mouths hanging open.

"It's just a thought," he added with a shrug. "Every man must surrender sometime."

"We're too young to surrender," Taariq said sternly.

"Yeah," Hylan cosigned. "Besides, you're like a living legend or something. If you retire—" He glanced at the others. "It affects all of us."

"Oh, cut me a break." Derrick turned up his beer bottle and took a long, hard swig. "Nobody wants to be dirty old men marrying women half their ages."

"Don't forget rich," Charlie said. "And I don't see anything wrong with being eighty and married to a twenty-four-year-old."

"Yeah," Hylan jumped in again. "Rich makes a difference."

"Speak for yourself." Stanley found his voice. "The only reason Amanda Easton went out with me was because I know Derrick. Same goes for Jennifer Givens or Monica

Kingsley. The sistahs wouldn't give me the time of day if it wasn't for you."

"Then maybe you should consider going back to your side of the fence. You catch my drift?" Taariq chuckled. "Hanging out with us is never going to make you a brother. You know this, right?"

Stanley scrunched his face as his neck turned beet red. "Yeah, I know that." He rolled his eyes, but was unable to wipe the hurt completely from his face.

"Sorry, man. I just— I don't know. All this partying is just getting old," Derrick said.

"Herman has finally gotten into you, hasn't he?" Taariq accused.

"That or that one chick you were grinding on at Visions the other night," Charlie guessed. "She wouldn't happen to have a sister or a cousin—"

"Hell, I'll date her momma," Stanley crackled, joining in on the high-fives. "Leave it up to Derrick to score with the finest woman in the place."

"Hell, the one I caught should be having my baby," Charlie chuckled and then tossed back the rest of his beer.

"You know how I do," Hylan said, pumping his chest.

"I scored two fly honeys who had to be gymnasts," Taariq boasted. "Their mounts and dismounts were worthy of gold medals."

Laughter roared and a few of the guys pounded Taariq's back in congratulations.

Only Stanley, with his tall lanky frame and flaming-red hair went home alone, but his boys were good about not commenting on it.

When the fuss died down, everyone returned their attention to Derrick.

"Seriously," Charlie asked. "You're really trying to break ranks with that chick?"

"Nah." Derrick shook his head. "Denise was beautiful and all," he admitted. "But we were just dancing. I'm not going to see her again."

"Then you won't mind if I try to hit it?" Stanley asked.

The boys tried to muffle their laughter, but failed.

Taariq leaned over and wrapped a muscled arm around Stanley's thin neck. "C'mon, man. You know better than playing with grown folk's toys."

Stanley reddened and laughed good-naturedly.

"Actually," Derrick said. "Denise is married."

"Ooh," his boys winced.

"Tough break," Hylan said, shaking his head. "Course you know, married chicks are off the hook. They're less clingy and they're some other cat's problem." He tossed back the rest of his beer and then released a long belch.

As Derrick's laughter died down, his mind drifted over Herman's constant lecturing. For years, he had laughed off the barber's lectures, but now he couldn't get the old man's words out of his head.

But monogamy? Heck, did he even have it in him? One woman—for the rest of his life?

"Uh, oh," Hylan said, snapping his fingers in front of Derrick's face. "I think we're losing him."

The weight of everyone's gaze landed on Derrick again and he quickly blinked out of his trance. "C'mon, guys. Haven't you, at least, thought about it?"

"Sounds like we need to do an intervention," Taariq said somberly. His eyes still trained on Derrick. "He's forgotten the BBD golden rule."

Stanley nodded. "Yeah. Never trust a big butt and a smile."

"Cut it out." Derrick plunged his hands into the bowl of potato chips and took another swig of beer. "You can't go the rest of your lives living and partying like drunken college students. It's time to grow up, settle down—even have a few kids or something."

"This is more serious than I thought," Charlie said.

His three buddies sat back and glanced at each other.

"If it ain't broke don't fix it," Hylan quipped. "It's not broke, is it?"

Derrick hedged, wondering how to tell his boys the truth. Men didn't talk about *feelings*. Well, they could express anguish or joy about their favorite sports team. Anger was celebrated especially if it was attached to plans of vengeance, but tedious soliloquies about longing, loneliness or emptiness was a definite no-no.

"Derrick?" Stanley elbowed him.

"Nah." Derrick shook his head and flashed everyone a quick plastic smile. "No. It's not broken."

After a week in Atlanta, Isabella regretted agreeing to let Waqueisha give her a complete makeover—especially now that every bone and muscle in her body ached in revolt.

"Very good," the striptease instructor praised from the front of the classroom. "You all are doing much better today."

Better must've meant they hadn't had to call the paramedics, Isabella thought. Of course, if she had to put in another full hour of bending, twisting and sliding down a slippery pole it might be her turn for an emergency room trip.

Cookie, the instructor who looked more comfortable on a stripper pole than walking, glided up beside Isabella and helped her arch her back and extend her leg higher. "That's it. Just like this."

Nothing about the supposed erotic pose made Isabella

feel the slightest bit sexier and neither did the other class participants, judging by their pained expressions.

"C'mon, ladies. Work with what your momma gave ya."

Isabella groaned and shot a look over at Waqueisha, the teacher's pet. "Are you sure all of this is really necessary?"

Waqueisha sprang high onto the pole, flipped upside down and flashed a bright smile. "Oh, yes. When you come back from your honeymoon, you'll want to name your first kid after me."

"Don't get your hopes up," Isabella mumbled under her breath.

Somehow, probably through the grace of God, she managed to make it through the rest of the class and collapse into a heap on the floor.

Waqueisha laughed and pulled on Isabella's arms for her to get up.

"I can't move. Just leave me here to die."

"Hey. You're the one that wanted to do this, remember? We can quit at any time."

Remembering her humiliation at her own engagement party, quitting wasn't an option. Whether or not she did go through with this wedding, she vowed to become the kind of woman who knew how to keep her man happy in the bedroom. She wanted to be more than a political trophy.

Isabella released one last groan and then climbed back up onto her ridiculously high-heeled shoes and draped a towel around her sweaty neck.

"That's m'girl," Waqueisha praised. "Let's get you over to Monique's, so we can pick you out some wonderful lingerie pieces. Nothing says sex kitten like silk and lace."

Isabella perked. Finally, something fun. After waving goodbyes to their exhausted group, Isabella allowed Waqueisha to pull her out of the workout room and across the gym.

Derrick, drenched in sweat while running five miles on the treadmill, caught a glimpse of a familiar face and temporarily slowed his pace. In a flash, he lost his balance, hit the console and then fell backward on the spinning belt.

Taariq and Charlie, who were running on opposite sides of him, shut off their machines and quickly came to his rescue.

"Dayum, man. Are you all right?" Taariq asked.

Derrick hardly heard them as he peeked around their legs in the direction he had last seen Isabella and then jumped to his feet when he didn't see her.

On seeing that he was fine, Charlie laughed. "D, I've never seen anyone bust their butt like that."

Their comments drifted in one ear and out the other as Derrick sprinted off to make sure what he'd seen wasn't a mirage.

Taariq and Charlie looked at each other and then chimed together, "Must be a woman."

Derrick weaved through treadmills, step machines and one corner of the free weights section in chase after what logic told him was impossible. He made it to the railing that lined the second story gym and peered down to the first floor.

Nothing.

"I must be going crazy," he chuckled. Turning away, he saw Isabella, rounding a corner on the lower floor. "It can't be." Derrick raced down the stairs.

"Hey, watch where you're going," a few gym members shouted in his wake.

"Sorry," he said over his shoulder, but refused to slow down. Derrick caught a glimpse of an outfit: short shorts, halter top…and high heels?

"Hey, wait!" he shouted, but the woman rounded another corner.

Derrick picked up the pace until he was at a full run and then raced through the first door he came upon. Before his brain registered his mistake, sonic waves of hysterical screaming pierced his eardrum.

Shutting his eyes, he performed a 180 and raced back out of the women's locker room, apologizing the whole way. Once he was safely back out into the hallway and before a long wall of windows, he saw his mysterious woman from Washington, or her look-alike, climb into a SUV. Before he could reach the door, the vehicle peeled out of the parking lot and disappeared into traffic.

Chapter 9

Isabella's makeover went from bad to worse.

Lingerie shopping turned out to be one of the most humiliating experiences of her life. But after hours with Waqueisha and the best-looking drag queen she'd ever seen, Monique, Isabella's B cups were pushed up to C and her flat behind had been upgraded to bootylicious.

"What happens when I have to get naked?" she innocently asked. "Don't you think this is false advertising?"

Monique rolled her eyes and cradled her hips. "Honey, after you do your little striptease number, your man is only going to be interested in getting to *one* thing."

"Amen to that," Waqueisha co-signed and gave the boutique owner a high five.

Isabella couldn't stop glancing at her image and feeling like a fraud.

Handing over her credit card, Isabella charged a ridiculous amount of money for very little material. Next stop was Prestigious Hair Salon.

"I don't know," Isabella said after hearing what the stylist, Aubrey, had planned for her long locks.

Aubrey cradled Isabella's shoulders and leaned close so their gaze would meet in the mirror in front of them. "Sweetheart, trust me. You'll be looking fierce when I get through with you."

Isabella looked over at Waqueisha, who was talking and texting half of Georgia in preparation for the Kidd Rhymes CD release party that night. "I don't know," Isabella hedged.

"Hold on just a minute," Waqueisha told her caller and then lowered the phone to speak with Isabella. "Izzy, trust my girl Aubrey. She's the best."

That was not the support Isabella was looking for.

"What do you say, girlfriend?" Aubrey asked.

"Okay," Isabella said through gritted teeth. "I'll do it."

An hour later, Isabella was in tears.

"It's orange!"

"Now calm down," Aubrey said, trying to shush her and calm her growing hysterics.

"I can't calm down," Isabella screeched. She jumped out of the stylist's chair to edge closer to the vanity mirror. Maybe it was just the lighting.

No. Her hair was orange.

Isabella pivoted toward Waqueisha who stood frozen with her eyes wide and her mouth hanging open. "I can't go anywhere with my hair looking like this!"

"Uhm. Er." Waqueisha blinked. "It's actually...kind of...cute." She glanced at Aubrey. "Sort of a golden auburn."

"What?" Isabella swiveled back to the mirror, but through her tears her hair looked like a pumpkin.

"Honey, don't panic." Aubrey jumped into action and led her back to the chair. "If you don't like it, we can tone the color down a little."

"A little?" Why had she trusted this stranger with her

hair? She would have been better off if the woman had shaved her bald. She couldn't stop the tears even if she tried. Once they started, it looked like there was no end in sight.

"Trust me. I'll take care of it," Aubrey promised, glancing over at Waqueisha.

Waqueisha, however, stood staring at Isabella's orange hair with bulged eyes and a slack jaw. What could she say?

An hour later, Aubrey had not fulfilled her promise. And when she at last consulted the product she was using she discovered the hair color was permanent and not temporary as she had originally thought.

"Oh, Isabella. I'm so sorry," Aubrey apologized profusely.

"Sorry isn't going to fix my hair," Isabella sobbed.

"We can always buy you a wig," Waqueisha suggested.

"Or I can give you a nice little cut and you can rock a slanted bob," Aubrey tossed in.

Was she serious? After screwing up her hair color, did this woman really think Isabella was going to trust her with a pair of scissors?

"No, thank you. I think you've done enough." Isabella snatched the cape from around her neck.

But Waqueisha placed a restraining hand against Isabella's shoulder. "We have to do *something* with it."

"I am. I'm going to find a pharmacy and buy some black hair color and change my hair back."

"You can't do that," Aubrey and Waqueisha exclaimed.

Isabella blinked at the force of their protest. "Why not?"

"Because your hair will fall out," Waqueisha advised gently and then pried the cape out of Isabella's tight fingers. "You know the color is not that bad."

If she was lying, Isabella couldn't detect it.

Waqueisha finished snapping the plastic cape around

Isabella's neck and then took her hand into hers. "It's just a radical difference because we've never seen you with much color. But trust me. After a nice cut and a visit to the M.A.C. counter, you're going to look like a new woman."

"I already look like a new woman: *Rainbow Brite's* black sister."

Aubrey laughed but quickly clammed up after twin smothering glares from the sorority sisters.

Waqueisha gave Isabella's hand an affirming squeeze. "Trust me."

Isabella reluctantly settled back in the stylist's chair and tried to prepare for the worst, if there was such a thing.

Chapter 10

"I'm not going," Isabella declared after staring at the stranger in the mirror for the past hour. She had signed up for a makeover—not to look as though she'd enlisted in the federal witness protection program where she could only be identified by fingerprints.

"Of course you're going," Keri said, sliding a gold hoop earring through her ear. "You look fabulous."

Waqueisha bobbed her head in agreement as she slipped into a red backless number and then jumped into a pair high-heel pumps.

Instead of Waqueisha's place, they had all agreed to dress at the downtown Ritz Carlton because it was closer to *The Zone*—where the CD release party was being held.

"You didn't do all this hard work for nothing. Just think of tonight as a practice run for when you return to D.C."

"I show up like this and I'll probably be disowned and Randall may not give his ring back."

"Sounds like a win-win situation," Keri said and glanced at her watch.

Isabella didn't miss the "amen" looks that passed between her sorors. In truth, since she had removed her ring, it felt as if a heavy burden had been lifted from her shoulders. She would enjoy her small time of freedom—at least try to anyway. She rubbed the bare space on her ring finger again, dreading when she'd have to put the pretty shackle back on. And she *would* have to put it back on. Her father would see to it.

"We better get a move on, girls. We're running late."

Isabella twisted and turned in a white Chanel number better suited for the red carpet. Her bright hair color did look better with the slanted bob and her new makeup transformed her from ordinary to…different—at best. She took another long look at herself in the mirror. "I'm *not* going," she announced. "I can't."

"C'mon, Izzy." Keri wrapped an arm around her shoulders and gave them a hearty squeeze. "You're going to have a good time."

"Trust me," Keri insisted with another hearty squeeze. "Would I steer you wrong?"

Derrick and his boys entered through the doors of *The Zone* ready to play. One look around at the exotic décor let everyone know that no expense was spared. But what drew every man's eye were the scantily clad women in pearl thongs and breast pasties.

Stanley sighed and looked like he was ready to start drooling. "Did we just die and go to heaven?"

The boys laughed.

"Stan, my man," Hylan said, wrapping his arm around Stanley's pencil thin neck. "If *you* can't score tonight, you won't have to ever worry about when to retire your playa's card. We'll take it from you."

During a rumble of laughing agreement, Stanley turned ten shades of red.

"Thanks, guys. No pressure."

"Go get 'em, tiger." Taariq pounded Stanley's back and then gave him an encouraging shove.

"Drinks?" a feminine voice floated from behind them.

Derrick turned toward a smiling ebony beauty wearing the themed pearl thongs and pasties. After nodding his appreciation of her feminine curves, Derrick placed his drink order.

"Looks like someone's not so sick of the game anymore," Charlie chuckled before placing his own order.

Derrick didn't bother to defend himself. Just because he was getting tired of the playa's life didn't mean he couldn't appreciate a fine woman when he saw one.

Minutes later, the guys separated and melted into the crowd. A few times, Derrick made it onto the dance floor with barely-twenty-one Kidd Rhymes groupies dropping it like it's hot. Though he was having a good time and enjoyed the couple of drinks that had already hit his bloodstream, Derrick longed for something more.

Isabella felt like a fish out of water the moment she entered *The Zone*. Seeing so many hip and beautiful people milling about pushed all of her insecurity buttons. Who was she kidding? She could never blend in with this crowd. She was a straight-laced tax attorney and daughter to one of the most powerful men in Washington.

She didn't belong here.

"Relax," Keri shouted over the ridiculously loud music. "You look like you're ready to turn tail and run."

That was exactly what she wanted to do.

"Yeah, loosen up," Sylvia shouted above the music.

Waqueisha tapped her on her left shoulder and also yelled, "I gotta go play hostess. Have a good time."

Before Isabella could say abracadabra, Waqueisha disappeared into the crowd.

"Drinks?" a honeyed baritone questioned.

Isabella turned and her mouth dropped open at the sight of the waiter's mountain-size and chocolate-covered muscles. She might have licked her lips at his cut abs and his itsy-bitsy loincloth, but she wasn't sure.

"Sure," Keri responded first. "I'll have you in a tall glass."

"Make that two," Isabella co-signed and then blushed at hearing the words come out of her mouth.

Keri and Rayne laughed at her boldness.

"Look out, Atlanta," Keri boasted. "Izzy is letting her hair down tonight."

The waiter winked at Isabella and she nearly died in embarrassment.

"Make it two grape martinis and walk away slowly so we can drool."

"You got it," the waiter said with a wink and then did exactly what Keri bided.

"I can't believe I said that." Isabella covered a hand over her face.

"I'm proud of you," Keri said, bumping her hips against Isabella's. "There just might be hope for you yet."

Encouraged, Isabella brightened and tried to relax.

That was also when she saw *him*.

There, bumping and grinding against a Ciara look-alike, was the incredibly handsome Derrick Knight. Isabella blinked once, twice and then finally a third time before she believed her eyes weren't playing tricks on her.

Keri followed her stare.

"C'mon. Let's dance," Keri whispered in her ear, giggling before she grabbed hold of Isabella's wrist and dragged her toward the dance floor.

"No. Wait," Isabella protested.

Keri marched on, giving no sign that she heard or felt Isabella trying to dig in her heels.

Keri ignored the fact Derrick was in the middle of getting his groove on and tapped him on the shoulder.

Isabella's breath hitched when he cast a glance over his shoulder and froze.

"Hey, Good-looking," Keri shouted, beaming her pearly whites. "Care to join us?"

Isabella noticed the woman he'd been dancing with spear Keri with a contemptuous glare, but another man quickly stepped in and she resumed dancing as if nothing happened.

Keri started dancing too, but Isabella couldn't get her brain to issue orders for her hips and feet to start moving.

Derrick smiled, undoubtedly reveling in Isabella's discomfort. "I'd love to join you." He took the middle spot between her and Keri and started swaying his hips.

Isabella tried not to stare, but watching him move accelerated her body's temperature and dried her palate. She desperately needed a drink.

"What's the matter?" Derrick chuckled. "You don't know how to dance?"

From behind him, Keri was bugging her eyes and rolling her hands trying to get Isabella to join in on the fun.

"It's easy," he said, settling his large hands on her hips. "Just follow my rhythm."

She tried. Honest to goodness, she did, but the feel of his hands on her body caused a near sensory overload.

Derrick moved closer. "Like this." He moved her hips from side to side.

Isabella followed his lead and after a few beats, he drew their bodies even closer, until the tips of her breasts brushed against his hard chest. She drew in a small gasp and lifted her gaze to his intense stare. After that, the rest of the world melted away.

"This is a pleasant surprise," he murmured. "I thought I would never see you again."

Neither did she, but she didn't tell him that—mainly because she seemed to have forgotten how to talk.

He continued on as if he hadn't noticed she'd been struck dumb. "If I didn't know better, I'd say that you didn't like me. But just in case I did say something foolish to offend you, I hope you'd now accept my apologies." His gaze again slid over her body. "Forgive me, but was your hair orange the last time we met?"

Gasping yet again, Isabella stopped dancing and lifted a hand to her short bob.

"It's—" Derrick struggled for the right word. "Different."

Isabella whirled around on her heel with intentions to march away, but Derrick's hands returned to her waist and he spun her around so in the end, she'd made a complete circle.

"Oh, no you don't." He chuckled. "You're not running away from me this time. At least not until we're finished dancing."

At long last, she managed to unglue her tongue. "Dance with—" She glanced about; but was surprised, though she shouldn't have been, to see Keri had disappeared.

"C'mon now. I can't be that repulsive," Derrick said, following her gaze. "Before meeting you, I found that most women liked my company."

"Then I'll leave you to your fan club," Isabella replied bitterly and then made another attempt to strand him on the dance floor.

"My, my, my. That's quite a temper you have there."

"What? I do not!" she snapped and then during his resulting laughter realized that her tone contradicted her words. "Oh, whatever." She made a third attempt to escape, but his firm hold was having none of that.

"Let go," she growled and despite the loud music she knew that he had heard her.

Derrick ignored the order. "If I let go, you'll run away."

"That is the idea," she said sweetly.

"And the reason I'm *not* letting you go." He shared a magnanimous smile. "Looks like we have a stalemate."

Isabella couldn't remember ever being so angry. Who did this idiot think he was?

"So why did you change your hair?" Derrick asked, ignoring her narrowed gaze and darkening face. "I liked it long...and black."

"Nobody asked you what you liked," she spat.

Derrick shrugged, never missing a beat while moving to the music. "I just figured that you'd like a man's opinion. I imagine it's the reason for this drastic change in your clothes and makeup. That or you're looking for a drastic change in careers. A lady of the evening, perhaps—or video vixen?"

His words completed her humiliation and tears stung her eyes.

Seeing her distress, Derrick stopped his teasing and loosened his hold. "Oh, I'm sorry. I—I didn't mean to upset you."

"No? Telling a woman that she looks like a hooker was meant to be a compliment?"

He winced and finally stopped dancing. "I'm sorry," he said, and truly looked as though he were. "I was just trying to say I liked you the way you were."

As quickly as his harsh words had wounded her pride, the new ones had mended it and even caused a warm flush of pleasure to blaze through her body.

Derrick's keen gaze caught how the apples of her cheeks darkened and he was pleased that he'd finally wrangled his way onto her good side. "All's forgiven?"

When Isabella lifted her tranquil maple-brown eyes to his, a strange rush of emotion flooded his senses. His brain scrambled, trying to make some sense of what was happening to him; but the only answer that seemed to fit came from an old familiar voice.

When you look into her eyes and her soul speaks to you. That's a love worth dying for.

Derrick broke eye contact to search for her engagement ring. At the sight of her bare, slender fingers, his smile bloomed wider. "What do you say we head over to the bar?"

Her hesitancy frightened him a moment. What could he really do if she'd said no? After she made a few cursory glances around her, she responded, "One drink."

He complied with a simple nod and then led her off the dance floor with one arm still locked around her waist in silent possession. However, it took a little work finding a spot at one of the club's multiple bars.

"Two Incredible Hulks," Derrick yelled to the bartender.

"Two what?" Isabella inquired.

Derrick turned up the charm to full blast. "Trust me. You'll love them." He moved his stool closer so he could have her all to himself in a private alcove. Instead of getting upset, this time his mysterious woman smiled.

"So when are you going to tell me your name?"

She hesitated. "Isabella."

He repeated the name and then shortened it to, "Bella."

"I guess anything is better than Izzy," she confessed. "My friends call me that."

His brows quirked in surprise. "If you don't like it, why do your friends call you that?"

"Old habit. I let them get away with it in college and it stuck." She shrugged. "I guess I was hoping it would grow on me."

"And it hasn't?"

She laughed as she shook her head. "I hate it."

"Your drinks, sir." The bartender set the radioactive-looking drinks down on the bar. "Enjoy."

Derrick lifted his drink and proposed a toast. "To your new nickname 'Bella.' May you think of me every time you hear it."

Isabella laughed at the absurd proposal, but lifted her drink anyway. Together they took their first sips, their gazes locking above the rim of their glasses.

She couldn't describe the charge of emotions his smoldering black gaze caused nor could she rationalize why this gorgeous man seemed so interested in her. Even with her enhanced figure, there were bigger breasts and bigger booties to chase on the dance floor. Yet, Derrick Knight seemed to only have eyes for her.

It was a glorious feeling and it was one that she hoped to enjoy for at least a little while longer.

"So," Derrick said, setting his drink aside. "Read any good books lately?"

Isabella choked.

Chapter 11

"I think your daughter is having second thoughts," Randall complained, pacing around Senator Kane's desk. Now that he'd spat out the words most heavily on his mind, the muscles around his heart nearly squeezed him to death.

"Don't be ridiculous," the senator said, not bothering to glance up from his piles of paperwork. "Isabella knows how much I want our families to join forces. This is the perfect political move." He finally glanced up. "For both of us."

Randall bobbed his head in agreement, but Kane's words failed to ease his anxiety. After all, he wasn't marrying the senator.

"You know it would have helped if you had tossed in a few words about love when you proposed."

Randall took great care to not bust out laughing—but love? Cut him a break. Anyone who had known him more than five minutes, knew that Isabella Kane was not his type. He was a T&A man, leaning heavily toward the A part. While Isabella wouldn't scare anyone out of a dark alley, she also never roused his lust either.

"I was nervous," Randall offered weakly. "Plus, she left me on bended knee for so long I began to take root."

The senator dismissed the event with a low growling grumble.

"Isabella has been down in Atlanta with her sorority sisters for nearly a week and she has not called me once." Randall continued to worry. "I, on the other hand, have left message after message."

"Ah." Kane finally lifted his chin and removed his reading glasses. "Now we get to the truth of the matter. Has my daughter managed to wound your pride? Perhaps you care for her more than you like to admit?"

Careful not to offend, Randall chose his words wisely. "Of course I have feelings for her. We're engaged."

The senator leaned back in his massive leather chair. "In this town, love and marriage have very little to do with anything. I'm sure you've learned that much."

Hell, he had learned it in childhood. Leon Jarrett, a crafty lobbyist turned congressman learned the importance of marrying up when he left Randall's mother, whose great crime was being the daughter of a man who owned some shady strip bars in Alabama, for his stepmother, Eunice Temple. Eunice had the good fortune of graduating from Oxford and had a political lineage that ran all the way back to the first African-American congressman, Joseph Rainey.

The right political pairing was crucial to one's career.

"You're really worried about this thing, aren't you?" Kane asked. His keen gaze studied Randall.

"I just don't like any surprises. That's all."

The senator nodded. "Very well. I'll have another talk with her and reinforce my stance on the marriage."

Randall relaxed. One thing he knew about his fiancée was how much of a daddy's girl she was. "Thank you, sir."

He turned to leave, but the senator wasn't through with him.

"Since we're doing favors for one another," Kane barked when Randall's hand landed on the doorknob. "Maybe you can do one for me as well."

Randall turned, his ready smile died on his lips at the sight of Kane's steely gaze. "Sir?"

"Your girlfriend," the senator clipped out. "Maybe it's not a good idea that you continue to see her during your brief engagement."

Randall's hand tightened on the doorknob while he grinded his teeth.

"It's considered bad form," Kane added.

"Yes, sir." Without another word, Randall jerked open the senator's office door and stormed out.

"Are you all right?" Derrick asked as he lightly whacked Isabella on the back. In truth he was amused to have caught her off guard.

After her coughs subsided, Isabella nodded her head and took another sip of her drink. "I'm fine. I'm fine. Thank you."

"I'm sorry. I don't mean to pry, but the last time we saw each other, you looked like you were up for some interesting reading. Did you learn anything?"

"Actually, I was, uhm—was giving those away as uh, gifts," she said.

Derrick laughed at the obvious lie but didn't call her on it. "For someone having a little trouble in the bedroom?"

"Uhm, yeah. Something like that."

"Oh." He nodded as if he completely understood. Plus, he enjoyed the way the apples of her cheeks kept darkening with each lie she told. "Well, I guess that makes you an exceptional friend. What? You bought her ten—twelve books?"

"Thirteen," she supplied and took another gulp of her potent drink.

"Wow. Thirteen." He chuckled under his breath. "Well, did it help you?"

"What?" She almost choked again.

"Her. I meant her," he covered smoothly. "Did the books help your friend?"

Isabella shrugged and averted her gaze. "I guess so."

"Hmm." He nursed his drink for a few seconds and then replied. "I'm not surprised." That caught her attention.

"You're not? Why?"

Derrick hunched his shoulders lazily. "C'mon. Sex isn't something you read about. It's something you experience. Something you—practice." He stole a sidelong glance. She hung on his every word. "Take someone like you," he said, facing her. "I'm sure you're a well-experienced woman."

"Yeah, uhm, of course."

"That's what I thought." His smile broadened. "Now, you tell me. Don't you think there's a difference between experiencing a man's touch and reading about it?"

"I, uhm—"

When Derrick eased closer and covered one of her hands with his, her eyes dropped and followed his slow, gentle stroking. "No two people are turned on the same. One of the joys of sex is discovery." He stilled his hand, but maintained contact. "A man is always curious about what will make a woman sigh." He resumed his stroking and he watched intently how she drew in a deep breath. "What will make her quiver, moan and cry out your name." He fell silent until her eyes slowly traveled back to meet his gaze. "Isn't it the same for you?"

Isabella refrained from fanning herself, but instead drained the rest of her drink.

"Easy now," Derrick warned. "That drink has a way of sneaking up on you."

"I'm a big girl," she sassed. However, she wasn't prepared for Derrick's dark gaze to caress her every curve.

"That you are, Bella." His smile turned sly. "Another drink?"

"The agreement was for one drink."

"I'd hoped my winning personality would convince you to stay for another."

Isabella blinked. Could it be this man, this incredibly handsome man, was truly attracted to her? The answer seemed obvious but she wasn't sure she trusted the obvious. "I better go. It was nice meeting you again." She hopped off the stool, but the sudden movement made her lightheaded and she wobbled and then slipped into Derrick's arms.

"Smooth," he said, tilted forward until their lips were inches apart. "I was wondering how I was going to get you into my arms." Before she could push away or utter a protest, Derrick kissed her.

A real kiss—like the ones she'd seen in the movies.

Isabella had never experienced anything like it. Soft, full lips laced with a hint of alcohol and peppermint proved to be a heady combination. Isabella enjoyed the sensation of being suspended in midair.

His tongue slid between her lips and performed an erotic mating dance with her own. The ache between her legs was instant and the images flashing in her head were similar to the ones on the pages of her "research" books.

Gone was the reality of being an engaged woman.

Gone was the average wallflower that no one ever noticed.

Wrapped in Derrick's arms, she was acutely aware of being one-hundred-percent woman. She didn't want that feeling to end.

Moaning, she wrapped her arms around his neck and encouraged him to deepen the kiss.

He obliged.

She moaned again as her nipples hardened and her toes curled.

"Get a room," someone sneered nearby.

Much to her regret, Derrick broke the kiss and the reality of their surroundings came crashing back.

"Well, it looks like I've figured out what makes you moan," he teased, with sparkling eyes.

Reluctantly, she pulled out of his arms.

"Please tell me that you didn't learn to kiss like that out of a book," he said.

She should respond. She wanted to respond, but all she could manage was a lopsided smile while waiting for her heaving chest to slow back to its normal rhythm. If kissing him was that explosive, what would it be like making love to him?

She gasped. She needed to snap out of this. She had played with fire long enough. Or had she? Her gaze returned to his lips and she wanted to taste them again. She wanted to feel them on other places too. Fleetingly, she wondered how a woman asked to go back to a man's place or back to her hotel room. What would he think if she did? Hell, she didn't even know what to do once she got there.

Derrick licked his lips and asked, "Do you want—"

"Yes, I'd love to go to your place."

"—want another drink?" he finished.

Isabella's entire body flushed with embarrassment. "I, uh." Was there any way she could crawl under the bar?

Maybe if she was lucky she would die in the next few seconds from embarrassment.

"Actually—" He tossed down the rest of his drink. "I think I like your idea better. Let's go."

Chapter 12

First things first, Isabella scoured *The Zone* and found Waqueisha just before she was about to go on stage and introduce the rapper of the hour, Kidd Rhymes. Isabella lied and said that she was tired and was returning to the hotel. Her friend made a weak attempt for her to stay, but being rushed to the stage, she just bid Isabella good night and expressed her hope that she'd feel better by morning.

If everything went according to plan, Isabella was going to feel great in the morning.

She didn't dare try to find Keri or Rayne to give them the same lame story. Keri would have seen right through the lie and then question her about Derrick.

She didn't want anyone questioning her about that—not even herself.

Even as she slid into the leather seats of Derrick's sleek BMW, Isabella knew this was wrong, but she lacked the will and the desire to turn back.

"Buckle up," Derrick instructed before closing the passenger door. From the other side of the windshield, he winked while his sexy lips curved higher.

In the brief quiet while Derrick walked to the other side of the car, Isabella drew a deep breath as she reached for her seatbelt. Derrick's seductive cologne lingered in the air—that and his Fresh Mountain Rain-scented car deodorizer.

You can still get out of the car, her voice of reason whispered. It's not too late. You're an engaged woman. Isabella glanced down at her fingers. Even though she'd removed her engagement ring, she could still see its ghostly circular impression. Guilt settled on her shoulders as the magnitude of her actions began to scroll through her head.

One night, she pleaded with her conscience. Was it too much to ask to have one night when she wasn't the soft-spoken, do-as-she-is-told politician's daughter? It was bad enough she'd agreed to marry a man she didn't love. But before she walked down the aisle, she wanted one night.

Who was she fooling? She couldn't do this.

With a trembling hand, Isabella reached for her door handle, just as the driver's door opened and Derrick dipped inside and flashed a wide smile. Isabella's hand returned to her lap. She wasn't going anywhere.

"Are you ready?"

She bit her lower lip and nodded—mainly because she didn't trust her voice to be steady.

Derrick started the car and then reached for her hand. "Are you sure you want to do this?"

She heard the words, but her eyes had dropped to their joined fingers. Heat simmered beneath her skin and traveled the length of her arm. Within seconds, other parts of her body tingled too. Shifting her eyes back up, she met his direct gaze and nearly melted beneath its intensity.

"I'm sure," she whispered.

Derrick's luscious lips parted again as he leaned forward; his warm breath caressed her face. Isabella closed her eyes and waited in anxious anticipation for that magical moment when their lips would touch again. When it finally happened, it was…more. More potent, more wonderful—more everything.

For long seconds after their lips parted, Isabella's eyes remained closed while she relished his sweet aftertaste. Not until Derrick's low chuckle did her eyes flutter open, but her heart remained lodged in her throat at seeing him hover less than an inch from her face.

The seconds ticked while they soul gazed. "You're a fascinating woman, Isabella," he stated with naked honesty. "Has anyone ever told you that?"

She shook her head.

"I don't believe that." He shifted the car into Reverse and pulled out of the parking space. They stopped briefly to pay the parking attendant and then exited the parking deck—but he never once released her hand.

A comfortable silence settled inside the car. Isabella remained content to be seduced by her senses. Derrick Knight looked good, felt good and smelled good. And for the night, he was all hers.

Within minutes, they arrived at the parking deck of a luxurious midtown high-rise and the night continued to feel surreal. Who knew—maybe it was a dream.

Somebody pinch me.

Then again, she would probably kill that person if they woke her from this dream.

Once Derrick shut off the engine, he was out of the car and opening the passenger door in a snap. If she didn't know any better, she would think he was just as nervous.

That was impossible.

He looked the very definition of calm, cool and collected. She, however, was a rioting mess. What was the protocol for situations like these? At what point do you tell the guy that you don't know what the hell you're doing—or sadly that you're a twenty-seven-year-old virgin?

Isabella hesitated, just for a second, but then slid her hand into his while he helped her out. Before they stepped away from the car, Derrick pulled her pliant body against his and nuzzled her neck, lining kisses along the way.

"I'm thrilled you suggested this," he whispered, and then nibbled on the lobe of her ear.

Her knees folded, however, she quickly steadied herself by gripping his sinewy arms.

If Derrick detected her brief moment of weakness it didn't show. Instead, he kept a possessive arm around her waist while he led her into the building, past the night watchman and into a waiting elevator.

When the doors closed, Derrick drew her back against his hard, muscled body and wrapped his other arm around her. She had barely drawn a breath before their lips connected. It amazed her how each time he kissed her, the emotions behind it intensified.

Or was that all in her mind?

Derrick broke away, breathing hard. "I want you to know, you don't have to do anything you don't want to," he rasped, and then nuzzled her neck again.

A long winding moan fell from her lips and filled the small boxed compartment.

"If you want, we can just sit and talk." Derrick's hand drifted down the length of her body, curled around her hip and then glided along her thigh. "We could put on some music, dim the lights and…talk."

Talk, hell, she thought. If he kept this up, she was going to rip his clothes off right here and now.

The bell chimed and the elevator doors slid open, but neither moved from their cozy cocoon. In fact, Derrick chose that moment to brand her with another earth-shattering kiss.

Isabella's arms slid around his neck and locked him in place. If she had her way they would remain like this for all eternity. Instead, their private interlude was interrupted when someone cleared their throat.

Breaking away, Derrick and Isabella's gaze swung to a tall, handsome elderly gentleman with a grin the size of Texas. "You two lovebirds plan on staying in here all night?"

"No, Mr. Roberts." Derrick laughed, lowering Isabella's leg and then gently escorting her out of the elevator. "It's all yours."

"Uh-huh." Mr. Roberts shook his head as he stepped into the elevator, but a chuckle escaped. "You two enjoy the rest of your evening."

"We will," Derrick whispered for Isabella's ears only.

Isabella hung her head low in embarrassment. How could she have forgotten they were in a public place? She and Randall had never displayed public affection—or private for that matter. Yet, there was a sliver of pleasure that rippled through her. She had never in her life been so bold or acted so brazen.

She loved it.

Glancing back, she saw the elevator doors close and she released the air pinned in her lungs.

"That was exciting," Derrick said, stopping in front of door 1018 and whipping his keys out of his pants pocket.

Isabella didn't respond, but secretly agreed. If only her friends could just see her now.

Scratch that.

Derrick opened the door and gallantly gestured for her to enter. "Beauty first."

She blinked. The steady stream of compliments kept

throwing her off. At seeing his somber sincerity, Isabella allowed a small smile to curve into place before crossing the threshold into his apartment.

Derrick moved in behind her and clicked on a light. Dark, rich mahogany and a variety of eclectic paintings showcased an apartment created by someone with an artistic eye.

"Nice place," she complimented, moving deeper into the stunning high-rise. Though everything was immaculate, certainly not what one would expect from a bachelor, she couldn't help but think it was missing something.

A woman's touch?

As soon as the thought crossed her mind, she scolded herself. This was the very thing men accused women of doing. Still, a few plants would be nice.

Derrick moved behind her and slid off her thin jacket, exposing her bare shoulders before covering them with warm kisses.

Isabella's eyes fluttered closed, while she savored his touch. His hand slid around her waist and glided upward until it cupped her left breast. She gasped, tilted her head back while her nipple hardened and poked into his palm.

"What do you say we go into the living room and I fix us something to drink and put on some music?"

She didn't want anything else to drink. She still had a low-grade buzz from her drinks at the club—or maybe it was his kisses that were affecting her blood sugar. "That would be nice," she lied.

Linking their hands together again, he guided her to the living room. Once there, she stepped onto a carpet so soft and plush, she wanted to kick her shoes off.

"Make yourself comfortable," Derrick instructed, releasing her hand to cross over to the hanging CD player on the wall behind the corner bar. Within seconds, Jill Scott's melodic song "My Love" drifted from unseen speakers and filled the apartment.

"I love her," Isabella gushed.

"Yeah, the sister has skills," Derrick said, pulling out two wineglasses. "This CD has been in the player since I bought it seven months ago."

She laughed and tried to relax, but then he dimmed the lights and approached, carrying two wineglasses.

"For you," he said, handing one of the glasses over.

Isabella's heart rate escalated, her palms suddenly felt slick, her nerves now tangled into an impossible knot. She reached for it, praying he wouldn't see how badly her hand shook.

He did—it was impossible not to.

"Why don't we sit down?" he suggested, his eyes filled with compassion.

What choice did she have? At this point she needed to either sit or fall down. Her trembling legs weren't going to hold her up much longer.

After trading off the wineglass, Derrick recaptured her free, though moist, hand and led her over to the leather sofa. It was like sliding into a lush mattress, her muscles relaxed considerably once nestled in its comfortable folds.

"Better?" Derrick asked, taking the space next to her.

Isabella nodded and avoided his gaze while she took that first sip of wine. It did wonders for the knot in her stomach.

Derrick's laugh rumbled around her. "I meant what I said earlier. We don't have to do anything tonight." His arm hugged the back of the couch. "I'm just happy you're here."

Against her will her eyes darted to his to gauge his sincerity. Then a question was out of her mouth before she could stop herself. "Why?"

His eyes twinkled. "Because I find you fascinating—orange hair and all."

If it was a lie, he was a damn good liar.

He smiled.

Her heart raced.

"Tell me about yourself," he said, setting his wineglass down and focusing his full attention on her. "What do you do? Where did you grow up? What happened to your engagement ring?"

Isabella choked.

Derrick quickly took her glass and began whacking her back. The act only succeeded in bringing tears to her eyes and rattling her lungs. "Boy, you really don't know how to handle your alcohol."

"I—I'm…f-fine," she lied and waved his rescue efforts off before he killed her.

He stopped, waited while she sucked in a few deep gulps of air, then he jumped up and disappeared for a few seconds before returning with a box of Kleenex. "You're sure you're all right, Bella?"

She nodded but snatched a few Kleenex to dab her eyes. When she'd managed to pull herself together, her smile quivered at the edges.

For a full minute Jill Scott's powerful vocals pulsed between them. Derrick's eyes held a question while Isabella's begged him not to ask it.

So he made a statement that *sounded* like a question, "You don't want to talk about it."

A horrible image of this wonderful night crashing to an abrupt end flashed through Isabella's mind. The last thing she wanted to talk about was her *perfect* fiancé, but now that the subject came up, Randall's presence filled the sparse space between them, stealing her one and only moment of freedom away from her.

Taking a deep breath to steady her nerves, Isabella's

gaze fluttered to her bare fingers. Before she could open her mouth, Derrick's strong hands covered her own.

"It's okay. I understand if it's too painful for you to talk about it," he said, his voice thick with sympathy. "I recently broke up with someone, too."

Jealousy reared. She didn't like thinking about him with other women, though it was unrealistic to believe he didn't have a line of single women that reached clear to the west coast.

Yet, here he was. Holding her hand and undressing her with his eyes.

"Forget our exes," he said, suddenly upbeat. "Let's talk about something else."

She frowned. *Exes?* Then it hit her. He thought she was no longer engaged. Amazingly, she started to correct him, but caught the words before they leapt off her tongue. A confession would keep her from her ultimate goal: his bedroom.

"You're trembling," he noted.

Isabella glanced down and saw she was shaking like a leaf. She laughed as an attempt to cover her nervousness, but then decided to drain the rest of her wine. Once her glass was empty she chanced another look at him. His handsome features disarmed while his light but heady cologne seduced.

Courage, undoubtedly gained by the different combinations of alcohol, surged through her veins. "I want you to make love to me," she said.

Derrick lifted a lone brow and then took his time dragging his heavy gaze over her upturned face. He couldn't remember the last time he'd seen anyone look so adorable. But the question was whether this was a genuine proposition or a case of the booze talking. Clearly Bella didn't realize her innocence and inexperience radiated from every pore of her body.

Then again, her ex-fiancé's loss was his gain.

He must have taken too long to answer because she started shaking again.

"We don't have to if you don't want to," she amended and started glancing around the room. "I just thought, well—"

"Oh, I want to," he said and then watched her eyes widen with surprise. "I just don't want you to get the wrong idea," he added, finding humor in letting her play the aggressor. "I don't usually do this sort of thing on the first date."

"Oh." Her cheeks darkened. She looked uncertain where to go from there.

Having mercy on her, Derrick stood and with a look asked her to do the same. "Why don't we dance for a little while—some cheek to cheek action to get us in the mood?"

Isabella only nodded and glided into his embrace. He had to admit that he liked the way she fit against his frame, liked how his body responded, but he absolutely *loved* the way she stared up at him.

Herman was right. This was a connection he'd never felt before. She was different and, in turn, for the first time in his life, love seemed like a possibility.

Their bodies rocked slowly in sync with the music. Lyrics of love and empowerment strummed the cords around Derrick's heart.

My God. She's the one.

Slowly, Derrick's hand drifted across her back, his fingers quickly and stealthily found the tiny zipper on her dress and pulled. He knew she was cognizant of his actions by the way her body quivered again. Her innocence continued to charm and fascinate him.

Despite the many invisible notches on his bedpost, Derrick had never seduced a virgin—not even when he was one himself. The pressure to make the night special was a challenge he was rising to accept.

The zipper reached the end of its track and he slowly peeled her thin straps from her shoulders and watched the dress as it fell and pooled at her feet.

Isabella stopped dancing and grew very still.

Derrick's heart skipped a beat, fearing that she'd finally come to her senses and was about to change her mind. Hoping to sway her back to a night of seduction, Derrick curved his head into the nook between her jaw and collarbone and peppered the area with tiny kisses.

She sighed and moaned her pleasure and he relaxed when she melted against him. They started moving to the music again while Derrick's hands explored the flat planes of her back and then slipped beneath the lining of her panties to curve around…around—*what on earth?*

He stopped and pulled out a strange padding.

Isabella shrieked and raced from the living room.

Chapter 13

Isabella locked herself into the first room she came across. She had never been so humiliated in all her life. How had she forgotten about her new pair of padded panties? Now she was huddled in the bathroom with one butt cheek substantially bigger than the other and a confused man on the other side of the door.

"Bella?"

"Go away," she wailed and back-handed her streaming tears.

"C'mon, Bella. Open the door," he coached. "It's not a big deal."

"Not a big deal?" she thundered. "My butt just came off in your hand!"

"Well, I admit I was a little surprised," he chuckled. "But it's not the end of the world. I'm sure you're—*we're* not the first couple this has happened to. We should look at it like a sort of ice breaker. The worst is behind us."

Isabella jutted her bottom lip as she reached inside her push-up bra and removed the additional padding there, as well.

"Bella?"

"Oh, please just go away," she moaned. "This is the worst night of my life."

Derrick didn't respond.

Regret, relief and disappointment fused together and overwhelmed her. She just wanted this one thing and she'd messed it up. She hugged her legs against her chest and rested her head upon her knees and sobbed softly.

"I wish you wouldn't do that," Derrick said. His honey-eyed baritone carried notes of genuine concern.

The door shifted against her back. Was he leaning against it?

"I'm sorry you're not having a good time," he said. "I was enjoying it."

He was just trying to be nice, she told herself; but a part of her wanted to believe him.

"Can I ask you a question?" he said, and then plunged ahead without waiting for her consent. "Why are you trying so hard to hide yourself?"

"I'm not—"

"The hair, the clothes, the—enhancements?"

Isabella swallowed, wishing he really would leave her alone so she could wallow in her misery.

"I liked you the way you were," he said.

She glanced over her shoulder and frowned at the door.

"Granted, you were a little rude in the bookstore. But you sort of made my day when I saw your adorable face turned up at me in the rain. Then you went back to treating me like something stuck on your shoe when we shared that cab. But I have to admit, I've thought of you often since that day."

"Why?" she whispered, but the question bounced off the bathroom's natural acoustics.

"Because I like you," he said simply. "I thought that much was pretty obvious."

Stunned speechless, Isabella just stared at the door.

When he didn't get a response, Derrick sighed and tried to get used to the idea of spending the night camped outside his bathroom. This was certainly a first.

He folded his arms and settled back against the door; but at that precise moment, it swung open and he fell back and slammed his head against the floor.

"Ow." Derrick blinked the stars from his eyes and wondered if she'd just given him a mild concussion.

"Oh, I'm so sorry," Isabella exclaimed, kneeling beside him. "Are you okay?"

Despite the stunning pain, he smiled up at his puffy-eyed, mascara streaked angel with the orange halo. "I'm better now." He allowed her to take his arm and help pull him into a sitting position.

"Are you sure you're okay? You hit your head pretty hard. How many fingers am I holding up?"

Derrick saw the two digits, but answered, "Four."

"Oh gosh," she panicked. "Maybe we should get you to a hospital."

He laughed and shook his head. "I'm joking with you. Calm down. You had two fingers up."

"Oh." She lifted her quivering smile and struggled to find something to say.

"Thanks for opening the door." Gently, he cupped her tear-stained cheek and erased her mascara's dark tracks with the pad of his thumb. "I meant every word I said. I like you."

Whatever reservations she had, Derrick watched them melt away as her eyes softened. How was it that this unique flower didn't know how beautiful she was? He couldn't imagine that no one had ever told her. Derrick smiled and pulled her heart-shaped face close so he could taste her lips again. Surely he was now addicted.

The way their tongues danced, sliding and caressing one another made him anxious to get her into bed. Yet, he had to remind himself to take it slow. It was her first time, after all.

His heart skipped a beat at the reminder. There was something exciting and exhilarating about being her first. It tugged all his tender heart strings and made him more possessive.

When he pulled away, her eyes stayed closed—a perfect picture of serenity. Taking advantage of the moment, Derrick leaned forward and peppered kisses along her neck, collarbone and then finally the small swells of her breasts.

He noticed their drastic reduction, but smothered a smile in the valley between the two. His Bella was certainly a bundle of surprises and he loved every one of them. "What do you say we get out of here?" he asked, though if she wanted, he was more than willing to make love to her right there on the bathroom floor.

"I'd like that," she said, her nervousness still evident by the slight quiver in her voice.

Together they climbed back onto their feet. Derrick took her hand and led the way to the apartment's master bedroom.

Isabella followed as though she was in a dream and when she crossed the threshold into his bedroom, it looked and felt like she'd stepped into an expensive hotel suite. The room held Derrick's signature scent of spice and sandalwood. The downy carpet beneath her feet felt as soft as the bed looked. The king-size mattress was encased in red silk with a headboard the same rich mahogany that graced most of the high-rise.

Derrick turned toward one of the walls and lowered

the lighting with the sliding dimmer switch. Next to it, he punched a few buttons and then Jill Scott's melodious voice floated into the room.

"There," he said, returning his attention to her. "That's much better."

She agreed. As if by magic, the night resumed its romantic course as if her padded booty incident had never happened. Thinking of which, she reached behind her and removed the last bubbled-pad from her left butt cheek and held it up.

They both glanced at it and snickered.

Derrick removed the pad from her fingers and tossed it over his shoulder before pulling her back into his arms.

She watched his head's slow descent through the fan of her faux eyelashes and then locked her arms behind his neck and then welcomed his kiss like a starved woman. She didn't feel it when he unsnapped her bra, but Isabella certainly felt the room's cool air kiss her nipples when the thin material fell to the floor.

Wanting to mimic his boldness, Isabella lifted his shirt and smiled in satisfaction when he aided in taking it off. She marveled at the feel of his silky skin as she glided her hands across his muscled chest and then wrapped her fingers around his hard biceps. His body was like a wonderland and for the first time in her life, she was ready to play.

While he pulled at her panties, her hands suddenly shied at his pants buttons. Sensing her waning courage, Derrick helped her out again and was nude before she could blink an eye.

She gasped and ogled the multiple mountains of hard muscles along his chest that quickly morphed into toned, sharp ridges down his abdomen, but then ended at the small, inky-black thatch of hair that fringed his large erection.

"Oh, my." She swallowed. Despite all her research, nothing could have properly prepared her for something so erotic and…beautiful. That was the word that described his nude form. He was the very definition of a man—aesthetically perfect.

She couldn't stop staring.

"You're going have to stop that," he laughed and stepped forward, his sex brushing against her soft belly. "You're going to make me blush."

And he was going to make her faint. Did women faint anymore?

She stepped back, her panic rising at an alarming rate and Derrick quickly counteracted with another mind-blowing kiss. She wouldn't have thought it was possible, but Derrick's erection grew even harder and though she wanted to burn every detail into her memory, she had a devil of a time remembering how they'd made it across the room and onto the bed.

All she knew was the sensation of being pressed into the center of the firm mattress and his hot mouth blazing a new trail down her body until his tongue made teasing laps around her left nipple. At the same time, she was aware of one of his hands coasting upward in between her thighs and then lightly caressing then grazing the velvet entrance with his fingers.

Her body tingled with heat and desire until she thought that she couldn't stand it anymore. "Derrick…please."

She had no idea what she was begging for, but she trusted that he knew what she needed. In answer, he finally closed his mouth on a marbleized nipple while simultaneously slipping a finger inside her dewy passage. Her legs opened automatically, giving him better access to the aching pulse at her core.

Isabella absently stroked the curve of his back while

adding her own melodic moans to the music that surrounded them. She was vaguely aware that she should be doing something for him, but it was so difficult to emerge from the vast sea of pleasure that his wonderful stroking created.

He slipped in a second finger and then shifted to worship her right breast. The air thinned in her lungs as her hips moved on their own volition, trying to keep time to the rhythm he'd set.

While she concentrated on his hand, Isabella lost track of his mouth. That is, until it replaced his exploring fingers. His breath was warm, his tongue cool. Their wild combination sent her scurrying up the bed, overwhelmed by the pleasure.

She didn't get far.

Derrick's arms locked around her hips and held her in place while his tongue probed her lower lips, diving deeper this time. He groaned as her juices flowed against his lapping tongue. A canopy of stars twinkled behind her closed eyelids—at least she thought they did while she squirmed and moaned helplessly. However, the more his tongue filled her, the greedier she became.

Isabella's legs crossed behind his head and held him in place like a vise. Her fingers roughly massaged his head while simultaneously urging him on.

Soaring through the stars, her winding moans slowly transformed into short halting gasps as ecstasy unfolded from her throbbing center and then exploded to every part of her body.

Yet, Derrick didn't stop. His tongue stroked.

Stroked.

Stroked.

It all became too much. Isabella uncrossed her legs and

resumed trying to inch away, pleading for mercy all the while.

Relentlessly, he suckled and teased and before she knew it another explosion erupted and wiped all thought from her mind and left her body limp.

Then and only then did Derrick release her. He crawled up the bed to hover above her; on his lips hung a sly smile. "I hope you don't think I'm done with you, Bella."

Somehow, Isabella managed to open her eyes. She honestly didn't think she could take much more.

Derrick crawled higher and then reached over to the nightstand. From the drawer he withdrew a condom. "Would you like to help me put this on?"

There was a beat of hesitation and Derrick kindly smiled into her eyes. "If you want to stop…I'll understand."

Her brows arched in disbelief.

"I'll need a very cold shower, but I don't want you to do anything you're not ready for."

A few seconds stretched between them. Finally, in answer, she reached for the condom and tore it open.

Chapter 14

Randall was at the end of his rope.

After a fitful night of sleep, he woke early Sunday morning determined to get his fiancée on the phone, but call after call was transferred to Isabella's hotel voice mail.

What the hell was going on? He no longer believed Senator Kane that this little tiff between him and Isabella would blow over. Maybe he had pushed too hard. Isabella wasn't like his other girls who would curse, scream and give as well as they got.

She was fragile.

Delicate.

Perched on the edge of his bed, he looked down at the glittering ring between his fingers and tried to decide on his next move. A part of Randall argued that he should cut his losses and find someone else to take her place. However, that idea wouldn't exactly go over well with his father or Senator Kane.

The other part of him didn't like to lose. When Isabella stormed out, she had activated his competitive nature and it was apparent he wasn't going to rest until he slid the ring back down her finger.

Randall reached for the phone next to his bed. His constant calling was beginning to feel like a bad habit he couldn't break. When he asked the front desk for Isabella's room again, he could hear the irritation in the woman's voice when she asked him to "please hold."

But just like the hundred times before, the call was soon transferred to voice mail. He hung up. Called back. This time, he asked for Keri Evans's room.

Keri picked up on the first ring.

"Where the hell is she?" Randall thundered before Isabella's best friend finished saying hello.

"Who's this?" Keri asked, her voice thick and scratchy.

"It's Randall." He stood from the bed and started pacing. "Now where is she? Is she in your room? Why isn't she answering her phone? When are you girls coming back?"

"Whoa. Whoa," Keri said, perking up. "I'm a grown woman and you don't sound nothing like my daddy."

Randall sucked in a deep breath, forced himself to count to ten and then tried again. "Sorry. I'm a little worried. I've been calling Isabella for a week and she has yet to return any of my calls."

"Well, maybe she doesn't want to talk with you. Have you thought about that?"

"Did she tell you that? Is she in the room with you?"

The woman curled in his bed stirred.

He turned his back and marched out of the bedroom with the cordless phone so he would have some more privacy.

"What Izzy and I talk about is none of your concern," Keri retorted snidely. "And *no* she's not in my room."

Once in the hallway, Randall's anger simmered back to

the surface. "Keri, I know what you're doing and it's not going to work. Isabella and I are going to get married."

Instead of locking horns and joining him in verbal combat, Keri just laughed and said, "I'm going back to sleep. That party wore me out."

"Party?" Randall questioned. "What party?"

"'Night, Randall."

"Keri. Keri!"

She hung up.

Randall pulled the phone from his ear and stared at it. "What the hell is going on in Atlanta?" Stabbing the end button, Randall marched back into his bedroom, knowing what he needed to do next.

"Oh, there you are, baby," the soft feminine voice floated from the bed as the woman stretched out her hand. "What are you doing up? Come back to bed."

Randall forced a smile on his face, but it felt like a grimace despite the tempting picture she posed. She wasn't his main girlfriend, but she was certainly in the top ten. "I can't. I gotta go." He returned the phone to its cradle. "Get up. I need for you to get dressed."

The woman's hands snaked out and caught his wrist. "Go?" she pouted. "You said that we could spend the whole weekend together."

Leaning down, he planted a brief kiss against the expensive pair of breasts he'd invested in. "Change of plans. I have to fly to Atlanta."

Isabella sighed and stretched along her cloud of satin sheets. Every limb ached; yet at the same time, she'd never felt better in her life. There was a nice little hum—as if her mind, body and spirit were perfectly in tune. Images of last night's sexcapades flashed through her mind, but even now she couldn't believe some of the things she'd done *and* the many different ways she did them.

Maybe it was all a dream.

Maybe when she opened her eyes, she would wake up at home, curled up next to her favorite teddy bear. Her heart fluttered a bit, fearful that might be true.

She drew a small breath and opened her eyes.

"Good morning, Bella."

A warm smile slid across her face as she gazed into his beautiful brown eyes. "Morning." She pressed her body against his and sighed again when his arm slipped over the curve of her hip. "How long have you been up?"

"A little while."

"Why didn't you wake me?"

Derrick's lips sloped unevenly. "I like watching you." He leaned over, brushed a kiss against the tip of her nose. "Sleep well?"

"You know I did."

"And how do you feel?"

She knew what he was really referring to. Last night, there had been no hiding the fact that she was a virgin. Not after the ear-splitting scream she'd unleashed when he'd first entered her. It was embarrassing, really—especially since she wasn't being split into two and wasn't dying like she initially thought.

Derrick turned out to be a big guy—a very big guy.

Mercifully, the pain she experienced was brief, and within a few strokes a part of heaven opened within her.

"I feel wonderful," she admitted.

"Really?" he asked, leaning forward again. This time, he peppered light kisses over her cheeks, nose and eyelids. "Because I was thinking—" his lips lowered to sweep against her neck "—that if you were up to it, we could, uh, play some more?"

Isabella giggled when his warm breath tickled a sensitive spot beneath her earlobe, but when she squirmed, her hard nipples brushed his toned chest and she was instantly ready for another round.

"Can I..." She stopped herself. Maybe she was getting a little too bold.

"Can you what, Bella?"

She flushed, loving her new nickname. But she was still feeling too shy to ask.

"C'mon. What is it?" Derrick nudged. His curiosity made his eyes twinkle.

"I was just wondering if...if I can take the top position again." She bit her lower lip and dropped her gaze to study his Adam's apple.

Derrick chuckled and then tilted her chin up so he could steal a kiss. "Don't be silly. We can do anything you like." He pulled her body on top and he rolled over onto his back.

Now familiar with where he kept his condoms, Isabella reached for the nightstand drawer and removed a gold packet.

Derrick folded his arms behind his head and watched as she ripped it open, but his eyes started to droop when her slender fingers curled around his proud standing erection.

Isabella noticed how her lover tensed when she touched him and a jolt of power surged through her. Instead of immediately sliding on the condom, she tightened her grip around his thick penis and started stroking.

He sucked in a sharp breath and tilted his head back farther while a look of unmistakable pleasure covered his features.

Smiling, she continued stroking and pumping while Derrick inhaled and exhaled in small puffs. However, watching only turned her on more and she became anxious to get in on the action as well. It took her twenty-seven years to have sex and now she couldn't get enough.

Isabella quickly ripped open the packet and rolled on the condom. As she tried to position herself, Derrick's hands lowered, gripped her hips and lifted her up. They sighed in combined pleasure as her body lowered back onto his hard shaft. Using her knees, she lifted up again and slid back down.

Slower this time.

Then again even slower.

"Oh, baby. Stop teasing. You're killing me."

She didn't change her rhythm—not until he started begging.

"Please, baby. Please," he croaked.

Finally she gave in; picking up the pace until she literally bounced against him. That was about the same time she was having trouble keeping air in her own lungs. Her body's temperature rose until she felt feverish, but then that wonderful feeling unfurled. She tossed back her head and her mouth sagged, not realizing she looked like a woman in reverent prayer as much as an insatiable goddess lost in orgasmic rapture.

Derrick, spurred on by her eager and wild response, dropped one hand from her hip to slip it between their joined bodies. He watched as her eyes widened with surprise, but drifted closed again as the pad of his bent finger rubbed against her clit.

Seconds later, Isabella released a long winding scream as she neared her explosion.

"C'mon, Bella. Come for me," he rasped.

"Oh, God!" she cried, exploding. A million stars flashed behind her closed eyes.

Rolling her over, Derrick quickly took the top position

and hammered into her hot, slick passage until his toes curled and his own orgasm erupted and drained him dry.

He collapsed. Sated. Exhausted.

If he thought he was going to be able to rest for long, he was sadly mistaken. The woman cocooned inside his bed was like his own personal Energizer Bunny. They made love in the shower, the hallway, the living room, the kitchen and finally back in the bedroom. She even had the opportunity to put a few of her newly acquired stripper moves to work.

His little Bella wanted to try everything and he was more than happy and willing to be her love slave.

The morning morphed into the afternoon and it was now drifting toward evening. The condom box was now empty and if they were planning to eat, he needed to take a trip to the grocery store. He seized the opportunity when Isabella finally drifted off to sleep.

He threw on a sweat suit, jotted a brief note that promised he would be back shortly and rushed toward the door, but not before stealing a few minutes to watch her curled up in bed, snoring.

In that time, he envisioned stealing such moments for years to come. Hot damn. He'd actually found *The One*.

It was a miracle.

For the second time, Isabella woke up in a strange bed with a delicious ache in between her thighs. This time when she opened her eyes to make sure she wasn't dreaming, Derrick's handsome face wasn't there to greet her.

She bolted up, startled. But one glance around the unmistakably masculine room and it was enough to convince her that the past 24 hours had been no dream.

Smiling, her gaze fell to the note placed on the pillow beside her. Pleased that she hadn't scared the man off, she relaxed back among the pillows and reviewed some of her favorite memories.

She felt wicked, strong and beautiful. All things that, up until last night, were foreign to her. She couldn't wait to tell Keri.

"Keri!" Isabella bolted up again and raked her fingers through her very tangled hair. Her sorority sisters were probably going out of their minds with worry. Glancing around, Isabella located the phone that was knocked off the hook next to the empty box of condoms and she made a mad dash for it and quickly punched in the number for the Ritz.

Within seconds she was transferred to Keri's room and nearly had her ear blasted off before she could finished saying, "Hey, Keri. It's me—"

"Izzy! Oh, thank God."

Isabella cringed. "I'm sorry. I know I should have called."

"Where in the *hell* are you?" Keri barked. "You told Waqueisha that you were coming back to the hotel last night. We've been banging and calling your room all day. We even had the manager open your room and we could tell you didn't stay there."

"I know. I—"

"We were debating whether we should call the police."

"Again. I'm so—"

"And that's not the worst of it. Randall has been calling and—"

"Oh, forget about him," Isabella snapped and reared back against the pillows. "It's over between us."

Keri finally shut up for a moment and then said, "Come again?"

"I'm not marrying Randall," Isabella announced and smiled at the relief and strength those words gave her.

"Izzy, where are you?"

"I'm…with someone."

Keri gasped. "You didn't!"

Isabella giggled. "I did."

"OH—MY—GOD!"

Isabella could then hear Waqueisha and Sylvia shout, "What? What? What did she say?"

"Izzy popped her cherry!" Keri screeched to the girls. "She's not a virgin!"

Isabella pulled the phone from her ear when a trio of screams shot through the line. The whole scene felt reminiscent of college when the girls would get caught up in the gossip grapevine.

"Tell us. Tell us. Tell us," Keri shouted over the other girls. "We want to know all the juicy details."

"Yeah," Waqueisha co-signed. "Like what's his name?"

"Derrick Knight," Isabella confessed.

"Who? Who?" Her clueless sorors hooted.

"Derrick Knight," Keri repeated, and then asked Isabella to confirm.

Isabella quickly filled them in on her night—minus the padded panties disaster.

"Well?" Waqueisha pressed. "Was it everything you hoped for?"

Drawing out the suspense, Isabella clammed up and allowed silence to fill the phone line.

"Oh, stop it. You're killing us," Sylvia shouted.

Finally, Isabella couldn't contain it anymore and squealed a loud, "YES!" She pulled the phone away from her ear again as equally excited screams echoed back.

"How do you feel?"

"When can we celebrate?"

The questions hurled at such a rapid pace, Isabella couldn't catch who was asking what, but she gave the answer they were all waiting for. "It was amazing," she sighed dreamily. "It was better than I ever thought it could be. In a way, I can't believe I waited this long."

"None of us can believe it." Keri laughed. "Well, what's going on now? Where's Derrick? We should send him a box of cigars."

"Very funny." Isabella rolled her eyes but kept smiling. "This is what it's really like to be in love."

The three voices on the other end stopped their giggling. "Love?" they shouted in sync.

"It has to be love," Isabella countered dreamily. "The earth moved, stars collided and I swear I heard angels singing."

"Oh good God," Waqueisha moaned. "Stop being so dramatic."

"Yeah," Sylvia agreed. "It was just sex."

Isabella ignored their words. "You guys don't understand," she said. "It was more than that. We connected. We—oh, I can't put it into words. I just know how I feel."

Silence hummed over the line.

Despite that, Isabella just laughed and trudged on. "I don't expect you guys to understand. I just want you to be happy for me...and supportive," she added. "When I return to Washington, I fully intend to end things with Randall once and for all."

"What about your parents," Sylvia inquired. "They're going to hit the roof."

No truer words had ever been spoken and, in truth, Isabella suspected her father would take the broken engagement harder than Randall. "It'll be hard," she admitted. "But I'll get Daddy to understand."

"Ha! Good luck," Keri laughed.

"I think it's great," Waqueisha finally spoke up. "If this is what you want, Boo."

"Thank you, Kiki."

A door slammed in the apartment and Isabella quickly jumped out of the bed. "I gotta go. He's back," she said.

"Wait," Keri barked. "When are you comin' back to the hotel? Randall called and said he was on his way here."

"What?"

"He said—"

"I can't deal with that right now," Isabella said. "Just stall him until I get back."

"Which is when?"

"I don't know. I'll call you." Isabella ended the call. She grabbed the top sheet and wrapped it around her before racing out of the bedroom. As she ran down the hall, her heart rammed against her ribcage in anxious anticipation. Maybe they'd make love in the living room again.

"Derrick, I've been waiting for you," she sing-songed. When she rounded the corner, her feet skidded to an abrupt stop and her mouth sagged open in shock.

A drop-dead gorgeous woman decked out in a form-fitting, peach-colored dress gaped back at her. "Who in the hell are you?" she barked.

Isabella blinked—several times, but failed to recall her own name.

"Where's Derrick?" the woman snapped, slamming her clutch bag down on the nearest table.

"He—uh, went out." Isabella swallowed and then tightened her grip on the bed sheet. "Who are you?" she managed to ask.

"I believe I asked you first."

"I'm Isabella."

The woman's eyes raked over Isabella while her lips curled in disgust. "Well, Isabella. I'm Meghan. Derrick's fiancée."

Chapter 15

Derrick was in love.

He didn't know how or why it happened. He just knew that it had and he'd never been happier in his life. He was thirty-two, but felt sixteen. He promised himself that when he returned to the apartment that he would learn everything he could about Bella. What were her favorite things? What did she do for a living? What was her last name?

Smiling and humming, Derrick quickly perused the grocery aisle for the ingredients for his signature lasagna dish. When he reached the small florist section of the store, he combed through their small selection of roses and settled on a few stems that looked like they'd live for at least a few days.

"Well, you look happy," the cashier, a short, squat, African-American woman with a face full of freckles commented and then picked up his bundle of roses. "Ah. Food and flowers." She eyeballed him. "You must have done something serious."

"No. No," Derrick said, shaking his head. "Can't a man buy his woman roses just because?"

"Not according to my husband," she said and shared a laugh.

The cashier grabbed the box of condoms and Derrick couldn't believe he was actually blushing, but when his gaze returned to the cashier, she wore a smile the size of Texas.

"Some women have all the luck," she said.

"No. You got it wrong," he corrected. "I'm the lucky one."

After checking out, Derrick hopped back into his car and raced back to his apartment. In the short drive, he'd almost caused three accidents while bits of memory from last night popped into his head. Just remembering Bella's husky moans, floral-scented skin and the way her warm body pulsed around him...

The driver behind him blew his car horn, jarring Derrick out of his daydream. Seeing that the traffic light was green, he gave the man behind him an apologetic wave and then raced through the light.

Nothing would sour his mood today.

Whipping his car into his designated parking spot, Derrick jumped out of the car and grabbed the few bags of groceries and of course the bundle of roses.

"Good afternoon, Mr. Knight," the building's watchman greeted.

"Hey, Al," he said, punching the button for the elevator. "Don't you ever take a day off?"

"Once in a blue moon," Al joked. "You must be running late. Meghan is already upstairs."

Derrick nearly dropped his bags. "What?"

Al jumped to attention at the sudden change in Derrick's posture. "Uh, she, uh, arrived about twenty minutes ago."

"And you let her up?"

Al sputtered.

The elevator bell dinged and the doors slid open. Derrick rushed inside and jabbed the number 10 button. "C'mon. C'mon," he chanted impatiently while the elevator doors took their time sliding closed. The lift to the 10th floor took forever and when he finally reached his destination, he bolted out of the doors and nearly crashed into Mr. Roberts.

"Whoa. Slow it down, buddy. I just got this new hip."

"Sorry, Mr. Roberts." Derrick kept running.

"Well, where's the fire?"

"Can't talk now, Mr. Roberts," he said over his shoulder and raced the rest of the way to his apartment. "Hurry. Hurry," he coached himself, but then started cursing when his hand trembled so badly he couldn't get his key into the lock.

"Bella," he shouted the moment he threw open the door. He raced inside, dropped his bags onto the first table he came upon.

"Hello, Derrick," Meghan said from the kitchen's entryway, her arms crossed.

He only gave her a cursory glance and then turned down the hallway, shouting. "Bella!" His heart pounded, blood surged to his head and still he held out hope that when he opened the bedroom door, she would still be cocooned where he'd left her.

The bed was empty.

"If you're looking for that tramp that was here earlier," Meghan sneered, "don't worry. I got rid of her for you."

Derrick whirled and slammed his fist into the bedroom door—just inches away from Meghan's head. "Where is she?"

Meghan jumped, her eyes wide with fright. "She's gone."

"Where?" he growled.

"C'mon, Derrick. You can't be serious. That mousey nobody with the orange hair? I just figured you had a little too much to drink last night and—"

He slammed his fist into the door again and roared, "Where?"

"I don't know. She just ran out of here crying."

"Goddammit!" He ground his teeth and turned away from her. Halfway down the hallway, he stopped and Meghan crashed into his back. "What the hell are you doing here? And what did you tell her?"

"I've had time to cool off. I—I came back to—to see if we—"

"No," he answered coldly. "It's over. Now what did you tell Bella?"

Meghan thrust up her chin; tears glistened in her defiant eyes. "I told her the truth. That you're a lying playboy that will screw anything that moves."

Derrick had never wanted to strike a woman in his entire life, but he calmly held out his hand and asked for his building and apartment keys back.

Meghan maneuvered around him and retrieved her clutch bag from the living room and handed over the keys, after which he promptly showed her to the door. Something he should have done months ago. "I've *always* been honest with you. You chose not to listen."

"Whatever." She rolled her eyes. "Trust me when I say that she's better off without you."

Derrick slammed the door in her face.

Isabella tried, but couldn't stop crying.

It had gotten so bad the cab driver had passed her a new packet of travel-size Kleenex. "Th-thank you," she croaked and quickly tore it open.

"Are you going to be okay, lady?" the cabbie asked.

She bobbed her head, but her heart screamed no. Those words of love she had expounded to her girlfriends now haunted her. They had tried to warn her; after all, it was just sex.

Just sex.

"Honey, you're not the only girl Derrick has cheated on me with, but in the end he always comes back to me."

Suddenly Isabella was laughing and crying at the same time. The cabbie glanced back through the rearview mirror, a look of weary caution on his face.

"Don't worry. I'm not crazy," she said. "Just—sad."

When he finally pulled up to the curb of the Ritz Carlton, Isabella raked through her purse several times before she found the two twenties at the bottom. "Here. Keep the change."

She bolted out of the backseat and nearly broke her neck trying to wobble and walk on a broken heel.

A few patrons gasped when she rushed by, but Isabella paid them no mind during her mad dash to the elevator bay. She knew she looked like hell, but she didn't care. The only thing that mattered was getting to her room so she could take a long, hot shower. With any luck, she would be able to erase every trace of Derrick from her body.

Her humiliation extended when she had to ride up to her floor with a compartment full of hotel guests—each of them darting questioning glances her way.

She ignored them all.

When she finally spilled into her hotel room, she immediately pulled at her clothes while her tears fell in earnest. The shower's water was scalding hot, but Isabella stood beneath its brutal lashing and scrubbed her skin as if she wanted to peel off every layer.

When she finally emerged from the shower, her skin

had been scrubbed raw and her puffy eyes were now the size of baseballs. But at least she was all cried out.

Wrapping a towel around her body and another one around her wet hair, Isabella traipsed out of the bathroom like a doomed woman walking to the electric chair. She calmly made her way over to the bed and crawled in beneath its cool sheets. For a long time, she just lay there listening to the silence and willing her emotions to go numb or at least for sleep to come and steal her away for a few hours.

Neither happened.

Instead, the pain of her raw skin lessened and in its place Derrick's remembered touch resurfaced—as well as the taste of his minty-hot mouth. It was like being seduced all over again.

She closed her eyes. One last tear tangled in the fan of her lashes. Why did this hurt so much? She hardly knew Derrick.

Hadn't she gone home with him on the sole purpose of a one-night stand? When did she allow her heart to get twisted up with this?

Sometime while he was screwing your brains out.

There was a knock at the door.

She ignored it.

The knock grew louder.

She still couldn't get herself to move.

The knock became a hammering. "Isabella, answer this door!" Randall's voice roared.

At the sound of her fiancé's voice, her eyes finally flew open. What was left of her heart lodged its way into her throat. *He knows!*

The hammering rattled the door.

"Hey. Hey. What are you doing?" Keri's voice filled the

hallway while Isabella scrambled out of bed, wondering what she should do.

"I came to speak with my fiancée," Randall thundered. "I'm tired of her avoiding my phone calls. I want to know what's going on!"

"Quiet," Keri hissed. "You want everyone in this hotel to hear you making an ass out of yourself?"

Isabella calmed a bit. If anyone knew how to handle Randall it was Keri.

"Where is Isabella?"

There was a pause. "She's not here."

"If she's not with you then where is she?"

There was no mistaking the note of suspicion in Randall's voice. In a blinding panic, Isabella rushed to the door before Keri was placed in the position to tell the truth or lie to cover for her.

"Randall," Isabella exclaimed after jerking open the door. "I thought I heard someone out here."

Two pairs of startled eyes flew in her direction and she forced on a smile that rivaled the practiced ease of her father's. "I was in the shower," she explained though no one had asked a question. "What are you doing here, Randall?"

Randall glanced between the two women; his expression was still lined with distrust. "You haven't returned any of my phone calls," he drawled.

"Well—" She swallowed. "This was supposed to be a little break—remember?"

Randall stepped toward the door and then his brows lifted when Isabella didn't budge. "Aren't you going to let me in?"

She hesitated, cast a glance over at Keri.

"Izzy, you don't have to do anything you don't want to."

"Will you please butt the hell out of our business?" Randall rounded on her. "This is between Isabella and me."

Keri's hands settled on her hips. She looked like an Amazon warrior; prepared to go to war, but Isabella agreed with Randall. This was between him and her. "It's okay, Keri. He can come in." She stepped back from the door.

Randall and Keri glared at one other until Isabella spoke up. "Randall."

Finally he turned away from Keri and stormed into the room. Isabella gave her best friend a woeful look, but mouthed the words "thank you" before shutting the door.

Chapter 16

Derrick hadn't smiled in two months.

He hadn't laughed, told a joke and he *tried* to avoid his frat brothers at all cost. However, they stuck to him like glue—each taking it as their personal duty to try to cheer him up.

Nothing worked.

Only one thing would, but Isabella was out of his life for good.

"Yo, D. You've got to snap out of this," Taariq said from his chair in Herman's barbershop. "I'm tired of you trippin' over your bottom lip. You need to dust your shoulders off and find yourself another girl. For real. I mean, Stanley has even found himself a woman."

Stanley jutted up his thumbs and slid on a smile of a well-sexed man. "Baby girl gives it to me all night long," he bragged.

Everyone in the shop groaned and hoped they wouldn't have to listen to Stanley queue up again with exaggerated stories about his sexual prowess.

Derrick sighed. "I'm just not interested in dating right now. I need a break."

Herman removed the trimmers from Derrick's edges to chuckle under his breath.

"Find something funny, old man?"

Herman's laughter grew louder. "Yeah. You." He swiveled the chair around so Derrick would face the mirror while he started edging up the back. "Looks to me that you've finally got a taste of your own medicine. Can't say I didn't see this coming or that I didn't warn you."

Derrick could only simmer like a scolded child.

"One thing that all the religions have in common is the belief that what you put out in the world comes back to you."

"You don't understand," Derrick said defensively.

"Well, let's see if I can gander a guess, hmm? I'd say you fell for a woman and that woman didn't exactly return your affection." He turned the chair around so that he could meet Derrick's gaze head-on. "How did I do?"

"You hit the bull's-eye," Charlie commented from the sidelines in his own chair. Reclined back with a steaming towel over his face, Charlie continued, "I don't think I've ever seen him so lovesick in all the years I've known him."

"That makes two of us," Hylan co-signed.

"Ah, leave him alone. I remember you two 'dawgs' were whipped a time or two yourselves," Taariq said, looking up from the Sunday sports section.

Stanley opened his mouth.

"Some of us more times than others."

Stanley closed his mouth.

Charlie and Hylan were silent for exactly two seconds.

"Whatever man," Charlie said. "I still say he needs to find a new chick in order to get over the old. That's the only remedy for this sort of thing. And Kappa men don't have any trouble in the ladies department."

A chant of "Amen," circled around the shop.

"Aw, shut up with the Kappa men do's and don'ts crap," Derrick snapped. "And while you're at it, stop talking about me as if I'm not here."

Bobby, who'd suspiciously been sweeping the same spot on the floor since Derrick came in, shook his head as if he was witnessing the demise of his favorite superhero.

"I'm fine," Derrick stressed. "There's nothing wrong with me. I'm just…laying low for a while."

"You're really a lousy liar," Herman said, sweeping the loose hairs from off Derrick's neck. "Why can't you just admit you're in love with the girl?"

Because she doesn't love me back. "Don't be silly, old man. I hardly knew the girl."

"That doesn't matter," Herman chuckled. "I told you. It's all about how you feel when you're looking into her eyes."

Derrick clamped his molars together and counted to ten.

"Ah, you're a prideful bastard." Herman laughed at his insolent behavior. "Lawd. Lawd. Lawd. What I'm gonna do with you?" He slapped his hand on his hip, took a good hard look around his crowded shop. "What am I gonna do with all you clueless knuckleheads?"

Everyone suddenly pretended to be busy.

Shaking his head, Herman's piercing gaze returned to Derrick. "You know what I'm talking about, don't you?"

Derrick peeled off his cape. "Are we through?"

A blanket of disappointment covered the old man's face. "Do-you-love-her?"

Yes. "I…have strong feelings for her," he admitted, uncomfortable of having this discussion with so many eyes trained on him.

Herman stared—waited.

Everyone waited.

Then finally, "Yes," Derrick whispered. His answer was followed by a combination of snickers and syrupy "ahs."

The old barber blinded Derrick with his pearly-white dentures. "That wasn't so hard now, was it?"

Charlie peeked out from under his steaming towel. "Oh, God. Is he blushing?"

Laughter erupted around the shop.

"Now the question is," Herman continued, ignoring everyone else in the room. "What are you going to do about it?"

"There's nothing to do," Derrick said, resigning himself to having this conversation in public. "The woman disappeared into thin air. Besides, I can't make someone feel something they don't. I should know. Do you know how many women have proposed to *me?* Each of them looked into my eyes, begged *me* to feel something I didn't feel. It's like you said: I'm just getting a dose of my own medicine. And *yes,* it's bitter going down."

"But you don't *know* how she feels," Herman reasoned. "At least those women in your past put themselves on the line and took a risk. No, it didn't pay off for them; but they're better off than wasting years wondering. You go down this road you're on and you'll spend the rest of your life *wondering.*"

Derrick shook his head, pulled money out of his wallet and stuffed two crisp bills into Herman's front shirt pocket. "Keep the change."

February was exceptionally cold in D.C., but that didn't stop Isabella and her mother darting around town planning for her big day just eight weeks away. In the two months since her fiasco in Atlanta, Isabella had become quite a pro at pretending to be happy. With her hair back to its normal color, her risqué clothes packed up, she attended all of Randall's social and political functions without complaint and with a smile on her face.

Everyone remarked how much she'd changed since her trip, her mother and father thought for the better. Her sorority sisters thought quite the opposite. Isabella tried her best not to think about it at all—at least while she was in public.

When she was alone, that was a different story.

Her pillows had absorbed a river of tears and her body ached for something it couldn't have—or someone. Too many times, she had tried to rationalize her feelings and each time, she'd only grown frustrated with the effort. It had only been *one* night. Granted, it was one night of incredible sex, but still.

Her last hope was that this was how all women felt after sex and that she would feel wild sexual urges toward Randall after their wedding night.

Sex was sex, right?

Until then, whenever she closed her eyes, it was Derrick who awaited her. Each night, she relived that wonderful time when her name was Bella and she was entangled in red silk sheets and climbing to new heights with Derrick's muscular body thrusting into her.

But then each morning, she woke trembling and had to massage the throb between her legs to give her body the release it craved. Why did he have to be engaged?

Why did she?

"Earth to Izzy." Rayne waved her hand in front of Izzy's face and then laughed when she'd blinked out of her stupor and she was sitting back at her parents' dining room table. Her friends had agreed to a brunch to help her generate names and addresses for the final invite list.

"What? What were you saying?"

Keri slid a pointed look in Rayne's direction and then shifted it back to Isabella. "I was asking you how much time you were going to take off from your practice after you're married."

"Oh." Isabella straightened in her chair. "Sorry. I have so much on my mind. Uh, Randall thinks that I should only take the week off for the honeymoon and get directly back to work. He thinks I'm on the fast track to making partner."

Keri settled back in her chair and crossed her arms. "Oh, does he now?"

"Of course, we'll get started on kids right away. Randall wants at least one of each. A boy definitely to keep the family name going."

Rayne also settled back and crossed her arms.

Isabella smiled blithely and continued, "It'll be hard for a little while starting a family and pursuing partnership, but Randall thinks I'm more than capable and supports me one hundred percent."

"Is he also going to put a bib on you and cut up your food?" Keri asked.

Isabella sighed. "Keri, I really do wish that you'd at least *try* to get along with Randall. He *is* going to be a part of my life now."

Keri grunted.

"Randall said—"

"Oh shut up about Randall already," Keri barked. "Has the man brainwashed you or something? Everything out of your mouth for the past two months is 'Randall said this' and 'Randall said that.' What happened to your own thoughts and opinions?"

Isabella bit her lip. She had expected this blowup from Keri. "I know you don't like him. But this is what I want," she said, reaching out and covering Keri's hand with her own. "I'd appreciate it if you could be a little more supportive. If not, then I'll understand if you want to back out of being my maid of honor."

Keri held her gaze, undoubtedly to see whether Isabella was serious. Brows high, Keri asked, "You're giving me an ultimatum?"

"I'm just giving you an out," Isabella said. "I don't want you to do anything you don't want to."

"Why not? You are."

The table fell silent. Rayne and Sylvia looked up from their list to watch the action.

Close to tears, Isabella drew a deep breath, counted to ten before she spoke. "I'm not going to fool you into believing that I'm in love with Randall. You girls know me too well for that," she started. "But in all honesty, I think love is overrated—especially in a marriage. Love disappoints. But a marriage built on sturdier things: friendship, respect and a commonality have the potential to last. A different kind of love can be cultivated from that. Randall and I have more in common than you think. We could do great work together."

"You've been in love all of what—one time? For less than twenty-four hours and now you're an expert?" Keri looked insulted. "And since we know each other so well, don't think I don't recognize your father's regurgitated speeches. It insults my intelligence."

"I think I'm going to go get us some more tea," Sylvia said, standing. "Rayne, you want to come?"

Rayne shook her head, riveted to the brewing fight.

"Rayne," Sylvia insisted.

"Nah. Nah. Go ahead."

Sylvia exhaled, and stormed off.

"Keri, I don't want to fight," Isabella said, exhaling an exhausted breath.

"Too late. We're already fighting," Keri said. "I think you're making the *biggest* mistake of your life."

"Then it's my mistake to make," Isabella shouted back.

Keri blinked at the fury in her friend's voice. "So you *do* know how to stand up for yourself. Bravo. Now if you can just focus that anger on the people trying to run your life instead of the ones trying to get you to take charge, then we'll be in business."

"This discussion is over," Isabella fumed.

"Izzy—"

"And stop calling me that!" Isabella exploded out of her chair.

"What?" Keri asked, truly mystified now.

"Izzy," Isabella yelled. "It's a horrible nickname. I hate it. I've *always* hated it."

Keri glanced over at Rayne, who could only shrug. "Okay, what about Belle or Bella?"

Isabella flinched and looked as if Keri had physically struck her. She glanced down at the floor and whispered. "Don't call me Bella either. Just…" Finally tears leaped over her eyelashes and streaked down her face. "Where's that damn tea?" She stormed out of the dining room.

"What about Randall's list?" Rayne called after them.

Isabella disappeared.

"Just send an invite to everyone in his day planner," Keri said and then took off after Isabella.

Isabella pushed through the door to enter the kitchen and stopped when Sylvia and Randall jumped away from each other. Her gaze darted between the two.

Keri entered the kitchen behind Isabella, her gaze also swung around the room. "What's going on?"

Chapter 17

"Nothing," Sylvia answered quickly. "We're out of tea and…Randall was just helping fix a new pot."

Calm, cool and collected, Randall set the tea kettle on the stove. "Actually, I was in the study with your father and came out to the kitchen." He finally noticed Isabella's face. "Have you been crying?"

Isabella quickly mopped her face dry. "We were just laughing at some thing," she lied expertly; her practiced smile bloomed.

For a long awkward minute the foursome darted curious and searching gazes around the room, and then finally Randall asked, "So how's the invitation list coming along? Did you get the day planner I left with your mother?"

Isabella nodded and busied herself helping Sylvia with the tea.

"Good," Randall said. "There are a few names I have highlighted that I preferred you not invite. In all, it's about two hundred names. My parents are coming up with their own list. I'll make sure they get that list to you this week."

Again, Isabella nodded.

Keri glowered.

And Randall met her look with a smile. "Hello, Keri. You're looking nice today."

Isabella's heart leapt into her throat while her eyes begged her best friend to be nice. She got her wish when Keri elected to say nothing at all.

Randall excused himself and returned to her father's study.

"Okay, Sylvia," Keri said the moment they were alone. "What the hell was really going on?"

"Nothing," Sylvia said, defensively. "I was surprised to see him just like you were."

Keri held her friend's stare.

Isabella frowned. "Why are you so suspicious, Keri?"

"Why aren't you suspicious at all?" Keri snapped back.

"Nothing happened," Sylvia insisted, looking offended by her friend's disbelief.

"Fine. Nothing happened," Keri said, turning her attention back to the door. "But a woman can never be too careful. A man like Randall I'd trust about as far as I could throw."

Derrick needed to find a new barber.

Everywhere he went, no matter what he was doing Herman's words of wisdom chased him. What did the old man expect him to do? Bella left him high and dry. What was he supposed to do, run off to D.C. and comb every bookstore and restaurant?

The question lingered until he shook it out of his head and increased the speed on the gym's treadmill. In response, Derrick's muscles screamed; but he pushed through the pain—welcomed it even. Pain was a nice distraction from the other aches his body suffered.

"Easy, D," Charlie said from the treadmill on his right. "You don't want to bust your butt again."

Derrick blocked Charlie out, blocked the whole world out. He just wanted the pain.

"What are you trying to do—kill yourself?" Taariq asked from his left.

Derrick upped the speed again.

This time his running partners said nothing and left Derrick alone with his demons.

Two hours later, Charlie and Taariq each had one of Derrick's arms thrown around their necks and carried one leg as they tried to hike him into Derrick's high-rise apartment building.

"Careful. Careful," Derrick moaned when Charlie accidentally slammed a foot against the elevator wall when he turned and pushed the correct button for Derrick's floor.

"Stop whining," Charlie snapped. "You did this to yourself."

Taariq grumbled an agreement. "I still think we should take him to an emergency room."

"I don't need a doctor," Derrick said testily.

"Yeah, you do," Charlie said. "A shrink."

"Ha. Ha."

The elevator doors slid open. Mr. Roberts blinked and took in the scene. "I take it he still hasn't talked to her?"

"Nope," Charlie and Taariq answered and carried their friend out of the elevator.

Mr. Roberts just shook his head.

"What? Does everyone know my business?" Derrick asked.

"What business?" Taariq asked. "Even Stevie Wonder could see something's wrong with you. If that Bella chick rocked your world this badly, I'm gonna have to agree with

Herman. You need to find this girl before you lose what's left of your mind."

"Or break our backs," Charlie added, reaching into his pocket and digging for his copy of Derrick's apartment key.

"Amen," Taariq co-signed.

Derrick glowered while he remained cradled between them.

"Oh, Mr. Knight!" A feminine voice floated down the hallway.

Taariq and Charlie turned, banging Derrick's feet and head against the doorframe while he slipped dangerously close to the ground.

"Uh, guys?"

His question fell on deaf ears as a curvy, petite woman approached them.

"Hello. Are you Derrick Knight?" she asked Taariq.

"No. That would be me," Derrick said, grabbing her attention as the invalid in the middle.

The woman's lips parted in a bright smile. "Hi. I'm Marcia Walker. I just moved into the building, but I've received some of your mail today by accident." She held out a few envelopes, but Derrick wasn't exactly in the position to grab them.

"I'll take that for him," Charlie said, dropping one of Derrick's legs. It hit the floor with a thud.

Derrick closed his eyes and clamped back a curse as stars burst behind his eyelids.

"Hi, I'm Charlie Masters, by the way."

"Hello," the woman flirted back. "Do you live in the building too?"

"Uh, no. But I visit my friend here, quite often."

"Excuse me," Derrick rudely interrupted. "But could you please get me into the apartment before someone mistakes me for being a part of the carpet?"

"Oh, right." Charlie slid the key into the lock and opened the door, but left it up to Taariq to drag Derrick inside. "Now where were we?"

"So much for loyalty," Derrick muttered.

Taariq laughed. "Can you blame him? I haven't seen curves like that since Jessica Rabbit." He finally deposited Derrick on his leather couch. "I'm grabbing a beer. You want one?"

"Sure." Derrick shifted around to get more comfortable.

When Taariq returned from the kitchen with the beers, Charlie was at his side.

"That was quick," Derrick said.

"Her husband showed up," Charlie grumbled and tossed the mail on Derrick's chest. "Lucky bastard."

Taariq laughed.

Derrick frowned at one of the envelopes.

"What is it?" Charlie and Derrick asked in unison.

"It's from Randall."

His two friends looked at each other. "Randall who?"

"Jarrett." Derrick tore open the envelope. "It's a wedding invitation."

Charlie popped a squat next to Derrick to read over his shoulder. "He's inviting *you* to the wedding?"

Derrick tossed the envelope to his friend. "See for yourself."

Taariq handed Derrick his beer. "Guess my Nanna is right. We are living in the last days."

Charlie nodded in agreement and handed the invitation back. "This definitely qualifies as a miracle."

Derrick had to agree. He chugged down half the bottle of beer and when he came up for air, he scanned the invitation again and stopped on the name: Isabella Elizabeth Kane.

Isabella.

Bella.

His Bella?

For a long time, he sat staring, once again, tuning out his friends while calculating the odds. "Nah. It couldn't be."

Chapter 18

On the first day of spring, the good residents of Virginia woke to a torrential downpour and nearly sent both Isabella's mother and her future mother-in-law into cardiac arrest.

"We're going to have to move the wedding inside," Katherine worried. "There's no way we can fit that many people in the house."

Isabella calmly poured her morning coffee. "The wedding is a week away. The meteorologists are reporting the rain will all be gone by then."

"It better be," Eunice spat like she was prepared to go to battle with Mother Nature.

"Coffee anyone?" Isabella held up the carafe, waiting to see if anyone would take her up on the offer. Both women passed on her offer.

Eunice stopped pacing to eye her future daughter-in-law. "I must say, Isabella, you have turned out to be one of the calmest brides I've ever seen. Haven't your wedding jitters kicked in yet?"

Isabella smiled blithely. "What's there to be nervous

about? You and Mom have taken care of everything. I've just had the lonely task of comprising the invitation list. All that's left for me and Randall to do is just show up, say our 'I do's' and then run off to Aruba for our honeymoon."

"You still have to get your marriage license. We can't take care of that for you."

"We're taking care of that first thing tomorrow morning."

"Good. Good." Katherine nodded. "Your father's parents are flying in from Martha's Vineyard on Thursday so I have to make sure I have my Valium refilled."

Eunice snickered. "I hear you. My in-laws came in last night and I've already doubled my dosage. Look at this." She held her hand up horizontally. "Steady as a rock."

Isabella laughed, but when she picked up her coffee mug, her hands were nowhere near as steady.

Randall's hips hammered away between the sexiest pair of legs he had ever had wrapped around him. The closer his wedding day drew on the calendar, the freakier his girlfriend became. Today started with a sexy striptease and then ended with a wonderful feather stroking him in places that had him shooting off one orgasm after another.

Not only that, but the sex talk grew so dirty it would make Larry Flynt blush. Randall loved every minute of it. Of course he knew why his longtime lover was going through such extremes: she'd hoped to change his mind about marrying her sorority sister.

But that wasn't going to happen.

When they collapsed exhausted in a sweaty heap, he still managed to place a few love-nips against the column of his lover's neck. "Have I told you lately how much I love you?" he asked.

"You sure do have a funny way of showing it," she said, pushing him off.

He expected the anger. It had a habit of showing up after her orgasms. In response, he just rolled over and propped himself up on the pillows. "Look. I didn't ask you to come over," he reminded her. "In fact, you keep taking risks by showing up here. Isabella—"

"I don't want to talk about her."

"All right." He shifted to his side and began playing with one of her perky breasts. "What do you want to talk about? My strategy for running for my first public office— or how about the number of lobbyists and interest groups who extended an invitation for dinners and lunches since my engagement?"

"Screw you," she spat and turned away from him.

"Face it, sweetheart. My plan is working. This marriage is going to jumpstart my career."

She sprang from the bed, snatched her clothes from the floor.

Randall didn't stop her. If she left, she'd be back. She always came back. And he would be waiting for her, married or not.

Derrick never sent in his R.S.V.P. for Randall's wedding. He couldn't make up his mind whether he wanted to accept the surprise olive branch. Why now? Why after all this time would Randall approach him? Certainly a strange way to solicit his vote should the day come when he did run for president.

"Maybe you should go there and ask him," Charlie said. "I'm tired of you asking us."

"Well, you talk to him regularly."

Charlie stopped chomping down on his second serving of fried chicken long enough to flash a smile at his mother when she placed her peach cobbler on the table. "Momma, you're spoiling me."

Faint lines crinkled around Arlene Masters's warm brown eyes as she smiled back at her son and patted him lovingly on the cheek. "It's my duty to spoil you." She looked pointedly across the table at Derrick. "And you too since your mother is living in Florida now."

"What can I say? I've tried everything to lure her back to Georgia but she won't hear of it. I'm an orphan."

She rounded the table and swatted him on the arm. "Nonsense. You want some cobbler?"

"Now, you know you don't even have to ask that question. I just hope you have another one of these baking in the oven, 'cause I'm eating this one myself."

Charlie grabbed his fork. "I'll fight you for it."

Arlene chuckled. She loved it when they fought over her food. "Y'all behave. You know I've made plenty."

Derrick and Charlie remained in a mock war crouch, forks in hand.

Arlene gently took hold of Derrick's chin and forced him to look at her. "Child, you got a new barber or something? Don't tell me Herman's messed your lines up this badly."

Charlie snickered. "He doesn't go to Herman's anymore."

Derrick shot his best friend a warning look, but it went unheeded.

"Herman's on his back about getting married."

Arlene's ears perked up like antennae. "Oh, really?" She eased into a chair between the boys. "Is there a particular girl he has in mind?"

Derrick knew before the day was over, Arlene would be burning the telephone line to Florida to let his parents in on all the juicy details.

"Some girl he met in D.C.," Charlie continued like a reporter on CNN.

"Charlie, do you mind?" Derrick snapped.

Arlene clasped her hands together excitedly. "Well, I think this is wonderful news." Her smile beamed. "Tell me all about her."

"There's nothing to tell," Derrick said, hoping in vain that would be the end of the conversation.

Arlene waited him out.

Derrick relented while Charlie snickered and dug into his peach cobbler. "Like Charlie said, I met her in D.C. We shared a cab, she didn't like me."

"Oh, c'mon," Arlene chastised. "What girl wouldn't like you?" She reached over and pinched his cheeks. "A handsome boy like you? She was probably trying to play hard to get."

"Or she was already spoken for," Charlie piped in between bites.

"Married?" The light in Arlene's eyes dimmed.

"Engaged," Derrick clarified. "Then some weeks later, we bumped into each other at party. No ring."

"And one thing led to another," Charlie added.

Derrick sent him a sharp kick under the table and his friend nearly choked on his food.

"Well." Arlene cleared her throat; her face blushed from the TMI details her son tossed out. "So what's the problem? You like her and I take her feelings for you had, uhm, improved."

"She—" Derrick searched for the right word. "Disappeared."

"Vanished. Poof. Gone," Charlie said, nodding.

Arlene frowned. "I don't understand."

Derrick expelled a tired breath, looked into Arlene's

eyes and felt the urge to tell the woman who'd been like a second mother to him everything. So he did.

When he was through, the only sound at the time was Charlie's endless lips smacking.

"So…*do* you love this girl?"

"I hardly know her," Derrick repeated.

Arlene held his gaze until the truth tumbled out. "Yes. I do."

Charlie finally stopped eating.

"It doesn't make any sense," Derrick added, shaking his head.

Arlene chuckled. "Love rarely does. How long do you think it took Adam to fall in love with Eve? I'm willing to bet it was love at first sight."

Derrick smiled. "I never thought of it like that."

"That's what I'm here for, baby." She pinched his cheek again. "Now go and find her," she urged.

"Looks like you have two reasons to go to D.C. now," Charlie boasted. "To look for your Bella *and* attend Randall's wedding."

The doorbell penetrated Randall's deep sleep. He moaned into the pillow, not ready or willing to get up. It felt too good to be nestled beneath his comforter while a spring breeze seeped into his bedroom. The bell rang again and the body next to him stirred.

Randall bolted upright. What time was it?

His head whipped around the room in search for the clock, he found it on the floor, a casualty of last night's sexcapades. "Damn."

"What is it?" his lover moaned from the bed's tangled sheets.

"I overslept," he growled, racing to the adjoining bathroom to grab his robe. When he came back, he barked for her to, "Stay put. It's probably Isabella." He slammed the bedroom door and raced to the foyer. By the time he answered the door, he'd painted on a generic smile.

"There you are," Isabella exclaimed, brightly and then pocketed her cell phone. "I was just about to call you when you didn't answer the door." Her gaze roamed over him. "You're not dressed. We're supposed to go for our marriage license. Did you forget?"

Randall nodded, embarrassed. "I overslept."

She laughed and Randall felt a sudden kick in the gut. When did she develop such a nice laugh?

"Well." She glanced at her watch. "Aren't you going to invite me in?"

"Oh. Yeah." He stepped back and allowed her in. He caught a whiff of her floral perfume. "You smell nice," he complimented and closed the door.

"Thanks." She folded her arms and rocked on her booted feet during the ensuing silence. Finally, she prompted, "Don't you think you should hurry and get dressed?"

"Oh, yes." He blinked out of his fog, not sure what it was that he'd found so attractive about his fiancée lately. Something was different about her since she'd returned from Atlanta. He was actually growing more attracted to her. "I'll make it quick." He turned and raced back to his bedroom.

"Is it her?"

Randall shot a glance over at the bed. "We have to figure out a way to get you out of here."

"How about I just march outside and we could all just have a nice talk," his lover threatened, bouncing out of bed. She marched toward him at the bedroom door.

"What? You think she's going to forgive you any better than she's going to forgive me?"

She arched a delicately groomed eyebrow high into her forehead. "There's only one way to find out."

She reached for the door and Derrick slapped her hand away. When it looked like she was about to scream out to Isabella, he clamped his hand over her mouth.

In the foyer, Isabella waited patiently. When Randall didn't answer the door earlier, she'd found herself hoping that he wasn't home and that they would have to get their license at another time. Like next year or something.

While she waited, a pair of hushed voices drifted toward the quiet foyer. Was Randall talking to someone? She took a step, turned her ear toward the hallway. When she thought she heard it again, she took another cautious step. Who could Randall be talking to?

A man like Randall, I'd trust about as far as I could throw.

Isabella took another step.

Silence.

Another step.

The doorbell rang and Isabella nearly jumped out of her skin. She rolled her eyes and laughed at herself. The voices must have come from the other side of the front door. "I'll get it," she shouted and opened the front door, but when her gaze crashed into Derrick Knight's piercing black eyes, she fainted.

Chapter 19

Derrick's keen reflexes sprang into action and he caught Bella before she hit the floor. Bella. His Bella. His brain was having a hard time wrapping around that notion. He lifted her limp body up, tapped her left cheek lightly to try and rouse her. Slowly, she started to come around. Her thin fan of eyelashes fluttered and then finally her beautiful brown eyes popped open.

"If you wanted me to wrap my arms around you, all you had to do was just ask," he joked.

She shoved at his chest and jumped away from him. "What are you doing here?" She glanced over her shoulder and back into the house. Apparently the coast was clear because she pushed him back onto the porch, joined him and closed the door behind her. When she looked back at him, her eyes were wide with fright. "Well?" she prodded.

Derrick had almost forgotten the question. "I came to see an old friend. I was invited to his…" A light clicked on. "Isabella Elizabeth Kane?"

She thrust up her quivering chin.

His hand shot out, grabbed her wrist and he glanced

down at the offending diamond ring. "Funny. I don't remember this when I was making love to you in my bed."

This time when the apples of her cheeks darkened, he didn't find it so adorable.

"I'm sure you gave your fiancée an engagement ring," she accused.

"Did she show you one?"

Isabella blinked, suddenly unsure of herself.

"I'm not engaged. I've *never* been engaged. Meghan was a jealous ex-girlfriend who was just trying to eliminate the competition. Had you stuck around to get my side of the story, I would've told you that."

Bella's wide eyes blinked up at him while her mouth slid open in surprise.

The front door jerked open.

"Isabella, who's at the…"

Derrick's head snapped up and his gaze clashed with his old fraternity brother.

Randall's eyes rounded as wide as his fiancée's. "Derrick?"

"Randall."

Randall's gaze bounced between him and Bella, before his next question snapped in the wind and confused him even more. "What in the hell are you doing here?"

Derrick stepped back and then he met the angry glare head on. "I came here to talk to you."

"About what? We said all we had to say years ago when you stole my *first* fiancée."

"What?" Isabella turned toward Randall. "You were engaged before?"

"It was a long time ago. We were in college," Randall answered without looking at her. "The question is: what are you doing here now, Derrick?" He wrapped a possessive arm around his fiancée. "Are you here to try and steal Isabella?"

Derrick and Bella's gaze shot toward one another. "Obviously, there's been some kind of screwup. He reached inside his black jacket and withdrew the wedding invitation. "I received this and thought you were extending an olive branch."

Randall reached out and snatched the invitation from his hands. "Damn right there was a screwup." He cast a glance at Bella.

"I don't remember seeing his name on the list. Maybe one of the girls sent it out by accident," she offered.

Derrick felt like a fool.

An unwanted fool.

Randall turned his baleful gaze back to Derrick. "There you go. It was sent by mistake."

"I get it." Surrendering, Derrick tossed up his hands, but his gaze slid back toward Bella. "I know when I'm not wanted." He stepped off the porch and backed away. Halfway down the walkway, Derrick stopped. "If you're interested in burying the hatchet, Randall," he said, but looked at Bella, "I'll be at the Hamilton Crowne Plaza." With that, he turned and rushed back to his rental car in the driveway.

Isabella and Randall watched the silver sedan pull out of the drive and then disappear down the road. It was then Isabella became aware of the voice in her head screaming: "Don't go."

I've never been engaged.

Her heart plunged to her toes. She had raced out of his apartment so fast that day it never occurred to her to question whether the woman standing in his apartment was telling her anything but the truth. It wasn't like she really knew Derrick, despite her heart pleading the contrary.

Dear God. What have I done?

"Well, we better get a move on if we want to get that license this morning.

Isabella didn't answer, but she did allow Randall to take her arm and lead her to his car.

Derrick paced the limited space in his suite like a caged animal. His thoughts churned at such an alarming rate, he struggled to make sense of it all. He'd showed up two days earlier than the other Kappa brothers for two reasons: to hire a private investigator to find his Bella—with the limited information he had—and to talk to Randall regarding mending the bridge of their friendship before just showing up at his wedding.

Doing the latter first turned out to be a smart move. However, the last thing he'd expected was for Bella to answer Randall's door.

Bella.

His Bella.

His stomach pitched, nauseated at the thought of her marrying Randall. His ex-best friend Randall.

Fate was too cruel.

What was he going to do? What was his next move? What *could* he do? The harder he concentrated on those questions, the more frustrated he became; mainly, because he didn't have an answer. The morning drifted to the afternoon and then into a somber evening. Derrick finally settled on the edge of the bed, bare-chested, shoes and socks off, his belt unbuckled and his trousers unbuttoned. His head ached from his missing all three meals of the day and his stomach growled its protest as well, but he had no plans of leaving his room until he sorted this mess out.

The soft knock on the door had barely penetrated his troubled thoughts. He frowned until he remembered he'd requested housekeeping to send up more towels so he could take a long shower.

At the second barrage of knocks, Derrick climbed back onto his feet and buttoned just the top of his pants while he marched toward the door. "I'm coming," he mumbled and then jerked the door open and for the second time that day, he was greeted with the unexpected sight of Isabella Kane.

Initially neither spoke. They just took their time in a commensurate stare.

The housekeeper arrived, dividing her own questioning look between the two. "Here are your towels, sir."

Derrick turned toward the stout Hispanic woman and accepted the delivery. "Thank you."

"You're welcome." She turned but moved away slowly.

Once the woman was out of earshot, Isabella licked her lips and asked, "Aren't you going to invite me in?"

He didn't answer but he stepped back and allowed her to enter.

She stepped inside, her stride small, her demeanor timid.

Derrick closed the door behind her. He wanted to speak; but a part of him feared that if he did, she would disappear into thin air again. He didn't want that. In fact, if she was indeed real, he might consider locking them in this room indefinitely.

Moving from the door, he circled around her like a hunter teasing its prey. He wanted to tell her he liked that her hair had returned to its original color. He liked the minimal makeup—her lips painted a subtle toffee, her wide eyes framed with just a hint of mascara.

Quite simply, she was beautiful.

"Aren't you going to say something?" she finally asked.

With so much to say, where should he start? "I miss you," he said; his voice surprised him when it cracked with pent up emotions.

In response, Isabella leapt into his arms. The towels hit the floor and they tumbled onto the bed.

Isabella wasn't thinking. She was feeling. From the moment she saw Derrick standing on Randall's porch up until when their lips crushed together in sweet homecoming, her body was riotous with every emotion she'd ever felt in her life. Nothing mattered more than this moment, this second when her heart was close to exploding.

Arms wrapped around his strong neck, she felt anchored amidst a wild storm of desperation. In the few months since their parting, she'd forgotten how much she felt alive in his arms—forgot how his hot mouth instantly caused an ache between her legs.

Derrick tugged up her skirt and pulled at her panty hose until she felt them tear.

She didn't care. She just wanted him to hurry—to touch her where she needed to be touched. Her stockings only went as far as her knees before he returned to pull at her panties—and they, too, rested at her knees before he returned for one final thing.

Isabella broke their savage kiss when her head sprang back with a gasp. Derrick's strong, nimble fingers invaded her body's warm, slick passage.

While she took advantage to fill her lungs with much-needed air, Derrick's mouth didn't try to reclaim hers, but instead traveled down to the small buttons on her blouse and proceeded to snap each one off with his teeth. Her blouse slid open; her soft pink bra thrust her small breasts high into the air.

Derrick groaned and then proceeded to kiss and suck at her nipples through the thin, lacy material.

Moaning and writhing, Isabella was going insane from the hot feel of his mouth and the maddening tempo of his plunging fingers. The slim barrier of her bra lost the war when Derrick's teeth tore the lace and gained full access to an exposed nipple.

Pleasure and pain commingled when he sucked the hard bud into his mouth. Her arms unhooked around his neck so that her hands could grip his bobbing head.

"I need you," she rasped. "I need you inside me. Now!"

Derrick was only too happy to oblige. His hand abandoned the hot heat between her thighs so he could pull back momentarily to unsnap that one pesky button on his trousers. After that, the rest of their clothes came off in a flurry of continuous motion until there was nothing but flesh pressed against flesh—and heat seared into heat.

Tears leaked from Isabella's eyes when he began moving inside of her. Her body swallowed his sex whole and seemed to vibrate to soundless music. Eyes closed, her face bathed in bliss, Isabella rolled her hips along with his deep thrusts.

Higher and higher their souls elevated. Their breathing rapid and ragged until their bodies exploded within seconds of each other and they clung together as though their very lives depended on it.

Chapter 20

"Isabella Elizabeth Kane, will you marry me?" Derrick slipped the two-carat diamond ring off her hand. In its place, he wrapped a long piece of string from the bed's comforter around her finger. A crooked smile sloped his kiss-swollen lips when his gaze shifted to stare into her eyes. "I know it's not much." He shrugged awkwardly. "But, uh, I promise to buy you a better one as soon as I decide to let you out of this room."

Butterflies fluttered beneath every inch of Isabella's body and tears poured from her eyes.

"None of these," Derrick said, lightly wiping her eyes dry. "You're supposed to be happy."

"I am," she croaked. "More than you'll ever know but…"

Derrick tensed, waited. When she didn't continue, he prompted her. "But what?"

She started to pull out of his arms, but Derrick tightened them and held her in place. "Don't tell me you're still going to marry him?"

She didn't answer but her tears continued to flow. Now

that she'd satisfied her body's hunger how would she go about telling him that she *had* to marry Randall—that this marriage was much bigger than just her? Isabella tried to recall her father's exact words, but with Derrick's body still pressed against hers, Senator Kane's political agenda was a long way from her thoughts.

Derrick's face hardened, but he still didn't release her. "I thought that by coming here you…that we…" At long last, he pulled away, climbed out of bed.

Isabella swallowed, watching his beautiful muscled body as it paced, struggling to keep her eyes from staring at his heavy sex.

"Do you love him?" he asked brusquely.

She realized this was her cue to lie, but she simply didn't have it in her. "No."

He stopped pacing, his dark gaze impaled her. "Then why?"

"It's complicated," she moaned, rolling from the bed and looking around for her clothes.

"Complicated?" he echoed and then marched to her side. "If it's so complicated, explain it to me. I promise you I'm smarter than I look."

Isabella picked up her buttonless blouse, her ripped bra, torn panties and pantyhose. The only thing that was still intact was the skirt.

"Bella?"

She nearly melted at hearing the beloved name. Her knees folded and forced her to perch on the edge of the bed.

Derrick claimed the spot next to her, reached over and took her by the chin and forced her watery eyes to level on him. "Do you love *me?*"

"Yes," she whispered. "I don't know how. You just learned my full name today." She laughed. "I know it's silly."

"No, it's not," he said. "Not if we both feel the same way. I *know* I'm in love with you." He smiled, leaned down and brushed his lips across hers once, twice—then Isabella dropped her clothes and wrapped her arms around his neck and melded their mouths in a fiery kiss.

Derrick leaned back, dragging her body on top of his and moaning her name like she was the only person who could save him. It had to be true because he was the only person who could save her.

The kiss ended and Isabella rested her lips against his throat. "I do love you," she confessed and knew right then she was in trouble.

"Does that mean you'll marry me?" he asked.

She lifted her head and met his unblinking gaze. "Yes," she whispered. "I'll marry you."

"In that case—" his lips parted into a beautiful smile as he wrapped his arms around her hips so she could better feel his hardening erection "—you've made me the happiest man alive."

"And I the happiest woman."

Derrick rolled her onto her back and proceeded to make love to his fiancée.

Isabella floated home on a cloud. The whole time it was nearly impossible to wipe the smile off her face. Perhaps that had a lot to do with the fact that she had replaced her blouse with one of Derrick's shirts and wore no underwear underneath it or her skirt. The whole ensemble had a way of making her feel wicked and wanton.

She liked it.

While her cab bustled through the late morning traffic, she sat nestled in the back, smiling blithely at the string wrapped around her finger.

Derrick Knight was in love with her. A delicious

warmth flooded her body each time the words drifted through her mind. It was hard to keep her tears of happiness from spilling when she thought about just how much she loved him too.

As the cab neared the Capitol Overbrook Condominiums, all her happy thoughts and feelings began to subside. How on earth was she going to call off her wedding to Randall just three days from the event? How big of an explosion would her father cause? And what would Randall do when he learned of her affair with Derrick?

Suddenly Isabella questioned her decision to go into the lion's den alone. Derrick had insisted that he come along with her for support when she broke the news, but she had felt, at the time, that this was something she had to do alone.

Her gaze traveled from the string ring to her watch. Right now she was supposed to be headed toward the Four Seasons for her bridal brunch.

Everyone was expecting her.

What was she going to say—"Hey everyone, thank you for coming, but I'm not marrying Randall Jarrett, I'm marrying his ex-best friend and fraternity brother, Derrick Knight, instead?"

Now all the hard work her mother and Eunice Jarrett had put into everything caused her stomach to loop into several knots. Could she face these people alone?

At long last, the cab pulled up to her condo and she exited the vehicle like a death-row inmate headed for lethal injection. She needed a speech, she needed time—she needed a valium.

"There you are!" Katherine shouted the moment Isabella opened her front door. "Where have you been?"

Isabella blinked at the immediate assault. She was also

struck dumb and couldn't recall how to speak English no matter how hard she tried.

Katherine's sharp gaze took in her daughter's appearance and suspicion flicked in her eyes.

"Is she back?" Keri asked, exiting the downstairs powder room. She stopped in the small foyer and also took in her friend's tussled appearance.

Katherine was the first to find her voice. "Upstairs, you," she directed, marching to Isabella's side and taking her by the arm. "We have a brunch to get to. A lot of people are waiting for us."

"Mom—"

"I don't want to hear another word," Katherine snapped. "Get upstairs and make yourself presentable. Keri, you go with her. We're pressed for time."

"Mom—"

"Later, young lady," Katherine's voice continued to rise. "Whatever it is, it can wait."

Maybe it was best to wait until after the brunch.

The moment she entered her bedroom, Keri pounced.

"Where have you been? Who were you with? Why are you wearing a man's shirt?"

"Derrick Knight is in town," Isabella informed her in a harried whisper as she peeled out of her clothes. Since she'd taken a shower before she left the hotel, she raced to the dresser drawer for clean ones. "I spent the night with him," she confessed.

"Izzy! I mean, Isabella, you're getting married in three days."

"I'm getting married, but not to Randall." She flashed her friend her ring finger.

"That's a piece of string."

Isabella flashed a bright, endearing smile. "I know. Isn't it sweet?"

Keri stared as if she'd lost her mind.

"I know what you're thinking," Isabella said.

"Do you?"

"Yes." She raced over to the closet and grabbed the dress she'd selected for the brunch. "And don't worry, I'm going to handle this mess…somehow."

"*You're* going to handle it?"

"Yes."

Keri folded her arms. Her dubious expression was mixed with wry humor. "You're finally going to stand up to your parents *and* the Jarretts and call off the wedding?"

"Yes!"

Her best friend tossed back her head and laughed. "I'll believe that when I see it."

Chapter 21

Something had gone wrong.

After leaving like the twentieth message on Isabella's cell phone, Derrick slammed the receiver back onto the phone and began pacing in his room. She should have called him by now. She should have returned to the hotel. He should have gone with her. Muttering a stream of curses, Derrick was torn between scouring the city and waiting for her return. What if she showed up after he left?

What if Randall had flown into a rage after discovering she was ending their engagement because of him? Worse, had he taken that rage out on Bella?

"Damn it! I should have never let her go by herself."

There was a knock at the door.

Derrick's heart leapt into his throat as he raced across the room in record time. But when he snatched the door open, his excitement drained from his face.

"Let the party begin. Kappa Psi Kappa is in the house!" Tarriq shouted, using his hands as a megaphone.

The small group of fraternity brothers marched into the room performing a few step-show moves. So exuberant in their cheer, none of them noticed Derrick's disappointment when he slammed the door behind them.

It wasn't until they were about to start the cheer over that Stanley glanced at him and asked, "What's wrong with you? Someone shoot your dog or something?"

"He doesn't own a dog," Charlie said, popping Stanley on the back of the head before turning his attention back to Derrick. "What's up, D? No luck finding your mystery lady?"

"I found her," he deadpanned.

"Ah," Hylan said, shaking his head and jumping to the wrong conclusion. "She told you to get lost, eh?"

Derrick opened his mouth, ready to confess all, but then quickly closed it. Though he was no longer on speaking terms with Randall, his four frat brothers were very much a part of his ex-friend's life. In fact, they had all come for this weekend's wedding.

The wedding Bella was supposed to be canceling.

He quickly swallowed his confession, choosing to wait until he'd heard from Bella. "Nah. Nah. Everything is cool," he lied.

"Well, then," Charlie approached and wrapped his arm around Derrick's neck. "Since the bachelor party isn't until tomorrow night, why don't we go out and paint the town red?"

The brothers shouted their agreement, but Derrick hedged leaving the suite.

"Uh, actually, I was thinking about hitting the sack. I want to get an early jump on tomorrow."

His four brothers glanced at their watches at the same time.

"It's seven-thirty," Charlie said lamely. "Surely that's a bit too early even for you, Grandpa."

"What's this?" Stanley bent over and retrieved Bella's torn bra.

"Ooooh," his brothers chorused and then bobbed their heads in understanding.

Hylan discovered the ripped pantyhose. "Damn. I'm surprised the girl was able to walk up out of here."

Charlie turned toward Derrick. "She *did* walk out of here, didn't she?"

"All right, guys," Derrick said, heading back to the door. "Now you know. I have other plans tonight so you guys are going to have to paint the town without me." He opened the door.

"My man. My man," Charlie snickered. "Came early and tracked her down. Good for you." He patted him on the back. "After we get Randall hitched, I suppose you're going to be next to walk down the aisle?"

It was on the tip of Derrick's tongue to correct Charlie about Randall's pending marriage, but instead he just bobbed his head in agreement and ushered his friends out of the room.

"Well, you're going to the bachelor party tomorrow night, right?"

Derrick stalled.

"C'mon, man," Hylan coerced. "You can't skip out on the main event. You know Randall knows how to throw some off-the-hook parties. I talked to Randall about an hour ago; he says he has the whole thing set up. Good music, alcohol and the finest strippers money can buy."

Derrick stared at him. "You talked to Randall an hour ago?"

"Yeah. He told us about you showing up at his place. Not a good scene, huh?"

"No. Not really."

"Don't worry about it. Charlie has all but convinced him

to let bygones be bygones. Christina Faye was a trouble-maker from jump street. Word is she's an addict and has been in and out of rehab for years. You did him a political favor by taking her off his hands."

"For the last time, nothing ever happened between me and Christina."

"That's what I told him," Charlie cut in. "You would *never* steal a girl from one of your frat brothers. You have too much class for something like that."

"Yeah," his buddies co-signed.

Derrick swallowed; his thoughts immediately of Bella. Stealing Randall's girl was exactly what he was trying to do. "Randall said an hour ago that the bachelor party was still on?"

"Sure did," Stanley boasted. "I got my stack of condoms and dollar bills ready."

"Pace yourself," Hylan sniggered. "Are you sure your heart can take you getting laid twice in one year?"

Stanley's smile widened. "It's a chance I'm willing to take."

"So come to the party tomorrow and squash this non-sense," Taariq encouraged. "I know I'm ready for you two to move on from this."

"I'll think about it. If all goes right, I'll have other plans tomorrow night."

"Man, you really are whipped," Stanley said, shaking his head. "My hero. Down for the count."

Derrick rolled his eyes and shoved Stanley out the door. "Catch you guys later."

"Well, let us borrow your rental car, in case we score a few ladies and don't have to cram them on our laps. Wait. That might be a good idea."

Derrick shook his head and retrieved his keys from the

table. "Silver sedan parked on the first level. The license plate number is on the key ring."

"Thanks, Bro."

Derrick closed the door and slumped back against it while one question wiggled its way to the front of his mind. *Why hasn't the wedding been called off?*

Isabella tried to call off the wedding…sort of.

The brunch went off without a hitch, but accepting gift after gift weighed heavy on her heart. A few times she pulled her mother aside, but each time her throat would close up and her body went clammy.

"Oh, you're finally getting hit with those wedding day jitters?" Her mother smiled gaily. "I knew you'd get them sooner or later. Here, take one of these." Her mother shoved two pills into her hand. "It'll calm you down."

She needed to calm down. Isabella popped the pills and washed them down with her champagne. The result: Isabella became *too* relaxed—to the point that even talking became too much of a chore. Sure she caught a few curious stares, especially when she took it upon herself to forgo refilling her champagne flute to start drinking directly from the bottle—er, bottles.

This act stunned her mother and Eunice Jarrett into silence. Keri was the only one who found her behavior amusing. The rest of the brunch passed in a blur and somehow the women had returned her safely to her condo and tucked her into bed.

When Isabella woke up, it was black as pitch outside her window and the condo was eerily silent. The clock on her nightstand read nine o'clock. She had slept the whole day away.

"Derrick." She bolted upright and then moaned at the

instant headache the abrupt motion gave her. She bounded out of bed, called a cab and performed a quick change.

It was ten p.m. when she rushed through the door of the Hamilton Crowne Plaza. She performed a sort of walk-run to the elevator bay. When she finally knocked on Derrick's door, it was instantly jerked open and she found herself being swept into her lover's muscular arms.

"Where have you been? I've been so worried about you." Derrick moaned into her hair and, before she could answer, he rained kisses down her face and neck.

She moaned and melted in his embrace. It had only been twelve hours since they parted, but if felt as if it had been forever.

Finally Derrick ceased his mini-assault and pulled her over to the bed. "Did you tell him? What did he say? Is he angry or hurt? Should I go talk to him?"

"No," she snapped, but then regretted shouting.

Derrick frowned and pulled away. His dark, intense gaze impaled her with suspicion. "You *did* call off the wedding, right?"

Her mouth was as dry as a desert and no matter how long she worked her jaw, words failed her.

"I see." He stood from the bed. "Then you're here to break your engagement to me?" he asked softly.

She jumped up, her voice finally working. "No. No. It's just that when I arrived at my apartment, my mother was there, rushing me to hurry for the bridal brunch and I couldn't tell her with so many people waiting for us."

He frowned, but then asked, "So you told her *after* the shower."

"Well, no."

Derrick stepped back.

Isabella moved forward. "I was such a wreck at the brunch my mother offered me two of her valiums and I'm afraid I mixed it with some—a lot of champagne. I was knocked out and I woke up about an hour ago and rushed right over here."

He stared at her.

"I swear it's the truth," she stressed. "I'll have to do it tomorrow. Besides, I should tell Randall before I tell my parents. We have an in-law luncheon tomorrow—I'll tell everyone then."

An awkward silence stretched between them before Derrick's sexy lips split into a smile. "All right." He pulled her back into his arms and tugged at her clothes. "Tomorrow—and I'm going with you this time. Afterward, we can hop a plane to Vegas and you can still be a Vegas bride by Saturday."

Isabella tensed.

"Don't try to talk me out of it," he added. "I want to be there to support you." He nibbled on her ear and smiled when she sighed. "I nearly went crazy waiting in this room all day." He peeled her blouse off her shoulders and then skillfully removed her bra.

Isabella was completely overwhelmed by the power of his touch. Somewhere in the recesses of her mind, she knew that there was no way she was going to take Derrick to meet her father while she was trying to end the marriage to his selected protégé.

That was asking for trouble.

When the rest of her clothes hit the floor, all thoughts of Randall and her parents fled. Derrick was her world now.

Derrick eased Bella onto the bed and then quickly scrambled out of his own clothes and grabbed a condom. When he lay down beside her, he was greedy for her touch and nearly came unglued when her hands glided to and then massaged his solid erection.

Groaning, he nuzzled his face between her breasts, inhaled her fading perfume. Her moans and sighs filled the room when he at last took a puckered nipple into his mouth. Teasing, he slid a hand between her thighs and played with her velvet curls.

"Ah, Derrick," she sighed when he finally glided his two fingers into her slick passage.

He worked his lissome fingers against her soft flesh while dexterously opening the condom. Her passion built until she begged for him to join their bodies.

"Please. Please." She peppered kisses around his face.

Derrick sank into her lush body and Bella's vaginal walls closed around him like a tight fist. He clenched his teeth, straining not to lose control too soon. He wanted to take his time.

And he did.

They made love all night.

But when he woke, she was gone.

Chapter 22

For the second morning in a row, Isabella rode home floating on a cloud, she definitely looked like a woman who had a pleasurable night. Though she didn't like that she had to sneak out of Derrick's hotel room, she knew without a doubt it would only make things worse when she called off her wedding.

Now, she needed to figure out how she was going to break the news to everyone at the luncheon. It was probably best to keep everything short and to the point. "Randall, I can't marry you," she practiced saying to the window.

The cab driver glanced back at her and Isabella blanched. Her condominium came into view and she drew a deep breath, but still dreaded the hours ahead.

Entering her condo, Isabella thought she had about an hour to get ready before Randall arrived to take her to their luncheon. Instead, when the cab pulled up, she saw her father's black Mercedes parked in front.

This was too soon; she wasn't prepared to talk to anyone yet. She had developed a speech that held every possibility of her being disowned.

"Ma'am," the cab driver snapped. "Would you like for me to keep the meter running?"

"No, no." She reached for her purse, handed the driver a couple of bills and exited the cab. In no hurry to face the music, Isabella loitered outside her door a full five minutes before she mustered up the courage to go inside.

Her father was waiting.

"I was afraid you weren't going to come in," he said calmly from the kitchen. "Coffee?"

Isabella shook her head and tried to match his poised composure.

Despite her answer, the senator poured two cups of coffee and then slid one mug across the breakfast bar for her to drink. There was a short standoff and then Isabella finally reached for the steaming coffee.

Her father nodded, satisfied, before reaching for his own cup. While he took his first sip, he stared at his daughter over the rim of his cup.

Uneasy, Isabella lowered her cup and then climbed up onto one of the breakfast bar stools. She wet her lips and cleared her throat. "Dad—"

"I want you to end it," he ordered, cutting her off.

She gasped, surprised.

"What? Don't you think I know what goes on with my own daughter?" he questioned. "Your mother said you came home yesterday morning, wearing a man's shirt. I happen to know for a fact that you weren't with Randall that night."

Isabella stared at her father like a deer trapped in headlights. After she got her bearings, she launched into what little of a speech she had prepared. "Dad, I can't marry Randall."

"Yes, you can. And you will—this Saturday."

"Dad, I love…"

The senator lifted a silencing hand, his dark eyes hard as he leaned over the bar. "This is *not* up for debate, Isabella." His tone successfully silenced her. "I told you before that this marriage was important. Randall has the potential to go all the way to the White House and he wants *you*." He set his coffee down and walked to her side of the bar. "A *Kane* in the White House. I can't tell you how much of a dream come true that'll be for me."

Tears welled in Isabella's eyes. "Dad—"

"I never got the son I wanted," he continued, his words punching her in the gut. "Don't get me wrong. You've been a wonderful daughter." He reached and brushed a lock of hair behind her ear. "A shy but bright girl who's accomplished everything I've ever asked her to do. But *this* is your chance to make me so proud—to elevate this family into the history books."

Isabella watched her father's face glow with an avaricious delight. "When I was coming up, the idea of a black man making it all the way to the White House was an impossible dream. Had I known, I would have elected to have a few less skeletons in my closet," he chuckled and then quickly resumed his somber speech. "But with a son-in-law as commander in chief, I stand to be one of the most powerful men on the Hill."

"You're already a powerful man, Daddy."

"One can never have *too* much power."

"But I can't," she said shaking her head. "I'm in love with someone else."

Muscles twitched along the senator's hard jaw and when he lifted a second hand, Isabella flinched. He didn't strike her. Instead, he gently cradled her head between his hands and spoke clearly with an underlining threat to his words. "Isabella, you will do exactly what you're told."

* * *

Derrick started his day the same way he spent the last two days—anxious and moody. Whenever he thought about the note Isabella left by the nightstand, his blood pressure elevated while his heart threatened to do him in. A part of him understood why Isabella felt that she needed to handle ending her engagement to Randall on her own, but Derrick didn't trust his college buddy to keep a level head about the situation.

Lord knows, he didn't the last time.

Derrick stopped pacing and dropped his weight onto the bed. What a cruel twist of fate this was. Accused of a crime he didn't commit years ago—only to become guilty of it now. Hadn't he once thought that he was above such duplicitous behavior? No woman was worth breaking a friendship bond—especially the one between the Kappa Psi Kappa men.

But Bella was like no woman he'd ever known. She was so fragile on the outside but there was so much more underneath. He wondered if she even knew how strong she really was. And funny. There wasn't a day that passed when he didn't think about the padded booty incident.

Derrick climbed back onto his feet, started pacing again while he tried to pinpoint what it was that he loved so much about Isabella Kane. Finally—he concluded that Herman had it right all along. He was in love with Isabella's soul. Whenever he looked into her eyes, her soul cried out to his heart. And he responded.

"I need to be there for her," he decided, marching over to the room's desk, he quickly looked for the invitation he'd received in error. The wedding was supposed to be held at the Kane's estate. He needed the address. But when he remembered Randall had kept his invitation, Derrick went to Charlie's room.

He had to bang on the door for a solid five minutes before his hungover best friend answered it with a murderous gleam in his eyes.

"You don't look like you're bleeding."

"I need to get the address off your invitation," he said.

Charlie perked up at this. "Oh, so you're going to go?"

"Can I just get the address?"

Charlie frowned, grumbled. "Wait a sec." He turned and walked back in the room, while Derrick held open the door. He heard the ruffle of sheets and a woman inquire who was at the door.

Derrick shook his head. Charlie didn't believe in going to bed alone.

When his best buddy returned, he handed over his invitation and rental car keys. "Thanks a bunch. Your car came in handy." He nodded to the bed over his shoulder.

"Glad I could be of some help," Derrick said dryly.

"I'd read the invitation, but I'm still seeing double. Just give it back to me later. You're still coming to the bachelor party tonight, right?"

Derrick didn't answer. After today, he knew Randall would never forgive him. Rushing into his hotel room to grab his coat, Derrick had traveled halfway across the room before he realized he had guests.

Four tall, muscular men—a variety of races—in dark non-descript clothing surrounded him.

"Who the hell are you?"

"Are you Derrick Knight?" the largest man in the group asked, stepping forward.

A voice in Derrick's head told him to lie, but Derrick had never been one to back down from a fight. "I am."

The four men smiled manically.

"The Senator has a message for you."

Derrick didn't have time to process the giant's words before the man threw a punch that knocked him out cold.

Isabella felt like a caged bird during the in-law luncheon at her parents' estate. Though it was primarily for the parents of the bride and groom, there was a semi-small gathering of the Kanes' and Jarretts' closest friends—political friends—that had joined in on the festivities.

Despite it being a beautiful spring day, where the various floral aromas from the estate's meticulously groomed garden wafted on the air, Isabella watched the gaiety surrounding her with a sinking heart. The beauty had been reduced to a monochromatic gray and the laughter sounded like evil cackles. Though she'd been groomed for this life, she was very much an outsider.

Always would be.

Randall, picking up on his fiancée's melancholy, leaned over and instructed her through his gritted teeth, "Honey, smile."

But what was there to smile about?

Randall waited for her to comply with his order, but she ignored him and reached for her iced tea and wished the caterers would serve her something a little stronger— perhaps one of those Incredible Hulks Derrick had introduced her to in Atlanta.

Derrick.

Her body tingled at his name.

She glanced over the rim of her glass and caught her father's disapproving glare. Even then, she couldn't muster the ordered smile and she glanced away.

"Excuse me," she said, standing from the table.

Her father's face hardened with warning.

"I'll be right back," she said and turned from the table. She knew that there were at least three sets of eyes that followed her to the house. A few minutes later, she locked herself in the bathroom and had herself a mini-breakdown.

What was she going to do? She couldn't marry Randall, but how was she going to get out of it? After her talk with her father this morning, she was more than a little afraid to cross him. But what choice did she have?

"Izzy?"

Isabella glanced toward the door, wiped at her tears. "Keri?" she asked shakily, fearful her ears were playing tricks on her.

"Let me in, Izzy."

Isabella swiped more tears from her face and opened the door.

Keri rushed inside.

"What are you doing here?"

"I figured you needed my help since I haven't received word about you calling off the wedding yet. Have you chickened out again?"

Isabella broke down again and related what happened at her apartment with her father. She waited for Keri to tell her that she should have stood up to her parents a long time ago or that she didn't have a spine, but instead Keri produced a set of car keys and said, "That's why we came: to kidnap you."

"We?" Isabella asked.

"We Delta Phi Theta girls stick together. Me and the girls are here to bust you out of this joint."

And that was exactly what they did.

During their high speed race from Arlington back to the D.C. capitol district, Isabella's only thought was to get to Derrick and convince him that they should hop the first plane back to Georgia—or Vegas—or wherever he wanted to go. She would follow him anywhere as long as they got out of town today.

Isabella was so enamored with the idea of breaking from her gilded cage and starting a new life, she allowed herself to think that her parents would eventually come around once they saw how happy Derrick made her.

Randall would be a different story—especially when he saw the engagement ring she'd left in the bathroom with a note that simply said: I'm sorry.

Keri, Waqueisha, Sylvia and Rayne were all crammed into the black Lincoln Navigator and giggling at their participation in the high-speed escape. But everyone's excitement died once they reached the Hamilton Crowne Plaza and discovered that Derrick Knight had checked out of the hotel and broken Isabella's heart with a simple letter he'd left behind at the front desk.

Isabella,
After much thought, I realized that things were going too fast. I'm not the man for you. We're simply too different. It would be selfish of me to keep you when I know in time my eye will wander, like it always does. We had some fun and I'll never forget you, but your place is with Randall.
Forgive me,
Derrick

Chapter 23

Something was wrong.

Sure, Charlie and the boys knew that the possibily of Derrick and Randall ending their feud was a thin possibility—especially once everyone learned that the wedding invitation had been sent in error; but Charlie didn't think Derrick would up and check out of the hotel without so much as a fond farewell. It was also strange that his buddy would wake him up for the address for the wedding if he never planned to go.

"I don't see the problem." Hylan shrugged. "He just changed his mind."

That logic didn't salve Charlie's growing unease. So he started blowing up his friend's cell phone. During the course of the day, he'd left close to a dozen messages.

At one point, word had reached the small group of Kappa men that the wedding had been called off, but a couple of hours later everything was back on. The boys had snickered that Randall's fiancée had come to her senses, but the whole thing had been chalked up to a bride with wedding jitters.

"C'mon. You're supposed to be enjoying yourself," Randall laughed, smacking Charlie solidly on the back. "Rules are to have a drink in your hand and a girl on your lap!"

Charlie laughed good-naturedly, not wanting to bring down Randall's bachelor party. Though he did wonder about the number of girls Randall had disappeared with in his bedroom. Where there was little doubt that Randall could one day smooth talk his way into power, Charlie suspected that his voracious appetite for women would be his downfall.

In the end, Charlie had to admit that it was one of the best bachelor parties he'd ever attended. He laughed, he drank, he disappeared in the back room himself a time or two, but through it all, he couldn't erase the nagging thought that something wasn't right with Derrick.

Every bone in Derrick's body hurt.

And judging by his numerous blackouts, he concluded he had a concussion as well; but every time he opened his eyes, the same four muscle-bound men hovered around him. Hours ago, he'd overheard one of the men repeating that their job was to keep him bound and gagged until Randall and Isabella were on the plane to Aruba for their honeymoon.

Derrick also learned that Isabella had come to the room while he was knocked out, but the men had checked him out by phone and checked-in under another name. No one knew that he was still at the hotel. No one knew that he was in trouble.

Screaming for help was not an option. The last time, he'd received another beating and his mouth was duct-taped shut. He had to figure out some way to get out of there, but his hopes dimmed as day morphed into night.

His boys were likely at the bachelor party. They

wouldn't miss him. They'd think he simply went home. His emotions fluctuated between anger and despair. And by the time the morning's mercurial predawn light colored the sky, he was in a state of full depression. In a few short hours, the love of his life was going to marry another man.

To no surprise, the Kappa Psi Kappa men all woke to horrible hangovers; but somehow they were all ushered into a limousine and carried back to their hotel so they could shower and get ready for the wedding. For Charlie, when the clouds parted, his thoughts returned to Derrick.

After his shave, he placed another call to his buddy's cell and home number. No answer.

He finished getting dressed and answered his door when Taariq, Hylan and Stanley knocked to see if he was ready. As they walked by Derrick's old hotel room, a maid was knocking on the door and was greeted with a gruff voice telling her to "go away."

The housekeeper muttered something in Spanish and then pushed her cart to the next door. They weren't taking a limousine to the wedding; the boys had agreed that they wanted the freedom to leave early just in case it was a boring affair. When they entered the parking deck, Charlie froze.

Derrick's rental car was still parked where he'd left it the day before.

Derrick had worked steadily through the night on the nylon rope binding his hands. He held the thin hope that if he could get loose, he could tackle his way out of the room. It was a good thing he'd stayed in shape since his college football days, otherwise these men could have inflicted more internal damage—or maybe they had and his anger prevented him from feeling the full scope of his pain.

"Just a few more hours, buddy boy, and you'll be a free man," one of the men leered.

Derrick restrained his attack and instead glared up at the man. His body vibrated with anger.

The man shook his head. "Tough break, kid. You picked the wrong woman to have a fling with."

Charlie, Taariq, Hylan and Stanley made it back to Derrick's floor. At least this time, Charlie had been able to convince the other boys something was indeed wrong since it didn't make sense for Derrick to check out of the hotel but leave his airport rental car.

The men surrounded the Hispanic housekeeper and tried to work their charm on her to open Derrick's door. When that didn't work, they slipped her a hundred-dollar bill.

She agreed.

Together, they all tipped-toed back to the door and watched as the housekeeper slipped the card key into the lock. When the green light flashed, they charged inside.

The cluster of Kappa Psi Kappa men startled the thugs inside, but Charlie and the boys took in the scene and went on the attack.

Adrenaline pumping, Derrick leapt to his feet and body slammed the giant closest to him. The man crumpled back, dazed and bleeding.

Derrick finally slipped his hands from the nylon rope and joined his boys, opening a fresh can of whup ass— even Stanley landed a few punches. A few minutes later, it was all over and the Kappa men raced from the hotel before the cops arrived.

They had a wedding to stop.

Chapter 24

Al hell broke loose when Derrick and his crew sped to the Kanes' sprawling Arlington estate. With most of the groomsmen in torn and blood-splattered tuxedoes, it surprised no one when security tried to prevent them from crashing the wedding; but when the men threw their invitations at them, they had no choice but to let the men pass.

The wedding guests parted like the Red Sea when Derrick's men stormed through the backyard. Everyone undoubtedly wondered what the hell was going on. Even through his boiling anger, Derrick appreciated that his friends brokered few questions, but made it clear that they had his back for whatever went down.

Randall flew through the crowd, trying to see who or what was causing such a ruckus at his wedding. When Derrick came into his line of vision, his expression twisted into sheer hatred. He approached, certain that he would be able to draw his old friend and nemesis aside to ask him what the hell he was doing there. Instead, Derrick delivered a punch that sent him reeling back.

"Isabella!" Derrick shouted. "Where are you?"

"What the hell?" Randall recovered and then launched his own attack.

An already bruised and battered Derrick took a couple of punches, but during his return attack, he continued to shout, "Isabella, I love you!"

Not to be outdone, a few of Randall's friends tried to jump in and help, which caused the other Kappa Psi Kappa men to join the foray. Within a few minutes, the nice, serene spring wedding became the scene of an outright brawl that continued when the two fiancés fell into the water fountain....

Isabella woke from her fainting spell to find that she was on a bed and surrounded by friends, family and her two fiancés.

"Hey, sweetheart," Derrick said, smiling down at her.

Randall and her father just glared.

"I hope you're happy, young lady," her father hissed. "You've turned this wedding into a fiasco. I still have half a mind to call the police."

Derrick stood and confronted her father. "By all means, call them. I have a kidnapping to report."

Senator Kane's angry face lost some of its color.

Katherine gasped and rounded on her husband. "You didn't!"

The senator sputtered, "I don't know what the boy is talking about." He was lying, and everyone knew that he was lying.

"Will someone tell me what in *hell* is going on?" Randall seethed. "How do you two know each other?" he challenged Isabella. "And why is he claiming to be in love with you?"

Isabella wet her lips and tried to sit up. Derrick and her mother aided her.

"Well?" Randall thundered. "I deserve an explanation!"

It was time to make a decision. Isabella reached for Derrick's hand and felt a surge of strength.

"Isabella." Keri moved to the bed. "There's something I have to say that will probably help you with your decision."

"Shut up, Keri," Randall rounded on her.

"No," she barked back. "I've been quiet for too long," she said, her eyes filling with tears. "I've been the worst kind of friend to you."

"Keri," Randall gritted through his teeth.

"Randall and I have been involved for years. We've been…" Keri couldn't finish.

"Isabella," Randall said, turning on his best politician smile. "Don't listen to her. It—"

Isabella climbed out of bed and smoothed down her wedding dress as she stalked toward Randall. "Is it true?" Her gaze shifted between him and Keri. "You've been sleeping with my best friend behind my back?"

Randall's jaw worked, but words failed him. At last, he turned toward the senator. "A little help here?"

"Who cares who's sleeping with whom," her father thundered. "We're in the middle of a crisis here."

Keri sobbed. "I'm so—so sorry, Isabella. I know you'll never forgive me."

"Forgive you?" Isabella said, surprised and then broke into a smile. "I thank you—for finally telling me the truth. Now I know why you've been so hostile about this wed-

ding and it makes it just a little easier to call off the wedding." She gathered Keri into her arms and hugged her.

"CALL—OFF—THE—WEDDING?" her father sputtered. "You'll do no such thing!"

"Oh, shut up, Tyler," Katherine snapped. "You've done
quite enough!"

The senator blanched.

Once again, Isabella slid her engagement ring off her
finger and handed it to Randall. "It's over."

Randall accepted the ring but looked like he was ready
to breathe fire.

Katherine moved to her daughter's side and took her
hand. "I'm sorry we forced you into this." She glanced
over at Derrick and then back at her daughter. "Do you
love him?"

Isabella shifted her adoring gaze to Derrick. "With all
my heart."

"Then that's all that matters, sweetheart."

"Well, it looks like you win again, Derrick," Randall
said, glaring. "She's all yours." He turned and marched
toward the door. He stopped beside Keri. "Well, are you
coming?"

Keri shook her head. "No."

Randall stormed out.

Derrick dropped his gaze. This was the final nail in
the coffin for his and Randall's chance for reconciliation;
but when he turned his attention to Isabella, he knew it
had all been worth it. He glanced down at the string still
tied around her finger. "What do you say we hop a plane
to Vegas? If we're lucky we can still get married today."

"I'll follow you anywhere." Isabella threw her arms
around his neck and kissed him so thoroughly she heard

her mother gasp while her bridesmaids applauded. It was just like the movies.

A wicked thrill coursed through Isabella and she knew without a doubt that the shy wallflower was finally ready to bloom.

* * * * *

SINFUL CHOCOLATE

This book, as always, is dedicated to my loyal
Byrdwatchers Group. I couldn't have asked
for a better group of women to cheer me on.
Best of love,
Adrianne

Chapter 1

"Surprise!"

Charlie Masters clutched a hand over his heart and jumped back from his front door. Before his mind could register what was happening, the large crowd of people crammed into his Buckhead high-rise broke out in song.

"Happy birthday to you! Happy birthday to you!"

At last a smile broke wide across his full lips as he finally crossed the threshold into his apartment where black-and-gold balloons showered down on his head. "You guys shouldn't have," he said in the middle of their song.

His smiling and jubilant friends parted like the Red Sea to allow a magnificent four-tier, circular chocolate cake to be rolled out to the center of the living room.

Charlie moved forward, taken aback by the decorative dessert. Each layer showcased multiple ribbons of dark and white chocolate. On top, the ribbons looked more like a gigantic Christmas bow with the number thirty-four sparkling in the center.

Impressed and touched by the gesture, Charlie blushed like a prepubescent teenager until his friends finally ended their song and erupted into a thunderous applause.

"Thank you, guys. Thanks. You're the best."

"Are you just going to stare at it all night, or are you going to make a wish and blow out the candles?"

Charlie turned to his right and beamed a smile toward his best friend and fraternity brother Derrick Knight and his wife Isabella. "Hold your horses, man. Can't a brother just enjoy the moment?"

The guests laughed heartily.

Derrick rolled his eyes, but his smile remained as wide as Charlie's.

To his left, his other three Kappa Psi Kappa brothers cut in, "C'mon man. Make a wish."

"Yeah. You're holding up the music," Taariq added.

Make a wish. Wouldn't it be great if he could fix his mounting problems by simply making a wish? Feeling the weight of everyone's stare, Charlie played the good sport by closing his eyes, leaning forward and finally blowing out the candles.

Another round of thunderous applause ensued and a second later, Rick Ross poured out of his surround-sound speakers, and most of the crowd paired off to get their grooves on. The rest of them crowded around Charlie and pounded his back in congratulations. It felt like most of the guys were trying to break his spine in half.

Before Charlie could ask his Kappa brothers how they'd managed to plan this whole thing without him catching wind of it, Hylan moved up behind him and jammed him into a headlock and razed the top of his head with his knuckles.

"Hey, old man. What did ya wish for?"

Charlie chuckled despite his inability to breathe.

"He can't tell you that," Isabella said, coming to his defense. "If he tells, then it won't come true."

Hylan grunted, but released Charlie before he passed out.

In retaliation, Charlie popped Hylan on the back of the head, and then the two raised their dukes as if they were really considering squaring off for a fight.

Taariq rolled his eyes and sucked his teeth. "You two cut it out."

Still smiling, Hylan and Charlie dropped their fists and instead gave each other a shoulder bump.

"Happy birthday, man," Hylan said. "You're…" Their conversation trailed off when a Halle Berry look-alike strolled past laughing and shaking her romp to the hard bass pounding all around them. "Excuse me, fellahs," Hylan said, adjusting an invisible tie. "But booty calls."

Charlie and the gang laughed as Hylan strolled off in a George Jefferson-imitation strut.

"A steak dinner says he'll strike out," Charlie said, sliding a hand into his pocket and rocking back on his heels.

Taariq frowned. "You know her?"

Charlie nodded. "Yvette. I tried to hook up with her a couple of years ago, but her *girlfriend,* if you know what I mean, nearly took me out."

The fraternity brothers chuckled then swung their heads back in Hylan's direction to watch in giddy anticipation of his crash and burn.

Yvette beamed a beautiful smile at Hylan and even fluttered a hand across her heart.

Taariq leaned toward Charlie when Hylan's mack game seemed to be working. "Maybe she's swung back to our side of the fence," he whispered.

"Oh ye of little faith." Charlie smirked. "Three, two, one."

Right on time, a three-foot-eleven woman rushed onto the scene and managed to work her way in between Hylan and Yvette.

Isabella gasped. "*That's* her girlfriend?"

Hylan stared down at the small woman in open confusion…right up until the time the woman dealt a deadly left hook into the family jewels.

"Ooooh." Charlie and the Kappa boys cringed and covered their own packages in union as they watched their brother double over in pain.

The angry little woman snatched her girlfriend's hand, and together they marched off into the dancing crowd.

Isabella couldn't help but join in. "I don't think I've ever seen anything like that in my entire life."

"Been there, done that." Charlie shook his head. "I wore a cup to the clubs for a full year after Mighty Mouse dealt me the same blow."

Taariq, Derrick and Isabella laughed.

A crouched Hylan returned to their intimate circle in defeat.

"So how did it go?" Derrick baited, wrapping an arm around his wife. "Get the digits?"

"I don't think she's my type," Hylan croaked. "Damn. Is it just me, or is the room spinning?"

"It's just you," the gang responded and then burst out laughing again.

Still chuckling, Charlie gave a quick scan of the room to survey the selection of beauties his buddies had rounded up for the evening. If anyone knew his type it would be his Kappa brothers.

After a week of battling to keep his company, Masters Holdings, from plunging into bankruptcy, Charlie needed a distraction. Burying himself into something along the lines of five-foot-nine with a lot of curves was right up his alley. The thicker the better.

Judging by the number of female gazes that drifted his way, Charlie was going to have a good night. A very good night.

Taariq threw the best damn parties in Atlanta, and it was clear he'd spared no expense for Charlie's thirty-fourth birthday bash. Actually, calling them merely women was a serious disservice. They were more like works of art.

"I know that look." Taariq laughed, swinging another hard pound against Charlie's back. "I guess that means we can give you our gifts early."

Frowning, Charlie faced the group again. In sync, they each rolled out a sleeve of gold-packaged condoms.

Isabella couldn't stop herself from giggling.

"Try not to use them all in one night," Derrick chuckled.

"Funny." Charlie rolled his eyes when the gang draped the condoms around his neck like Mardi Gras beads.

"You know I've been waiting hours so I can have a slice of this cake," Isabella said, drawing his attention from his search of women in the room.

Charlie took another look at the elaborate cake, once again impressed with the intricate details. "Chocolate. My favorite." He picked up the knife but hesitated slicing the beautiful dessert.

"Derrick told me you loved chocolate. So I got you something a little different: molten chocolate cake. The center is filled with raspberry jelly." Isabella beamed and clutched her hands together. "I found this wonderful new shop downtown. The owner is a master." She glanced around. "Where is she?" Isabella grabbed his hand. "I can't wait for you to meet her."

Charlie selected a corner and gently cut a slice. "Here

you go," he said, grabbing a paper plate and serving her. After handing it over, he noticed a smudge of frosting on his finger and licked it off.

"Hmm." His eyes bulged in shock at the sinfully delicious chocolate as it melted in his mouth.

Isabella lit up. "Wonderful, isn't it?" She grabbed a fork and then held out a piece of the cake for him to taste. "Here, try it."

"Heeey!" Derrick stepped forward and draped a possessive arm around his wife's waist. "I'm the only man you're supposed to be feeding cake to." He even managed to look wounded.

Charlie ignored Derrick's fake jealousy act and took a bite of the cake Isabella offered. "Hmm. Damn!" Hands down, it was the best cake he'd ever tasted. He better not tell his mother that.

Isabella's excitement grew. "Fantastic, isn't it? I swear this woman is going to be the next big thing," Isabella gushed and then turned toward her husband. "I'm telling you we need to invest in her shop."

Derrick sighed dramatically, but he wasn't fooling anyone. Where Isabella was concerned, Charlie's best friend would deny her nothing. After a year of marriage, the couple still behaved as though they were coasting on an extended honeymoon—probably to the dismay of Isabella's father, who had his mind and heart set on his only daughter marrying a prominent political ally and another Kappa Psi Kappa brother named Randall Jarrett.

No one ever mentioned how Isabella was once, technically, engaged to two men at the same time, or how her father had arranged to have Derrick held hostage while trying to force her to marry someone she didn't love. But they *did* talk and laugh every chance they could about Derrick, Randall *and* Reverend Williams falling headfirst into a Lady Justice water fountain and duking it out in front of Washington's political elite moments before Isabella was to walk down the aisle.

"Where's Stanley?" Charlie asked.

The group looked around.

"He's gotta be around here somewhere," Taariq said, frowning. "He better not bother the DJ. I keep telling that boy that white men can't rap and I better not catch him on the mic. I have a rep, you know."

"What about Eminem?" Charlie asked.

"I reserve judgment until I see the man's daddy. You know what I mean?"

"Yeah, whatever."

"All right, all right." Charlie popped his collar. "I know you have some Cristal floating around here."

Taariq reached out and grabbed two flutes from a passing server. "Yo, here you go, bro." He handed a glass to Charlie. "Cheers!"

"Check it. One, two. One, two," Stanley rapped into the microphone. "I'm a white boy and a frat boy—"

"All, hell naw," Taariq cursed. "They gave Stanley the mic. Charlie—"

"Yeah, I'm cool. Handle your business." Charlie chuckled and waved him off.

People in the crowd started booing.

Charlie sliced himself a piece of cake. As he chewed he couldn't stop moaning. He tried to stop, but damn. *What exactly is in this stuff?*

"Oh, there she is," Isabella said, glancing over Charlie's shoulder and waving.

Turning, Charlie froze as a stunning cinnamon-brown sister navigated her way through a throng of dancing people. Her long brown hair fell in loose curls across her shoulders while her deep sable eyes twinkled with excitement and two raisin-size dimples grooved into her apple cheeks. Entranced by the angelic vision, it took Charlie longer than normal to take notice of her statuesque curves.

He smacked his lips, but it had nothing to with the lingering taste of chocolate in his mouth and everything to do with a sudden longing to taste her strawberry-colored lips. Absently, Charlie pulled at his collar and wondered who in the hell turned up the heat.

In Charlie's mind, the woman was moving in slow motion—like a classier version of Bo Derek in the movie *10*. The beauty's breasts had a slight jiggle as she walked and her hips swayed in a strange, but hypnotic, rhythm.

"Happy birthday to me," Charlie mumbled under his breath while his erection pressed hard against the inseam of his pants.

Isabella looped an arm around the mysterious woman's waist and then led her to their small circle. "Gisella, I'd like for you meet the man of the hour, Charles Masters— but everyone calls him Charlie. Charlie, this is Gisella Jacobs, the owner of Sinful Chocolate. She made your cake."

"A pleasure to meet you," Charlie said, offering to take her hand. "The cake is delicious."

"Likewise." Gisella's accented voice was musical yet husky, a heady combination. "You have a lot of friends," she added, glancing around. "I hope you don't mind my crashing and networking for new business. Isabella assured me that you wouldn't mind."

Charlie cocked his head while the corners of his lips curled with open pleasure. "You're French," he announced, moving closer. "How erotic."

Gisella's arched brows rose in amusement. "Erotic?"

Even the way she said the word sent pleasure rippling down his spine and added a sweet ache to his throbbing hard-on. "Come on now," Charlie said, erasing the last remaining inches between them. "Surely I'm not the only red-blooded American man who's been enslaved by your..." His eyes roamed yet again. "Accent."

"Oh, he *is* good," Isabella whispered, turning toward her husband.

Charlie had forgotten about their audience.

Derrick nodded and proceeded to pull his wife away. "Let me get you out of here before you fall under his spell and I have to fight for you all over again."

Taariq and Hylan also didn't linger for a brick wall to fall on their heads. They quickly turned their attention to a couple of other women floating by.

Gisella looked stunned at how fast everyone disappeared and left her alone with a man with predatory eyes and a wolfish smile. Maybe she should grab one of the white napkins from the table and wave it as a flag of surrender.

"I'm glad Isabella told you to come. I like making new friends." Charlie couldn't stop his gaze from roaming again. By his shrewd calculations, her measurements were a perfect 36-24-36. Lord, this was shaping up to be one hell of a birthday.

"Interesting party favors."

"Huh?" Charlie followed her line of vision to the condoms draped around his neck. "Oh. Well. You want one?"

Gisella blinked and took a step back.

"Okay. *That* didn't come out right." He laughed.

Gisella took another precautionary step back. The man looked as if he was going to devour her right there in front of everyone. "Well, like I said. I'm just trying to drum up new business," she said, trying to swallow her nervous tremor.

"You're not going to have a problem with that once everyone tastes this wonderful creation. How long have you been baking?"

Her smile brightened again. "All my life. My *mère* and *grandmère* still run a shop in Paris."

Gisella's accent enraptured Charlie.

A woman to their right emitted a low moan of orgasmic pleasure. "Oh, my God, this cake is off the chain." The woman turned to her companion. "Here, taste this."

Gisella's cheeks blushed a rich sienna. "I love baking and cooking. Food is life, no?"

Charlie just smiled. "Have you ever heard that the quickest way to a man's heart is through his stomach?"

Eyes twinkling, Gisella's lips turned up into a sly smile. "If I wanted your heart, I would just take it."

Charlie cocked his head with a bemused grin, but when he opened his mouth for a quick retort, a pair of hands slipped over his eyes.

"Guess who." A high-pitched feminine voice floated over the shell of Charlie's ear while a small set of breasts pressed into his back.

Not now. He controlled his irritation while he forced a smile. "Let me see now," he said, wondering how to get out of a potentially sticky situation. "Could this possibly be my favorite woman in the whole wide world?"

"And who would that be?" the woman asked with attitude edging her voice.

Charlie reached to uncover his eyes. "Dear ole Mom, of course," he answered, pulling away the small hands and turning around with his ready-made smile still hugging his lips.

"Hey, you." He still didn't know the name of the smiling beauty, with a short spiked haircut and eyes the color of maple, but he was determined not to go down in flames. "You came!"

The woman's face lit up with pleasure. "I wouldn't have missed your birthday for the world." She inched closer and lowered her voice in a conspiratorial whisper. "Especially after that wonderful weekend last month."

Charlie was still clueless to the woman's identity. After all, that was four weekends ago, and he was never without company on any of them.

"Well, I'm glad you made it," he whispered. His mind scrambled for a way to get rid of her so that he could get back to Gisella.

"I hope you're saving one of those for me," she cooed, pulling one sleeve of condoms from around his neck. "In fact—" she leaned in close "—why don't we slip away upstairs and I give you your birthday gift?" She grinded her hips against his to ensure he caught her meaning.

Charlie's brows jumped at the suggestion. "Why don't you meet me up there in about twenty minutes? I gotta say hi to a few more people first."

The beauty sucked in her bottom lip and gave him a wink. "Don't leave me waiting too long." Still holding the sleeve of condoms, she turned and switched her hips as she moved through the crowd.

Charlie sighed and then turned back to address Gisella. She was gone.

Glancing around the perimeter of the room, Charlie's heart pounded in double-time. He moved through the crowd, searching.

"How about a dance?" a new woman asked, looping her arms around Charlie's neck.

"Not right now." He tried to pry the woman's arms away but she locked her hands together and kept him ensnared between her arms. "I'm looking for someone," he confessed.

"Another woman?" she asked, inching up an eyebrow.

Charlie glanced down and recognized Lexi—another fling from last month. "Oh, hey." He changed up his program. "How are you? I've been meaning to call."

"I just bet you have," she said, smiling though her tone held a lethal edge. "I should have listened to my girlfriends and stayed away from you."

Charlie's lips curled wickedly. "Then why didn't you?"

Lexi hesitated and then allowed her eyes to roam down the front of his body. "Because I wanted to see whether you'd live up to your reputation."

He arched an eyebrow, his ego expanding. "How did I do?"

She flashed him an incredibly white smile. "You're a cocky sonofabitch."

"*That* is what makes me so adorable."

"One of these days…"

From the corner of Charlie's eyes he caught sight of Gisella heading toward the door. He finally pulled Lexi's hands from around his neck and winked at her. "Hold on a second."

"Yeah. Right. I won't hold my breath."

Charlie plowed back into the crowd and tried to maneuver his way to the door. But every few steps another woman would grab him by the arm, the neck and even his crotch to ask why he hadn't called them in such a long time.

At the door, Gisella stopped and kissed Isabella on each cheek and then waved goodbye to her.

"No. Wait," he called after her, but the loud music swallowed his voice and a throng of women kept pulling at him. By the time he made it to the door and then glanced down the hallway of his Buckhead high-rise, Gisella was long gone.

Chapter 2

"He's not my type," Gisella repeated to herself. No matter how many times she made the declaration, a part of her rebelled at the notion. The thought just kept coming to the forefront of her mind how handsome—no—how *fine* Charlie Masters was. From the moment that six-two, golden brown Adonis strolled inside his high-rise apartment, Gisella could hardly take her eyes off of him.

The man exuded confidence and possessed an undeniable sexual prowess that dampened his fair share of panty liners whenever he walked by. And those eyes—playful hazel green—that sparkled if you were fortunate enough to hold his attention.

No wonder every woman in the room was practically drooling and shamelessly throwing themselves at him. It wasn't surprising that he looked as if he was reveling in his element.

From the moment she'd slipped her hand into his, there

was a powerful magnetic pull toward him, which was right on course since she had an affinity for bad boys, the very habit that she'd promised herself to break.

With a determined shake of her head, Gisella erased Charlie's image just as she arrived at her car in the high-rise parking garage. "Forget about him," she mumbled under her breath as she unlocked the car and slid in behind the wheel.

But that was easier said than done. After moving over four thousand miles to get away from the last playa extraordinaire who'd broken her heart, Robert Beauvais, she swore her next man would be the more stable kind—the marrying kind. When his name and image floated across her head, she couldn't help but roll her eyes. Of all the men she could have fallen for, she had to fall in love with an international male model.

If there was one life lesson learned, it was to never trust a man who's prettier than you are.

Gisella laughed at herself as she pulled out onto the highway and headed toward her half sister's apartment in downtown Atlanta. The distance wasn't too far, but with so many one-way roads, it was easy for her to keep getting turned around.

By the time she made it to Anna's place, it was beyond late, and her sister had already gone to bed for the night. It was just as well because the last thing she wanted to do was play Twenty Questions.

Since Gisella's move to America, Anna had taken her role as protector a bit too seriously. Gisella suspected it had a lot to do with Anna's obsession with police shows and forensic files. For her, trouble lurked around every corner, especially if there was a man involved. Where Gisella had one ugly breakup, Anna had a string of them.

Despite being beautiful, men had lied to, stolen from,

beaten up and slept around on Anna. You name it, she had been through it, and when Gisella called her crying about Robert's infidelity, Anna convinced her to leave France and start over with a new life in Atlanta.

Nine months later, Gisella wasn't exactly sorry she'd made the move, but she realized that she had underestimated just how broken and bitter her sister really was. Once a month, Anna and a handful of her college girlfriends would host the Lonely Hearts Club. It was supposed to be a book club, but its real function was for the women to get together and gripe about men.

At first Gisella welcomed the sisterhood meetings as a place to vent over the demise of her engagement, but at what point were these women going to move on?

Gisella used the meetings as the first step in healing.

Anna used the group as a monthly soapbox.

After tiptoeing to her sister's room, Gisella slowly turned the knob and opened the door, then eased her head inside. Under the soft glow of light from the nightstand table, Gisella found Anna's sleeping form curled up on her side with a thick book next to her. Smiling, Gisella eased into the room and made it over to the bed to gently remove her sister's reading glasses from her face.

Anna moaned and stirred, but she didn't wake. "Good night, big sis," Gisella whispered, leaning down and placing a kiss against her sister's forehead before turning off the light.

Gisella crept to her bedroom and quickly kicked off her heels and slid out of her clothes before heading toward the adjoining bathroom. In the short time it took for her to make it to the shower, Charlie Masters had eased into her thoughts, and a smile had curved its way back onto her lips.

Humph. Humph. Humph. It really should be a crime for a man to be that hot, that fine, that *sexy*.

Without meaning to, Gisella made a few calculations and realized it had been more than a year since she had last experienced the touch of a man. Never mind the whole seduction of kissing and...well, just getting laid.

Sighing as she stood underneath the spray of hot water, Gisella allowed her active imagination to take flight. Still smiling, she pretended Charlie had joined her in the bathroom's billowing steam and that it was his hands instead of the mesh sponge massaging liquid soap across her soft skin.

Gisella moaned and lolled her head back as if giving her imaginary lover full access to her slender neck.

"You taste like strawberries and chocolate," murmured Fantasy Charlie, nibbling on her ear. His slick hands now roaming around her body and then cupped her full breasts. Instantly, her dusky brown nipples puckered and then throbbed for attention.

Charlie's rich laughter bounced off the bathroom tiles before his head dipped low and took a hardened nipple into his mouth. Despite knowing this whole thing was just a fantasy, Gisella's knees still went weak as the shower's hot droplets substituted for Charlie's mouth and talented tongue.

"Does that feel good, baby?"

She barely managed to croak out a "Yes" while an army of strawberry bubbles roamed and marched toward the springy black vee of curls between her legs. Charlie's fingers followed the sudsy front line and then penetrated her with smooth gentle strokes.

Gisella hiked up one leg onto the tub's ledge and gave her fantasy lover better access to her pulsing cherry. There was also no mistaking the change in her breathing. Soon her temperature rose and it had nothing to with the hot cascading water.

Long strokes.

Short strokes.

Gisella's moans climbed higher and higher. In her ear, Fantasy Charlie kept urging her to, *"Come for me, baby. That's it."*

"Ooooh, yes," she sighed, her body tingling.

"That's a good girl."

Toes curling, Gisella's sighs and moans continued while she imagined the feel of Charlie's rock-hard erection pressed against her round bottom.

"You comin' for me?"

"Y-yessss."

"What's my name, baby?" he asked, his fingers now plunging deep into her core.

"Ch-Charlie." The moment his name crested her lips, her inner muscles tightened while she buckled against his hand. When her orgasm hit, her imaginary world exploded behind her closed eyelids, and her face was momentarily submerged under the shower's steady stream.

It was at that moment the heat disappeared, Fantasy Charlie vanished along with the shower's rolling steam, and the water turned into stabbing icicles. She jumped back and nearly tripped over the shower mat. Equilibrium restored, Gisella laughed at herself as she rushed to shut off the water.

Once out of the tub, she wrapped a plush towel around her body and made a second one into a turban over her wet hair. Walking back into her bedroom, her teeth chattered, and her skin pimpled with fresh goose bumps when the cool breeze from the air conditioner kissed her skin.

One thing was for sure: Gisella was a hell of a lot more relaxed after her session with Fantasy Charlie.

She giggled and then fell into a heap across the bed. The clock on the nightstand read one o'clock a.m. Gisella sighed contentedly and promised to get up in a moment to slip into her nightclothes and dry her hair, but before she knew it, she unfurled a few wide yawns and curled against her pillow.

Immediately, Charlie Masters resurfaced in her mind. "I'm not supposed to think about him," she mumbled. A man like Charlie was dangerous.

Plus, how desperate must she be to fantasize about a man she'd just met and had talked to for less than five minutes?

But what a man.

Burrowing herself into the bedsheets and comforter, the devil on her left shoulder argued with the angel on her right. In the end, Gisella saw nothing wrong with carrying on with her fantasy lover. As long as she never *acted* on her impulse or actually tried to hook up with the handsome playboy, what harm could it do?

"No harm at all," Fantasy Charlie whispered as he brushed a kiss against her satiny shoulder.

Gisella rolled onto her back and stared up into his hypnotic hazel green eyes.

"I have a question," he said, reaching beneath her pillow and then withdrawing her hidden vibrator. *"Mind if we play with this?"*

Chapter 3

Charlie woke up early Sunday morning the same way he woke up every Sunday morning: completely satisfied and with a curvaceous beauty at his side. What was the girl's name again—Marcia, Jan or Cindy? Maybe he was thinking of *The Brady Bunch*. Blair, Jo, Tootie—no, that was *The Facts of Life*.

The woman moaned softly as she turned and wiggled her rump against his hip—a silent invitation and a coy way of letting him know that she was no longer asleep. Hard and ready, he was more than willing to RSVP her invite when the phone rang.

Mentally, he wrestled with whether he should answer, but then relented when his gaze read the digital clock. Groaning, he snatched up the phone. "I'm up, Taariq."

"Yeah? Well, you're late," he said, irritation dripping through the phone line. "It's bad enough you dissed us at the party last night for that Beyoncé wannabe. By the way, how was she?"

Charlie glanced out of the corner of his eyes to skim over the woman's voluptuous form imprinted beneath the silk sheets. "A gentleman never tells."

"Has anyone ever told you you're one lucky S.O.B? You eased up on her two seconds before I did."

"You snooze, you lose." He smiled and sat up. "Give me about an hour, and I'll be right over."

"One hour." Taariq huffed. "I'm going to hold you to it."

"Whatever." Charlie hung up and turned his attention back to—Penny? No, that was *Good Times*. Well, when in doubt, he relied on his favorite pet name. "Hey, baby girl." He eased a hand beneath the sheet and caressed her soft skin. "I really hate to have to do this, but I, um, I'm afraid it's time to get up."

She emitted another soft moan, but then gracefully rolled over to her side to face him. Big, beautiful cat-shaped eyes fluttered open to reveal an intriguing shade of gray.

"Do we really have to get up?" she inquired, curling the corners of her full lips.

Charlie stared at the nymph in his bed as though it was the first time he'd seen her. Her face was devoid of makeup except the slightest hint of red lipstick. She was stunning. "Denise," he murmured.

"You remembered. I'm impressed."

"How could I ever forget? Denise just like in *The Cosby Show*," Charlie covered smoothly.

"Do you always try to do name associations with TV shows?"

Charlie blinked. "Not always."

"Then I guess the rumors are false."

"Rumors?"

Denise's tinted lips widened across her face. "C'mon. You have to know you're a man with quite a reputation." Her eyes traveled down his chest and settled on his erection. "Not all of it bad."

Charlie's ego inflated. "Glad to hear it."

Something stirred at the foot of the bed and since Charlie didn't have any animals, he jumped, but then quickly relaxed when the covers lifted and Samantha's—like in *Sex and the City*—tussled head peeked out. "Are you sure it's time to get out of bed?"

Charlie's smile slid wider. "Did you two have something else in mind?"

"As a matter of fact—" the beauty tossed the sheet back from her body to give him a clear view of what she was offering "—I have a *few* things in mind."

His erection throbbed and robbed him of sufficient oxygen for him to think clearly. At last a smile rolled across his lips. "To hell with Taariq."

"*You* let her meet Charlie Masters?" Nicole, Anna's busybody best friend roared incredulously. She pretended to rub wax out of her ears. "Please tell me I'm hearing things."

A bored and sleep-intoxicated Anna struggled to rake her fingers through her frizzy hair before turning her attention to her large mug of coffee. "Gisella is a grown woman and more than capable of keeping her legs closed."

Nicole's eyes narrowed. "No woman can think straight when Charlie is on the prowl. How many times have I told you girls that?" She glanced around the four-member Lonely Hearts Club.

"At least a million," Anna droned.

"Exactly." Nicole crossed her arms and glared at her best friend. "I knew this was going to happen. I swear

Charlie has like this radar whenever a beautiful new woman moves into this city. Hell, I'm surprised it took him nine months to find her."

The other women snickered at the joke, which only encouraged Nicole to stay perched atop her soapbox. "Wake up, Anna, your sister is exactly Charlie's type, and he'll be all over her like white on rice."

Jade, one of the founding members of the group frowned. "What's Charlie's type?"

"Anything with breasts and a pulse," Nicole shot back.

"Damn. I better hide Sasha, too." Anna bent down and picked up her orange-and-yellow tabby cat that kept mewing at her ankles.

"She's telling the truth," said Emmadonna, a plus-size beauty with a mountainous chip on her shoulder, nodding in agreement. "I met the famous dog at a club a couple of years back, thinking I was safe since he spent half the night dancing with the same old anorexic-looking chicks until he brushed up on me."

"Ooh?" the other women chorused.

"Next thing I know, he was all up in my ear, saying only a dog wants to play with some bones."

The women laughed.

"Girl, I played it cool for about two minutes before I jumped him and showed him how us big girls worked it out. Nahwhatimean?" She held up her hands and received a train of high fives while the room filled with new squeals of laughter.

"If you didn't see the devil horns and tail then you weren't looking hard enough," Nicole said, rolling her eyes.

"Oh, I was looking, all right," Emmadonna said. "All I saw was a tall brother with money, class, sophistication... and if I'm not mistaken, a dash of thug in him. Every girl needs a little thug in their lives."

"That man has a trail of broken hearts that stretches halfway around the globe." Nicole's hands settled on her thick hips. "Charlie's a diehard playa, and any woman who thinks she can change him, which is every woman he's ever come in contact with, is just kidding herself."

"Including you," Jade said, easing back into the leather couch with a knowing smile.

"Yes, including me." Nicole squared her shoulders. "Of course, *I* never became a notch on his bedpost. I had a little more sense than that."

Anna rolled her eyes and yawned. "Anyone want some more coffee?" She shuffled toward the kitchen. "If I have to wake up, I might as well do it the right way."

"I could've slept with him if I wanted," Nicole said to Anna's back.

"I hope you like Folgers."

"Ignore if you want, but back in college I was considered a fine catch myself," Nicole reminded her.

"Of course, I think we might have some Taster's Choice in here," Anna kept on, unfazed.

Nicole rolled her eyes. "Folgers is fine."

Anna rustled through the cabinets for a few minutes and then fumbled with the coffeemaker. All this talk about Charlie was hitting a little too close for home. She had her own history with the infamous playa and she'd rather just forget the whole incident. She certainly didn't want to talk about it.

Nicole glanced down at her watch. "It's noon. I bet you anything, Charlie is lying next to some chick right now trying to figure out the best way to get her out of there."

"Okay, now you're creepin' me out." Anna hit the Brew button. "You know just a little too much about the man's modus operandi."

"All playas have the same M.O. Hit and run."

"I still say Gisella is smarter than that. She was just hired to make the man's cake. She's hardly looking to leap back into another relationship after what her ex just put her through."

"Charlie doesn't *do* relationships."

"And Gisella doesn't believe in one-night stands."

Emmadonna, with supersonic ears for all things gossip, cackled from the living room. "Girl, please. Every woman has had at least one."

Anna and Nicole rejoined the women in the living room.

"I say," Nicole continued, "the only way a woman can avoid getting caught up in Charlie Masters's dog trap is to run the other way when you see him strolling down the sidewalk."

"Amen" circled around the room along with another series of high fives before the women burst out laughing.

Curious about the commotion in the apartment, Gisella finished dressing and joined her sister's friends in the living room. "What's so funny?"

The minute she walked into the room, all the laughter was suddenly sucked out of the air and everyone began straightening and fidgeting in their seats.

Gisella cast her gaze around the room as suspicion crept up her spine. "*Parlez-vous de moi?*"

Anna shooed Sasha off her lap and stood up. "Don't be silly, Gisella," she said, shuffling over and draping her arm around her shoulders. "We weren't talking about you—exactly."

"No, we were talking about your birthday boy last night," Nicole said, piping up.

Gisella's face flushed. Had her sister heard her in her room last night? Oh, Lord, hadn't she called out his name a few times?

Nicole pointed. "Look at her face. Something *did* happen last night."

Anna's arm fell from Gisella's shoulders. "You didn't!"

"Didn't what?" Gisella asked, thoroughly confused.

"Sleep with the enemy," Anna said. "Charlie Masters is the biggest man-whore in Atlanta."

"And that's putting it nicely," Nicole agreed.

Gisella groaned before she could stop herself. Didn't these girls ever give it a rest? Men were not the enemy. "Relax," she huffed. "Nothing happened. I went to network, remember?"

Unconvinced, Nicole planted her hands on her hips. "Did you meet the birthday boy?"

Four sets of eyes locked on to Gisella and waited.

"I met him." Gisella shrugged. "He said he loved the cake, and then I took off."

Anna smiled as her arm magically reappeared around her shoulder. "See? I told you she knew how to handle herself."

Ivy, the petite and soft-spoken member of their group, voiced her suspicions. "You mean Charlie didn't even try to hit on you?"

Gisella shook her head, even though the memory of their light flirting replayed in her head. "Nope."

"Damn." Emmadonna chuckled and eased back into her seat. "We really are living in the last days."

Chapter 4

Life had gone from bad to worse.

It was the only way Charlie could explain it. His company, Masters Holdings, continued to edge toward bankruptcy. Hopefully, his upcoming trip to South Africa would change all of that. His bid for a lucrative government contract was all that stood between him and financial ruin. The housing market combined with the credit crisis had formed the perfect storm to sink his financial ship. He was going to lose everything. The high-rise. The cars. The boat. The plane. His lifestyle.

To make matters worse, Charlie had been less than forthcoming with his frat brothers. How could he be, when they were still very rich and very successful in their own right? The last thing he wanted was to be labeled the failure of the group, nor did he want anyone's sympathy.

After all, he did have his pride.

No. Charlie shook his head. He was going to rebound from this. He had to.

First, he had to survive this basketball game. Hylan and Taariq were running rings around him today, and Derrick looked ready to kick him to the curb and pick Stanley as his partner.

But something was changing. Charlie felt it the moment Hylan passed Taariq the basketball and he launched into trying to block the next shot. Sure, he was in shape. He worked out five days a week at his local gym. Pumped iron, practiced kickboxing and swam like a fish in their indoor pool. And every Sunday afternoon, like today, he and his frat brothers got together on the half-court at Derrick's spacious estate in Stone Mountain for a few friendly games.

Bottom line: he was in shape.

So what was this change he was feeling in his body? The same change he'd been feeling since the moment he blew out the candles on his birthday cake.

I'm getting old.

Charlie frowned at the continuous thought circling his mind. Trying to dispel the notion, he pushed himself a little harder, ignored a few straining muscles and wiped the pouring sweat off his forehead with the back of his arms like windshield wipers in the midst of a thunderstorm.

Still, he didn't feel as aerodynamic as he had in college. Why weren't his other frat brothers struggling?

Taariq faked a shot, Charlie jumped and a collection of muscles in his lower back throbbed in protest. Recovering, he jerked to his left, intersected Taariq's running dribble for a clean steal.

"Yeah!" Derrick shouted as he did his best to clear the perimeter for Charlie to take his shot. Some people who'd watched them play in the past thought it was a bit odd for the teams to be divided as three on two. Those same people quickly understood when they saw how Stanley epitomized the term: white men can't jump...or shoot, dribble, block or run.

"Take your shot!" Derrick shouted. "Take your shot."

Charlie took aim and then launched the ball. Everyone stopped to watch its perfect arch. Taariq, Hylan and Stanley groaned when it swished beautifully inside the netting.

The game tied, Charlie and Derrick whooped in excitement and pumped their fists in the air.

Charlie took a moment to bend at the waist and chugged in a few deep gulps of air.

"You okay, hot shot?" Taariq asked, eyeing him up and down.

"Never better." Charlie righted himself and forced a smile.

Taariq shrugged off his concern and turned back to wait for Stanley to toss the ball back into play.

Charlie's resentment toward the other guys' boundless energy returned. Of course, they could be faking, too, he realized. He couldn't see any of them admitting to the pull of aging.

Kicking it into overdrive, Charlie tapped into the energy reserves he had left and started zigzagging in between the fellahs. But somewhere along the line, he lost his mind.

That was the only explanation for his delusion of being like Michael Jordan in 1989 and launching across the court with the song "I Believe I Can Fly" playing in his head.

Flying wasn't the problem.

It was landing.

The ball swooshed through the hoop, giving him and Derrick the winning two points. However, when Charlie's feet hit the concrete, his ankles folded like paper.

"Ooh, damn!" the Kappa brothers chorused and winced at the same time.

"Owww!" The sound that erupted from his throat wasn't unlike a roaring lion. But when Charlie looked down and saw the odd angle of his foot, his deep bass disappeared and he sounded like, what Derrick would later call, a wailing banshee.

"Oh, my God, I've died and gone to heaven," moaned Waqueisha, Isabella's good friend and Delta Phi Theta sorority sister, as she bit into another one of Gisella's chocolate truffles. "I know you said the girl was good, but damn!"

Waqueisha was the epitome of the round-the-way girl. She wore a lot of hair weave, tight clothes and was still rockin' bamboo earrings. Despite all that she was a very successful entertainment publicist.

"Everything just tastes so fantastic," said Rayne, another soror and a timid elementary schoolteacher. "I want two dozen of these chocolate coconut nuggets. Make that three dozen."

Gisella beamed at the women. "Isabella, I can't thank you enough," she gushed, rushing to fill the ladies' orders. "It's been crazy since that birthday party, and every day I'm getting calls and orders from people that say you've recommended my shop."

"You can thank me by agreeing to let me be your business partner," Isabella said. She'd given up tax law when she became Mrs. Derrick Knight and searched high and low for a career change. Since she found her courage and stopped being the person her parents wanted her to be, she'd spent the last year doing some much needed soul searching. She wanted to be involved in something that inspired her and elicited her passion.

"I'm flattered," Gisella said, shaking her head. "But going national just seems so grand, *oui?* I just like things simple. I bake and make treats because I like making people happy. I don't like making a big fuss of everything."

"You won't have to," Isabella said. "You bake, and I'll fuss over the big stuff."

"Yeah," Waqueisha said. "No one out-fusses our girl Izzy."

Isabella frowned and Waqueisha shrugged. "What? I was just trying to help you make the sale."

Isabella raced behind the counter and draped an arm around Gisella's shoulder. "Just picture it." She swept one hand up toward the ceiling as she described her vision. "Sinful Chocolate being packaged and sold in shops just like this one all across America, your grandmother's recipes putting smiles on millions of faces," she waxed enthusiastically.

"And depositing an insane amount of money into your bank account," Rayne added.

Gisella smiled and shook her head. "*Je ne pense pas.* Money is not the most important thing in the world."

Waqueisha and Rayne's mouths fell open.

"What?" Gisella asked, frowning at the two women.

"You really aren't from around here, are you?" Waqueisha said.

Gisella finally laughed. "Am I really all that different?" She glanced around. "I've seen you with your husband. Can you really tell me that the things that truly make you happy are attached to how much money he makes or what kind of car he drives?"

Isabella's face flushed a deep burgundy. "No."

"You see?" Gisella gave a smug smile to Waqueisha and Rayne. "Material things are what distract people when they're not following their hearts. Things like family, laughter, food and love are the real keys to happiness."

Waqueisha blinked. "Damn. That sounded like it should be on a Hallmark card."

Charlie and his frat brothers soon discovered that the emergency room was no place for an emergency. Bored and in no hurry, the E.R. nurses were more interested in exchanging gossip than helping the sick and injured. Instead, Charlie was stuck watching a bunch of unruly children run around hyped up on sodas and vending machine snacks while a loop of the same news from T. J. Holmes and the rest of the CNN weekend crew played every fifteen minutes.

Finally, Hylan had to ask. "Man, what the hell were you thinking?"

Derrick, Taariq and Stanley all covered their mouths and snickered.

"Charlie, you were really feelin' yourself," said Hylan, continuing to tease.

Taariq jumped into the fray. "I tried to tell you those Air Jordans will get a brother caught up each and every time."

Charlie rolled his eyes. "Ha. Ha. Very funny."

Another round of snickering and elbowing ensued.

After two hours of waiting to see a doctor, Charlie's patience neared an end. He'd almost convinced himself that he would rather go through life with a limp than to sit another minute in the E.R.'s hard plastic chairs.

"Charles Masters?"

"Over here," he called, struggling to his feet.

A shapely Latina nurse smiled when her eyes landed on him. "The doctor can see you now. Would you like for me to get you a wheelchair?"

That was like asking a starving man if he wanted a cracker.

A few minutes later, Consuela, according to her name tag, wheeled him through the crowded hallway behind the reception desk. Getting a room was too much to hope for apparently. Instead, the nurse rolled him behind a make-shift divider and told him that the doctor would see him in a few minutes.

It was another hour.

"Well, well. Sorry to keep you waiting," a voice boomed as the divider was pulled back, which jarred Charlie awake.

"Dr. Weiner?" Charlie asked, startled.

"Ah, Charlie!" A stunned smile spread across his personal physician's face. "What a surprise." He looked down at the paperwork Charlie had filled out at check-in. "I must be tired. I didn't really make a connection when I read your name on the folder."

Charlie squared his shoulders and felt a little better about being in the care of his primary doctor. "I didn't know you worked here at the hospital."

"Well, I fill in from time to time." Dr. Weiner closed the folder and leveled a serious look at Charlie. "You know my office has been trying to reach you."

Charlie instantly recalled the number of messages left on his home answering machine. But with all the trouble going on at the office, he kept putting off returning the doctor's calls. Besides, they probably just wanted to give him the results of his lab work for his upcoming trip.

"Tell you what," Dr. Weiner said after an awkward beat. "Let me take a look at your foot, and let's just have you come into my office in the morning."

"Tomorrow?" Charlie frowned. "Is there something wrong?"

Weiner hesitated again. "I don't have your chart from my office with me, so let's just go over everything then?"

Charlie's gaze lingered on the smiling doctor. He didn't like the sound of that at all.

Chapter 5

Charlie hated doctors. No doubt. His resentment went back to the day he was born, when some heartless doctor smacked him on the butt. Since then, he despised anyone wearing a white coat. Since that first day, medical professionals had put him through an endless ordeal of sharp needles, horrible-tasting prescription medicines, and as he got older, even subjected him to invasive finger-probing in unmentionable areas.

Now with an important business trip to South Africa coming up, Charlie had to deal with a lot of blood work, updating vaccinations and loading up on antibiotics. But it all needed to be done if he was going to save his company.

"Ah, Mr. Masters. You kept your appointment."

Charlie gave an odd-angled smile as he strolled into Dr. Weiner's office leaning on a cane to protect his sprained ankle. His brain quickly scrolled through his mental Rolodex for the name of the cinnamon-brown beauty at the check-in desk, but luckily he was rescued by her name tag. "Tammy, how are you?"

The roll of her eyes told him she knew he didn't remember her. "So what's the excuse this time? You lost my number? You had another death in the family—the dog, perhaps?"

"I don't own a dog," he said, unruffled by her irritation. He leaned over the counter and smiled into her eyes. "Besides I've been under the weather and have been laid up for a little while."

A spark returned to her disbelieving gaze. "Then maybe I could come over to your place and play nurse?"

"Now that sounds like a plan."

"Humph!"

Charlie glanced over his shoulder and then smiled at the nurse glaring at him. "Ah, Lexi." Embarrassment heated his face. "I didn't see you standing there."

Lexi shook her head. "You'll never change, will you, Charlie?"

He gave her his best puppy dog expression while his smile turned sly. "Can I help flirting when this office is filled with such beautiful women?"

"Sign in right here," Tammy instructed, her lyrical voice now flat.

Determined not to let the women see him sweat, Charlie scribbled his name and handed over his insurance card before Lexi led him to a room to wait for Dr. Weiner. A playboy at heart, Charlie couldn't stop thinking about Tammy's idea of playing nurse—especially if she wore a tight white dress, white fishnet thigh-highs and high-heeled shoes.

Thinking about the fantasy nurse uniform gave Charlie an instant hard-on just as he was sitting down on the doctor's table, giving Lexi a good eyeful.

"Um." She cleared her throat. "The doctor will be with you in a minute."

Charlie nodded and pretended not to notice her distraction as she walked backward. When she bumped into the wall, he gave her a smile.

"Oops," he said.

Lexi jumped and glared at him again before racing out of the room.

He chuckled. Women never failed to amuse him.

Twenty minutes later, when Charlie had just decided to take a quick nap, Dr. Weiner ambled into the room with his thick, black-rimmed glasses sitting on the edge of his nose.

"Ah, Dr. Weiner. Good to see you again," Charlie greeted.

The hunch-shouldered doctor came in with a thin smile and lifted his rheumy eyes toward him. "Afternoon, Charlie."

It was the tone that knotted Charlie's stomach muscles or maybe it was the fact that the chilly room had suddenly grown stuffy. "What is it, Doc?"

Weiner drew in a deep breath and closed the chart in his hand as he pulled up a stool and sat down.

Charlie could literally hear the blood rushing through his veins. He didn't like the look of this. He tried to brace himself the best he could, but he couldn't stop being impatient for the news. "Whatever it is, just tell me. I can handle it," he lied.

The doctor nodded gravely. "Your lab results came in…"

"And…?"

"And… It doesn't look too good." He leveled his serious gaze on Charlie. "You're dying."

Charlie stiffened. "Come again?"

"I know this is coming as a surprise, but the lab re-sults—"

"B-but I feel fine." The doctor's words hit him like an iron fist. It simply wasn't true. It wasn't possible.

Dr. Weiner frowned. "Didn't you tell me two weeks ago that you've been exhausted lately?"

"B-but that's because of work. I've been putting in a lot of hours. I—" Charlie swallowed. "What's wrong with me?"

"It looks like you have aplastic anemia."

"A plastic what?"

"Aplastic anemia. It means you have a low count of all three blood cells. I still need to confirm with a bone mar-row test—but with these numbers, I'm pretty sure."

The room roared with silence before the doctor at long last said, "I'm sorry."

Finally finding his courage, Charlie asked, "Okay, how do we treat it?"

The doctor hesitated. "Well, there're a few things we can try—all extremely risky but…."

"How long?" Charlie asked.

"I—I can't just give a date."

"How long?" Charlie insisted.

Dr. Weiner glanced back down at the chart. "Given these numbers, I'd say five to six months, tops."

Chapter 6

"I don't feel right leaving you here like this," Anna complained, setting her suitcase down by the door. "What if something happens while I'm gone?"

"I'm a big girl." Gisella laughed. "I think I can take care of myself."

Anna drew a deep breath. "Nicole and Jade's phone numbers are on the refrigerator. Call them if you need help with anything. I'm leaving to go to my company's headquarters in New York, but I'll call you every day."

"Yes, *Mom,*" Gisella sassed, bumping her hip against her sister's before marching out of Anna's bedroom. "Sasha and I will be fine."

Her sister followed her to the kitchen and watched her slip on her Kiss the Chef apron and then pull out a variety of bowls and ingredients from every cabinet. "You really do love doing this stuff, don't you?" she said, folding her arms and leaning against the kitchen's door frame. "You'd live in a kitchen if you could."

"Don't think I haven't thought about it," Gisella joked, measuring out flour and vanilla extract. "I'm still trying to crack *grandmère*'s famous recipe for her *Amour Chocolat*."

"Why don't you just ask her for it?"

"Now *that's* a novel idea." Gisella smacked her palm against her head. "Why didn't I think of it?"

"She won't give it up, eh?"

"She claims the recipe is top-secret because its effects can be dangerous for those who don't respect its power."

"Dangerous?" Anna repeated skeptically. "We're talking about chocolate, right?"

"Ah, but not just any kind of chocolate." Gisella waved a finger at her sister. "There is what you might call a culinary urban legend about *grandmère*'s *Amour Chocolat*. It is said that just one bite of the decadent treat ignites passion."

"What? Like an aphrodisiac? C'mon, people have been saying that about chocolate for years. It's not true."

"But, ah! This recipe is the real deal. Trust me. I know."

Anna lifted a single brow. "You've had it before?"

Casting her eyes down, Gisella bit her lower lip and tried her best not to look like a blushing fool.

"Gisella! Don't tell me there's a wild side to you."

"There's a lot you don't know about me," she sassed with a shrug of indifference. "Anyway, I'm no closer figuring out the recipe now than when I first started a couple of years ago, mainly because I have to rely on memory. But I *will* figure it out," she vowed.

"So whose bones did you jump when you ate this magical stuff?"

Gisella's smile faded when her mind tumbled back. "Robert's."

"Oh." Anna sobered. "There I go shoving my foot into my big mouth."

"Don't," Gisella said, waving off the apology. "The past is the past. All I can do is learn from it and move forward and create new memories."

Her sister's eyes narrowed on her. "Do you already have someone else in mind?"

"What? No!" Gisella lied, her face heating up with embarrassment. "I'm just saying that you never know what's in the future. That's all."

"Humph!" As usual, Anna rolled her eyes at Gisella's romantic fancy. "I already know what my future holds—a lot of romance novels and gallons of ice cream."

Gisella laughed guiltily as she turned toward the refrigerator and took out the milk, butter and eggs. "As much fun as that can be, I'd much rather curl up to a warm body at night."

"You'll learn. Men aren't worth half the trouble they cause. All a woman needs to be happy is a great career, some nice toys and a hearty stock of copper-topped batteries. Trust me."

Masters Holdings now operated with a skeletal crew. Commercial and housing construction in Atlanta had slowly ground down to a complete stop in the last four years. While puffed up economists, Wall Street analysts and the same tried-and-true politicians argued whether the nation was in a recession or not, companies like Charlie's were hemorrhaging money at a record pace.

When the first signs of trouble emerged, Charlie foolishly believed that his company could survive an economic slowdown. But this was like a financial drought that was on the verge of wiping him out.

Not that it should matter anymore.

Charlie's gaze drifted to his computer inbox and noted the number of messages from Dr. Weiner's office in the last week. He sighed and waffled again over picking up the phone. Why *was* he putting off making the appointment for the bone marrow test?

He leaned forward and put his elbows on the desk. Maybe he just didn't want to know the truth. He didn't know how to go about the business of dying.

How was that for denial.

"Mr. Masters," Jackson Boyett, Charlie's executive assistant chirped over the intercom. "You have a call on line one."

Charlie reached for the receiver, hesitated and then asked. "Who is it?"

"It's your mother."

Charlie's heart dropped. He'd been avoiding his mother's calls like the plague. Though a part of him was feeling incredibly guilty about it, another part of him knew it was vital not to let his mother even suspect that something could be wrong. But Arlene Masters's intuition was always sharp as a tack.

Today was Tuesday, and Charlie and his mother had a standing Tuesday night date. If she didn't have something planned at the senior center, his mother would usually cook him dinner. What was he going to tell her? What should he tell her? If he told her about his aplastic anemia, he knew she would move into his apartment before the end of the workday.

The real question was, could he fly under the radar of his mother's sixth sense? He stared at the red flashing light on the console, took a deep breath and finally answered the phone.

"Well, if it isn't my favorite girl in the whole world," he said, forcing humor into his voice.

"What's wrong?"

Charlie frowned. This was going to be harder than he thought. "Nothing's wrong."

"Come on, Charles. This is me you're talking to. I used to change your diapers. So trust me when I say I know when there's something wrong."

Charlie rolled his eyes as he leaned his head against the palm of his hand. "Trust me, Mom. Nothing is wrong. You know, it's always busy here at the office. I'm just swamped."

"I hope you're not trying to tell me you're not coming to dinner."

"Of course not. You know how much I look forward to your home-cooked meals."

His mother drew a deep breath, and he could tell she was still trying to detect whether he was being straight with her. "Well, I guess not." In the next second, she became bubbly with excitement. "Anyway, I called because I wanted to tell you that we are going to be trying a new dessert tonight," she said in a singsong tone.

"Oh?"

"Don't worry. It's chocolate. I found this new bakery downtown. You're going to love it."

At precisely seven-thirty, Charlie knocked on his mother's door. Dressed in casual jeans and a royal-blue cotton top, Charlie prepared for the performance of a lifetime. After thinking about it for the past few hours, he finally decided *not* to say anything until he had the results of his bone marrow test—that was, *if* he ever took the test.

As he waited for his mother to answer the door, he wondered what would happen to her if the test confirmed the fatal diagnosis. Given his financial situation, he wouldn't have anything to leave her in his will. He'd never thought about it before, and it seemed unnatural to be thinking about it now. Charlie's smile evaporated a second before his mother opened the door.

"Great, you're on—what's wrong?" she asked.

Charlie realized he'd been caught off guard and quickly chiseled his smile back into place. "Nothing." He leaned forward and planted a kiss against her round cheek. "I was just thinking."

"You sure have been doing an awful lot of that lately."

"You're complaining? I seem to recall you always telling me to think before I act, speak and—"

"All right, all right," she said, rolling her eyes. "Get on in here. I have chicken frying on the stove."

Charlie stepped into his mother's quaint and spotless apartment and drew in a deep breath. The heavenly aroma of fried chicken filled his nostrils and weakened his knees. Nobody could cook like his mother.

A second later his stomach growled in agreement.

Chuckling, his mother patted his firm stomach. "Sounds like you brought a healthy appetite with you."

"Still complaining?"

"Well, what the heck happened to your foot?" She glanced down at his cane.

"Sprained it playing b-ball with the guys."

She shook her head and frowned. "I swear, you boys." She shook her head and disappeared into the kitchen. "Have a seat. Dinner will be ready in a second."

Charlie almost followed her, but knew if he stepped a foot into her kitchen, she would have a hissy fit. His mother loved serving him as much as she loved cooking for him. Truth be told, he knew he would be lying if he said that he didn't love how she spoiled him.

Growing up in the heart of Atlanta in the 1970s and '80s wasn't exactly easy for him or his single mom, but they always seemed to manage walking the fine line between poor and broke. It helped a lot that he and Derrick were not only best friends, but so were their mothers. Together the two women kept both boys in line.

Derrick's mother eventually remarried, while Charlie's mother still seemed to mourn the loss of his father.

A sad smile ghosted around Charlie's face as he reflected on his childhood—the good and the bad.

Charlie's gaze floated across the dining room and landed on the multitude of pictures hanging on the wall. There were pictures of his mother when she was young. Some of his grandparents, and even one of his great-grandmother was smiling back at him. There were plenty of pictures of him, too. Some of them he didn't remember posing for and others that he had fond memories of.

At last his eyes landed on a picture of his parents together. They were teenagers. According to his mother, Jonathan Masters was often mistaken for a white man and as a result of genetics, Charlie had his mother's complexion but his father's eyes.

Jonathan Masters died a young man. He'd gone out on a cold winter's night for baby formula and ended up being an innocent bystander shot dead during a store robbery.

"He was so young," Arlene said, following Charlie's gaze. "There's not a day that goes by that I don't miss him." She looked at Charlie. "I hate that you don't remember him. He would've been so proud of you."

Charlie reached for his mother's hand and gave it a squeeze.

"Despite him dying so young, he lived a full life." She chuckled softly. "Everyone who knew Jonathan knew him to be a good man. Honest. Kind. Loving. And definitely a playboy. You definitely inherited that trait from him."

"What?" Charlie actually blushed. "I don't know what you're talking about."

"Uh-huh." His mother leveled him with a playful look. "I just know Jonathan had so many women beating down his door, his picture should have been in the *Guinness Book of World Records*."

Charlie laughed.

"I'm telling you he had it goin' on. All those girls plotting and scheming. All *I* had to do was invite him over for supper every Sunday. In no time at all I had him eating out of my hand." She glanced down and stared at the gold band still adorning her finger. She sighed. "Now I'm just waiting for you to come to your senses and settle down so I can have me some grandbabies running around here."

Charlie automatically rolled his eyes. "Oh, are we about to have that conversation again?"

"Nope. I'm going into the kitchen and get your food, but don't think I'm going to be around here cooking for you forever. Find you a girl who knows her way around the kitchen instead of the mall, and you'll have yourself a winner."

A few minutes later, his mother set in front of him a large plate piled high with fried chicken, candied yams, collard greens with bits of ham hock and her off-the-chain homemade cornbread.

Charlie looked over at his mother with tears in his eyes. "Have I told you lately how much I love you?"

"You better." Arlene lovingly patted the top of his hand and placed a kiss against his brow.

Charlie grabbed his fork but was quickly smacked on the back of the head.

"Now you know we say grace around here," she reminded him. She eased into her chair, took his hand and bowed her head. "O Lord, we bless thy holy name for this mercy, which we have now received from thy bounty and goodness. Feed now our souls with thy grace, that we may make it our meat and drink to do thy gracious will, through Jesus Christ our savior. Amen."

Arlene lifted her head, but was surprised when Charlie added more to the prayer.

"God of all blessings, source of all life, giver of all grace, we thank You for the gift of life, for the breath that sustains us, and for the food of this earth that nurtures life…"

He paused and Arlene opened her mouth to end with an "Amen" but her son wasn't finished.

"We also want to thank You for the love of family and friends for without which there would be no life…"

Another pause, Arlene opened one eye, waited and then opened her mouth again, only for Charlie to trudge on.

"For these, and all blessings, we give You thanks, eternal, loving God, through Jesus Christ we pray… Amen."

"Amen!" she jumped in and lifted her head to stare wide-eyed at her son.

Charlie shoved a forkful of collards into his mouth and then realized his mother was staring. "What?" he asked after swallowing.

Arlene folded her arms. "Are you sure nothing is wrong with you?"

"I'm sure," Charlie lied again, and shoveled more food into his mouth.

His mother stared.

When dinner was over, Arlene stood and went back into the kitchen and then returned with a red-and-gold cake box.

"Wait until you try this," she said. "I swear this woman could give me a run for my money."

Charlie's eyes widened at the gold script on the center of the box. "Sinful Chocolate," he read, remembering the

French beauty from his surprise birthday party. "Let me guess. Molten chocolate."

His mother's face lit up with surprise. "How did you know?"

"I met the owner."

"Really?" His mother voice registered her surprise. "She's a very attractive woman."

"You don't say," he said, amused.

"I *do* say. And if you asked me, *she's* the kind of woman you should be dating. Beautiful, smart—and if she can cook as well as she can bake—you two would be a match made in heaven."

Chapter 7

"I'm sorry, Mr. Masters, but we cannot approve you for this loan."

Stunned, Charlie blinked at the loan officer across the desk. A few erratic heartbeats later, he finally managed to sputter, "Why?" He straightened in his chair. "I have a triple-A credit rating, my paperwork is in order…"

The attractive dark-skinned beauty smiled. "Your debt to ratio is a major concern, and with this credit crisis we're taking a harder look at our loan applications. Unfortunately, you are what we call high risk at this time."

"High risk? I don't understand. I've never defaulted on a loan, and I've been banking here for over a decade."

The woman's smile remained firmly in place. "Again, I'm sorry. Maybe once you pay down some of your debt we can help you."

How was it that a bank only wanted to give you money when you didn't need it? After taking a deep breath, Charlie forced himself to relax so he could think clearly. How was he going to make next month's payroll? If he laid off any more people, Masters Holdings would undoubtedly fold before he made his trip overseas.

Sighing, Charlie started to thank the woman for her time when he caught the lazy way she was looking at him. Maybe this was an opening. "Tell you what. Why don't you and I discuss this over dinner?" he suggested.

A new spark lit the woman's eyes. "Dinner?"

Charlie turned on the charm. "I know this wonderful restaurant out in Buckhead. They serve the best seafood in Atlanta. I would be delighted if you could join me."

"Really?"

"Sure. We'll have a nice meal, some wine…" He allowed his sentence to trail off while he gave her a sly smile.

She leaned forward and folded her hands beneath her chin. "And then what?" she inquired huskily.

He shrugged. "Who knows?"

"Maybe you'll take me back to your place?" she suggested. "You'll put on some music, dim the lights and we could dance cheek-to-cheek?"

He smiled.

"Sort of like how we did six years ago when you came in for your last loan?"

Damn. Charlie's face fell. *That's why she looks so familiar.* "Dee."

"Yes, like the little girl from *What's Happening?* What's the matter, you stopped playing your little name game?"

Charlie coughed and then choked over the proverbial foot he'd just shoved into his mouth. "I think I better go," he croaked, reaching for his cane and suitcase.

"You damn right," she snapped.

He climbed to his feet. "Have a good day."

"It's the best damn day I've had in six years."

Charlie couldn't get out of there fast enough. He just hoped he could make it out before she caused a scene. Still wearing a plastic smile, Charlie limped across the bank as fast as he could.

"Charlie!"

He kept going.

"Charlie!"

He heard the clatter of heels racing behind him but before he could push through the bank's glass doors, a hand landed on his wrist and pulled.

"Wait, Charlie."

He finally recognized the voice and turned. "Isabella."

She smiled up at him while she tried to catch her breath. "Didn't you hear me calling you?"

"Oh, I—I, uh, guess I was a little distracted," he covered and then glanced over her shoulder to see Dee with her arms crossed and glaring at him from the door of her office.

"You remember Gisella, don't you?" Isabella asked.

He turned in time to see Gisella approach from his right. A new and more genuine smile caressed Charlie's lips. "I most certainly do," he said, holding out his hand. *"Bonjour, mademoiselle."*

"Bonjour. We meet again." Gisella slid her silky hand into his, and he felt a stirring in the pit of his stomach while his heart hammered against his rib cage.

"I haven't seen you since you disappeared from my birthday party before I could finish thanking you."

"Well, you looked a little *occupied* with your impressive fan club."

"Oh, that's all the time." Isabella laughed.

Charlie cringed. Surely his best friend's wife wasn't about to throw salt in his game. Not with this woman. Please, God, not with this woman.

"So what are you two doing here?" he asked, hoping to change the subject.

"We're about to become business partners," Isabella boasted. "Isn't that right, Gisella?"

"*Oui*." Gisella nodded. "*Ma nouvelle amie* here seems to think my little *chocolat* shop has quite a future ahead of it."

Charmed by her accent, Charlie's smile widened.

"I have to agree. I had another one of your cakes for dessert last night. It turns out my mother is also a fan. And trust me, that's a rarity."

"Then tell your mother I said *merci*."

Charlie couldn't stop staring. He couldn't get over just how absolutely stunning she was.

"Sooo what are you doing here?" Isabella asked.

Charlie continued to stare and smile.

"Charlie?" Isabella snapped her fingers in front of his face and broke his trance.

"What? Oh!" He blinked. "I, uh, was just here on business."

"What is it that you do?" Gisella inquired.

"I own a commercial development construction company." *Just barely.*

"Oh." Gisella nodded. "Impressive." She glanced down. "And what happened to your foot?"

"Oh, it's nothing. It's just a minor sprain from playing basketball with the fellahs." From the corner of Charlie's eyes, he saw Dee break away from her office door and march toward them.

Trouble, Charlie Masters. Trouble.

A wave of panic washed over him, telling him it was definitely time to take his leave. "Well, I gotta go. Itwasapleasuretomeetyouagain. Wemustdoitagainsometime," he said hurriedly and turned to leave.

"What? Wait, Charlie," Isabella said, grabbing him again. "I was just about to ask you to join us for lun—"

"Excuse me, ladies," Dee interrupted.

Charlie groaned as he caught the mischievous glint in Dee's eye.

"Are you two friends of Mr. Masters?"

Isabella frowned.

"If not, I only wanted to warn you that he's nothing but a low-down, lying, sex-crazed egomaniac that some vet needs to put out of his misery to save unsuspecting women from being nothing but notches on his bedpost."

Isabella was stunned speechless.

Gisella's eyes widened but then just as quickly seem to twinkle with amusement.

"And on *that* note," Charlie said, clearing his throat and barely holding on to his smile. "I'll be leaving." *Before I catch a case.* He turned and finally strode out of the bank, completely humiliated.

By the time Charlie made it to his Aston Martin V8 Roadster in the parking deck across from the bank, he was wishing he could go back home and start the day all over again. He slid in behind the wheel and then slumped his head back against the headrest. "You're losing your cool, Charlie," he mumbled. What happened to the days when being a playa was fun? Where did this rash of disgruntled lovers come from all of a sudden?

The problem with playing the field too long is that you forget names and faces. It was getting harder and harder to keep them straight and apparently to keep them happy. He replayed the incident in the bank's lobby again in his mind and was convinced that if he ever had the slightest chance of hooking up with Gisella it was completely erased now.

Just then, Isabella and Gisella marched around the bank's corner and headed toward the parking deck. They were laughing and shaking their heads. Hell, he didn't blame them. No doubt Dee's tirade gave them plenty to laugh about.

His eyes locked on to Gisella, and from the safety of his car he was free to just watch the French beauty. It was a cool spring day, and Gisella wore an amazing sky blue wrap dress that hugged her perfect hourglass figure. Hands down, she had the sexiest walk he'd ever seen. As her hips swayed, her breasts jiggled slightly and her onion-shaped bottom simply hypnotized.

"Where, oh where have you been all my life," he whispered.

Isabella said something and Gisella's face lit up and her musical laughter floated across the parking deck. He cocked his head with a lazy smile and continued to watch as her hair billowed in the gentle breeze. His eyes then zeroed in on her full lips and he felt that stirring in the pit of his stomach again while his erection throbbed against his leg.

The two women reached Isabella's red Mercedes, and he had to swallow his disappointment when Gisella disappeared from view. A few heartbeats later, he was shaking his head and telling himself he needed to change the direction of his thoughts. The last thing he needed to be thinking about is getting involved with another woman.

No matter how beautiful.

What was the point? He might have less than six months…

Isabella's Mercedes pulled out of its parking space then disappeared onto Fourteenth Street. After taking a few more deep breaths, Charlie's erection softened, and his heartbeat returned to normal. He started the car and backed up only a few inches when a thumping noise caught his attention. Shifting the car back into Park, Charlie climbed out of his car.

At first he thought that something must be wrong with his vision. But after blinking several times, he knew his eyes weren't playing tricks on him, and he was staring at two flat tires. Then something else caught his eyes. He stepped forward and noticed the hood where someone had keyed in the word *asshole*.

"Great," he groaned. "Just great."

Chapter 8

Saturday morning, Charlie strolled through the doors of Herman's Barbershop with his cane and smiled at the usual suspects as they chimed, "Yo, Charlie!"

"Morning, everybody," he greeted.

Herman Keillor, a tall robust man who was cruising toward his mid-seventies, had owned the busy shop for over forty years. Most of the guys filtered through to hear Herman's stories, tough love advice and sharp haircuts.

Charlie and Derrick had been going to the shop since they were six years old. The other Kappa brothers started coming on their recommendation.

"Right on time," Herman's voice boomed across the room. "I swear, Charlie. That's why you're one of my favorite customers. You don't believe in any of the CP time like the rest of these knuckleheads up in here," he lectured on the sly.

As usual the men just laughed and waved the old barber

off. Mounted high in the left corner, a twenty-seven-inch television screen was tuned in to SportsCenter.

"Come on over," Herman directed. "I've got your seat all warmed up and ready for you."

Charlie made his way across the shop and eased into the leather chair.

Men in the neighborhood filtered in and out daily, but Saturday had always been Herman's busiest day of the week. Six barbers ranging from old school to new school donned burgundy barber jackets with Herman's name scrawled across the back. For an old redbrick building, the shop still managed to look modern and brand-new.

"So what's been happening, Charlie?" Herman asked, smiling and draping a black smock around his neck.

Charlie hesitated a moment and then answered with his tried and true. "You know the drill. Same ole, same ole."

"Same crap, different day, huh?"

"You got it."

Herman's was the place to be to discuss women, politics and sports. The perfect place for men to just be themselves, to get and give advice and just plain bond with one another.

"I hear you had an off-the-chain birthday party," said Bobby, Herman's nineteen-year-old great-grandson, who was sitting in the leather chair across from him. Like everyone else in the shop, Charlie had watched Bobby move from sweeping up the floors to trying his hand at being a weekend barber.

"Yeah. It was pretty cool."

"Well, what does a young brother gotta do to cop an invite?" Bobby asked, pretending to be hurt by the exclusion.

"Are you kidding me? You're a college man now. Why the heck would you want to hang out with us? I'm sure there are plenty of honeys around you 24/7."

Bobby blushed while a sly smile hooked across his face. "Honeys? Man, you *are* old school."

"Lawd, Lawd," Herman mumbled, reaching for his clippers. "What you need to do is forget about those fast girls and put your nose deeper into those books."

"Relax, Gramps." Bobby smiled. "I got it all covered like Allstate."

Charlie laughed. It seemed like it was just yesterday that Bobby was pencil-thin with thick, black-rimmed glasses and a face covered in acne. Now, he'd filled out and his skin had cleared up and he was flexin' his playa's card. "You still pledging Kappa Psi Kappa?" Charlie asked.

"You know it."

The bell jingled above the shop's door and Taariq and Hylan entered the shop. After a round of perfunctory "Yo, whassup," Taariq and Hylan made it over to Charlie's chair to exchange a couple of knuckle bumps.

"What's happening, captain?" Taariq asked, grinning.

"You got it," Charlie said.

"You gonna let me hook you up today, Taariq?" Bobby asked, getting up out of his chair and gesturing for Taariq to take a seat.

For a full year now, Bobby had been harassing everyone who came in the barbershop, trying to build up his clientele by siphoning off Herman's loyal customers.

Taariq stared him down while he wrestled with his decision. "Man, if you jack this up it's gonna be just you and me out back."

Bobby beamed a smile at him and patted the leather chair. "Have a seat."

There was a round of snickering, all of them probably thinking that Taariq was being incredibly brave, seeing as how just two months ago Bobby shaved a bald spot in the middle of J. T. Caesar's hair because he'd gotten distracted by a thick romp shaker in a BET rap video.

"Better you than me," Hylan said, shaking his head.

"You ain't never lied," J.T. agreed with a flash of his front gold tooth. "Yo, yo, Hylan. I got that new Jay-Z underground joint. Five dollars."

"That's all right," Hylan chuckled.

"What about some DVDs? I already got that new Will Smith joint."

"C'mon, man. You know I don't buy none of that bootleg crap."

"What about some socks?" He opened his jacket and pulled out a massive bundle.

"What the hell?" Hylan asked. "Has anybody *ever* bought socks from you?"

"Yeah, man. That's my hottest selling item."

Charlie laughed. This place was just where he needed to be to forget about his troubles.

"Oh, by the way," Taariq said, returning his attention to Charlie. "I rushed that paint job for you. You can come by the shop any time and pick it up."

"Thanks, man. I owe you one."

"Uh-huh. Word around town is that you're starting to have women trouble lately. Vandalism, causing a scene at the bank—"

Charlie groaned. "How did you find out?"

"Isabella told Derrick, Derrick told me, and then I told everybody I could think of." He laughed.

"Thanks, dawg."

"Don't mention it."

Charlie suffered a few jeers.

Hylan rocked on his heels. "Losing your touch, ain't ya?"

"Say it ain't so!" Bobby said, wrapping a smock around

Taariq's neck. "I thought it was a sad day when pimp number one went down. Don't tell me that the replacement has lost his Midas touch."

"I take it you mean Derrick. And we're not pimps."

"Whatever. I just know the faster you old-school playas get out the game, the more *honeys* there will be for me."

Everybody roared at that.

"Man, if you don't get your rookie butt outta here," Taariq said. "You still got breast milk on your breath and you up in here thinking you a real playa."

Bobby's face darkened with embarrassment. "C'mon now. Stop frontin'."

"Yeah, man," Hylan stepped in and corrected Taariq. "He's been grown for at least two weeks."

The guys cracked up again, including Herman.

The shop's bell rang again and Stanley strolled inside with his customary wide smile. None of the regulars called the lanky redhead by his first name. Instead, they affectionately called Stanley "Breadstick" and sometimes "Whitey," probably because Stanley was the only white man to get his hair cut at Herman's.

"Yo, everybody, whassup?" Stanley greeted, acting more black than everybody else. At this point, everyone was used to it and welcomed him into the fold just the same.

"I know one thing," Bobby said. "I'm getting more action than *this* dude."

There was another roar of laughter, and Stanley tried to play off his confusion by laughing along with everyone else.

Herman shook his head. "Boys still playing at being men."

The guys pretended not to hear him, but in no time Herman felt like preaching. "You know ya'll need to take a page out of your friend Derrick's book."

Right on cue, the bell rang again and Derrick entered the shop.

"Speaking of the devil," Hylan said and waited as Derrick made his way over to them.

Derrick tossed everyone a slow nod.

"Now this one finally got it right and settled down," Herman said, pointing a firm finger at Derrick.

"Whoa. Whoa. What did I miss?"

"I was about to tell your friends about how nothing good can come from playing the field with all these different women. One of these days you're gonna roll up on the wrong one. Charlie already got one vandalizing his car. He's just one step away from taking a hot grits shower. If you don't believe me, ask Al Green."

"Who?" Bobby asked.

"Lawd, Lawd, please help these knuckleheads running around here—starting with my own."

Charlie smiled. Once Herman got started there was no stopping him.

"I'm going to agree with Herman," Derrick said.

Charlie and the rest of the Kappa brothers rolled their eyes. Derrick had been siding with Herman ever since he'd said "I do."

"Be still," Herman warned Charlie and then clicked back on his trimmers.

"For real," Derrick said, easing his hands into his pockets and rocking on his heels next to Hylan. "I don't regret a single moment once I finally turned in my playa's card."

"That's right." The trimmers were clicked off again. "There's nothing better than the love of one special woman. A man needs peace in his house—in his life."

"Yeah, yeah, yeah," Taariq droned, unconvinced.

"Mark my words. You learn sooner or later."

Herman's speech stayed with Charlie for the rest of the day while he thought about his past relationships. And there were a lot. With the clock ticking maybe it was time he tried to set things right.

There's nothing better than the love of one special woman.

Each time Herman's voice repeated those words, Gisella floated to the forefront of his mind. But just as quickly, he would shake off the image. That avenue was closed. If Dr. Weiner's diagnosis held, then the last thing he needed to be starting was a relationship. He needed to start focusing on making peace with his past.

As Charlie made it back to his apartment building, his thoughts muddled together. Tonight, he would pull out his thick little black book and start making some calls. Hell, it just might take him the whole six months to call them all.

When Charlie slipped his key into the apartment door and stepped inside, he received another shock of his life. Sucking in a breath, his eyes roamed across busted furniture, shattered glass and the word *asshole* scrawled across his white walls in red spray paint.

"Who in the hell is this chick?"

Chapter 9

Gisella's business was booming.

Word of mouth from Charlie's surprise birthday party continued to spread like wild fire. And now Waqueisha kept calling with outrageously large orders to fill for people in Atlanta's entertainment industry.

After running around like a chicken with its head cut off, she realized that she did need help and took Isabella up on her offer.

"Trust me," Isabella boasted. "By this time next year, Ms. Winfrey will be naming your chocolates as one of her favorite things."

Smiling, Gisella shook her head. "When you dream, you dream big, don't you?"

"You just concentrate on making your wonderful treats, and leave the business end to me."

Gisella drew a deep breath and resolved to do just that. The two new business partners huddled together over her sister's dining-room table and discussed everything from hiring more help to balancing their budget. The task was made a little difficult with Sasha constantly jumping on the table and waiting to be petted.

Finally, around ten o'clock, Derrick started blowing up Isabella's cell phone and urging her to come home.

On his fourth call, Gisella smiled at her new partner. "We better call it night," Gisella said.

Isabella agreed, though it was clear she was still excited about this latest career change. "I'll see you bright and early at the shop," she said, giving Gisella a final hug at the door.

When she turned to leave, Gisella could no longer ignore the anxious knot looping in her stomach. "Um…"

Isabella stopped with her hand frozen on the door. "Yes?"

Suddenly feeling foolish, Gisella shifted her weight nervously from side to side. "I was wondering if, um, you heard from Charlie again."

A single brow inched higher towards the center of Isabella's forehead. "Not since we saw him at the bank Friday."

Gisella nodded and swallowed the lump in the center of her throat.

"Why?" Isabella pressed.

Unable to stop the heat from rushing into her face, Gisella's brain short-circuited while she tried to come up with a sufficient excuse for her inquiry. When all she could manage was to bump her gums in silence, a knowing smile eased across Isabella's face.

"You like him, don't you?"

No. Just say no. "He's…interesting."

Isabella snickered. "I think that's putting it mildly— especially after that weird episode at the bank."

"Well, you definitely gave that loan officer a good piece of your mind," Gisella said, laughing.

"After I'd finally recovered from my shock. Poor Charlie. I just know he was humiliated."

"Well." Gisella tilted her head, hedging. "Are we sure that he didn't deserve it? I mean…I've heard rumors."

Isabella drew a deep breath and Gisella thought that maybe she shouldn't be questioning her about a friend. "I'm sorry. I shouldn't have—I mean, forget I said anything."

"No. No. It's fine," Isabella assured her. "I mean… Charlie does have quite a reputation. A lot of it is true, unfortunately." She took another breath. "Of course, Derrick had the same reputation, too, before we met."

Gisella nodded and remembered the covetous glances women made toward the handsome Derrick Knight at the party. She also remembered how he only had eyes for his wife. "You're a lucky woman."

"I am," Isabella agreed, blushing. "There's not a morning I don't wake up and pinch myself."

Gisella relished finding another hopeless romantic. "My sister seems to think there aren't any good single men out here anymore. She's given up."

Isabella cocked her head. "What about you?"

"Me?" Gisella echoed.

"Yeah, you. Has your ex turned you off to finding true love?"

"*Tell her*," Fantasy Charlie whispered against her ear.

"No." Gisella cleared her throat. "Of course not."

Fantasy Charlie chuckled and brushed a kiss against the back of her neck.

"Good," Isabella said. "I'm glad to hear it. I truly believe that if I could find true love, then surely someone as beautiful as you should have no problem."

Gisella frowned at the odd comment.

"And don't let the rumors about Charlie dissuade you."

"You should listen to the girl." Fantasy Charlie moved next to Isabella and folded his arms.

"Charlie is like a big kid. A lot of the women he's dated act like little girls. They just keep putting his favorite toys in front of him and then act shocked when someone with newer or bigger toys lures him away."

"She has an interesting way of putting things," Charlie said.

Gisella giggled.

Isabella smiled. "What I mean is, Charlie will act more like a man when he meets a real woman. Does that make sense?"

Fantasy Charlie shook his head. *"No."*

"It makes perfect sense," Gisella answered and then gave Isabella another departing hug. "I'll see you in the morning."

After Isabella left the apartment, Gisella closed the door and slumped back against it.

"I thought she would never leave," Fantasy Charlie said, easing up to her and brushing a kiss along her neck. *"What do you say we go back to the bedroom and have a little fun?"*

Gisella glanced up at him, thinking over Isabella's words about the real Charlie being a big kid. "Not tonight. I have a headache."

"Do you know anyone who'd want to do this to you, sir?" Officer Todd asked, with his notepad and pen in hand.

"Not off the top of my head," Charlie grumbled and massaged his throbbing temples. He took another hard look around his ransacked apartment and felt the blood boil in his veins.

"You said that you filed another police report yesterday about your car being vandalized?"

Charlie nodded and couldn't help but feel he'd been cast into some pathetic B-movie horror flick.

Officer Todd frowned. "Are you sure you can't think of anyone, sir? Perhaps an ex-wife or old girlfriend…or boyfriend?"

"What?"

"Sorry—but we never know. Since nothing was stolen, clearly this was a crime of passion."

Charlie flashed the man an irritated glare. "I'm not gay, and I've never been married."

"And your old girlfriends?" the officer asked undaunted.

"That's obviously a different matter," Charlie said, exhaling a long breath, racing through a list in his mind. When no woman stood out in his mind, a painful throbbing at his temples began to hammer double-time. "I'll have to get back to you on that one."

"All right." Officer Todd scribbled a few more notes on his notepad and then handed Charlie a card. "Just give us a call if you're able to think of anything else."

"Sure thing." Charlie slid the card into his pocket and then held the door open while the officer and his partner made their exit. Once they were gone, he shut the door and took another disheartening look at the damage before him.

With no other choice, Charlie rolled up his sleeves and got busy cleaning. Hours later, he gave up and decided the job was going to require real professionals. Close to midnight he limped over to the bar and found one unbroken bottle of Jack Daniels and poured himself a drink.

It took three before he was completely relaxed.

"An ex-girlfriend or boyfriend." He laughed. Hell, what

else was he going to do? As he continued to survey the damage, he reflected over his cavalier lifestyle and the numerous one-night stands. Up until now, he'd viewed it all as harmless fun. He'd never made or broken any promises, nor had he asked for any in return. He always made sure his dates had a great time, and then they were free to go on their merry separate ways.

Maybe he had been too naive.

Charlie stood up from the bar and hobbled to his bedroom—another disaster area. At least he was able to clear off a space on the bed so he'd have some place to sleep tonight. He reached underneath the mattress and hoped what he was searching for was still there. He panicked for a moment, but then his hand finally brushed against the spine of a book.

Smiling, Charlie set his whiskey down on the nightstand and pulled out his thick little black book. Such a book was the hallmark of every true playa. His didn't just contain the names and numbers of the beautiful women who'd been so gracious with their time and bodies, but also notes and a very intricate rating system he'd conjured up in high school.

The book was his most treasured possession.

He flipped through the pages, and a flutter of memories danced before his eyes. If the good Lord did decide his time was up, Charlie realized he'd lived one hell of a life—just not a complete one.

Charlie's smile disappeared as a lump of regret clogged his throat and reality hit him hard. Obviously, he had broken a few hearts over the years, and if he was facing the end of his life maybe he should be using this time to right a few wrongs.

He returned to the first page of his black book and

read the first name—Abby. "Three and a half stars." That wasn't too bad, he thought and picked up the phone.

As he dialed, he thought briefly about what he would say. He drew a blank while the line rang but before he could hang up, a woman answered.

"Hello."

"Uh, hello." He clutched the phone. "Is, um, Abby there?"

"This is she."

"Oh, Abby." He cleared his throat and tried to control a wave of panic. "This is, um, Charlie—Charlie Masters. You probably don't remember me—"

"Charlie Masters!" She perked up. "Oh, my God. I can't believe it's you."

He smiled at the reception. Maybe this won't be so hard after all.

"My goodness." She sighed. "How have you been?"

"Not so good. I'm dying," he blurted and then smacked a hand across his forehead.

"What?"

"That didn't come out right."

"You mean…" She gasped.

Charlie immediately knew she'd jumped to the wrong conclusion. "No. No. No. No. It's not what you thinking," he rushed to say. "I don't have a sexually transmitted disease," he stressed. "It's not that at all."

"What, then?" she asked, obviously confused. "Is it cancer?"

"No." He exhaled again and felt his migraine return. "It's aplastic anemia."

"It's a plastic what?"

"It's just a rare form of anemia."

The line fell silent.

"Hello? Are you there?"

"Oookay," she said hesitantly. "Sooo, why are you calling?"

"Well." He cleared his throat. "I was doing a lot of thinking, and I wanted to apologize for, uh…" He looked down at his notes in the book. "Standing you up that time."

"You mean…senior prom?"

Charlie frowned and squinted down at the book. Apparently his intricate system didn't include dates. "Yeah, well. Again…sorry."

There was another long silence.

"So, I'll let you go. It was nice talking to you." He quickly disconnected the call. "Real smooth," he said, rolling his eyes and reaching for his drink again.

Still, he thought after a moment, it didn't go too bad. He probably just needed to tighten up his speech a bit and try to just concentrate on the women outside of high school.

Charlie glanced at the clock and realized that it was getting late. He picked up the book again. Tomorrow he would call Allison…and Anna.

Chapter 10

"Is this some kind of joke?" Allison asked, frowning at him over her Belgian waffle.

Charlie glanced around the Georgia Diner, smiled at a few people he suspected were eavesdropping and shifted uncomfortably in his seat. "No. It's no joke," he said, praying there wouldn't be an explosion. He had no idea what possessed him to do this in person. It might have had a lot to do with the fact that he'd generally liked Allison. Once he remembered who she was.

They'd met in a public library. She had her nose buried in a mystery book. He was struggling with a term paper.

Allison was kind and nurturing. However, she was also a tad bit clingy and had a habit of laughing like a hyena.

"You mean you weren't a secret agent for the CIA?"

Oh, yeah...she was a little gullible, too.

"Sorry," he said, cringing. "I'm afraid not."

"What about that elaborate story about a covert mission to bring down the Hawaiian Mafia in New Jersey?"

Hawaiian Mafia? "Never been to New Jersey."

Allison lowered her fork and eased back in her chair. "So, what? I'm supposed to feel sorry for you because *now* you're about to kick the bucket? Is that it?"

"Not exactly." He shifted in his chair. "I just want to apologize and bring closure if you thought that I've done anything to—"

"Unbelievable!" Allison crossed her arms. "The only reason I slept with you was because I thought I had a patriotic and civil duty. You *said* you were leaving for a top secret mission in Mauritania and that you may not survive. I thought you were dead for the last fourteen years?"

Charlie cocked his head, thinking she was taking this a bit too far. "C'mon. That is *not* why you slept with me."

Allison rolled her eyes, but a smile teased the corners of her lips. "So what's the play this time? You have six months to live, and now you want me to take you back to my place for one last fling?"

Leaning his elbow on the table, Charlie pinched the bridge of his nose. "No. That's not it."

"Oh," she said, disappointment clearly in her tone. "Would you like to go back to my apartment?"

He frowned. "Aren't you married now?"

"Marcus doesn't get out on parole until next month."

"Uh, thanks, but…I'll pass."

Allison shrugged. "Can't blame a girl for trying."

Charlie's relationship with Anna was complicated. Even though they'd never dated or were intimate, Anna was perhaps the closest female friend he'd ever had. To him, she was like a sister—smart and easygoing. They met at a frat party back when he attended Morehouse and she the neighboring Spelman College. A friend of hers, Nicole something-or-another, had too much to drink and was unable to drive and Anna had never driven a stick shift.

Charlie and Taariq stepped forward and helped her out by driving them back to their dorms. It was the beginning of a nice friendship, especially when he discovered that she was a whiz in calculus. Unfortunately, their relationship was derailed a year later when Charlie grew interested in her new roommate Roxanne.

Roxanne had the hottest body on campus, and Charlie was just one in a long line trying to hook up with her. For an advantage, he started milking Anna for information about her roommate—on the sly. When he started seeing Roxanne, he kept it from Anna…until she caught them in bed together.

It wasn't until she was crying and cussing him out did he realize that Anna's feelings for him went beyond friendship.

She accused Charlie of using her.

And he had—unintentionally.

She never spoke to him again.

Anna's old number was no longer in service. Charlie spent an hour at his apartment Googling and searching the white pages online for an address. If there was one woman he truly wanted to make peace with it was Anna. As it turned out, he was in luck. She still lived in Atlanta, not too far from his downtown office.

Once Charlie wrote down the new address, he stared at it, contemplating. Did he really want to do this? Finally, he stood, folded the paper and slipped it into his pocket.

"Ah, this is the life," Gisella sighed, sinking deep into her bubble bath. She had waited all week for this. Sunday was the only day the shop was closed and she could use some R & R. She was determined to do absolutely nothing. With Anna still out of town, Gisella had the apartment all to herself. She could run around naked if she wanted. A tempting thought.

The first and only thing on her schedule was to pamper herself, which was why she'd borrowed one of her sister's romance books, globbed on a thick cucumber mask and poured a big glass of wine.

Fantasy Charlie showed up for a few minutes, but she quickly sent him away. After all, there was plenty of time to play with him later.

In no time, the stress of the past week seeped out of her body, and she fell fast asleep. When she awoke, the bubbles were gone, and the water was cold. Laughing, she climbed out of the tub with her fingers and toes nearly pickled and with the real challenge of removing the cucumber mask that had hardened into green concrete.

It took a lot of scrubbing, but when she was through, her skin was as soft and smooth as a newborn baby's. After blow-drying the ends of her hair, she hummed her way into her bedroom for some underwear, rubbed her favorite lotions into her skin and then danced to the kitchen for a big bowl of cereal.

No cooking today.

Still dancing, she scanned her sister's music collection. When she found an old 1980s classic, Gisella slipped the disc into the CD player and turned the volume up to full blast.

Charlie walked into the brownstone, puzzled by the sound of Deniece Williams's "Let's Hear It for the Boy" blaring out into the hallway. Was there a 1980s retro reunion party going on? When he realized that the music was coming from the apartment number written on his paper, he began to have second thoughts about this whole thing.

"All right, Charlie. Let's just get this over with," he coached, drawing a deep breath. He knocked on the door and waited. When it was clear no one heard him, he rang the bell and knocked again.

Still no answer.

He thought to wait for the song to fade, but it immediately launched into Kenny Loggins's "Footloose."

Now, he started hammering and shouting, "Hello!"

As a last-ditch effort, he tried the door and was surprised to find it unlocked. He paused for a moment, then slowly turned the knob. "Hello!" He entered the apartment.

Kenny Loggins continued to cut loose as Charlie inched further into the apartment.

"Hello! Anybody?"

Charlie rounded a corner and faced the living room. He stopped in his tracks. There, in all her Victoria's Secret glory, danced an ebony goddess holding an orange cat. The ability to speak or even to process thought grinded to a halt. Surely, he looked like a cartoon with his mouth hanging open and his tongue rolling onto the floor.

Gisella jiggled and wiggled and really got into the old movie soundtrack. She was completely clueless of Charlie's presence, much less how his erection was trying to steeple like an Egyptian pyramid in his pants.

Forget six months, Charlie had died and gone to heaven the moment he'd entered this apartment.

Then something incredible happened. Gisella turned around and flashed him a smile.

"Hello, lover," she singsonged playfully.

Charlie looked over his shoulder to make sure she was talking to him.

She was.

To his surprise, she danced and bopped her way toward him with a sly smile and the unmistakable glint of seduction in her eyes.

Hot damn. This is my lucky day.

When she was within inches of him, the scent of strawberries swirled around his senses, making him light-headed…and incredibly horny.

"How about a kiss?" she asked.

Before he could answer, she planted her full breasts against his chest and swept her sweet tongue inside his mouth. He moaned and started to wrap his arms around her waist when she suddenly jerked back and screamed.

Chapter 11

One should never scream while holding a cat.

The minute Sasha's nails dug into Gisella's arm, she was airborne. When the startled cat landed on Charlie, she turned into a weapon of mass destruction.

Charlie roared.

Sasha shrieked.

And Gisella screamed and ran from the room. "Oh, my God. Oh, my God," she chanted, slamming her bedroom door behind her. To calm down, she paced the floor and fanned herself. "That didn't just happen," she mumbled. "It didn't. It couldn't have." She rolled her eyes skyward. "Oh, God, please say that didn't happen."

She started praying in French.

Unfortunately, Charlie and Sasha's continued war prevented her from sinking into denial. Gulping in a few deep breaths, she raced over to her chest of drawers and slung clothes around until she found a pair of sweatpants and a white T-shirt. Once she was dressed, she still hesitated to leave her room. What was she going to say? How could she explain kissing him like that?

And damn. What a kiss.

Just thinking of it caused her heart to speed up again. Who on earth would ever believe that she kissed him because she thought he was a figment of her imagination?

Suddenly, the apartment was quiet.

Gisella inched toward the door. Was Sasha safe? Didn't someone say something about not trusting Charlie alone with anything with breasts and a pulse? Slowly, Gisella pressed her ear against the door.

Silence.

Did he leave?

She closed her eyes, held her breath and strained to hear the slightest sound.

"Gisella, are you in there?" came Charlie's low baritone.

She leaped from the door.

His tone was barely above a whisper, but it had the effect of an excited cheerleader shouting through a megaphone.

"Gisella?"

"Um." She hesitated. "What are you doing here?"

"Look. I knocked, but you had the music turned up so loud you wouldn't have heard a bomb going off." He chuckled.

"Oh," she said, unprepared for a logical explanation. But on second thought, that only answered why he was *inside* the apartment, not why he'd come there in the first place.

"Actually, I was looking for a friend."

She frowned. They were hardly friends. Hell, they barely qualified as acquaintances. "I never gave you this address," she said, still weary about opening her door.

"You didn't. I looked up the address on the Internet."

Okay. Was he a stalker?

"Why would you look me up on the Internet?"

"Oh. No. Not you," he rushed to explain. "No. I was looking for an old *college* friend, Anna Jacobs. Wait. Isn't Jacobs your last name?"

Charlie and Anna were old college friends? Gisella snatched opened the door and Sasha darted in between her legs with a loud meow.

However, the *real* war victim was clearly Charlie.

"*Mon Dieu.* Look at you!" Her eyes widened at the number of scratches covering his face, neck and arms. "Come here." She grabbed him by the wrist and led him toward her adjoining bathroom. "Here. Take a seat." She lowered the toilet seat and then rustled for some supplies.

Charlie sat and looked around. "I'm sure it's not as bad as it looks," he said.

"Nonsense," she said. "You're bleeding." Gisella twisted open a bottle of alcohol and pulled out a few cotton balls. "Now this is going to sting a bit."

Despite the warning, Charlie sucked in a shocked breath and bounced around on the toilet seat like a Mexican jumping bean.

"Be still," she instructed softly and then blew on a few deep gashes. "Is that better?"

Charlie grew still. "A little."

Gisella glanced up and their eyes locked. "You're a big baby, no?"

His cheeks dimpled. "I wouldn't say that."

For a few seconds, the bathroom tiles magnified their shallow breathing and Gisella swore it even picked up the sound of her heartbeat. Fantasy Charlie paled in comparison to the real deal. Charlie Masters could easily grace the glossy pages of fashion magazines instead of wheeling and dealing behind some office desk. He was just that beautiful.

Forcing herself out of her self-imposed trance, she returned her attention to cleaning a few more scratches, especially the long one across his right cheek. When she leaned forward, Lord help her, she could literally feel his warm breath rush against the exposed portion of her cleavage in her low-cut tee. It took every ounce of her willpower to keep her knees from buckling and depositing her on his lap. All the while, his gaze remained locked on her.

"I'm beginning to think you're a masochist."

She blinked. "A what?"

"Someone who enjoys torturing people." When she still looked confused, he added, "Either kiss me again or let me stand up."

She quickly backed away from him.

"I thought so." He stood and eyed a Band-Aid in the corner of the medicine cabinet. "May I?"

She nodded, swallowing the lump amassing in her throat.

Charlie leaned toward the mirror and applied an invisible Band-Aid against his cheek. "There. Good as new."

She smiled. "Sorry I threw Sasha at you."

"Sorry I frightened you."

They stood staring at each other, but Gisella knew what they were both thinking about.

That kiss.

"So," she said, hoping to deter him from asking about it. "How do you know my sister?"

He stepped back. "Anna is your sister?"

"Half sister," she corrected. "Different mothers, same father."

Charlie blinked. "Oh. I would have never thought—you two don't look anything alike."

That was true. Anna was tall and angular and Gisella was thick and curvy. Though both women were attractive, the facial features were stark opposites.

"Well, I take it she's not here." He laughed. "Know when she'll be home?"

"Actually, she's out of town for a couple of weeks. In the meantime, it's just me and Sasha."

"The killer cat."

Gisella laughed.

"Well," he said with a note of disappointment.

"When she calls," Gisella said, "I'll be happy to tell her you came by."

"That'll be great." Charlie bobbed his head and went back to staring at her. The memory of their kiss still threatened to become a topic of discussion.

"Do you want to leave a number so she can call you back?" Gisella offered.

"Sure. Um, you gotta pen?"

Gisella glanced around and decided against using a tube of lipstick to write a message. "There should be one up front," she said, leading the way.

As they walked back through her bedroom, Sasha curled into a ball on the edge of Gisella's bed and meowed at Charlie as he walked by.

"I don't think Killer cares for me much."

"She'll be all right." In the living room, Gisella found pen and paper.

Charlie jotted down his name and cell phone number and handed it over. After another beat of silence, he said, "I still can't believe you two are sisters."

"We have been all my life," she joked.

They stared at each other as if waiting for the other person to bring up the taboo subject. It was going to be a long wait if it was up to Gisella.

As if reading her thoughts, Charlie nodded and finally took his first step toward the door. "I guess I'll let you get back to your…uh, dancing."

Gisella's embarrassment rushed back. "Oh, I can't believe you saw that."

Charlie stopped and loitered for a few more seconds. "You have some pretty good moves."

"You, Mr. Masters, are a liar."

"Please. My friends call me Charlie."

She gave him a soft smile. "All right. Charlie…you're a liar." Even though she meant it as a joke, she could tell her words landed a blow by how his smile shrank a few inches.

"Well, I guess I've been called worse," he said with a sad, self-effacing humor.

At the odd flicker of emotions crossing his handsome face, Gisella wished she could take her words back but before she got the chance, he walked away.

She followed, trying to keep her eyes averted from his broad shoulders, firm butt and muscled legs, but it was impossible.

No. No. No. No more bad boys.

He stopped briefly to retrieve his cane from the floor, but then continued on to the front door.

"I guess I'll see you around," Charlie said after crossing the threshold. He waited, giving her one more chance to talk about the kiss.

Instead, Gisella lowered her eyes and nodded.

"Goodbye." He turned and walked away.

Gisella slowly closed the door—and locked it.

Chapter 12

Charlie had no memory of driving back home. All he could do was replay the image of Gisella dancing in her living room in a lacy blue panties-and-bra set. No way would he ever forget it. Every detail from the heart-stopping curve of her breasts, the roundness of her full hips and even her long, shapely legs were now permanently branded in his mind.

He squirmed in the seat of his rental car, trying to give his erection a little more breathing room.

And what about that kiss?

He never dreamed she could taste that sweet. With very little effort he remembered how her silken tongue swept through his mouth and stole a part of his soul. It was just that erotic and sensual. No woman had ever kissed him like that.

Ever.

The only frustrating part was that it ended too soon.

One moment he was lost in heaven, and in the next all

he saw was orange fur and sharp claws. But even the attack of the killer cat was worth that brief moment of intimacy. By the time he took a break from his long daydream, Charlie was back at his apartment and sprawled across his bed.

Seconds later, he was groaning and wishing the kiss had been longer or that he had reached out to feel the weight of her breasts in his hands. He did remember them being pressed against his chest and confirming that those babies were indeed real.

What he wouldn't give for the chance to see if her luscious mounds were just as beautiful as the rest of her. Charlie's breath thinned in his lungs as he closed his eyes and allowed the memory of strawberries to fill his senses.

Sighing, Charlie lost himself in the short memory and wondered why he'd never felt like this before. He ached just to be able to run his fingers through her hair or rain kisses along her collarbone.

For a woman who spent her life baking sugary treats, Gisella had a body any Hollywood celebrity would kill for. Small waist. Round hips. Flat stomach.

He wondered if her nipples were the color of brown sugar or maybe amber with a hint of gold. Charlie played with the images in his head like it was a hologram in his mind. He gave it some serious consideration and finally decided her nipples would be the color of brown sugar and then went on to wonder about other intimate parts.

Brazilian wax?

Groomed?

Au naturel?

More important than that was, what did the other parts of her taste like? These were mysteries he was now obsessed with solving. And he *will* solve them.

Behind his closed eyelids, Gisella's saucy smile beamed, and her seductive walk entranced him. Now he pictured her crawling up his bed. Fantasy Gisella reached inside his pants with the promise to ease the ache of his throbbing erection.

Her hands were soft and smooth as silk, and their gentle stroking was torturously long and slow.

"Oh, God," he moaned, his toes curling against the bed. He wanted this woman, more than he'd ever wanted anyone. If fantasizing was the only way he could have her, then it would just have to do.

For now.

"*I know what you want,*" Fantasy Gisella whispered huskily in her erotic accent.

He didn't answer. He just watched as she positioned herself to straddle him and then eased down with all the grace of a ballerina.

Tight.

Warm.

Wet.

As she began to ride, breathing became secondary to the intense emotions swirling inside of him. "Gisella... Gisella..."

It was all he *could* say and all that he *wanted* to say. He exploded like a rocket, every ounce of his energy zapped in an instant. But he was far from being satisfied.

It wasn't wise to pursue a new relationship. Not with all that he had on his plate. It was too late for that. He was closing chapters in his life, not starting new ones. It wouldn't be fair for him or her. Yet, he *had* to see her again. Even though reason and common sense told him to stay away, his heart and body had plans of their own.

Gisella opened her shop bright and early Monday morning. It was a new day, and she was determined to put yesterday's embarrassment to the back of her mind.

But it wasn't working—just like it hadn't worked yesterday.

There was a serious issue at play here. The craziness that she couldn't tell the difference between a fantasy and a real man standing in her living room was too disturbing.

Two of Gisella's part-time workers, Krista and Pamela, darted wary glances Gisella's way every time she'd slammed down a pot or dropped a tray of eggs. They had never seen her like this, and with all the mumbling Gisella kept doing they were too afraid to ask what was wrong.

After making one too many mistakes, Gisella snapped. "Okay! So you kissed him." She slammed her fist into a pile of flour and caused an atomic white mushroom cloud to cover her face.

Krista and Pamela crept toward the front of store in case their boss turned postal. Death by chocolate didn't sound so cute today.

Choking and waving the flour from her face, Gisella turned and marched to the large walk-in cooler to calm down. By the time Isabella breezed through a few hours later, Gisella had pulled herself together and was at least managing to get *some* of her recipes right.

Isabella reviewed a few spreadsheet issues with her, but by the time she left the shop, Gisella realized that she hadn't heard a single word the woman said.

Gisella sailed into the afternoon, edgy and distracted. Edgy because she thought everyone knew what she'd done and distracted because Charlie's phone number was burning a hole in her pocket. She was supposed to give the number to her sister last night when she called but she never quite got around to doing it. Not that she didn't have the opportunity, it's just that, well, she wasn't exactly comfortable with her sister calling her...what? Fantasy lover?

She did, however, casually bring up his name. This

time she listened carefully to what her sister said as well as what she didn't say. Anna couldn't be baited; she just smoothly changed the subject.

What did that mean?

Were Charlie and her sister an item back in college? *That* thought was more troubling than the kiss. She dropped another pan, cursed a blue streak—both in French and in English.

Krista cleared her throat. "You have a visitor."

Gisella frowned. "Who is it?"

"I don't know." Krista shrugged. "Some guy," she said, her eyes sparkling. "Some incredibly handsome guy, if that helps."

Charlie. Gisella blinked stupidly up at her.

"Is everything all right?" Krista asked.

When she didn't readily respond, Krista asked, "Do you want me to get rid of him?"

"Uh, no." Gisella stood. "Just…tell him I'll be right up."

Frowning, Krista nodded and walked off.

Gisella quickly tried to dust the excess flour from her apron, but after surviving a large white funnel cloud, she gave up. Acknowledging that she was both excited and nervous, Gisella coached herself to stay cool. "You can do this." At least she hoped she could. This was like being a teenager all over again.

For an extra touch, she removed the hairnet and clip from her head and then strolled to the front of the shop with her heart in her throat.

But it wasn't Charlie waiting for her.

"Hello, Gisella."

"Robert?"

Chapter 13

"Sorry, Mr. Masters, but the Johannesburg contract has gone to McGraw-Hill Construction."

Charlie's heart sank as he gripped the phone receiver. "How is that possible? There wasn't supposed to be a decision until next month," he said, exasperated. "I've already booked my flight to South Africa."

"I'm sorry, but they announced their decision this morning," the nameless executive said emotionlessly.

Charlie plopped back in his chair, barely able to restrain his stream of curses. He didn't need this right now, but what else was there to say? No point in shooting the messenger.

After a couple of deep breaths, Charlie nodded against the phone. "Thank you for your time," he said gruffly and then dropped the hand unit back onto the cradle.

For a while, all he could do was sit in his chair and stare at the phone. What was he going to do? Disgusted when he couldn't think of a plan of action, he swiveled his chair and stared out of the window.

Charlie remembered the first time he'd looked out on the concrete-and-glass landscape. He felt like he was sitting on top of the world and there was nothing he couldn't accomplish.

Now…he felt lost.

Everything, it seemed, was falling apart, crumbling at his feet.

"Mr. Masters, you have a call on line one," Jackson announced over the speakerphone.

"Thank you." He turned around to the console and picked up the call. "Charles Masters."

"Charlie, I'm glad I've finally caught up with you."

Rolling his eyes, Charlie dropped his head against the palm of his hand. "Dr. Weiner, I've been meaning to call you."

The ensuing beat of silence hinted that the good doctor didn't exactly buy that line.

"I called to see if we can get you scheduled for that bone marrow test. It's important we get this done as soon as possible."

"Of course, um…I'll need to check my schedule…"

There was another awkward silence before Dr. Weiner said, "Look, Charlie. I know that this must really be hard for you. It's not uncommon when patients get this kind of news that they go into self-protection mode. Denial. They think the longer they don't know something the better. This isn't going to go away. In this case, it could be a fatal mistake. What you don't know *can* hurt you."

"I just…" Charlie stopped and drew a deep breath. "I just need some more time."

"You don't have much of that, Charlie."

But I feel fine!

"Look, I'm not going to lie to you. If your numbers are as severe as your blood work indicates, your chance for survival is extremely low. We have to get on top of this now."

After the doctor listened to Charlie's breathing for a few seconds, he added, "I'm going to have the nurses schedule you for the test at two o'clock on Friday at Northside, all right?"

Charlie nodded and then remembered that the doctor couldn't see him. "I'll be there," he lied.

"Good."

"Robert, what are you doing here?" Gisella asked with a sense of awe and suspicion.

International fashion model Robert Beauvais slid on his multimillion-dollar smile. "I came to see you," he said. He swept his arms open. "Now how about a kiss for your fiancé?"

From behind the sales counter, Krista and Pamela sighed.

Gisella crossed her arms. "You mean *ex*-fiancé, *n'est-ce pas?*"

"Semantics." He shrugged.

"We broke up over a year ago."

The reminder failed to erase his smile, and since she didn't rush dramatically into his arms, he took the initiative to close the gap between them in two strides. When his long muscled arms wrapped her into a smothering bear hug, Gisella thought she'd gag off his overpowering cologne.

"Ah, Gigi, you don't know how much I've missed you," he murmured against her ear.

Despite his handsome looks and his perfectly proportioned body, Gisella wasn't the least bit turned on. Pushing him back, she wiggled out of his grasp. "This is not the time or place," she warned.

He released her and then watched her march back behind the counter.

"Gigi—"

"Stop calling me that!"

"But—"

Mercifully, Gisella was literally saved by the bell when two women entered the shop. "Hello, can I help you?" she asked, slapping on a bright smile.

A plus-size older woman with a sharp silver bob haircut smiled warmly. "Yes. I heard so much about your shop. I'd like to buy a dozen of your chocolate-strawberry mousse truffles."

"Excellent choice!" Gisella exclaimed, a tad animated.

"Oh, I'll get them," Pamela volunteered.

"I'd like two dozen of the coconut clusters," the other woman added.

"I'm on it," Krista said.

Gisella could've chewed nails when she was once again stuck with having to deal with her ex.

"I missed you," Robert said, reaching for her hands.

She jerked them back across the counter and folded her arms across her chest.

"Paris is not the same without you," he continued undaunted.

"Robert…"

"Now," he said, holding up a hand. "I know I've made some mistakes, but I want you to know that I'm a changed man. I came here to apologize."

"You flew all the way here *just* to apologize?"

He nodded, but then added, "I also have a fashion shoot over at—"

"Figures."

"C'mon. Don't be like that." He cocked his head and leveled his best puppy-dog expression on her.

The shop's bell rang again, and this time the store experienced an afternoon rush.

However, Robert surprised her when he just stood back, content to wait. Forty-five minutes later, he pulled her aside again. "I mean it. I miss you. Come back to me."

Gisella stared, dumbstruck. Was he for real?

Confidence radiated in Robert's smile. *"J'ai t'aimé toujours."*

"If you loved me you wouldn't have cheated on me." She rolled her eyes and tried to walk away.

Robert grabbed her by the hand but she twirled around and snatched it back. "No, Robert. It's over. I've moved on." Too angry to notice the shop's sudden silence, Gisella moved forward and jabbed her finger into the center of his chest.

"You broke my heart," she hissed. "While I was off foolishly planning to spend the rest of my life with you, you were off sleeping with half of Europe."

Robert realized they were the center of attention and smiled awkwardly. "Could you lower your voice? Everyone is watching us," he whispered.

Gisella shook her head. It was hard to believe that at one time she thought he hung the moon and stars. It wasn't until she left France and did some soul searching with the Lonely Hearts Club did she realize just how unhappy and unfulfilled she was in their relationship. She suffocated under Robert's ego and resented the fact that he never encouraged her to pursue her own dreams, even if it was just to run a small bakery.

Now, there she was standing before one of the handsomest men in the world and she felt…nothing. Absolutely nothing. "Go home, Robert," she said in the kindest voice she could manage.

"Gigi." He cocked his head. "It's me you're talking to. There's no need to play hard to get. I *know* you miss us being together."

"Robert—"

"Do you know how many women that would *love* to take your place?"

"As far as I'm concerned they're more than welcome to have you."

Disbelief rippled across Robert's face. A second later, it turned into suspicion. "Is there someone else?"

Mon Dieu!

"Is there?"

As if summoned by some magical power, the shop's door opened, and in walked Charlie.

Seizing the opportunity, Gisella practically flew to Charlie's side. "Ah, sweetheart, there you are!"

Frowning, Charlie glanced around. When he saw that there was no one behind him, he pressed a hand against his chest. "Who, me?"

Gisella laughed and wrapped her arm around his waist. "Stop being silly, darling. Of course I'm talking to you." She leaned up on her toes and pressed a butterfly kiss against his lips. Her performance was undoubtedly worthy of a Razzie Award for Worst Performance by a Non-Actress, but she smiled up at Charlie, praying desperately that he would play along.

The woman must have a split personality, Charlie thought. He looked from her to the tall brother that was glaring at them and put the pieces together. Easing on a wide smile, Charlie slid his arms around Gisella. "Well, I'm glad to see you're over that little lover's spat we had last night," he covered and then swooped down for a real kiss.

A deeper kiss.

A longer kiss.

Krista and Pamela sighed.

Gisella's pretense easily melted beneath the heat of such overwhelming passion. Her hold tightened around his waist when his tongue wickedly mated with her own. In no time at all her body overheated and the delicious sensations coursing through her left her trembling like a leaf.

Robert cleared his throat.

Charlie and Gisella kept kissing.

Robert tried again, this time sounding like he was trying to hack up a lung.

Charlie finally pulled away, mainly because Gisella lacked the strength.

"I take it that this is your new boyfriend," Robert droned sarcastically.

"What?" Gisella's eyes fluttered open. "Oh, yeah." She started to step back, but Charlie's arms locked into place. It was just as well since she doubted her legs would hold up on their own. "Um, Robert this is Charlie. Charlie, honey, this is Robert...my *former* fiancé."

"Former fiancé?" Charlie finally glanced at Robert.

"I'm sure she's mentioned me," Robert said confidently.

"No. Not really."

Robert's smile dropped.

Gisella forced back a laugh.

The men's keen gazes slowly assessed one another and, judging by their faces, neither was too impressed with the other.

"Well, I see you two are quite an item," Robert said and then clenched his jaw. "How long have you been dating?"

"Six months," Gisella answered the same time as Charlie replied "Two months." They glanced at each other and then switched positions.

"Two months."

"Six months."

Suspicion crept back into Robert's eyes. "I see."

An awkward silence drifted over the shop.

"I have to tell you," Charlie said. "I've never been happier since Gisella came into my life."

"Thanks…sweetheart." She laughed awkwardly. "I feel the same."

"I mean, the sex is like…incredible."

Gisella's eyes bulged.

A few women snickered and reminded Gisella that they had an audience. "Okay, *honey*. We don't need to talk about that."

"At first I didn't think I'd be able to keep up," Charlie added almost conspiratorially. "But my baby here was determined to coach me out of my shell. Ain't that right, *sweetie?*"

Instead of answering, she leaned forward and hissed, "I'm going to kill you."

"I love you, too, baby." He locked her chin between his fingers and silenced her with another kiss.

Forgotten once again, Robert coughed. "Well, that's that. I guess I should wish you two luck."

"Thanks, man. I appreciate that."

"Don't mention it." Robert's gaze drifted to Gisella. "It was nice seeing you again, Gigi. *Bon chance*."

"*Au revoir,* Robert."

His smile gone, Robert turned and walked out.

Gisella sighed in relief.

"You know," Charlie said. "You come up with the damnedest reasons to kiss me when all you have to do is ask."

Chapter 14

"You're incorrigible," Gisella said. "I swear I would slap you if I wasn't so grateful for you helping me out of a sticky situation."

Charlie's brows cocked in amusement. "You're welcome."

The shop hummed with activity again. "The drama up here beats anything I've seen of *General Hospital* in the last ten years," one woman said, laughing.

"The men are better-looking, too," her friend added as they left the shop with their arms loaded down with cake boxes and store bags.

Charlie leaned forward and whispered in Gisella's ear, "Frankly, I thought the leading lady was pretty hot, too."

She rolled her eyes but couldn't stop a smile from carving onto her face. "What are you doing here anyway?"

Charlie decided to dance around the truth. "Well, I was out feeling sorry for myself and thought that maybe one of your delicious cakes would cheer me up. Had I known that you were giving out chocolate kisses all willy-nilly, I would've come by sooner…and more often."

He watched as her cheeks darkened and he had another urge to kiss her. This time when he leaned forward, she leaned back.

"What are you doing?"

"What does it look like, sweetie?"

Belatedly, Gisella realized that she was still locked in his embrace. She cocked her head up at him with a sneaky suspicion that he was more than content to hold her. "You can let go now. The show is over."

"Are you sure, love muffin?" He pressed her closer. "Maybe we should keep the ruse up just in case he's outside watching us."

Gisella's gaze darted to the storefront window. Her eyes scanned the outside perimeter. Just when she was about to sigh in relief, her eyes caught sight of Robert sitting behind the wheel of a black Escalade across the street.

"*Mon Dieu.* He is out there."

"He is?" Charlie tried to turn to see for himself.

"Don't look." She pulled his body around, but only succeeded in placing her back against the glass and giving Charlie the street view.

"Ah, there he is," Charlie said, frowning. "What's the story with this guy? Is he a stalker or something?"

"No." Gisella shrugged. "I don't think he is, anyway."

"Maybe we should give him a good show." Charlie lowered his head but only to brush their noses together.

"What are you doing now?"

"You want to make it look good, don't you?"

She hesitated, but then forced herself to relax. "Why won't he just go away?"

"Maybe he's whipped," Charlie said, grinning. "You

look like the kind woman that could whip a man without batting an eye. You probably do adorable things like dance around the house in sexy lingerie and then throw a killer pussy in a man's face."

She gasped.

"A pussycat…I meant a pussycat."

"Sure you did." She tried again to wiggle out of his arms only to have him tighten his hold.

"Wait. Wait. Wait. He's looking again."

Before she could verify, Charlie swooped low and kissed her. This one was even more intoxicating than the last. He didn't understand what was happening. He just couldn't get enough. When they broke apart, they were both out of breath and had to rest their foreheads together.

"Is he still watching?" Gisella asked, panting.

Charlie cast a quick sidelong glance. The Escalade was gone. "Yeah. He's still there."

"Maybe I should go out there and talk to him again. I can't imagine what made him think we could get back together."

"Maybe *I* should have a talk with him."

She chuckled.

"What? Even with a bad ankle I can take him."

"It's not that," she laughed.

"Then what?"

"I don't know. You just struck me as being a lover, not a fighter."

Charlie's cheeks dimpled as a sly smile hooked into place. "You picked up on that, did you?"

"Actually I think it was the warning about you being a low-down, lying, sex-crazed egomaniac that some vet needed to put out of his misery to save unsuspecting women from being nothing but notches on his bedpost."

Charlie's hold loosened. "Damn, woman. That's one hell of memory you got there."

"I only remember things worth remembering."

Completely charmed and fascinated, Charlie took a chance and said, "Go out with me."

"No," she answered simply.

"No?" he repeated. "You don't want to at least think about it?"

"Hmm…no."

"Damn. You really know how to hurt a man's feelings."

She reached behind her back and pried open his arms. "You're a big boy. You can handle it."

Even though her words were soft and her smile was kind, the rejection felt like a steel punch to the gut. "May I ask why?"

Gisella quirked up her brows. "Honestly?"

"Go for it."

"To go out with you would be no different than going out with Robert. Both of you aren't looking for anything serious. You view women as playthings and give very little thought to their feelings as you cast them aside when you're done with them."

Charlie's arms finally fell to his sides. "That's not true… entirely."

"Sorry if I hurt your feelings." She flashed him an apologetic smile. "I better get back to work."

Charlie wasn't ready to give up. "What if I said that I was a changed man?"

"I wouldn't believe you."

"You don't pull any punches, do you?"

"I believe in being honest."

"Oh. Is that right?" Charlie's face lit up. "Then maybe I should go outside and share a little honesty with pretty boy Robert about our so-called relationship?" He took one step toward the door.

"No!" Gisella grabbed him by the waist again.

"Ooh. I love it when you play rough." Charlie laughed at her panic-stricken face.

Pamela, Krista and a couple of new customers whipped their heads in Gisella's direction.

"Sorry," she said to the small crowd and then narrowed her gaze at Charlie.

"Sounds to me that someone is a bit of a hypocrite," he said.

"All right. You got me. Sometimes honesty is *not* the best policy."

"Go out with me."

"No."

"Then I have to talk to Robert." He faked another move toward the door.

Gisella's grip tightened. "That's blackmail."

He shrugged with a crooked grin. "Sometimes a man has to take desperate measures to avoid eating alone. Trust me. I'm not exactly proud of myself right now." He glanced out the window. "Oh. He's looking again." Charlie's lips attacked. This time he made up his mind to take his fill of her. As a result, there was a lot of moaning and pressing together.

"Damn. Get a room already," a male customer commented as he exited with his purchases.

At long last, Charlie pulled away while Gisella wobbled on her legs with her eyes still closed.

"Say you'll go out with me."

"I…"

"Tomorrow night," he pressed. "I promise I'll be on my best behavior. I'll take you to the best restaurant."

Her eyes fluttered open. "I…can't."

"You gotta eat. A woman can't live off chocolate alone."

"I...shouldn't."

Sensing victory, he smiled. "But you will."

Their eyes locked. Gisella nibbled on her bottom lip, contemplating. "Just dinner?"

"Just dinner," he promised.

After listening to both the devil and the angel on her shoulders, Gisella took a leap of faith. "All right. I'll go out with you."

Charlie tried to celebrate by stealing another kiss, but Gisella whipped her head and peered out the window. "Heeey. He's not out there." She whirled back toward Charlie. "How long has he been gone?"

"Ten, fifteen minutes." At her gasp, he delivered a quick peck on her nose and winked. "Pick you up tomorrow at seven-thirty."

Chapter 15

"What in the hell was I thinking?" Gisella asked herself for the umpteenth time. She stumbled into her sister's apartment with her arms weighed down with groceries. "There's no way I can go out with him. I'm supposed to stay away from his kind," she argued. "He's a womanizer. A dog."

In the kitchen, she plopped everything onto the counter and nearly slumped to the floor herself. "And on the other hand, the man sure can kiss." She sighed.

Sasha meowed and danced around Gisella's feet. "Don't worry. I haven't forgotten about you," she said, gathering up her energy and retrieving a can of cat food from the cabinet.

After setting down Sasha's food and water, Gisella headed toward the shower, debating whether she needed to make it a hot one or a cold one since her mind and body kept responding to the memory of Charlie's kisses.

She settled on hot. When she closed her eyes to enjoy the pulsing water against her skin, Charlie floated around in her head with his soft lips and talented tongue. It was as if he had made love to her mouth. That was the only way to describe it.

Where was her shame, standing in the middle of her shop, *in front of Robert,* and allowing Charlie to hold and seduce her like that? And why was it that she craved for him to do it again?

She sighed, remembering how each time his tongue dipped and caressed her own, her heart had skipped a beat, but that was nothing compared to how her body tingled whenever the tips of her breasts pressed against his chest.

"I don't know why you're fighting it," Fantasy Charlie whispered in her ear. *"You know you want me."*

That was an understatement.

Before her imagination got carried away, Gisella shut off the water and climbed out of the shower. She dried off and rushed through her regime of oils and lotions as an attempt to keep Fantasy Charlie at bay. To be more contrary, she dressed in her old two-piece cotton pajamas instead of anything lacy or satiny.

"I still think you look sexy," Fantasy Charlie said, stretching across the bed.

"Oh, go away," she said. She climbed into bed and gave him her back.

Fantasy Charlie chuckled.

Maybe she should cancel the date. What was the point in going out with him? She still didn't know the story between him and her sister. The last thing she wanted was Anna's leftovers.

Plus, would she be able to handle herself and keep her knees locked against a man so charming and charismatic?

"You're kidding, right?" Fantasy Charlie rolled over and

laid his head against her arm. He smiled. *"We both know how tomorrow night is going to end."*

Her heart raced at the thought of their different shades of brown skin rubbing against each other.

Fantasy Charlie winked.

She swallowed.

"You shouldn't have agreed to that date," the angel on her shoulder scolded.

"Hey, I'm a changed man," Fantasy Charlie protested.

Gisella glanced up into his dancing hazel eyes while doubt crept around in her mind.

The devil on her left shoulder laughed. "I say we jump his bones the minute he shows up at the door."

"I second that motion," Fantasy Charlie said.

"You stay out of this," Gisella snapped.

He held up his hands in surrender. *"All right. But maybe you should answer the phone."*

She frowned at him and in the next second, the phone rang. Gisella whipped her head toward the nightstand and then back toward Fantasy Charlie.

He was gone.

Hesitantly, she answered. "Hello."

"I'm dreaming about tomorrow night," the *real* Charlie informed her in a deep, sexy baritone. "What about you?"

Gisella hedged on how to answer.

"Hello?"

"Yeah, I'm here," she said.

"You're not thinking about canceling, are you?" he asked with a note of trepidation.

She shrugged. "What if I said yes?"

"I'd remind you that we made a deal. One date in exchange for my silence. Remember?"

"Yes, but—"

"I'd hate to have to drive over to the Ritz Carlton and knock on Robert's room to have a man-to-man talk."

Gisella frowned. "You know where he's staying?"

"Let's just say that I like to take out insurance when brokering important deals." He chuckled.

She groaned.

"And don't bother trying to make me feel guilty about blackmailing you," he added. "I've already prayed for forgiveness."

Finally laughing at the situation and his tactics, Gisella gave up. "All right. You win."

"Touchdown. Picture me dancing in the end zone."

His laugh was infectious. Gisella smiled, turned off the light on the nightstand and burrowed beneath the sheets. "How did you get this number?"

"The Internet, remember."

"You're a regular detective."

"I view it as going after something I want."

"Do you always get what you want?"

After a long silence, he answered, "Not always. No."

There was unmistakable note of sadness in his voice. Gisella wondered at its source, but hesitated in asking.

"Anyway," Charlie said, snapping out of his melancholy. "I called because I wanted to tell you to dress sexy-casual tomorrow night. The more leg the better, but if you want to tease me with some cleavage action, too, I won't complain."

She laughed at his audacity. "Thanks for the information."

"Don't mention it. Can you dance?"

"I can hold my own...as long as my partner isn't a stripper pole. I'll leave that fine art to some of the other women you date."

"Ooh. Frenchie has claws. No wonder you and Killer get along so well."

She giggled. "Sasha is not a killer."

"Yeah, right. That orange puffball is lucky there's no such thing as a kitty jail, or I would have had her butt hauled downtown."

Gisella warmed at the sound of his laughter and realized that it was something that she could easily get used to hearing.

"It's late," he said. "I better let you get some sleep."

She didn't want to hang up, but wouldn't allow herself to admit it.

"Sweet dreams, Gisella."

"Sweet dreams."

Charlie disconnected the call and then smiled up at the ceiling in his darkened bedroom. With everything that was going on in his life, he couldn't believe that he'd found something so precious. He couldn't believe how much he was looking forward to his date with Gisella. He already missed holding and kissing her.

I've picked a hell of time to fall in love.

He flinched and his smile evaporated. Why on earth had he used the L-word? Surely, he wasn't *in love*. He hardly knew the woman.

Sure she was beautiful and charming. And maybe there was something about the way she looked at him that in one minute he felt like an awkward teenager and in the next he felt dominant and masculine.

Charlie rolled onto his side and stared at the wall.

Maybe there was something about the way their bodies snapped together like pieces of a puzzle when he kissed her. It was as if they were a natural extension of each other.

And whenever their mouths melded together, it was explosive.

No. He couldn't wait for tomorrow night.

"Remember, you promised to be on your best behavior," Fantasy Gisella said, suddenly appearing next to him.

"Trust me. I'm going to be the *perfect* gentleman."

The next day crawled at a snail's pace. Every five minutes, Charlie's gaze found its way to a watch or a clock. Once, he tried to tell the time by the angle of the sun. During meetings and conference calls, his mind kept drifting to the night's possibilities.

Charlie attempted a few more black book calls, but the majority of the B's and C's had either changed or disconnected their numbers.

Taariq dropped by and invited him to the Jocks and Jill's Sports Bar for lunch. He agreed but hardly paid attention to the food or the conversation.

"Are you all right, man?" Taariq asked. "I feel like I'm boring you or something."

Charlie blinked out of his trance and shook his head. "Sorry, bro. What were you saying?"

Taariq eyeballed him and then lowered his fork—an event that never happened when red meat was in the vicinity. "What's up with you? Me and the fellahs have been noticing you haven't exactly been acting like yourself."

"I don't know what you mean," Charlie lied.

"C'mon, man. What do I look like to you?"

Charlie almost laughed, especially since he was trying not to stare at the large bald spot Bobby had shaved on the side of his head.

"We're boys, remember?" Taariq said. "We've known each other for sixteen years. I know when something's up with you, man. Why don't you just spit it out?"

Guilt erupted in Charlie like a geyser. Here he was calling old flames and readily confessing the doctor's prognosis and he'd yet to tell the truth to the closest people around him. Mainly because once they knew, his life would irreversibly change. He wasn't ready for that right now.

"Nah, man. Everything's fine," he insisted, this time with his best poker face.

Their eyes locked for a long time before Taariq gave him a slow nod, but his eyes called him a liar.

Gisella tried on every dress in her closet—twice—and still didn't like any of them. Breaking sister rule number one, she went into Anna's room to raid her closet. It didn't help since 1. they had different body types, and 2. Anna's evening clothes were purchased back in the 1990s.

Sasha apparently found the whole thing amusing and followed Gisella from room to room.

In the end, Gisella decided on a short pale peach number that fell mid-thigh with a bubble hem. She felt self-conscious about her arms in the spaghetti straps, but confident that Charlie would be more than pleased about the amount of cleavage the dress displayed.

She accessed the various angles in the mirror about a hundred times and was just about to convince herself to change yet again, when the doorbell rang.

"He's early," she gasped. She turned toward Sasha curled up at the foot of the bed. "How do I look?"

Sasha cocked her head and then quickly dismissed Gisella to focus back on her own grooming needs.

"Thanks a lot." She took a final glance into the mirror and then rushed to answer the door. However, when she opened it her heart dropped.

"Nicole…Emmadonna…Jade…what are you girls doing here?"

The members of the Lonely Hearts Club shared their own astounded looks as their gazes raked over her.

Nicole jutted out a hip and crossed her arms. "We came to take you out," she said. "We figured with Anna still out of town that you'd want some company. Looks like we were wrong."

"Uh, er…"

Without waiting for an invitation, Nicole waltzed into the apartment. Her two cohorts followed.

Jade shook her head. "Here we are planning a girls night out, and you're creeping out the back door. Who's the hot date?"

Gisella's eyes bulged. No way was she telling this group she had a date with a man they considered to be the undisputed enemy to womankind. "Um, no one," she said, finding her tongue. The lie would have been more convincing if she wasn't standing in front of them in a three-hundred-dollar dress. "I have a business engagement."

"A *business* engagement," Nicole echoed. "What, did I just fall off the turnip truck this morning?"

Deciding to come clean, Gisella tossed up her hands. "All right. I have a date, and he's going to be here any moment."

Emmadonna chuckled. "Is that French for 'get lost'?"

"Must be." Jade laughed.

Gisella felt desperate. "Ladies, please. Thank you so much for thinking about me. Maybe we can do it another time."

The women stared.

"Promise?" Gisella added.

"All right," Jade said and straightened her shoulders. "We'll leave…but let me use your bathroom first." She turned and marched toward the hallway.

"I'm after you," Emmadonna chimed.

Gisella panicked. They were stalling. "Ladies, ladies, please." She raced behind them.

"Ooh," Nicole smirked. "This must be serious. You really don't want us to know who this guy is."

Emmadonna planted a fist against her plush hips. "What's the matter? Is he ugly?"

"No," Gisella protested.

"Fat?" Jade suggested.

Emmadonna looked heated. "What, you got something against plus-size people?"

"No. I. Don't." Gisella was close to losing her patience. "Now will you please…?"

Jade stepped into the bathroom and closed the door.

Gisella tossed up her hands and swore in French.

Emmadonna's neck swiveled around. "Girl, you're acting like you're scared we're going to try and steal your man or something."

"Yeah. Calm down," Nicole said. "We're just going to check him out for you. Make sure his ass is on the up and up. What you got to drink up in here?" She headed toward the kitchen.

The doorbell rang.

Gisella froze.

"Ooh. That's must be him now," Nicole whooped. "I'll get it."

"No. Nicole, wait." Gisella rushed behind her, but Nicole had amazing speed for a woman in heels. Toward the end, the race seemed to move in slow motion.

Nicole's hand landed on the doorknob, Emmadonna and Jade cackled in the background, and Gisella screamed, "No," because she, alone, knew what was about to happen.

"Come on in, lover boy," Nicole sang, opening the door.

All playfulness died when Charlie stood smiling in the doorway.

He looked good. Damn good in a pair of white slacks and a pale green top. In his hand, he held a single long-stemmed rose. Definitely casual-sexy.

"Good evening," he said.

"Hi," Gisella greeted breathlessly behind Nicole.

The ever busy busybody whipped around and stabbed Gisella with an accusing glare before swinging it back to Charlie.

"Oh. Hell. Naw," Nicole shouted and then promptly slammed the door in Charlie's face.

Chapter 16

What just happened?

Charlie blinked at the closed door and hit instant replay in his head, but it didn't help. However, he could hear angry voices on the other side. He leaned forward and pressed his ear against the door. A mistake, given how his name seemed interchangeable with *dog, jerk, asshole* and a few other words that weren't fit for Christian ears.

Clearly, Gisella's friends weren't exactly fans of his.

When he'd heard enough, he straightened up and knocked on the door with his cane's handle. To be safe, he braced for anything.

Thankfully, Gisella answered the door, but he noticed her smile was strained. One glance at the three glaring witches was a sufficient explanation. "Ladies." He tilted his head in a half bow. "Problem?"

"You damn right there's a problem," snapped the obvious leader. "You've lost your rabbit-assed mind if you think we're about to let you take our girl out tonight."

Gisella whipped her head around. "Nicole!"

"Gisella, girl. This man—"

"Enough!"

Charlie frowned. "Nicole, Nicole..." He searched through his mental Rolodex. A few images popped but none that resembled... "Wait a minute." He snapped his fingers and then entered the apartment. "I know you."

Nicole crossed her arms and cocked her head.

"Yeah. I remember now. You're Anna's friend from college." His lips quirked up. "The one that used to always pass out drunk at all the fraternity parties."

Nicole's face darkened. "Not always."

The friend to her right grabbed her by the arm. "Let's just go, Nic."

Charlie turned his attention to the attractive plus-size woman. "I know you, too, don't I?" He waited for his recollection to kick in.

"You sure do," the third woman said, with an unbelievable high-pitched voice. "You two hooked up at a club—"

"Jade, hush!"

"What, Em? You said—"

"That's it." Charlie snapped his fingers. "You tried to rape me at a bar once when I asked what you were drinking. Said something about dogs and bones and then jumped me."

"Emmadonna!" Her friends gasped.

Gisella snickered.

"*You* said that he was the one that—"

"I never said no such thing. Now let's go." Emmadonna clenched her purse strap, threw up her chin and then marched out of the apartment.

"But, Em," Jade said, rushing after her.

Nicole was the last to take her leave, but when she reached Gisella by the door, she cast a final glare at her. "Just wait until I talk to your sister."

"I make my own decisions, Nicole," Gisella said.

"Humph. We'll see." Nicole looked over her shoulder at Charlie. "As for you, try to keep it in your pants tonight." At last, she left the apartment.

Gisella closed the door behind her.

"Interesting group of friends you got there."

"Actually, they are my sister's friends." She drew in a deep breath. "I'm sorry about that."

"Don't be." He walked over to her, his limp less noticeable. "I'm the bad boy with the bad reputation. One that I unfortunately earned."

She gazed at him. "I have a long list of reasons why I shouldn't go out with you tonight. Your reputation being number one."

"I thought it was because I was blackmailing you," he said, smiling.

"That's number two."

He took a deep breath, fearing what she might say next.

"Like I was saying," she continued. "I have a long list of reasons *not* to go out with you and only one for why I should."

"And that is?"

Her beautiful, plump lips widened. "Because I *want* to."

"Sounds like a good reason to me." Charlie handed her the rose.

"Thank you." Gisella placed the delicate petals against her nose and inhaled its light fragrance.

To his surprise she stepped forward, leaned up on her toes and brushed a kiss against his cheek.

Charlie's eyes lit up. "Wow. What would I have gotten if I brought you a dozen?"

"I don't know." She shrugged. "Next time, bring a dozen and we'll find out."

He loved the way her eyes glinted when she flirted. Of course, he had to restrain himself from grabbing her and ravishing her on the spot. "Next time, eh?"

Gisella rolled her eyes.

"By the way, you look beautiful this evening."

"*Merci*. You look rather handsome yourself—but I think you know that."

Charlie winked. "Are you ready to go?"

"Let me just grab my purse and the wrap that goes with this. I'll be just a minute," she said.

"I'll wait right here."

Gisella left the living room just as Sasha made her grand entrance. Man and animal eyeballed each other, neither one trusting the other. The orange cat marched back and forth like an armed security guard parceling out meow warnings.

"I'm ready," Gisella said, returning and catching the ending of their tense stare down. "You two play nice." She laughed.

"I'm cool if she's cool." He opened the door.

"Mind if I ask where we're going?"

"Actually, I want it to be a surprise."

And a nice surprise it was, Gisella thought as they were escorted through the elegant Prime restaurant. The soft lighting and the contemporary elegance of the place made Gisella feel as if she was joining the city's posh elite.

"Would you like a bottle of wine?" their server asked.

"The house wine will be fine," Charlie said.

Gisella continued to look around, her face glowed when she stared out at the city's twinkling skyline.

"Do you like the restaurant?" he asked, watching her.

"It's lovely." She smiled. "I wasn't expecting grand. You said casual."

"This is casual, but if you want we can rush out of here and catch Arby's before it closes."

She laughed. "Maybe next time."

"Again with the next time." He leaned forward in his seat. "I'm beginning to suspect you like me."

"Maybe…or maybe I just like to play dress up every once in a while."

"Nice play." He wagged his finger. "You don't want me to get a big head."

"Don't you mean a *bigger* head?"

Charlie drew a deep breath and settled back in his chair. "You know, I think I'm heavily misunderstood."

Her delicate brows stretched. "Do you?"

"Absolutely," he said, putting on a serious face. "Women see a man like me, and they transfer their own perceptions of what I'm all about onto me. I very rarely have a say on the matter."

Gisella shook her head, smiling. "You said earlier that you earned your bad reputation. Which is it?"

He shifted in his chair. His Cheshire smirk wobbled into place. "I guess it would depend on one's definition of bad."

"Oh, really?"

"The definition varies between the sexes. For men, bad could be a good thing. Just as too much of a good thing could be bad. I like to think women believe I'm too much of a good thing. Anyway, I have a whole charting system on this if you ever want to come back to my place to study up on it."

Gisella's laughter was like music to his ears.

"Does that line usually work?" she asked.

"What line?" he asked innocently.

Their server returned and presented a bottle of the house

wine. Charlie nodded and waited as the cork was popped and their glasses were filled before returning to their conversation.

"So tell me about Sinful Chocolate. It looks like you have quite a lucrative business going."

Gisella took a sip of her wine and wondered where to begin. "It looks that way. I'm really happy how it's all working out. I can't remember a time when I wasn't cooking or baking. In my family it's an expression of life… love…everything. When you cook for people there's a connection. For some it's even an art form. Just like music or a painting, it can create and elicit memories. Let's face it, no one is sad when they are eating a good meal."

Charlie looked at her as if she was an angel descended from heaven. "If you cook half as good as you kiss I'm going to have to start calling you Mrs. Masters before long."

"If it's a princess-cut ring you just might have yourself a deal."

Charlie chuckled and then slowly realized that he hadn't stopped smiling since their date began. He adored how she had the tendency to talk with her hands or how her accent muddled some words and made others sound incredibly sexy. When their server returned, she allowed him to order for her and then when the food arrived, he was turned on by the many sounds she made when eating.

He hardly tasted his food. He was so enamored with everything about her he wasn't interested in anything else. Where had she been all his life, and how cruel was it for her to show up now?

"Charlie?"

Charlie reluctantly pulled his gaze away from Gisella to see an attractive woman head their way. He knew her. He was fairly certain.

She stopped at the table.

Joan? Lynn? Mya? No. That was that Girlfriends *show.*

"It's Lexi," she supplied. "When are you going to learn that TV name game doesn't work?"

Actually, she would be surprised, he thought.

"And who is your beautiful friend here?" Lexi asked.

Charlie shifted in his chair. A person would have to be deaf, dumb and/or stupid not to pick up on Lexi's thinly veiled jealousy.

"This is Gisella," he answered. "Gisella, meet Lexi."

"*Bonjour.*"

"Ah, French," Lexi cooed. "You're reeling them in from across the water now. Good for you. I think it's just so generous of you to *spread* the love."

Charlie's smile tightened. "Well, it was good seeing you again, Lexi."

Her fake smile dropped at the dismissal. "Fine. I'll see you around." She glanced at Gisella with a calculating sneer. "Have a…fun evening. It's likely all you're going to get."

Charlie and Gisella watched her leave.

Charlie relaxed.

Gisella asked, "Old girlfriend?"

"Something like that." Charlie grabbed his wineglass and drained it dry in one gulp.

"Humph." Gisella shook her head. "Bad boys and their forgotten toys."

Charlie didn't respond and hoped the subject would just drop.

Their dinner plates were removed, and dessert arrived with much fanfare, but it paled compared to Gisella's new orgasmic moans.

"You're killing me," he said playfully, hoping to reclaim their earlier mood.

"Oh, I'm sorry," she said, teasingly or innocently. He couldn't tell which.

"There's just so much moaning I can take," he warned. They lapsed back into their easy conversation, neither noticing how the restaurant was emptying.

"I have to ask you a question," she said after fidgeting for a while.

"Okay. Shoot."

She hesitated. Bit her lower lip.

"Must be serious," Charlie commented.

"What's the story between you and my sister?"

"Oh, that." Charlie stopped smiling.

"Where you two an item?"

"No." That part of the story was the easy part. "I misinterpreted her feelings toward me back in the day."

"Sounds like a habit of yours."

He blinked at the casual observance. "You might be right," he admitted.

"Tell me the story."

He did just that. From how they met to the ugly fight where Anna accused him of using her.

"To this day she was my only real female friend that didn't involve…you know."

Gisella nodded and looked much relieved.

"What did she tell you?" he asked.

"I haven't talked to her about it." She glanced up sheepishly. "I haven't *exactly* delivered your message yet. Sorry."

"Not *exactly* dependable, are you?" His smile returned.

"I was just afraid that you two…and I…forget about it."

"No, no, no. This sounds interesting." He leaned closer. "What were you afraid of?"

"Nothing. Forget I said anything."

"All right. But I'll get the truth out of you someday—somehow."

"There's just one thing I don't get," Gisella said. "Why did you look her up now? I mean, this happened so long ago."

Charlie dropped his gaze, his smile gone.

Gisella waited through the silence, sensing that wave of sadness again.

"No reason," he finally said. "She just crossed my mind again. Who knows, maybe you reminded me of her."

She couldn't prove it, but she thought he was lying to her.

Charlie glanced around. "It looks like we're the last ones here." He looked over at her empty plate. "Are you ready to go?"

She wasn't, but he clearly was. "Sure."

Gisella excused herself to the ladies' room while Charlie took care of the bill. At the vanity, she washed up and retouched her makeup. The entire time, she wondered if she'd said something wrong. When she returned to their table, he was back to being his old charming self.

Maybe she'd imagined the whole thing.

It was past one a.m. when they returned to her apartment building. Gisella's nerves were so frayed over the thought of a good-night kiss that it felt as if the Cirque du Soleil troupe was performing in the pit of her stomach.

Should she invite him in? What would happen if she did?

"You know what will happen," the devil said, popping up on her shoulder.

"Well, I guess this is it," Charlie said, stopping in front of her door.

"Yeah. I guess so." She smiled through an awkward pause and then unlocked and opened her apartment door.

"I, um, had a great time."

"So did I," he said, picking up on her nervousness. Usually, about now, Charlie would calculate and strategize on how to get invited in for a nightcap. But for some reason he didn't want to rush things with Gisella. This time, he wanted to do everything right. "Good night." He leaned forward and swept his lips against hers.

The electric jolt was instant and, as expected, their bodies snapped together completing the perfect puzzle. In truth, he could've held her all night and overdosed on the sweetness of her lips. He wanted her to know how special she was to him and in order to do that, he *couldn't* sleep with her.

He frowned at his conclusion. Had the day finally arrived Charlie Masters was *not* going to have sex with a beautiful woman?

Gisella was ready to throw caution in the wind and invite Charlie in for a nightcap and for anything else he wanted. She knew there was very good chance that she would regret her decision in the morning, especially if she woke to just a note on a pillow. There was little doubt this scene was routine for him, but there was also no denying just how much she wanted him. Maybe it would be worth the risk—as long as she reminded herself not to fall in love.

Then again, maybe it was a little too late for that, too.

When the kiss ended and the invitation was on the tip of her tongue, Charlie smiled and murmured a final, "Good night, Gisella. Sweet dreams." With that he turned and walked away, leaving Gisella standing in the hallway with her mouth open.

Chapter 17

One month later

"**Y**ou *still* haven't slept with him?" Waqueisha thundered before tossing her head back with a roar of laughter. "What did he do, turn in his playa's card?"

"Waqueisha," Isabella hissed. "You're not helping."

Gisella whisked a bowl of ingredients like she had a vendetta against eggs and flour. "We've been going out for a full month. A *month!* And all he does is drops me off at the door with a kiss good-night."

"Well, how are the kisses?" Isabella inquired gently.

"Wonderful...fantastic!" Gisella slammed the bowl on the counter. "Kissing isn't the problem. Getting him into my bed is. Hell, last night I was tempted to strip in the hallway just to get his attention. I mean, where is this sex-crazed egomaniac I keep hearing about? And why won't he have sex with me?"

"Don't forget the low-down, lying dog that needed to be put out of his misery part," Waqueisha reminded her. When the women glared at her, she turned defensive. "I'm just saying."

Gisella tossed her hands. "You know what? I don't even want to talk about it anymore. In fact, I'm not even sure I'm going to see him again."

"Sounds like somebody's in heat."

Isabella jabbed her hands on her hips. "Waqueisha, you're not helping."

"What? I'm just saying that your girl wants to get laid, and this Charlie dude needs to catch a clue."

Isabella started to argue when Gisella cut in, "She's right. I'm ashamed to say it, but I'm horny as hell, and Charlie is as cool as a cucumber."

"Have you thought about taking him to a seafood bar and feeding him oysters all night? They're supposed to be like some kind of aphrodisiac."

"I thought of that," Gisella said. "He's allergic to shellfish."

"Ms. Jacobs, there's a delivery for you," Krista said, poking her head back in the kitchen.

"Coming." Gisella sighed and washed her hands in the sink before rushing up front.

"Are you Ms. Gisella Jacobs?"

"Yes, sir," Gisella said, walking toward the UPS man.

"Sign here."

She quickly raced over and signed the package. "Amélie DeLorme. It's from *ma grandmère*," she said, stunned and walked to the back office. What on earth was her grandmother sending her?

Sitting down at her small desk in her matchbox-size office, Gisella ripped into the package. Buried beneath a mountain of packing popcorn was a large decorative wooden box.

"*Recettes secrètes.*" Gisella gasped. Her *grandmère*'s secret recipes. Barely able to contain her excitement, Gisella bounced in her chair and then carefully pulled open the top. Immediately, she recognized the beautiful pen strokes on the three-by-five decorative postcards. "I can't believe it."

Gisella glanced back at the UPS box and wondered if there was also a note. She searched through the packing peanuts and withdrew a lavender-colored envelope with her name written in the same elegant penmanship.

Grabbing the letter opener from her desk, she ripped the top and unfolded the delicate lavender stationery.

"Is it something good?" Isabella asked. She and Waqueisha popped their heads into the office.

"It's more than good," Gisella sighed. "She sent me the recipe for *Amour Chocolat!*"

The announcement left Isabella and Waqueisha clueless.

"This means my little problem with Charlie Masters is over."

"You need to file bankruptcy?" Taariq braided his large hands and leaned over his desk. "Brother, I didn't even know you were in trouble. Why didn't you come to me sooner?"

Charlie drew in a deep breath and worried whether his massive migraine was going to do him in. "Nobody knew. I haven't told anyone. The last couple of years, I've done everything I could to stay afloat, but I'm going to have to shut down the office soon. I won't be able to make payroll past next week.

"This market has just dried up in Atlanta. There are too many commercial contractors like myself playing cut-throat politics for the few contracts that come available. Hell, I've even lost the bid on a few government and foreign contracts. Man, it's just time to just cut my losses and move on."

He looked over at his friend and appreciated the absence of sympathy and pity in his expression. "Can you help me out?"

"Sure." Taariq shrugged. "I just thought that you had your own set of corporate lawyers for this kind of thing."

"If I can't make payroll I certainly can't bankroll a team of expensive lawyers."

"I'm not exactly cheap, either," Taariq reminded him. A playful smirk hooked the corners of his lips. "But I guess I can see about getting you a discount, being that you're like family and all."

A genuine smile bloomed across Charlie's face. "Thanks, man. I appreciate that." He placed his fingers against his temples and gave them a vigorous rub.

"Are you all right, man?"

"Yeah. Sure. I've just been suffering from some killer migraines lately." Charlie flashed him a weak smile. "Probably from all this stress from the job."

"With Masters Holdings folding, how are you doing—financially, I mean? Is there anything I can help you with?"

"Nah, man. Thanks. Most of my personal situation is separated from the company. I still might have to give up a few toys until I launch into a second career, but other than that, I'm doing good. Thanks for asking."

Taariq nodded.

"Well, I better go. I'll get the financials together from the accounting department to you by the end of the week."

"Trust me. It's going to take you longer than a week to get everything we need together. But don't worry, if you need for me to roll up my sleeves to help out, you got it."

"Thanks, man. I appreciate it."

"Appreciate hell. You see about getting me an invitation to Momma Arlene's meals, and we can just about call this transaction square."

Charlie laughed. "Consider it done."

The men shook on it.

However, when Charlie stood to leave, he experienced a severe case of vertigo and wobbled on his feet before plopping back down.

"Whoa." Taariq leapt from his chair and raced around his desk. "What's going on with you?"

"I'm cool. I'm cool." Charlie shook his head. "Any way I can get some aspirin?"

"Sure. Hold on." Taariq quickly buzzed his assistant.

Less than a minute later, Charlie was handed two pills and a large glass of water. The whole time he could feel the weight of Taariq's gaze.

"Have you seen a doctor? You don't look so good."

Charlie chuckled and tried to dismiss his concerns. "It's just a migraine. Nothing serious."

"You've been having a lot of those lately."

"I already have one mother."

Taariq's hands shot up in surrender. "Hey, don't shoot the messenger."

"Don't worry, man. As soon as these pills kick in, I'll be good as new."

She didn't know what she was looking for. It was the second time she'd managed to gain access to the exclusive high-rise apartment and broke in to Charlie's bachelor pad. It was easy to do since her brother was head of security.

The last time she was in here, she'd totally trashed the place. But that, just like when she vandalized his car, she'd hoped the act of revenge would make her feel better.

It didn't.

Especially now that it seemed like the philandering playa had a new girlfriend.

French bitch.

In the last month, she'd followed them all over town. Every other night it seemed they were either going to some play or movie or concert or eating at the most exclusive restaurants. At first she thought she was mistaken about their relationship. As far as she could tell, Charlie and his foreign-exchange girlfriend had yet to spend the night together. It made no sense because just watching him with her, she could tell he was crazy about her.

Always smiling.

Always touching.

Always kissing.

The constant public show of affection was enough to make her gag. There's no doubt about it, Charlie Masters was in love.

So why weren't they sleeping together?

Was that the secret to winning his heart—keeping your legs closed? What kind of prehistoric thinking was that?

She drew a deep breath as her anger returned in full force. Her friends told her to stay away from him. Why didn't she listen?

She took another glance around the apartment, looking for something—anything—she could use to extract her next wave of revenge. But as soon as she walked into his bedroom, she was caught up in his world.

In his closet, she roamed her hands over his suits and shirts. At his chest of drawers, she sniffed his cologne and even dabbed a little bit on her wrists. The pinnacle, of course, was when she climbed into his bed and hugged his pillows against her chest.

Lost in her own fantasy, she almost didn't hear when the apartment's front door opened and then slam shut.

He's home.

She jumped off the bed and scrambled around in a circle, trying to think. Soon his heavy footsteps filled the hall.

I'm going to get caught.

She had seconds to find a hiding place.

After a hard day, Charlie entered his bedroom and started peeling out of his suit. He was looking forward to his date with Gisella. Just being around her was like a soothing balm to his soul. She calmed him. Grounded him.

She was everything a man could hope for—beautiful, funny and smart. As much as he wanted to make love to her, he was proud of himself for holding back. Without sex, he was free to discover Gisella the woman. He might not have appreciated her if he'd, like he usually did, rushed to sex.

Tonight, she said she wanted to cook him a homemade meal. She bragged that she could go toe-to-toe with his mother. If she could, he just might have to go through on his promise and buy her a ring.

He was leaning toward buying her one anyway.

Of course, he didn't know how she would feel about marrying a man who was on the verge of losing everything and whose days were possibly numbered.

Charlie ignored the pinprick of guilt for not keeping his doctor's appointments and for even ducking the bone marrow test. The main reason he'd bypassed the test was because he felt fine. How could he be dying when he felt as healthy as a horse?

Most of the time.

He thought about the increasing number of migraines he'd had, but he wasn't convinced that they weren't products of the amount of stress he'd been under on the job. Then there was the vertigo.

"I'm fine," he insisted with a firm shake of his head. He refused to think about the matter anymore. He needed to rush. There was just enough time for a quick shower before his date.

Charlie turned toward the adjoining bathroom and stopped cold. His hackles rose unexpectedly and he cast a curious glance around the room. Something was wrong. Something wasn't quite right about the room.

His gaze skittered over toward the bed and he noticed the sheets were wrinkled. Didn't the maid come this morning? Just then he sniffed the air, but he only smelled his cologne.

"Okay, old boy. You're imagining things." He laughed and left the bedroom.

Underneath the bed, she watched Charlie disappear into the bathroom. She held her breath until he turned on the shower. Relieved, she dropped her head against the carpet and waited for her heartbeat to return to normal.

Soon after, Charlie started singing a lame version of New Edition's "Candy Girl," and she crawled out from her hiding place. Despite knowing that she needed to get the hell out of there, she instead crept toward the bathroom with the overwhelming desire to see Charlie naked.

You're going to get caught!

It was a real possibility, she knew. When she was just a few inches from the door, she stopped and stood there a full minute, debating.

Finally, she backed away and rushed to leave his bedroom. But at the door, she stopped again. Something caught her eyes.

A book.

She picked it up and flipped through its page. "Well, I'll be damned." A broad smile stretched across her face. She had just hit the jackpot.

Still singing, Charlie shut off the water and grabbed a towel. He walked back into his bedroom, patting himself dry when he heard the unmistakable sound of his front door slamming shut.

Chapter 18

It had been so long since Gisella had tried to seduce a man that she worried whether she even remembered how. Luckily, she had a secret weapon. Once she'd received her grandmother's recipe box, she immediately left the shop in search of the foreign ingredients for *Amour Chocolat*. Of course, once she told the women at the shop the urban legend surrounding the recipe they'd all clamored for a piece of the action.

"A date-rape cake," Fantasy Charlie said. He shook his head. *"It's a sad day in Gotham."*

"Stop it." Gisella frowned, carefully setting the night's dessert down on the kitchen counter. "It's not a date-rape cake...it's date-*enhancer* cake," she corrected.

"You say tomato."

"Desperate times call for desperate measures," she said.

"I'm starting to think that you're getting sick of me."

"No offense. But I'm ready for the real thing." She smiled and winked.

Like a tornado, Gisella hit the kitchen and prepared her favorite roasted herb chicken, steamed some vegetables and made sure that she had plenty of red wine. Since it was her first time cooking a home-cooked meal for Charlie, she wanted everything to be perfect.

After a record-breaking shower, a rush through some hot curlers and tossing on a simple black dress, the doorbell rang.

"Showtime." Fantasy Charlie's voice floated around in her head.

Sasha meowed from the corner of the bed.

"Wish me luck, girl." Gisella raced to the door. "Good evening."

Charlie, holding yet another single red rose, took his time allowing his gaze to roam over her body. "As usual, you look lovely," he praised.

"And you look equally debonair," she returned, accepting the rose. Gisella inhaled its fragrance and then turned to add it to the near two dozen, in different stages of bloom, sitting in a vase in the entryway.

"It smells wonderful in here," Charlie said.

"I hope you brought a hearty appetite." She closed the door behind him. "I plan on giving your taste buds a night they'll never forget."

"Be still my heart. You're talking the language of love now." Without warning, his arms snaked around her waist and pulled her pliant body toward him.

When he pressed his pillow-soft lips against hers, Gisella emitted a submissive whimper. She loved how easily he dominated her body or how with a flick of his tongue she was reduced to putty in his hands.

"I missed you," he panted when he pulled away.

"It hasn't even been twenty-four hours since our last date," she said breathlessly.

"It still felt like a lifetime."

Gisella knew exactly what he meant. Her body seemed to count the seconds from their last touch. "Did you remember the movie?"

He held up a video box. "Your favorite. *Mahogany*."

"Good boy. I just might keep you around."

Smiling into each other's eyes, they held each other a little while longer and swayed to the music inside their heads. In what was becoming the norm, Charlie pulled away when the outline of his erection pressed against her belly. She didn't understand why he continued to resist his attraction toward her.

"Now let's see if you can back up all that trash talk about being able to beat my momma's cooking."

"Oh, I can back it up. I just hope you brought my ring."

Charlie laughed as she led him by the hand toward the dining room. "Can I help you with anything?"

"You can light the candles and pour the wine," she said before heading off toward the kitchen.

Minutes later, Gisella set their dinner plates on the table. "*Bon appetit*."

Charlie closed his eyes and dramatically inhaled the food's rich aroma. "Damn, woman. You already have my mouth watering." Before digging in, Charlie stood and pulled back her chair.

"Ah, a true gentleman." She sat down.

"I gotta take care of the cook." He brushed a kiss against her cheek and then returned to his seat. "I really appreciate you wanting to cook for me."

"It was my pleasure, and I fully expect for you to return the favor in the near future."

He laughed. "I don't know my way around the kitchen too much, but I can work a mean grill."

"Then barbeque it is."

Charlie took her hand and recited the Lord's prayer. Afterward, he clapped his hands and rubbed them together. Ready to dig in.

Anxious, Gisella watched. She wouldn't admit in a million years that she was actually nervous for his critique. As if sensing her anxiety, Charlie took his time cutting, inspecting and even smelling it again.

Gisella finally smacked him on the hand. "Stop it. You're killing me."

Laughing, Charlie took his first bite. Instantly, his eyes closed while he released a long moan of pleasure.

Gisella smiled as her chest puffed with pride.

"Oh, woman. You put your foot in this," he praised.

The smile melted off her face. "I did not!"

Charlie's eyes sprang opened before he rocked back in his chair laughing. "That's a Southern saying. It just means you put your best foot forward. You know. You gave it all you got."

"Oh." She fluttered a hand across her chest in great relief.

Charlie cut bigger and bigger pieces of his chicken and then moaned louder and louder. The biggest compliment came when he blinked his big hazel eyes at her and asked for seconds. "I have to be honest. I didn't think you had it in you, but I'm going to have to give it to you. You can give Momma a run for her money."

"Thank you." She beamed, handing him his second plate.

"I just need to know whether you want a church or an outdoor wedding."

"I don't know. I'll have to get back to you on that." They

laughed and then fell into easy conversation. Gisella imagined them doing this for years to come. She could picture them gray-haired with a loving family surrounding them. In that moment, she was the happiest woman on earth.

"You make sure you save room for dessert," she said. "I made something special just for tonight."

"Bring it on."

Gisella disappeared into the kitchen and then returned with the cake. Lifting the glass lid, she presented the intricate design of flowers and ribbons. *"Paraît bon?"*

"Looks beautiful." Charlie patted his stomach. "I'm going to have to double up my time in the gym being with you."

"There's other ways of working off extra calories," she said teasingly.

Charlie caught her meaning. "Is that right?"

She shrugged and then sliced him a piece of cake.

"Now what do we call this?" he asked accepting his dessert.

"It's a special recipe from my *grandmère*. It's called *Amour Chocolat*."

"'Love chocolate'?"

"More like 'chocolate love.'"

Charlie's brows sprang up. "Sounds erotic."

"It is. Wait until you taste it."

"All right." Charlie dug in and his face immediately collapsed with pleasure. "Oh, this is gooooood," he moaned, and then stuffed another piece into his mouth. When he cleaned his plate, he turned to her. "I mean it. You have to marry me. Say you'll marry me."

"Stop it before I think you're being serious."

"I am serious."

It was hard to tell whether he meant it or whether it was

the food talking. However, Gisella started to panic when he then sliced himself another piece of cake…a larger piece.

Was it possible to have too much? Could a person overdose on passion?

"Are you not going to have some?" he asked.

Gisella blinked out of stupor and sliced herself a thin piece. But one bite also had her moaning and shoveling it in.

"Wow." Charlie pulled on his collar. "Is it me, or is it getting hot in here?"

"It *is* a little warm." She checked the thermostat, but it read a cool seventy-four degrees.

"Everything looks normal," she said, returning to the living room. Gisella arms started tingling and then the sensation raced across her body. Suddenly she was very aware of her lacy bra brushing against her nipples as she walked.

Charlie watched her intently as she came back into the living room. She still had the sexiest walk he'd ever seen.

Those legs.

That butt.

Those hips.

Those breasts.

That face.

Charlie shifted in his chair, trying to give his erection a little more room. "That dress…you sure look good." He licked his lips.

Gisella watched the intriguing path of his tongue and stared fascinated at how it left his lips glistening beneath the candlelight. "Oh, goodness."

Charlie smiled and suggested, "Maybe we should go watch that movie now." The glint in his eyes said that the movie was the last thing on his mind.

"All right," she said, feverishly.

Charlie stood and carried their two wineglasses.

In the living room, Gisella turned on the ceiling fan, hoping the breeze would cool her down. She walked over to the DVD player, fumbled with the buttons before she realized she didn't have the movie. "Whew. Where's my head?" She turned around but bumped straight into Charlie's hard chest.

That was all it took to ignite the fire.

Chapter 19

Gisella and Charlie came together in a flurry of movements. He yanked her dress down from her shoulders, and she pulled his shirt over his head before attacking his belt and pants. They were hot and ravenous for each other's taste.

Charlie leaned her back and stooped his head low and tore at her lacy bra with his teeth. She whimpered when he managed to suck her enlarged and erect nipple into his mouth.

Together they crumpled to the floor.

Charlie's mouth roamed from breast to breast while his hands explored the rest of her. Every move and stroke inflamed her passion and made her greedy for more.

This was what she wanted. This was what she needed.

Charlie didn't know what was happening to him, but he sure as hell was going to enjoy it. As his lips brushed and his fingers touched, he could feel himself fall deeper and deeper into an abyss. Nothing pleased him more to see that her beautiful nipples were, indeed, the color of brown sugar and tasted just as sweet.

"Oh, Gisella." He sucked in a ragged breath. "What are you doing to me?"

"Th-the cake."

He was sure he misunderstood her and continued to travel down her body until he was dragging off her panties with his teeth. Once he'd cleared them from her ankles, he tossed them across the room where he was sure they had landed over a lampshade.

As he climbed back up her body, he had a breathtaking view of the small spring of curls between her legs. He glided upward, raining tiny kisses along the way. When he reached her center, the scent of strawberries overwhelmed him and caused his mouth to water.

"Open up for me, baby," he instructed hoarsely.

Slowly, her knees lowered and pointed in opposite directions. Charlie's erection threatened to punch a hole through the floor when he took two fingers and spread her brown lips to see her luscious cherry pulsing like a heartbeat.

Like a moth to a flame, Charlie dove in, lips first, and sapped her glistening juices.

"Ooh, Ch-Charlie."

Gisella's head rocked from side to side while every limb quivered and writhed. Where it was hot before, the room now encroached on being sweltering. Her body forgot how to breathe. When his tongue made lazy circles, she would pant, but when his tongue would dip in deep, she would hold her breath until she was ready to pass out from the pleasure or simply from lack of oxygen.

To add to the merciless torture, Charlie eased in one finger and then two while his tongue just focused on polishing her clit. His fingers began to stroke, and Gisella lost all ability to think.

She could only feel.

"Damn, baby. You taste so good," Charlie praised and went back to his real dessert.

Her hands roamed over his head and then her fingers dug into his broad shoulders. Then with little warning, her body exploded. At least that was what it felt like. Surely, she had shattered into a million pieces.

Charlie left her lying on the floor, her body quivering from aftershocks to search for his pants. "Please let there be a condom in here. Please," he begged.

God answered his prayers.

He ripped open the packet and sheathed his large erection before crawling back toward her like a prowling panther.

Awakening from her daze, Gisella pulled herself up from the floor and with a strong urge to prove that she could give as well as she could take. In the end her strong panther gave little resistance when she directed him to "lie back."

Charlie's hazel green eyes lit with undeniable lust while his lips curled into a grateful smile. What a woman, he thought when she climbed on top.

"I hope you forgive me in the morning," she said.

Again, Charlie didn't understand her meaning. Whatever it was, he was more than happy to talk to her about it…in the morning.

Gisella eased down, inch by glorious inch. Charlie sucked in his breath, thinking her inner muscles were going to milk the life out of him before they really got started. When she had at last taken in every inch of him, she nearly caused his eyes to roll out the back of his head when her hips rolled in perfect circles.

"Oh, baby."

"You like that?" she purred.

Like it? He loved it. He tried to speak again, but found the job nearly impossible.

The circles were replaced with a gentle back-and-forth action. Then she set a nice rhythm where she combined the two. Words tumbled out of Charlie's mouth, but he doubted that they made much sense. He just didn't want her to stop.

Charlie's hands glided over her hips and then climbed up to cup and squeeze her full breasts. Her nipples were hard as marbles pressing against his palms. Even that turned him on.

To up the ante, Gisella started to bounce. Charlie's hands fell away to grip her hips again. Soon the sound of their bodies slapping against each other filled the room. Wanting to double her pleasure, Charlie's hands continued to roam until they slid in between their moving bodies.

Her rhythm faltered when the pads of his fingers rubbed against her clit. And just like that, he was back in control.

Stars danced behind Gisella's closed eyelids. The sound of her rushing blood roared in her ears.

"You coming, baby?" he asked softly.

She couldn't speak as he rolled her onto her back. He hiked her legs over his shoulders and braced his weight on his folded knees.

"Hmm? You coming?"

Awkwardly, she nodded.

"Wait for me," he instructed. "I'm going to come with you." He folded over and took one of her bouncing nipples into his mouth.

Charlie's lips roamed over one luscious curve after another as he tried to sink deeper into the nectar of this sweet honeycomb. Yet, no matter how long or hard he stroked, he couldn't seem to reach his destination. Sure, she matched his rhythm and at times accelerated past him, but he would always catch up.

He wanted…no, he *needed* more from her.

He shook the bizarre thought from his head and then lost himself in the low melodious moans spilling from her lips. Even her voice was an aphrodisiac, he realized as sweat beaded his forehead, and his hands kneaded her soft, round breasts.

Harder.

Faster.

Her muscles tightened into a smooth sheath and Charlie's breath hitched in anticipation. Ecstasy was just a few strokes away. He could feel it.

"You ready, baby?"

In answer, she cried out his name.

In the next heartbeat, a white light flash behind his eyes and his body exploded as he growled against her shoulder. A calm and something undeniable filled his heart.

"Gisella," he whispered, closing his eyes and gathering her close. "I love you, baby."

Chapter 20

"You drugged me?" Charlie asked, chuckling.

Gisella glanced down where Charlie lay between her breasts. "Not exactly," she hedged. "It was more like a… stimulant."

"Oh, really?" His eyes twinkled.

"No different than if I'd served you a plate of oysters."

"I don't know what kind of oysters you eat over in France, but that cake could put Viagra out of business." He laughed while lazily rolling her puckered nipples between the pads of his fingers.

Gisella smiled as her eyes fluttered closed so she could enjoy the wondrous sensations her man stirred within her. They had made love for most of the night. Both were surprised and pleased by each other's stamina and, judging by what she was feeling rising against her leg, they were far from being done.

"Are you upset?"

"What, for seducing me?" He laughed. "Oh, yeah, I'm *real* mad about that." He climbed her body and pinned her hands above her head. "I better hold you here so you're not tempted to lure more unsuspecting men here with that dangerous chocolate." Charlie's eyes lit up. "You wouldn't happen to have a pair of handcuffs lying around, would you? That could be fun."

Giggling, Gisella tried to buck him off of her. "Well, I had to do something. I was getting tired of taking cold showers."

"Aww. Do I make you horny, baby?" Charlie asked in his best Austin Powers impression.

She tried to reach a pillow so she could hit him with it, but only succeeded in rocking against him even more. She finally went still when she felt the head of his morning erection against the apex of her sex.

He snickered. "So you *do* know how to behave. Good to know." He slid his cock back and forth along the top of her clit.

Gisella's eyes glazed with desire.

"You want to know why I resisted making love to you before last night?" he asked.

Their gazes locked.

"Because from the moment I saw you, I knew that you were special, and I wanted to treat you as such. I didn't want just one thing from you. I wanted *everything.*"

A tide of emotion swelled within Gisella. "I want everything, too." Tears trickled from the corner of her eyes.

Charlie smiled. "I meant what I said last night."

She blinked up.

"I love you." He leaned forward and brushed his lips across hers. "I've never said that to any other woman."

Gisella's vision blurred as her tears became a flood. "I love you, too."

"Does that mean you'll marry me?"

She nodded vigorously, not having to think twice on her answer.

Charlie's smile stretched as he finally dipped his hips and entered her in one smooth stroke.

Gisella gasped and then wrapped her long limbs around his waist. At the feel of his deep, long and steady strokes, she thrashed her head among the pillows. She didn't know how much more she could take, but there was one thing she knew for sure—heaven indeed existed on earth.

He released her hands, and she quickly glided them around his broad shoulders and then dug her short nails into moist skin. While their bodies rocked, their mouths locked and sealed their souls together.

This wasn't sex.

This was making love.

They wanted this moment in time to last forever, but as their bodies' friction drove them to higher planes, a familiar and powerful sensation tried to rob them of breath.

Feverish, she couldn't understand the words tumbling from his lips. But seconds before her orgasm detonated, Charlie's words were clear.

"IloveyouIloveyouIloveyouIloveyouIloveyouIloveyou."

With those words ringing in her ears, Gisella came.

"I'm glad you're back," Nicole said, leading the march behind Anna as she entered her apartment. "You need to nip this whole Charlie Masters thing in the bud."

Anna shook her head. "Believe me. I'm going to have a loooong talk with her."

Nicole sucked her teeth. "I tried that, but Ms. Thang told me how grown she was and that she made her own decisions. I *told* you Charlie was going to be on her like white on rice. Now didn't I?"

"Sho did," Emmadonna co-signed.

"Well, she is a consenting adult," Jade added in her pipsqueak voice.

The three women stopped in the apartment's entryway, turned and looked at Jade as if her middle name was Judas.

"What? I'm just stating a fact."

Emmadonna settled her hands on her thick hips. "Charlie is a dog. That's a fact, too."

"Amen," Anna and Nicole praised.

"Just like it's a fact Em lied when she said she'd slept with him."

"I never said that," Emmadonna said.

"You did, too."

"Ladies," Nicole interrupted. "Focus."

Anna turned around and nearly tripped over Sasha. "Hey, baby," she cooed and then glanced up at the table. "What the hell? Is she starting a floral shop now, too?" she asked, noting the large vase of roses.

"Hmmph. We're probably too late," Nicole said. "He's had her all to himself for a month. That's more than enough time for him to have the girl whipped."

"A month," Anna said. "I've been calling her at least every other day, and she hadn't said a word."

"Like I said…" Nicole snapped an imaginary whip.

"Since when does Charlie date someone for a month?" Anna said. "He doesn't *do* relationships. Remember?"

Jade shrugged. "Maybe it's serious."

Again, the three women stared at her.

"What?"

Anna rolled her eyes and walked away. She didn't get far. The sight of dirty dishes and an open bottle of wine left on the dining room table snagged her attention. "What the hell?"

"Hmm. Looks like someone had a hot date last night," Nicole said.

Anna walked away from her rollaway luggage to check out the living room. Half-empty glasses of wine were left on the coffee table, but it was the lampshade that drew everyone's eye.

"What the…is that what I think it is?" Emmadonna said.

"Interesting place to hang your panties," Jade snickered.

Anna kicked a pair of male slacks on the floor and then bent to pick up the wallet that was hidden underneath.

"Any bets on who the mystery man is?" Nicole asked.

Anna hadn't realized that she was holding her breath until she flipped open the leather wallet and stared at Charles Masters's driver's license. "I'm going to kill him."

Charlie discovered that Gisella was ticklish. Not just a little, but extremely ticklish—and just about everywhere.

"Stop, stop, stop," she begged while whacking him over the head with a pillow.

He had no intentions of stopping. He attacked under her arms, her sides and a few times on the soles of her feet. "Who's the best?" he taunted. "Tell me who's the best."

"No!"

Bam! Bam! Bam!

Gisella's bedroom door rattled on its hinges, instantly ending the lovers' naked horseplay.

"Gisella, I need to talk to you!"

"Anna," Gisella gasped.

"I guess that means she's back home," Charlie said.

"Hide! She can't see you."

"I know Charlie's in there," Anna said, letting them know she could hear them.

"Yeah, we know he's in there," Nicole chimed.

Gisella groaned.

"Strange echo," Charlie said.

"It's the Lonely Hearts girls," Gisella muttered.

"Whoa. I don't do groups."

Grabbing a pillow, she whacked him on the head and watched him fall back in a dramatic death scene. "Will you stop playing? We gotta do something."

"What? She knows I'm in here." He shrugged and then folded one arm behind his head.

For not taking the situation serious, Gisella gave him one good shove and flipped him over the edge of the bed. He landed with a loud thud and then quickly popped his head up.

Gisella slapped a hand over her mouth to stop herself from laughing.

"When we're married, I won't put up with domestic violence from you."

"Gisella!"

Bam! Bam! Bam!

"Hide in the bathroom," she directed, scrambling out of bed and wrapping the top sheet around her body. "Take a shower or something."

He frowned. "What, are you ashamed of me now?"

Why was he being so difficult? "Please," she begged.

"Oh, all right." Charlie struggled to his feet, but when he took two steps he had to grab hold of the bed.

"Are you all right?"

"Just a little dizzy," he chuckled. "Must have gotten up too fast." He stood again and walked a crooked line to the bathroom.

She watched him, frowning, until her sister continued to shout her name. "I'm coming," she snapped and stomped toward the door. When she cracked it open, Anna looked like she was ready to breathe fire. "Yes?"

"What are you doing," she hissed.

Gisella cocked her head. "Surely, it hasn't been *that* long for you."

Anna sucked in a breath. "You're making a *big* mistake." She shoved Gisella and Charlie's clothes through the door. "That man is nothing more than a roaming dog searching for a place to bury his bone."

Gisella laughed. "Did you come up with that on your own?"

Her sister glared. "Trust me. He'll only break your heart."

"Why, because he broke yours?" she challenged. At Anna's stricken look, she tried to apologize. "Anna—"

"So he told you?"

"Told her what?" Emmadonna planted her nose into the conversation.

The sisters stared at one another. After a long pause, Anna's voice dropped into a trembling whisper. "That was a long time ago. I thought…we were just friends."

"It's not important," Gisella said, matching her sister's tone. "He actually came here last month looking for you. Said something about wanting to apologize—"

"Look, Gisella. What happened or didn't happen between us in college doesn't matter. What matters is his reputation. He doesn't stick around. He never has, and he never will."

"It's not like that with us."

Nicole chimed up. "Girl, do you know how many women have thought that?"

"Nicole," Anna snapped. "This is an A-and-B conversation. Will you please C your way out of it?"

"Let's just talk about this later," Gisella said.

The shower came on in the bathroom.

Her sister crossed her arms. "I want him out of here."

"No."

Anna's brows arched. "What?"

"I pay rent. This is my apartment, too, and I say he stays."

"Gisella…"

"I love him." Judging by the pain that stretched across her sister's face, one would have thought Gisella had stabbed her. "And he loves me."

Anna jabbed a hand onto her hip. "What? He told you that?"

"As a matter of fact, he did. So you might as well get used to seeing him around…because we're getting married." Before any of them could respond to that, Gisella firmly closed the door in their faces.

Charlie stood beneath the shower's steady water flow with his arms braced against the tile. He waited for this latest wave of vertigo to pass. The episodes were happening more often and were frankly scaring the hell out of him.

The test. He needed to take the test.

He shook his head, confused as to what he was doing. How could he possibly be making plans to marry Gisella when he didn't know what the future held?

He was being selfish.

"So what if you are?" the devil on his shoulder asked. "What's wrong with grabbing hold of a little happiness before you kick the bucket?"

The angel on his right refuted that. "You have to tell her the truth."

"No way, José," the devil said. "Who wants to deal with all that crying?"

Charlie thought about all the women he'd spent the last month calling, seeking and hoping to give closure to any open-ended issues. How easy it had been to tell *them* he was dying. But the woman he loved? He shook his head.

I can't tell her.

"Mind if I join you in there?"

Charlie turned toward Gisella's smiling face and felt his strength return. "I can always use a good back scrubber."

In the shower, Charlie and Gisella spent more time being dirty than getting clean. It wasn't until the water heater gave out and started pelting icicles on them did they finally scramble to get out.

Dried and dressed, Gisella's stomach rumbled. "I'm starving. We already missed breakfast. You want to head down to Oscar's for some lunch?" she asked.

"Sure, but for future reference, this brother can always eat."

She laughed. "I'll keep that in mind." She started toward the door and stopped. "Aww, damn." She sighed. "I know those ladies are still out there, ready to pounce."

"C'mon." He kissed her on the cheek. "Just ignore them."

When they left the bedroom, it was just as Gisella suspected. The women were all sitting in the living room, casting evil glares their way.

"We're going to head out and get something to eat," Gisella said. "Can we bring you anything back?"

Anna kept her mouth clamped while stroking Sasha's thick fur.

Nicole, Emmadonna and Jade were steady fanning themselves.

Gisella's eyes fell to the small plates with unmistakable chocolate crumbs. "Um, did you eat some of that cake in the dining room?"

Anna sighed. "They did. I didn't have much of an appetite."

"Um, hmm. It was good, too."

The women licked their lips and eyeballed Charlie with blatant desire.

"God, it's hot in here," Nicole panted.

Gisella spun around, grabbed Charlie's hand and yelled, "Run, Charlie. Run."

Chapter 21

Life was beautiful.

Gisella had never been happier. Charlie had filled the past three weeks with love and infused her night with passion. There were plenty of times she thought she should be ashamed of just how insatiable she was when it came to their lovemaking.

She no longer made *Amour Chocolat* cake, but she did alter the recipe to make truffles—with a little less potency and with a big warning label. The result: business had quadrupled. She and Isabella had to hire more employees and were now considering opening a second shop out in the suburbs.

"Godiva, eat your heart out," Isabella sassed as she rung up another sale.

Gisella laughed and turned her attention to the next customer in line. "May I help you?" she asked.

The woman smiled. "Well, hello."

Gisella cocked her head at the familiar face and struggled for a name.

"It's Lexi," she said.

Gisella remembered the woman from the restaurant. "Oh, *bonjour.*"

"I see you still have that cute little accent."

"Just like you still have yours," Gisella said, wondering what this woman really wanted.

"Charming," she said. "I can see why Charlie has taken an interest in you. He always did like women who were… different. How *are* things going with you and Charlie?"

Isabella turned from the register and eyed the woman.

"He's wonderful. As always," Gisella said, determined to remain pleasant.

"I hear you two are still dating?"

"From whom?"

The woman shrugged. "Around. Atlanta may be a big city, but in a lot of ways it's very small. It's not hard to get information when you really want it."

"I have no idea," Gisella said. "I don't spy on people. I think it's tacky." Her growing irritation only seemed to amuse Lexi.

"Humph. I hope you don't believe that you're actually going to nail Charlie down or get him in front of a preacher." Lexi plopped a thick book on the counter.

"What's that?"

"Charlie's little black book. It has all the names of all the women he's ever…dated. I'm sure they'll be more than happy to talk to you."

"And how did you get it?"

"I have my ways." She smirked. "Let me tell you something, sweetheart. You're no different from anybody else. In time, he'll get bored, and he'll dump you like he's dumped *all* the rest. It's what he does."

* * *

"What in the hell do you mean you're getting married?" Taariq roared.

Everyone in Herman's barbershop stopped what they were doing and swiveled their necks toward the Kappa Psi Kappa brothers.

Charlie slouched down in Herman's chair, surprised by their reaction. "Damn, y'all. My name isn't H. F. Hutton."

Suddenly they all tried to talk at one time. Questions like, "Are you crazy?", "Have you lost your mind?" and "What the heck have you been smoking?" were tossed at him.

Herman was the most amused. He clapped and rubbed his old leathery hands together. "Lawd. Lawd. Lawd. You still performing miracles."

Charlie rolled his eyes. "This hardly qualifies as a miracle."

A light flashed, temporarily blinding Charlie. He looked up to see Bobby aiming his camera phone at him. "What are you doing?"

"Capturing this historical moment. I'm putting this up on my Facebook and Myspace page. I think I'm going to title it 'The Death of a Playa.'"

"Very funny."

"Well, who's the lucky girl?" Hylan asked, frowning. "I didn't even know you were seeing anyone serious."

"I think I know," Derrick said. He sat smiling in the barber chair across from Charlie. "Gisella Jacobs."

"Who?" all the men in the barbershop chorused.

"You know. The woman Isabella hired to make his birthday cake for his party."

"The one she went into business with?" Hylan asked.

"Yep."

"Damn, bro." Taariq folded his arms. "That must have been one hell of a cake."

Hylan scoffed. "You probably need to check the ingredients. She probably put roots on you."

Charlie chuckled, remembering Gisella's *Amour Chocolat* cake.

J.T. stopped hawking his CDs for a moment to agree. "Yeah. I heard about chicks like that. Is she Creole? You know a Creole woman will put the roots on you in a heartbeat. My grandmother said that one stole her third husband like that. Fixed him a bowl of gumbo, and he was out the door."

Charlie sighed and wondered why he'd bothered to say anything. It probably had a lot to do with him just being happy as hell. For the past three weeks, he and Gisella had spent every free moment together making love. In fact, he would much rather be home with her now than sitting here jaw-jacking with this group of knuckleheads.

Herman patted Charlie on the shoulder. "Tell us something about your little lady. When are you going to bring her by here so we can get a good look at her?"

Bobby smirked. "I bet she's fine. My man Charlie here only strolls with the finest chicks. Ain't that right?" He looked at Charlie. "She's fine, ain't she?"

Herman clucked his tongue, a signal that he was annoyed with his great-grandson. "That's exactly why you're going to fall in love with a big cockeyed woman. God gonna get you back for always trying to judge with just your eyes."

Bobby shuddered at the thought. The other men laughed.

Herman went back to edging Charlie's sides. "Well, I'm proud of you, son. I know your daddy would be proud of you, too."

Charlie smiled. "Thanks, old man."

"I guess it's true what they say. When one door closes another one opens," Taariq said.

Charlie glared.

"What?" Taariq eyed him suspiciously. "Don't tell me you haven't told her."

The rest of the Kappa boys frowned. "Told her what?"

"Nothing," Charlie said, hoping Taariq would catch the hint and let the matter drop.

He didn't. "Far be it from me to tell you how to run your business…"

"Then don't."

"But keeping secrets is no one way to start off a marriage—or even an engagement."

"True. True," Herman chimed.

Stanley scratched his head, looking lost. "What? Are you talking about him being broke and filing for bankruptcy?"

Charlie's jaw clenched. "You told them?"

Taariq didn't bother to look contrite. "It slipped out."

"I swear you guys are the worst kind of gossipers."

Hylan held up his hand. "Heeey. We don't gossip. We *share* information. Totally different from gossiping. Women gossip."

Everyone in the shop nodded at that assessment.

Derrick didn't. "That has to be the most sexist thing I've ever heard."

"Chill out, D.," Hylan said. "Isabella isn't here." He returned his attention to Charlie. "You know you can't marry a woman without telling her you're broke."

"Especially a sista," Taariq agreed.

J.T. stumbled over and opened his merchandise-laden raincoat. "Well if you're looking for something on the cheap, I can hook you up. I got a couple of rings that looks one hundred percent zirconium. She'll never know the difference."

Charlie cracked up. "J.T., get out of my face with that crap, man. I'm not trying to put something on her finger that's going to turn green. Are you crazy?"

"Nah. Nah. Check it out. What you do is, every night when she goes to sleep, you just slip the ring off and put a tiny coat of clear nail polish on it. She'll never know."

The men laughed.

"Man, please. You stand a better chance of me buying some socks from you."

"Whoa. Whoa. I got some out in the car. Hold up. I'll be right back."

Charlie looked at his friends. "That brother got issues."

"Yeah, but he drives a Mercedes," Bobby said.

"An '82," Charlie countered.

"A Mercedes is a Mercedes. Somebody's rich butt sat in it at one time." Bobby handed a mirror to the nervous customer sitting in his seat.

It was the first time Charlie thought the young barber had actually done a decent job.

"All right, Hylan. You're next," Bobby said as his customer climbed out of his chair.

"Boy, please. I'm not about to have you messing up my head."

Insulted, Bobby frowned. "But you're bald. How am I gonna mess up your head?"

"Yeah. Well, I want to remain bald, not scalp-less."

Another round of laughter ensued.

"Y'all wrong, man." Bobby shook his head. "Y'all wrong for that."

Herman turned off his clippers and then folded his arms. "So when is the big day?" he asked, bringing the conversation back to Charlie.

At this point, Charlie knew that he should keep his mouth shut, but good news was hard to keep to oneself. "I bought the ring this morning. I plan on giving it to her this evening. If all goes right, I might be looking at a wedding in the next couple of weeks."

"A couple of weeks?" the shop clamored.

"What's the damn rush?" Taariq asked. "Her daddy got a shotgun after you or something?"

"Hardly."

Still mystified, Taariq kept shaking his head. "Whatever happened to long engagements? You know, date a couple of years, and then be engaged for a couple of more."

"She's a woman," Charlie said. "Not a bottle of wine."

"Yeah, man. That's not how it works," Derrick said laughing. "When it's love, you instantly know. All that stalling and dragging your feet is just a brother fighting it."

"Ain't nothing wrong with a good fight," Bobby interjected.

Taariq pointed at the young man. "See, now even the rookie is talking sense."

Bobby proudly puffed out his chest.

"Nah. I think my man, Derrick, is right on this one. When it's right, you know," Charlie said.

Herman sighed. "Y'all gonna get an old man crying up in here. I'm so proud. I've been cutting Charlie's head long before he even knew what to do with a girl. Now to see this new level of maturity, it just does my heart good."

It was Charlie's turn to puff out his chest.

Herman brushed off Charlie's neck and removed the smock.

Charlie handed him a folded bill and stood up from his chair. "Well, boys," he said, thinking about the ring he had waiting for Gisella. "I'm going to go make it official tonight. Wish me luck."

Taariq, Hylan, Stanley and Bobby grumbled.

Derrick and Herman boomed a clear, "Good luck."

Laughing, Charlie slapped his hand down on Taariq's shoulder. "Get the marbles out of your mouths and dust off your tux."

"I'll believe it when I see you at an altar," Taariq said.

Charlie shook his head and started toward the door. He'd taken only a few steps before pain exploded in his head and the room spun beneath his feet.

"Charlie?" Derrick called out.

Charlie dropped like a stone and banged his head on the floor.

"Someone call 9-1-1!"

Chapter 22

"Welcome back to the land of the living," Dr. Weiner said, smiling. "You gave everyone quite a scare."

Charlie groaned. His head felt as if someone had taken an axe to it and had a damn good time. When he moved, pain exploded at the back of his head and forced him to collapse back onto the pillow.

"Easy, now," Dr. Weiner warned. "We don't want you to overdo it."

Charlie wasn't going to argue. He closed his eyes to retreat from the room's bright light and exhaled a long breath.

"Your friends tell me that you took a rather nasty fall."

Had he? He couldn't remember. He opened his mouth to speak but his parched throat grated like sandpaper. "W-water."

"Hold on a second." Weiner turned toward the desk next

to the hospital bed and poured a glass of water. "Here you go," he said, tipping the cup toward Charlie's lips.

It was the best water Charlie had ever tasted. He drained the plastic cup in less than two seconds. "More."

The doctor complied and then said, "I have to ask you a few questions. They may sound silly to you, but I need to make sure there hasn't been any bruising or severe brain injury from your fall. Can you tell me your name?"

"Ch-Charles Masters," he whispered.

"Very good." Weiner retrieved a pin light from his breast pocket and then flashed it into Charlie's eyes to check their dilation. "What day is it?"

"Saturday," Charlie answered, trying not to be irritated by such mundane questions.

"Do you remember what happened?" Weiner asked.

At first, nothing came to mind, but after concentrating, bits and pieces of images surfaced. "Yeah, I—I think so."

"What do you remember?"

Charlie pushed himself through the pain of talking. "Barbershop. My head started hurting. I got dizzy. Fell."

Dr. Weiner nodded. "I'm going to order an MRI, but I believe you have a grade three concussion. We should probably keep you here overnight for observation. You'll live…for now."

Charlie's eyes fluttered open.

"While I have you here—"

"No."

A long silence followed. Dr. Weiner's hands gripped the bed's steel railing. "Charlie, you're making a grave mistake."

"It's mine to make," he countered. He glanced away when angry tears stung the backs of his eyes. "I-if I am sick, I don't want to spend what time I have left running in and out of hospitals."

"I've always known that you were hard-headed, Charlie, but I'd hoped that cracking your head open had knocked some sense into you." He paused. "I saw the look on your friends' faces out there. They care a lot about you. Have you thought about how they're going to feel when they find out you kept this illness from them?"

Charlie ground his jaw in stubborn silence. The last thing he wanted was a sermon.

"You have a responsibility to those you love. That includes telling them the truth. No matter how painful."

Charlie closed his eyes again and was greeted with the image of Gisella lying in his bed of satin sheets and smiling seductively. How could he tell her he was dying after he had allowed her to believe they were preparing for a future together?

"You're being selfish."

So what? Why couldn't he grab happiness while he still had a chance? Charlie pressed a hand against his forehead, but no matter how hard he fought against it, the doctor's words seeped into his thick skull.

"I'm not going to lie to you. You're at a major crossroad," Weiner continued. "It's not up to me to judge. You have to make your own decisions. But I gotta tell you, I think you're making the wrong ones."

Charlie's picture of Gisella then changed into one of his mother greeting him Tuesday nights with a kiss and then one of him and his Kappa brothers laughing it up every Saturday morning at Herman's and then his thoughts returned to Gisella.

"All right. All right. I'll take your damn test," Charlie snapped.

Weiner drew and released a satisfied breath. "I'll order for a nurse to come take you upstairs. The test won't take but a few minutes."

"Now?"

"I'm not giving you a chance to back out of this… again."

Gisella stared at Charlie's little black book.

She wasn't going to call anyone. What was the point? The women listed in there were all a part of his past. She was his future.

Right?

It was a good pep talk. One that worked for the first hour, but by the second, third and even the fourth, those words started to have a hollow ring. Even Lexi's sneering voice refused to stop echoing in her head.

"In time, he'll get bored, and he'll dump you like he's dumped all the rest. It's what he does."

Was she telling the truth? Despite their dating for the last seven weeks, there was still plenty Gisella didn't know about Charlie. How many times had she sensed that he was keeping something from her? How many times had she caught him staring at her with an odd sadness in his eyes? Was he already getting bored? Was a breakup just beyond the horizon?

Yet, there was so much she *did* know—and loved—that had nothing to do with him being good-looking or good in bed—*great in bed*, actually. Charlie was intelligent, loyal to his friends, funny, kind and endearing. There was something about the way he held her that made her feel like the quintessential woman. In his arms, she was sexy, alluring, strong and powerful—all at the same time. With him in her corner, there was nothing she couldn't do. No challenge too hard, no dreams impossible.

How could she *not* fall in love?

Gisella's gaze returned to the little black book. How many other women had felt the same way about Charlie?

"Krista, could you take over?" she asked, removing her apron. "I'm going to head home."

"Sure." Krista smiled. "I don't know how you put in the hours you do anyway."

At home, Gisella's anxieties increased. When she phoned Charlie, all her calls were transferred to his voicemail. If she could just hear his voice maybe she would calm down.

Curled up on the living room sofa with Sasha purring softly on her lap, Gisella stared at the black book as if in a trance. In the last hour, she had thrown the book in the garbage several times only to fish it out minutes later.

"In time, he'll get bored, and he'll dump you like he's dumped all the rest. It's what he does."

There was laughter in the hallway seconds before Anna and the Lonely Hearts breezed into the apartment. Clearly, they'd spent the day shopping, judging by the number of shopping bags. However, they sobered when they spilled into the living room and saw Gisella.

"You're home early," Anna said casually. A clear reflection of how their relationship had been strained since she'd learned about Gisella and Charlie's relationship. "What are you doing?"

"Nothing."

"We can see that," Nicole said. She lowered her bags near the coffee table and plopped on the cushion next to Gisella. "You look like a zombie."

"What's this?" Emmadonna asked picking up the black book and joining them on the couch.

"Charlie's little black book."

The Lonely Hearts gasped.

Nicole snatched the book from Emmadonna's hands. "Girrrl, how did you get your hands on this?"

"You mean men actually have those things?" Jade squeaked.

Excited, Emmadonna grabbed the book back. "Are you going to call any of them? Let's do it now."

"No."

"Where's the phone?"

"I *said* no."

"No?" the women chorused.

"Why the hell not?" Nicole asked.

Still standing in the living room's archway, Anna stared at her sister. "What's the matter, Gisella?"

"Nothing. I—I just…" She shook her head. "I was just thinking."

Anna set her bags down and climbed over her friends' legs and forced them to scoot over so she could sit next Gisella. "Do you want to talk about it?"

Sasha abandoned Gisella's lap for her owner's.

Talk about what? That she had this unexplainable anxiety over a relationship that everyone kept warning her to stay away from? One look at her sister and Gisella could tell that she was just jumping at the bit to say, *I told you so.*

Besides, Charlie hasn't done anything. It was just a feeling that bad news was just around the corner, caused by the seeds that Lexi woman planted in her head.

Gisella forced on a smile and unfolded her legs. "You know what? I think I'm just going to go and see my man."

"You mean *everybody's* man, don't you?" Emmadonna thumbed through the pages. "Damn, do you know the mayor is in here?"

Gisella tried to grab the black book. "And I'm giving him his book back."

"Whoa!" The ladies jumped to their feet.

"Let's not be too hasty there," Nicole said. "Apparently, you're too emotional and aren't thinking clearly. You do *not* give a playa his little black book back. That's like giving a recovering alcoholic a bottle of Jack Daniels."

Gisella snatched the book. "No offense, Nicole. But I'll start taking man advice from you when you have one of your own."

Chapter 23

The bone marrow test didn't take long. All that was left for Charlie to do was to wait. But he wasn't going to do that in a hospital. After insisting to be released, the Kappa Psi Kappa brothers drove Charlie back to his apartment. The ride was like a funeral procession. His boys clearly didn't know what to say to him and he certainly didn't know how to get the conversation started.

Once at his apartment, it was odd to see the Kappas, big, strapping manly men, fussing over him like a group of mother hens. Before he knew it, they had him propped up on the sofa with pillows and blankets and arguing who was better qualified to stay and watch for the night.

Derrick suggested calling Mama Arlene, and Charlie threatened him within an inch of his life when he'd picked up the phone. "I'm all right, man. There's no need to worry her. It's just a bump on the head."

Grudgingly, Derrick placed the phone back on the receiver and then shared a look with the other boys.

"Just spit it out," Charlie said.

Taariq crossed his arms. "Actually, we're waiting for you to tell us what's going on. What was up with all that extra testing?"

For a brief moment, Charlie thought that he could downplay the whole situation. "It was nothing. It…" He glanced at their solemn and dubious faces and knew that the jig was up. Time to come clean. "Dr. Weiner thinks I'm dying."

Everyone quickly collapsed into the nearest chair.

"Go on," Hylan said.

Charlie started from the beginning. How he'd gone to the doctor's to prepare for a business trip and ended where he'd finally was cornered into taking the test an hour ago. When he was done, the silence condemned him.

"And this is called a plastic what?" Derrick asked. He scooped out his cell phone so he could search WebMD.

"Aplastic anemia," Charlie repeated. "I didn't *really* believe the diagnosis…until the headaches and dizzy spells. I mean, most of the time I feel fine."

"It's just when you cracked your head on the floor that gave you pause?" Hylan asked.

Stanley looked on the verge of tears. "I don't understand. Why didn't you tell us? I thought we were boys."

Here we go.

"It's complicated, Stan," Charlie said. "I didn't want you guys to start…"

"What?" Derrick folded his arms. "You didn't want us to start what?"

"Treating me different," Charlie said.

"We wouldn't have done that," Stanley protested.

The rest of the Kappas chorused in agreement.

Charlie laughed. "Please. Look at you. I've been in the

apartment less than an hour and you guys got me snug as a bug in a rug. Hell, dawgs, a minute ago I was scared one of you were going to stick a thermometer up my butt if I asked for some aspirins."

A couple of them hung their heads in guilt.

"All right. All right," Hylan said. "Maybe we overreacted. But it was a little disturbing to see you wipe out the way you did at Herman's. You scared us."

"Sorry, man." Charlie shrugged. "I was just trying to do the right thing."

They bobbed their heads, but Stanley was barely keeping it together.

Having pity on him, Charlie said, "C'mon. Let's hug it out real quick." He stood and the Kappas came together for one big group hug and then broke away as if the incident never happened.

"But why would you call old girlfriends and tell *them?*" Hylan asked.

"Trying to bring closure to whichever one of them vandalized my car and trashed my apartment. Whoever it is is still messing with me. Things keep disappearing around here."

"Should've listened to Herman," Derrick said, waving his finger. "He warned you about being out of the field too long. Look at you now. You're in the middle of some fatal attraction soap opera." He glanced at his other brothers. "It's gonna happen to you guys too. Watch."

Hylan rolled his eyes. "Can we save the preaching for Sundays?" He turned to Charlie. "So where does all this 'I'm getting married' stuff fit in? Does your girl know about all this—or are you keeping this from her just like the whole bankruptcy thing?"

It was on the tip of Charlie's tongue to tell the guys that

it was none of their business what he did and didn't tell Gisella, but he hesitated too long and they had their answer.

"Man, what the hell are you thinking?" Derrick exploded out of his chair. "Are you really that damn selfish? How are you going to marry someone and *not* tell her you may be dying?"

Hylan was equally outraged. "Bump that. Do you even really love this girl or are you just swept up in the moment because you think you're getting ready to kick the bucket?"

The accusation had Charlie jumping to his feet. "What the hell kind of question is that? Of course I love her!"

Stanley, who was still hunched over in his chair, calmly asked, "Are you sure?"

"Damn right I'm sure." Charlie's face twisted in disgust. "Gisella is the best thing that has ever happened to me."

Taariq shrugged. "But you have to admit it's a little convenient your falling in love at the twelfth hour. *You,* a man who ran only second to Wilt Chamberlain in the number of women he'd slept with, finds the love of his life the moment he finds out he's dying. Do you know what the odds are on that?"

Charlie blinked.

Taariq shook his head. "C'mon, dawg. Who are you fooling? Us? Or yourself?"

"Or Gisella?" Derrick added.

Charlie opened his mouth to protest...but no words came out.

Gisella arrived at Charlie's high-rise apartment with her heart in her throat. In just a few minutes she would see Charlie, and all the anxieties of the day would melt away. At least that's what she was hoping. She waved at Todd at the security desk as she headed toward the elevator bay.

At Charlie's door she elected to knock first instead of

using the key he'd insisted on giving her. The last person she expected to answer the door was Isabella's husband. "Derrick?" She blinked up at him and then tried to glance around his large shoulders. "What are you doing here?"

"Hey, Gisella," he said, looking equally caught off guard. After a beat of silence, she wondered whether he intended to let her in.

"Is Charlie here?"

"Who? Oh, Charlie. Yeah. Um, come on in." He finally stepped back from the door.

Gisella gave him an awkward laugh before crossing into the apartment. The surprises continued when she found Charlie in the living room propped up on pillows and surrounded by three other guys.

"Gisella," Charlie said, standing. "I didn't know you were coming by."

Her curious gaze darted around the men's strange expressions.

"Oh. Um. You remember the guys from the birthday party. This here is Hylan, Taariq and Stanley," he said, touching each one on the shoulder.

"Hello," they greeted her, smiling.

"Bonjour."

"And of course you remember Derrick there."

Every fiber in her being told her something was wrong. The men were acting like she was an undercover cop who'd just busted them on an illegal act.

After the introductions were done, the silence in the room became a living, breathing thing.

Finally, Derrick broke the silence by clapping his hands together. "Well, I guess we'll be heading out."

It sounded more like a command than a suggestion. The other Kappa brothers quickly agreed and gathered their belongings. The situation made Gisella feel as if she should be apologizing for breaking up the private party.

"It was nice meeting you," Stanley said as he filed past her.

She nodded weakly as they all headed out.

"Bobby was right. She *is* fine," one of them whispered.

Both she and Charlie remained silent until they heard the front door close. "They seem nice," she said, easing into the room, trying to break the ice.

Gisella knew the Kappa boys more by the stories Charlie and Isabella shared with her than anything else. Her gaze took in the pillows and blankets spread out on the sofa again. "Camping out?"

"Sort of," he said sheepishly. "I, uh, sort of had an accident at the barbershop today. Hit my head. Got a concussion."

"What?" She instantly flew to him and tried to examine him for herself.

Charlie stopped her by taking her hands into his and kissing them. "It's all right. It's going to take more than a cement floor to bust open this head."

She laughed and until that moment, didn't realize how much she needed to do that. "That must be why I was so worried about you today," she said in relief. "I kept having this bad vibe ever since…" She shook her head and allowed Charlie to lead her to sit down and pull her into his arms. "I had the strangest visit from that Lexi woman, and I can't believe I let her get into my head."

He frowned. "Lexi?"

Gisella opened her purse and pulled out Charlie's black book. "She brought me this."

"What?" Charlie removed his arm from around her and took the book. "Lexi?" He shook his head as his rising anger caused visible lines along his jaw. "I should have known." He slammed the book on the table.

"She suggested that I call—"

"And did you?" he snapped.

"Of course not! I would never do that." She paused. "But it's a thick book."

"So?" He stood up and started pacing.

She blinked at him. "So…I didn't really realize how many women you had in your life."

"What…you wanted a number?"

Now Gisella jumped to her feet. "I never said I wanted a number, I'm just saying you've slept with a lot of women— even the mayor is in there!"

"Oh, so you read it?"

"No. Nicole—"

"Nicole? You let your *friends* read my personal property?"

"Nicole is not…" She stopped and drew a deep breath. "Okay. Are you purposely trying to start a fight with me?"

He stopped pacing long enough to breathe fire toward her. After a long minute passed, he finally glanced away. He didn't know if he could go through with this. After talking to the Kappas, he was suddenly confused on so many things.

Gisella forced herself to calm down. When she glanced back at him, she remembered his concussion. "Let's just drop this. Clearly, Lexi gave me the book for this very thing to happen." She smiled and walked over to him. "But I'm not going anywhere, baby. In fact, I'm going to take care of you tonight. We'll stay in, and I'll cook us something to eat and we can sit here on the couch and watch a movie." She kissed his cheek. "Would you like that?"

Charlie eased away.

Gisella's heart dropped. "What's wrong?"

"Nothing." He shrugged. "What makes you think something is wrong?" he asked, avoiding eye contact. He couldn't believe he was about to do this, but maybe everyone was right. Up until now, he was being selfish, planning a future when he didn't have one and wanting her to fall in love with him when he was just going to break her heart. Was this what the song meant when it said, if you love someone set them free?

Gisella studied him and was convinced that she could literally see the wheels in his head spinning. In that moment everything became clear.

"You want to break up with me," she said simply.

He looked at her then.

She waited for him to deny the accusation.

And waited.

And waited.

"I see." She shook her head and grabbed her purse from the couch. "You know, you're a real piece of work."

"Gisella—"

"Save it. You've already wasted enough of my time." She stomped away from him and marched toward the door steadily cursing him out in French. If he thought for a second that she was going to throw some temper tantrum, he had another thing coming. So intent on her leaving, she was caught off guard when he grabbed her wrist. "Gisella." He spun her around.

Out of reflex, she slapped him. "Drop dead."

Chapter 24

"Mission accomplished," Lexi murmured under her breath. It didn't take a rocket scientist to know that the look on Gisella's face when she stormed toward her car in the high-rise parking deck meant one thing: everything had gone exactly as planned.

Now she felt vindicated. Of course she still had one more bomb set in motion, but she had no doubt that when all was said and done, Charlie Masters would learn a valuable lesson.

Gisella slammed her car door and revved the engine. A second later, tires squealed, and a cloud of white smoke jetted out of her exhaust pipe when she peeled out of the parking deck. To Lexi's surprise, she experienced a nugget of sympathy but quickly shook it off. "Trust me, Frenchie. I did you a favor."

Charlie leaned his head against the front door while the left side of his face still throbbed from Gisella's powerful slap. He felt as low as a man could get. Now Gisella believed that she was no different than the already forgotten faces and names in his damn black book.

He squeezed his eyes tight, but tears still managed to escape and race down his face. This morning he was looking forward to officially proposing to Gisella. He would have never believed that the day would end with her hating his guts and with him hating himself.

The only thing that prevented him from running after her was Dr. Weiner and his frat brothers' words. He couldn't continue to be selfish. It wasn't fair. However, there was one thing he now knew for sure—he was definitely in love with Gisella. It wasn't fear of fading mortality. The gut-wrenching sickness he experienced now could only be love.

Somehow he managed to pull himself away from the door. Seconds later, he was in his bedroom pulling out the small royal-blue box from the top nightstand drawer. Before he could open it, he eased down on the edge of the bed and held his breath.

Ready, Charlie opened the box and stared at the elegant two-carat princess-cut diamond ring. Now he would have to continue to use his imagination of how the ring would've looked on Gisella's finger. After a long while, he finally exhaled and accepted the pain in his heart. It was worse than anything he'd ever experienced.

He lay back on the bed and wondered how long he would have to endure. Surely it would ease soon. *Please, Lord, let it ease soon.*

"A plastic what?" Isabella asked her husband. It was late and they were getting ready for bed when he dropped this bombshell on her.

"Aplastic anemia," Derrick repeated. "The whole thing

is messed up," he said worriedly. The idea of losing not only his best friend but a man who was like his brother was hard to wrap his brain around. "We're all waiting for his test results. It can take up to seven to ten days. Until then, we're not to breathe a word…not even to Mama Arlene."

Isabella's heart ached for her husband. She loved Charlie. He was like family. And seeing him so happy these past two months had given her hope that he was finally ready to settle down.

"What about Gisella? Does she know about this?"

Derrick stopped pacing, guilt flickered across his expression.

"Don't tell me he hasn't told her."

Derrick hedged. "Look, honey. There's a real good chance Charlie and Gisella may be breaking up."

"What? But Charlie's crazy about Gisella. They're supposed to be getting engaged." This didn't make sense.

Derrick started pacing again.

Isabella eyed her husband suspiciously. "Why would they break up?"

Derrick remained quiet.

"Who broke up with whom?" she needled.

"C'mon, honey. I don't butt into Charlie's business."

"Since when?" She climbed out of bed. "The Kappas huddle together at that barbershop every weekend and do nothing but gossip and high-five each other."

He tried to look insulted, but didn't quite pull it off.

"Charlie broke up with her and didn't tell her why, didn't he?" Isabella asked. "And something tells me the Kappas had something to do with it."

"That's not true," Derrick protested.

Isabella crossed her arms and tapped her foot.

"We just asked Charlie to evaluate his motivations for

getting married. We thought it seemed like an awfully big coincidence his falling in love the same time he'd been given a death sentence."

"Oh, did you now, Dr. Phil?"

"C'mon, Bella. Don't be like that. What he was doing wasn't fair to Gisella. Surely you can see that."

"I'm calling Gisella." She rushed back to the bed and reached for the phone.

Derrick flew across the bedroom, dove over the bed and jabbed his hand against the receiver to hang up the line. "We promised Charlie we wouldn't tell her."

"*You're* not. I am," she said. "Gisella is *my* friend…and my business partner. I can't keep something like this from her. She deserves to know."

Derrick cocked his head. "It's not our place."

"It wasn't your place to tell Charlie to break up with Gisella, but that didn't stop you, now did it?" She watched another flicker of guilt cross his features. "I expected this kind of behavior from Taariq and Hylan. A party ain't party unless Charlie Masters is there, right? But you…"

"So what are you saying?" Derrick challenged. "You want her to fall in love with Charlie just so she can watch him die? Is that what you want her to do?"

"It should be her choice."

"No. It's *his* choice," he argued, his eyes glossed with tears. "It's Charlie's decision, and we *will* respect that." He watched her jaw harden and then added. "Please, Bella. For me."

Isabella's resolve held until she watched a tear streak down her husband's cheek. She cupped his face and pressed his head against her bosom. "All right…we'll do things your way."

"Thank you, baby."

* * *

Gisella promised herself that she wasn't going to cry.

For seven days, she kept that promise…until Sunday morning when she was soaking in her hot bubble bath with her green cucumber mask. One moment she was fine, and in the next she was a blubbering mess.

How could she have been so stubborn, hard-headed and foolish?

Breaking up with Robert had been hard, but the pain in her heart now was stronger than anything she'd ever experienced. Reviewing the past week, Gisella realized that she had been more or less a walking zombie. She opened the shop at the crack of dawn and didn't leave until the dead of night. She did everything she could to keep busy.

At night, she fought the temptation of even fantasizing about Charlie, but lately, even that was getting harder and harder to do. She *did* want to see his face again, hear his voice. As her sobs bounced and echoed off the bathroom tile, she wondered how a man could make love the way he did and not feel anything.

Thereafter, every sentence started with *how* and *why,* and it continued until her head pounded mercilessly with a migraine.

"Gisella?"

At the sound of her sister's voice, Gisella made a lousy attempt to stem the flow of tears.

"Gisella, are you all right in there?"

She tried to respond, but all she could manage was more crying and sobbing.

The door flew open, and Anna rushed into the bathroom. Despite the water, bubbles and even the hardening cucumber mask, Gisella wrapped her arms around her big sister and cried until her heart was content.

"Shh. It's okay," Anna assured her. "Shh. It's going to be okay."

An hour later, Anna helped her sister out of the cold water, scrubbed her face and got her into bed. She instantly shifted into mother mode and fixed her something to eat and gave her aspirins for her headache.

She stayed with Gisella until she'd curled up in bed and fallen into a deep, exhausted sleep. This was exactly the heartbreak Anna had hoped her sister would avoid. But when Charlie Masters entered the picture, she and the Lonely Hearts knew that it was just a matter of time.

Still, there had been a sliver of hope that Charlie had changed, but life just proved that you can't teach an old dog a new trick. Anna sat on the edge of her sister's bed and lovingly finger-combed a few strands of hair from her sleeping face. Seeing Gisella look so childlike and vulnerable tugged at her heartstrings and renewed her anger.

Anna returned to her sister's bathroom and picked up the wet towels and straightened up when her gaze snagged on something in the small wastebasket.

A pregnancy test.

A positive pregnancy test.

Charlie wasn't going to answer the phone. He lacked the strength or even the desire to talk to anyone. A second before the call transferred to voice mail, he shot an arm out from beneath the piles of sheets and comforters to grab the receiver.

"Y-yeah."

"Mr. Masters, this is Todd down at the front desk. You have a visitor down here."

Charlie groaned. "N-no. No visitors tonight, Todd."

"Yes, sir. But she's insisting that you'll want to talk to her."

"If it's your crazy sister Lexi—"

"No, sir. She says her name is Anna Jacobs."

Charlie sat straight up. "Anna?" He tried to defog his brain. "What is she doing here?"

"I don't know, sir. Should I ask her?"

He scrambled out of bed, trying to think. Was it Gisella? Had something happened?

"Sir?"

"Uh. Uh." He glanced at himself in pajamas and a week-old beard. "Send her up." Charlie slammed the phone down and rushed to make himself presentable. All the while, his brain conjured up horrible scenarios of why Anna was there. Surely it was to deliver bad news. An illness? An accident?

When the doorbell rang, Charlie raced to the front door while still pulling a T-shirt over his head. When he finally jerked it open to his old college friend on the other side, he didn't greet her with the traditional "Hello" or "How are you?" But with a "Is she okay?"

Anna's eyebrows climbed. "I'd love to come in. Thank you." She stepped into his apartment. "It's good to see that you look like crap, too."

Charlie rolled his eyes, shut the door and waited with his heart clogging his throat. When she seemed content to inch her way through the apartment, pretending to be interested in the paintings and the knickknacks on the wall, his patience snapped. "Just spit it out. What's wrong with Gisella?"

Anna glanced over her shoulder and speared him with an icy glare. "Why do you care? Surely you've moved on to the next chick, right?"

Feeling the room tilt, Charlie closed his eyes and braced one hand against the wall. "Look, it's not what it looks like."

"Oh?" She crossed her arms. "And what does it look like *exactly?*"

Charlie sighed. Surely if something had happened to Gisella she would have said so by now. "That I'm…up to my old ways. That—that I was only after her for one thing."

"And you're suggesting that's *not* what happened?"

He shook his head, convinced she wouldn't believe him. Instead of the expected yelling and cursing, Anna remained silent.

Charlie glanced up and was stunned by the tears streaming down her face.

"I wish I could believe you," she said. "But I have a sister at home crying her eyes out, and I know your reputation firsthand."

"Look, Anna. I don't expect you to believe me, but I love your sister."

"You have a funny way of showing it."

Tears now splashed down Charlie's face. "Trust me. I'm doing what's best for her."

"And will you do what's best for your *child* as well?"

Stunned, Charlie stared. "Gisella's…?"

"I think the word you're looking for is *pregnant*. The question is, are you man enough to do the right thing?"

A baby. His laughter started as a low rumble and grew into a loud raucous roar that vibrated off the walls.

Anna cocked her head, wondering about his sanity.

Charlie couldn't get over how cruel life could be. He made the mistake of removing his hand from the wall and when he took a step, he dropped like a stone.

"Charlie!" Anna rushed over to him.

He tried to laugh the incident off, but Anna wasn't buying. "What the hell is going on with you?" she asked. "And I want the truth."

Chapter 25

Gisella cried so much that she became used to the taste of her salty tears. By morning, she promised to pull herself back together. She was a strong woman, and somehow, someway, she would get through this. She just wished it didn't hurt so bad. She hugged the bed's pillow tighter while her heart continued to break.

"It's okay. Don't cry," Charlie's voice drifted over the shell of her ear.

No. No. She didn't want Fantasy Charlie there. If she couldn't have the real thing, she didn't want anything at all.

"It's okay, baby. I'm here."

A soft kiss was pressed against the back of her neck and caused a delicious tingle to ripple down her spine. She moaned, slowly allowing this fantasy to play out. Arms slid across her body and pulled her back to settle into a comfortable spoon position.

"I'm so sorry, baby." He kissed her again. "I'm so sorry I hurt you."

His hand now caressed her belly. "Can you ever forgive me?"

She desperately wanted to, but she couldn't get the words out.

"I thought I was doing what was best," he whispered. "I love you. I never stopped loving you. I swear there's no one else." He pulled her even closer. "I was so stupid."

It was probably the sound of his broken sobs that finally penetrated her foggy brain and forced her to open her eyes. This was no fantasy.

Gisella covered the hand over her belly and rolled over to face the man lying beside her. She was shocked at his haggard look, his scruffy beard and watery eyes. And yet, he was still able to steal her breath.

"Hey, you," he whispered.

Fresh tears blurred her vision while a whirlwind of emotions swirled inside of her. "What are you doing here?"

"I came to beg you for forgiveness…and to tell you the truth about why I pushed you away." With the pads of his thumbs, he wiped her face dry and started from the beginning.

By the time he was through, she was crying again. She hammered him with questions and mentally tried to rebel against his doctor's diagnosis. When she realized that she was acting just as he'd feared, she showered him with words of encouragement.

"Don't worry, sweetheart," she said. "We can get through this…together."

There was no doubt that she'd forgiven him. She was kissing and holding him so tight that he could scarcely breathe. But Charlie had no complaints, especially when she pulled her nightgown over her head and revealed the provocative curves he'd spent the last week trying to forget.

As always their bodies snapped together like the perfect puzzle. She lay back with her eyes sparkling while he stretched above her. He entered her with ease. Their mouths fed hungrily upon each other. Arms circling his neck, Gisella squeezed her inner muscles for each slow thrust of his hips.

"Oh, Gisella," he moaned, losing himself in her sweet body. Their rhythm picked up speed and the lovers grew wild with passion and their bodies soon became dewy with sweat.

Gisella was coming, surging over the edge and calling out Charlie's name.

They shuddered together in an orgasm that seemed to go on forever. She kissed his shoulders and he pressed his lips against her forehead.

"I still want to marry you," he whispered. "That's if you'll have me."

She hugged him tight and smiled up at him. "I'll marry you anytime, anywhere and anyplace."

Charlie quickly rolled over and retrieved the blue box from the pocket of his pants strewn on the floor. "I was supposed to give this to you last week."

Gisella popped open the box and gasped.

"This makes it official," Charlie said. He kissed her again and slid the ring onto her finger. "I love you."

"I love you, too." She hesitated. "There's something I have to tell you. I'm pregnant."

A new smile exploded across Charlie's face. He didn't want to ruin the moment by telling her that he already knew about the baby. Instead, he pulled her close and made love to her again.

And again.

And again.

* * *

"I don't understand," Charlie said. "Swing that back by me."

Dr. Weiner shifted awkwardly in his chair. He braided and unbraided his fingers several times before he repeated the results of Charlie's lab work. "I don't know how this mix-up happened, but I want you to know that I'm extremely sorry."

Charlie shook his head and prayed that his hearing hadn't failed him. "So, I *don't* have aplastic anemia?" he asked for the third time. "I'm not dying."

Embarrassed, the doctor shook his head. "The best we can figure is that there was some kind of screw-up at the lab. Your samples were switched with another patient's."

"Switched?"

"Oh, baby." Gisella grabbed Charlie's hand and squeezed. When Dr. Weiner had called them that morning, they had dropped everything and rushed right over. They agreed that they were in this together. No matter what the diagnosis, they would face it head on—and they would fight.

Fight for their love.

Fight for their future.

While happy tears filled Gisella's eyes, Charlie was busy connecting other dots. "Dr. Weiner, does Lexi Thomas still work here?"

Gisella's head swung toward the doctor. "She *works* here?"

Dr. Weiner blinked, clearly surprised by the question. "Nurse Thomas left the practice last month. Why?"

Charlie drew in an angry breath. "I don't believe this."

"You don't think she was crazy enough to deliberately switch your lab results?" Gisella asked.

"Of course she would. She vandalized my car, trashed and stole things out of my apartment. With her working here, how hard would it have been to switch my lab results?"

"Whoa. Whoa." Dr. Weiner held up his hands. "I don't know what you're talking about, but the accusations you're leveling are serious. Do you have proof of any of this?"

Charlie laughed. "Of course not. She's too clever for that." He clenched and unclenched his fist. He wished he could do more than issue a restraining order. At this point he was just glad that he didn't own a pet rabbit.

"What about his headaches and dizzy spells?" Gisella asked, patting Charlie's arms in hopes to calm him down. "If he doesn't have aplastic anemia something has to be wrong."

"There is." Dr. Weiner drew a deep breath. "All tests indicate that you have type 2 diabetes, and, of course, we've always known about your borderline high blood pressure. The dizziness and vertigo can occur when your blood sugar shoots up. It's definitely the culprit behind the migraines."

"That's it?" Charlie asked almost laughing. "Diabetes?"

"Diabetes is still a serious matter. The Centers for Disease Control and Prevention considers diabetes to be a pandemic in America. The good news is now that we know what's wrong with you, we can work to control it."

"But it's not exactly the same as having a couple of months to live," Gisella cut in. Her relief was so strong it caused her to laugh.

"No. With any luck Charlie will be with us for a long time." Dr. Weiner looked at Charlie. "Again. I want to express my sincere apology for this lab screwup. I find it hard to believe that any member of my staff would have purposely switched lab results. I also want to point out that if you'd come in earlier for the additional testing then this wouldn't have carried out as long as it has."

At this moment, Charlie was too happy to be upset. "Can we have a few minutes alone?" he asked.

Weiner nodded. "Of course." He stood and left his office.

Immediately, Gisella launched into Charlie's arms and peppered his face with kisses. "Can you believe it, baby?"

He couldn't. After being so scared for seemingly so long, he felt as if he'd been given a second chance on life and in his arms was all he needed for happiness.

"You know what this means, don't you?" Gisella said. "I can't feed you any more of my chocolate."

Charlie laughed. "There's only one kind of chocolate I want from you, and I plan to have all I can eat every night."

Epilogue

One month later

Gisella and Charlie's hands overlapped as they gripped the knife and together sliced into a Sinful Chocolate popular creation—white chocolate and lemon cake. The happy couple smiled at the wedding photographer and then toward each other before shoving a handful of the decadent dessert into each other's faces.

Laughter rippled among the large gathering of friends and family and then a cheer went up when Charlie then tried to kiss and lick his wife's face clean. Armed with a new diet and medication, Charlie had learned to strike the perfect balance between having his cake and eating it, too.

"I love you, baby," he whispered, snapping their bodies together and dipping his head for a long soulful kiss. She tasted so sweet.

"Je t'aime aussi," she responded when he allowed her to come up for air.

Charlie groaned at the instant hard-on he acquired whenever Gisella spoke French. Now that they'd said their "I do's," Charlie was ready to skip right to the honeymoon phase. So much so he found himself asking Gisella every five minutes, "Can we leave now?"

"Behave." She giggled and then allowed Anna to pull her away.

"I'm so happy for you, Gisella," Anna said, wrapping her arms around her baby sister. "I don't think the Lonely Hearts will admit it, but you've renewed our faith in love."

Gisella smiled and wiped away a stray tear from her sister's face. "I owe you so much. If you hadn't gone to see Charlie that night…"

Anna gave Gisella's waist a gentle squeeze. "I'm sure you would've done the same for me."

"In a heartbeat." She paused. "He's out there, you know. There's a perfect guy out there for you."

Anna shrugged. "Maybe. But until then, me and Sasha are going to be just fine."

Gisella smiled as her eyes snagged on Taariq as he walked across the lawn. *Maybe…*

Charlie laughed as his mother gripped his cheeks and tried to pinch the blood out of them. "My baby has made me so proud. Not only did you give me a beautiful daughter-in-law, but I'm finally getting my grandbaby."

"Anything for you, Mama." He kissed her cheek.

"Of course you know I was right," she added, releasing his cheeks. "Didn't I tell you if you found a woman who could cook like your mama then you had a winner?"

"That you did, Mama." He wrapped his arm around her.

"I just wish your father was here to see this day," she

said. "Married and about to become a father. He would be so proud. I am."

"Thanks, Mom." He kissed her lovingly on her upturned cheek.

"Mama Arlene," Taariq greeted her with a wide smile. "I don't know if Charlie told you, but we talked it over, and he's completely cool with calling me 'Daddy.' All you have to do now is accept my proposal. I'll make an honest woman out of you."

"You're so bad." Arlene blushed as she gave Taariq a welcoming hug. "Now when are *you* getting married?"

"As soon as you say yes."

She rolled her eyes. "You just love me for my fried chicken."

"That's not true. You make a mean potato pie, too."

Arlene laughed and then continued to giggle like a schoolgirl when Taariq asked for a dance. As he led her to the pavilion before the band, Charlie was left to shake his head.

"So you finally did it," Hylan said, slapping his large hand across Charlie's back. "You waved the white flag and surrendered to the enemy."

Charlie laughed and rolled his eyes. "Don't start that with me."

"What?" He hunched his shoulders. "I'm just saying. We were supposed to be playas for life. Remember?"

Derrick rushed up behind Hylan and quickly put him into a headlock. "Whatever he's saying, don't listen to him."

"Oh, he's harmless." Charlie chuckled. "I'm just waiting for the day when he starts waving his own white flag."

"It'll never happen," Hylan croaked from under Derrick's arm and tried to tap out.

"It doesn't make any sense to be so hard-headed," Derrick said, releasing him.

Hylan sucked in a deep breath and then playfully sent a left jab against Derrick's shoulder. "Mark my words. A brother like me ain't going down without a fight. You'll have to pry my playa's card out of my cold dead hands."

"All right," Derrick said. "We're going to hold you to that."

"Charlie, man," Stanley said, joining the group. "Your wife's cake is off the hook. What's her secret, man?"

"She didn't make this cake. Her assistant Pamela insisted on making the cake as a gift. She did a good job."

"Pamela, huh? Where is she?" Stanley turned to survey the crowd. "Maybe I'll marry her."

"I'm sure she'll be thrilled to hear it." Charlie laughed. "Start with baby steps. Try to get a date first."

"Or try to get a woman to stand still long enough for you introduce yourself."

"Ha. Ha. Y'all gonna get enough messing with me." Stanley scanned the crowd again. "There's gotta be someone here I can hook up with. Weddings are the best places for single people to hook up. That and funerals."

Hylan and Charlie just stared him.

"What? It's what I heard."

"We're going to pray for you," Hylan said.

"Whatever." Stanley moved closer to Charlie. "So now that you're off the market, what do you say to passing a playa like me your infamous little black book? I've heard that it's a pretty thick book."

"A playa like you?" Hylan snickered. "If anyone should inherit the Holy Grail from my man here, it should be me."

"Guys, guys. As much as I'd like to improve your whack game, I can't. Gisella and I had a nice farewell ceremony and then tossed the book into the fireplace."

Hylan and Stanley blinked and then both pointed at him accusingly. "Judas!"

Derrick and Charlie laughed.

"What do a couple of married women have to do to get a dance with their husbands?"

Derrick and Charlie turned toward their smiling wives.

"Not a thing," Charlie said, taking his wife into his arms. "Of course I'm looking forward to a little private dancing," he whispered as he led her toward the music.

"Oh, you'll get your dance, Mr. Masters. That and a whole lot more."

"That's what I'm counting on, Mrs. Masters. That's what I'm counting on."

* * * * *

Welcome to Club Babylon: where the A-list VIPs come to play...

BEYOND THE VELVET ROPE

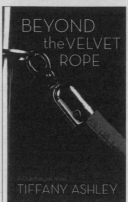

TIFFANY ASHLEY

Club Babylon is the hottest club on the Miami strip, a magnet for major South Beach movers and shakers. And New York promoter Thandie Shaw is about to meet the biggest player of them all.

Babylon owner Elliot Richards is macho, arrogant and sexist—everything Thandie doesn't want in a boss or lover. He's also the most erotic man she's ever met. As he tries to seduce her into a world of intense passion, she knows it's too good to last...especially after she uncovers Elliot's explosive secrets.

A Club Babylon Novel

"This book combines humor, heat and great dialogue. The characters were so well written that I didn't want the book to end." —*Night Owl Romance* on *LOVE SCRIPT*

Available July 2014 wherever books are sold!

REQUEST YOUR FREE BOOKS!

2 FREE NOVELS
PLUS 2 FREE GIFTS!

KIMANI™
ROMANCE

Love's ultimate destination!

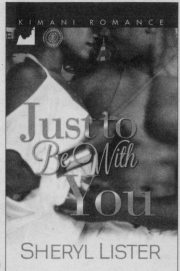

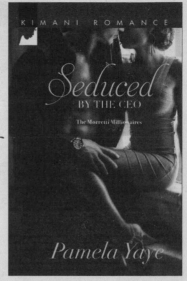